DESCENT INTO CHAOS

BROCK E. DESKINS

Azerick scrambled to his feet with a snarl, pointed his staff, and unleashed arcane fury into a knot of creatures that had observed Daebian's arrival and were set on rending him to pieces. The firelight afforded Daebian plenty of shadows in which to flit about the battlefield in a dance of death that left spawn bleeding and missing limbs, many without ever having seen their attacker.

The spawns' snarls and cries of pain brought their brethren racing toward the newcomers, and they focused all of their murderous hatred onto Azerick and Daebian. Azerick narrowed his focus onto single targets, not knowing where his son might appear next and did not want to catch him with a spell by accident. He was sure he would never hear the end of it.

Limiting himself so, several monsters managed to overwhelm his defenses and hurled themselves against his wards. Most went careening off, trailing smoke, and leaving behind the stench of charred flesh and burnt hair. Others dashed in, obsidian blades clutched in clawed hands that cut through his ward, weakening it with every strike. Azerick twirled a free hand over his head, and his ward turned into dozens of arcane blades that spun around him like a small tornado of death, cutting the spawn into pieces.

Azerick let the swirling maelstrom of magic dissipate and raised another ward just in time to intercept a ravager leaping at his back. It rebounded off the barrier with a loud spark of electricity only to have Daebian's sword cut it in two before it hit the ground. He pointed his sword at a pair of ravagers trying to flee into the night, but Azerick was not about to allow them to escape.

With an up-thrusted clawing motion of his hand, stone spikes sprang from the ground beneath both creatures, impaling them and leaving them flailing uselessly a couple of feet off the ground. Azerick slashed with his staff as if he were scything wheat. A crescent of cerulean light spun across the span, cleaving through stone spires and spawn alike.

CHAPTER 1

A zerick tore open a gate and stumbled through it into his old lair. He snapped the portal shut the moment the others crossed the threshold behind him.

"Azerick, what's going on? What happened?" Rusty asked, his tone pleading.

The sorcerer paused in his scramble to gather the few possessions he had and took a deep breath before facing the others. "I saw their army."

"What are we facing?" Daebian asked.

"Four, maybe five thousand soldiers, but they're not my biggest concern."

Daebian nodded with a grunt. "Whoever, or whatever, kicked your ass halfway across the western sea."

"It was their rulers' daughter, and it wasn't even her. She was just an astral projection aboard one of their ships."

"She must have been nearby though," Rusty said.

Azerick shook his head. "Maybe, but I don't think so. I got the impression she was far from their armada. Maybe back in their homeland."

Rusty's face blanched. "That's impossible. Projecting an astral form that far is extremely difficult. To strike from that distance is...impossible."

"Apparently not. I got a look at her aura. It was beyond anything I've seen before except among a few of the most powerful beings I've ever encountered."

"Are you saying what their people say is true, that their sovereigns are gods?" Andrill asked.

Azerick paused to think a moment before answering. "No. I don't think she could have struck me had I not also been an astral projection, and while her aura was extraordinary, it was not on the level of the gods or the Scions."

"So what do we do?" Rusty asked.

Azerick grit his teeth as he grimaced. "We can't fight them. Not here. Not just us. It would be foolhardy."

"So, we just let them have Southport, after all we did to win it back?" Rusty asked, his tone heated.

Azerick shoved the last of his few possessions into a bag and turned to his friend. "We don't *let* them have anything, not a drop of water, a crumb of food, or an inch of ground. We make them pay in blood for it. Conceding to reality is not the same as surrendering. The battle for Valeria is just beginning, but we have to fight from a position of strength and not simply throw ourselves on their spears."

"What's your plan?" Andrill asked.

"I'll take everyone we can gather and is willing to fight out of the city and link up with Marley and the mages in Freehold. We will have to get word to Ellyssa and North Haven so they can prepare to meet The Order and react accordingly. Rusty, I want you to do that. You are a trusted friend to both Miranda and her mother as well as Ellyssa. From there, I have to get word to King Miles. He and the heads of Brightridge and Argoth have the only standing armies capable of mounting an effective resistance."

Andrill nodded, his mouth turning down with the grim acceptance of their fate. "Me and my people will be staying here. I'm too old to be trekking about in the woods and playing soldier. I'll use the skills at my disposal and make a nuisance of myself as best I can from the shadows."

Azerick nodded. "I assumed as much, but you know you will have to be especially careful. This legion on the horizon is not likely to repeat the same mistakes of their predecessor. It's going to require a much more subtle hand."

The old thief grinned. "You don't think I can be subtle? I'm not going to run around setting fire to half the city like some people I know. Not unless they leave me no other option."

"Elias and Trisha will go with you of course," Rusty said. "As mages, they can't stay here."

"I'm going too," Vera said.

"Like hell you are!" Rusty snapped.

Vera matched her father's scowl and tone. "Like hell I'm not!"

Rusty pleaded with his youngest child. "The Order won't bother you. You're safer staying with your mother and grandparents."

"I don't care about safe. I fought these despots here, and I'll keep fighting them out there. I've done more than enough to prove I'm capable."

Rusty released a heavy sigh as he laid his hands on his daughter's shoulders. "It's not about your capabilities; it's about keeping my family as safe as I can. For Trisha and Elias, that means coming with me. They simply don't have any other choice, but you have an option, and the smart one is staying here."

Vera pursed her lips and met her father's eyes. "If it's a choice, then I choose to fight."

Rusty spun to face Azerick. "Please talk some sense into her."

"She's right," he held up a hand to forestall Rusty's rebuke, "but so are you." Vera's triumphant expression melted under the sorcerer's gaze. "You will serve us best by staying here. You have equipment and access to materials we won't have outside the city. If you truly want to do the most good, stay with Andrill and learn everything you can about these people and how to destroy them."

Vera took in a deep breath and slowly let it out. She tried to detect any condescension in Azerick's words or tone, but there was none, and she had to concur with his logic.

She pursed her lips and said, "Fine, I'll stay here until the situation becomes untenable."

Azerick smiled and touched a hand to her shoulder. "You're doing a good thing. Your fire bombs might just be the key to winning this war."

Rusty wrapped his daughter in a fierce embrace. "Look after your mother and grandparents. They'll need you as well. Whatever you do, stay safe."

"I will," Vera replied, her voice muffled against her father's chest.

"We can get you out and beyond the walls at the canal entrance," Andrill said.

Azerick and the others followed the old thief and smuggler through the sewers until they emerged next to the floodgate that kept the water flowing into the tunnels to keep them relatively clean.

Andrill turned to Azerick, blinking against the harsh sunlight. "It was good to see you again. If anyone can purge this infestation from the land, it is you."

Azerick shook the man's hand. "It was good to see you too. Andrill, the sewers are not likely to be safe much longer. The Order will know of how we used them to defeat their advance forces and won't make the same mistake again. My—Vera's chamber is well hidden and magically warded, but you'll want to secure all your entrances, and don't count on being able to use the sewers to traverse the city unseen."

Andrill smiled back at him. "I know. I've already sent word. We thieves have more than one way to stay out of sight."

"I thought you would. Good luck to you."

"And you."

Rusty caught Andrill's eyes with his own. "Look after my daughter. Don't let anything happen to her."

"I won't. They'll get her over me and my men's dead bodies, and I'm not one to die easily. You have my word on that."

A trio of gliders flitted over the wall too far away to hear. More aerial groups and individuals began flying past, some close enough they could hear the droning of the magic that kept them aloft.

"We best get moving," Azerick said.

He cloaked his group in concealing magic, hoping it was subtle enough to not draw The Order's attention. They made it to the edge of the forest without being spotted and made it into the woods just as the sun was setting. The added concealment helped them avoid the glider scouts, but it also slowed their trek through the forest as darkness set in.

The spawn were a bigger threat. Azerick and Daebian could handle small groups on their own without resorting to magic that might give them away to The Order. Rusty and the other mages had little in the way of martial training, and if a large pack found them, the resulting clash might end this war before it ever got started.

With help from Daebian's unnatural vision, Azerick located the portal arch that would take them to Freehold after more than three hours of stumbling through the woods. Luck was with them as they managed to reach the arch without running across any spawn.

Azerick fed power into the arch, and the air within the shape's confines shimmered a moment before resolving into a scenescape indistinguishable from that which lay just on the other side. The moment they stepped through, a voice commanded them to stop. Azerick felt at least three people drawing the Source not far away as four figures stepped from the darkened confines of the forest surrounding the archway. One gripped a sword, another a spear, and two held bows with arrows knocked and ready to loose at the first sign of trouble.

Azerick raised his hands in front of him. "It's Azerick and Daebian and a few friends," he said with a sidelong glance at his son, whose hands rested on the hilts of his blades.

Sybil pushed between the boughs of a pair of trees and smiled at the pair. "I welcome you back, Azerick. If you're here to escort your Academy friends home, I'm sure Marley will welcome you as well."

Azerick's lips tightened into a thin line. "I'm afraid my return is not likely to improve our relationship."

"Smart money bets it goes downhill and ends in a climactic crash of fire and destruction," Daebian quipped.

A look of concern replaced Sybil's smile. "Things didn't go as expected then?"

Azerick took a deep breath. "Yes and no."

"Mostly no," Daebian clarified.

The mage turned and waved over her shoulder for the pair to follow her. They trailed her through the dark woods for twenty minutes before reaching the hidden village tucked deep in the Heartwood Forest. The sod-covered buildings came into view as they pushed into the tree-dotted clearing.

Men, women, and children stood watch, worked, or engaged in other activities. Their body language suggested they were on heightened alert with eyes flicking toward the sky every few moments, ready to dart beneath the cover of the grassy roofs at the first sign of danger.

Kord stood outside the lodge hall with his arms crossed, his balled fists making his already ample biceps bulge out even more. Another man with a bandaged stump for a left arm glared hatred at the pair, his focus almost entirely upon Daebian. Daebian noted his ire and smiled at him in return, welcoming any challenge he might wish to present.

Kord moved aside and opened the door, not bothering to demand the father and son leave their weapons outside since he knew it would not make any difference should they decide to become hostile. Azerick spied Marley sitting on his log throne at the end of the hall before his eyes snapped to the visage of Headmaster Florent and several Academy mages sitting amongst a few of Freehold's citizens.

Marley's face broke into a wide smile that held little warmth or welcome. "Given the number of those flying machines I've gotten reports of, I assume the battle did not go according to plan."

"On the contrary," Daebian retorted. "It was a rousing victory that lasted nearly three hours before a ghostly woman ejected Father over the city wall with a swift kick in the ass."

Marley's eyebrows crawled higher up his brow. "Indeed?"

"My son likes to embellish, but it isn't far from the truth," Azerick replied. "While we did evict the few surviving invaders from Southport, their main host arrived on a flotilla of ships. I visited the lead vessel in astral form where I met the projected image of their princess. She...ejected my scrying spirit back into my body with significant force."

Headmaster Florent interrupted Marley before he could voice the questions written plainly across his face. "You saw only her projection? Were you able to discern her true location? I assume she was aboard one of the nearby vessels if not the ship you approached."

"I do not believe so. I think she was back in her native land."

The elder wizard's jaw fell slack. "Projecting that far should be impossible given the distance we assume lies between our land and theirs. To strike you with magic even if it were is..."

"Impossible?" Daebian sneered. "Perhaps you can convince Father to drop his trews and display the dainty yet deeply embedded footprint painted in brilliant scarlet upon the pasty canvas of his derriere? Let us then speak of impossibilities."

"Then this talk of theirs claiming to be gods must have some merit after all," Headmaster Florent said in a low voice.

Azerick nodded. "I will not speak of gods just yet, but their rulers are clearly powerful."

Marley cleared his throat. "I feel as though you are going to give me more bad news, something concerning me and my continued hospitality," he said, his eyes settling on Headmaster Florent.

"It changes some things," Azerick conceded.

"I don't see that it does. You asked me to house the wizards until you kick this Order out of Southport. You have done so, albeit only temporarily. It seems to me that the arrival of an even larger force means it is now a greater imperative that they leave, as you promised they would."

"The argument is the same. There are now more arcanus and the aerial scouts who will be looking for any signs of resistance, and you will need all the help you can get to remain hidden," Azerick insisted.

Joah had been silent until now, although his expression conveyed a great deal. "Then you are reneging on our deal and will force us to house them for an indefinite period of time?"

Azerick shook his head. "This is your land and your people. I will not usurp you," he said to Marley. "If you insist, I will take my leave along with the Headmaster and her people. I will lead them to North Haven and pray we get there unseen and before The Order does. Know that doing so puts your people in great peril as I am certain our enemy, and make no mistake that The Order is *our* enemy, will put significant effort into finding every last mage in the kingdom and put them in shackles, including yours. They also take a very dim view on anyone who engages in any sort of criminal activity, including extortion and highway robbery. You'll find no shortage of such examples hanging from gibbets within Southport."

Marley rubbed at the stubble on his chin. "What are your plans now?"

"I need to get to North Haven and warn Miranda and the duchess not to resist The Order. I imagine they will seek to occupy the city in short order, and fighting them with as few soldiers as Mellina has at her disposal will be a waste of lives."

"You don't intend on fighting them then?" Marley asked, his inflection rising in surprise.

Azerick glowered. "I intend on fighting them every step of the way, but unless I can get King Miles to raise an army of significantly greater forces, it will have to be on my terms, not theirs. I won't see people die needlessly."

"Then you'll be heading to Brelland next?"

"I have asked my friend Rusty to bring word to Mellina and Miranda. Even if I can convince the king to answer the call of battle, there's no way his army will make it back here before The Order begins spreading across the countryside, pacifying every town and city in its path."

"I can go to North Haven with Magus Cossington, assuming our host has another of his portals to hasten our journey," Headmaster Florent said. "You and your son should get to Brelland as swiftly as you can."

"I can get the both of you several days closer to your destinations," Marley said to the two spellcasters.

Azerick's eyebrows knitted together. "How many gates do you have?"

Marley's smile returned. "A few."

Azerick took a deep breath as he considered her offer. "Miranda and her mother were not fond of the Academy the last I knew. Unless your relationship has changed over the years, I think Daebian should go instead. Ellyssa is there, and between the two, they should have no trouble getting Miranda to convince her mother to do as I suggest. Headmaster Florent should stay here to help defend the village while I'm gone."

Daebian wagged his head. "As much as I would love to leave your company, you will need me with you more than Ellyssa does. Pen a note for Rusty to take to her so they all know it's your words and desires he conveys. That should be sufficient."

Azerick grinned at his son. "If I didn't know better, I would say you were concerned for my well-being."

"I'm more afraid you'll overestimate yourself again and cock it up. You seem to have a habit of forgetting that you left the best part of you in the abyss."

"That's not surprising. I also left the best part of you as stain on my bedsheet," Azerick quipped without missing a beat.

Daebian stared silently into Azerick's eyes for the span of two breaths, smiled, and nodded. "Nicely done, Father. There might be hope for you yet."

A snorted chuckle escaped Marley's mouth. "I'll send a few of my people with your friend and whoever he wishes to take among his group. I recommend keeping the party as small as possible."

"If you can have a couple of decent woodsmen to guide Rusty and his two children, that should be more than enough to deal with any trouble that might arise," Azerick said.

"Yes, the spawn have been increasingly active of late," Marley said. "I'll assign three of my hunters to accompany them. The faster we can resolve this invasion, the sooner you can all leave my town and the happier we'll all be."

CHAPTER 2

Azerick and Daebian emerged through the magical gate about two days walk from Brelland. They had wasted no time in departing, and the sun was setting as they began their trek east toward the kingdom's capital. There was no time to rest as it was most assuredly a race. The Order would form ranks and march toward every population center as quickly as they could, and with their hovering troop wagons, they could move much swifter than he and Daebian.

Azerick just hoped they would take some time to debark their ships and get organized. Hopefully long enough for them to reach Brelland and convince Miles to marshal every available fighter there and throughout the kingdom to meet this powerful enemy on the battlefield. If they could hit them hard, before they got themselves fully prepared, they might just be able to drive them back into the sea. Azerick knew the odds were slim, but it was the only chance he saw.

Darkness surrounded them as night fell. Azerick let Daebian take the lead and followed closely behind. It was still slow-going despite Daebian's perfect vision since Azerick could barely see his feet.

"It's going to take us twice as long to reach Brelland if you cannot move any faster," Daebian snapped.

"I don't possess a demon's eyes anymore."

"Then make a gods-be-damned light, or can you no longer do something that simple either?"

"We risk their scouts seeing us if I do."

Daebian stopped so abruptly that Azerick bumped into his back. "I'm not suggesting you make the sun rise above your thick head. We are surrounded by scores of miles of untamed forest and are nowhere near a road. The odds of anyone seeing a light out here is infinitesimal.

Even the glow of a single candle would be enough illumination to allow you to move at more than a snail's pace, and I doubt their scouts are going to stop for every single lamplight they spy throughout the whole of the kingdom!"

Azerick stared at his son in silence for a moment before the arcanum ball on his staff lit up with a flickering orange glow and cast light similar to that of a small lantern.

"Thank you," Daebian said between clamped teeth before spinning back around and stalking forward.

"You're welcome," Azerick replied congenially and grinned at the rude gesture Daebian cast over his shoulder.

Daebian stopped again less than an hour later as they crested a hill. "You didn't go and make the sun rise just to mock me did you?"

Azerick stepped up next to Daebian's side. "Of course not. Why?"

Daebian pointed to a spot of orange light on the far side of the small valley lost in the darkness before them.

"That's a fire," Azerick said. "A fairly large one if my estimation of its distance is accurate."

Daebian nodded. "It is, and it isn't a simple conflagration. It is burning in a ring."

"A ring?"

"My guess is that it is surrounding a small town."

Azerick's eyes flicked toward his son. "The Order?"

Daebian shook his head. "Not unless they have changed tactics and started burning villages."

Azerick gritted his teeth. "Spawn."

"That would be my guess."

"Can you shadow step us there?"

"Do you see any damn shadows?" Daebian snapped.

"I didn't know if darkness worked the same as shadows," Azerick bit back.

"No, it doesn't. Not exactly. Can you gate us there?"

"Can you see the damn ground?"

"Of course I can."

"Well I can't, so unless you want to risk ending up fifty feet above or below it, that's not an option either."

Daebian shrugged. "Looks like we're hoofing it then. Try to keep up, old man."

Azerick ran after his son who bolted down the hillside, nimbly leaping over fallen logs and obstacles with an ease that would have made an elf nod in appreciation. Azerick had to increase the brightness of his light to see farther ahead. Given the large blaze in the distance, he figured light discipline was no longer important.

The ground leveled out, and even Azerick could see the dark forms racing and leaping about in the fiery backdrop in the distance. He saw that a trench encircling a wall of raised earth perhaps ten feet high contained the blaze. Sharpened stakes protruded from its steep, sloping face and rim. Atop the palisade, men with bows, crossbows, and spears struck at any spawn that managed to leap over the fire and not impale itself on the stakes.

It was a large attack with at least a score of the monsters pacing around the fire in search of a way past an unprotected section of the wood and earthen bulwarks. Azerick could see that only a handful of the town's defenders wore armor and appeared to be trained fighting men. The bulk of the defending force was made up of ordinary citizens desperately fighting to repel the invaders.

Daebian looked over his shoulder at Azerick with a grin, "Better hurry up, old man, or there might not be any left for you to kill!"

Azerick slashed the air with his staff, opened a portal, and crossed the fifty or so yards separating the two in a single step. He emerged just ahead of Daebian and to his left. Azerick flashed his son a devilish grin, stuck the butt of his staff out to the side, and laughed as Daebian went tumbling headlong with a vile invective before he disappeared.

Azerick turned his gaze back to the spawn just as his foot came down in a pothole in the road. His ankle rolled beneath him, cutting off his mirthful chuckling as he too went sprawling. He rolled to a stop with a curse every bit as vitriolic as Daebian's had been. He glanced behind him as he clambered onto his hands and knees and saw his son emerge from a shadow a few paces behind him.

"Make way!" Daebian shouted.

Azerick let out a whoomph when Daebian crushed him against the road by placing a foot onto his back and leaping high into the air. With blade in hand, Daebian sailed at the nearest spawn and cleaved its head from its body with a single, gravity-assisted blow. He went into a tumble, sprang to his feet, and opened the guts of another.

Azerick scrambled to his feet with a snarl, pointed his staff, and unleashed arcane fury into a knot of creatures that had observed Daebian's arrival and were set on rending him to pieces. The firelight afforded Daebian plenty of shadows in which to flit about the battlefield in a dance of death that left spawn bleeding and missing limbs, many without ever having seen their attacker.

The spawns' snarls and cries of pain brought their brethren racing toward the newcomers, and they focused all of their murderous hatred onto Azerick and Daebian. Azerick narrowed his focus onto single targets, not knowing where his son might appear next and did not want to catch him with a spell by accident. He was sure he would never hear the end of it.

Limiting himself so, several monsters managed to overwhelm his defenses and hurled themselves against his wards. Most went careening off, trailing smoke, and leaving behind the stench of charred flesh and burnt hair. Others dashed in, obsidian blades clutched in clawed hands that cut through his ward, weakening it with every strike. Azerick twirled a free hand over his head, and his ward turned into dozens of arcane blades that spun around him like a small tornado of death, cutting the spawn into pieces.

Azerick let the swirling maelstrom of magic dissipate and raised another ward just in time to intercept a ravager leaping at his back. It rebounded off the barrier with a loud spark of electricity only to have Daebian's sword cut it in two before it hit the ground. He pointed his sword at a pair of ravagers trying to flee into the night, but Azerick was not about to allow them to escape.

With an up-thrusted clawing motion of his hand, stone spikes sprang from the ground beneath both creatures, impaling them and leaving them flailing uselessly a couple of feet off the ground. Azerick slashed with his staff as if he were scything wheat. A crescent of cerulean light spun across the span, cleaving through stone spires and spawn alike.

A quick glance around, with the only sound they could detect coming from the crackling fire, Azerick and Daebian concluded that the battle was over. They turned toward the men standing atop the earthen berm. The townsfolk still clutched their weapons in tight grips and looked at the newcomers with uncertainty.

Azerick raised his hand in greeting. "Ho there. I hope you don't mind us intruding into your troubles."

One of the men who appeared to have combat training was the first to speak. "No sir, not in the least. We thank you much for your help. This was a big bunch, and I'm not sure we would have withstood them this time. Not without a great many more wounded and dead. I'd invite you in for a drink, but I'm afraid the town's closed until the fire burns down."

"It's not much of an impediment if you don't mind having us."

The man nodded. "I thought it mightn't. You're welcome here, sirs. I'll have Norbert open the inn and pour us all some pints."

"Sounds good. Leave me an open area about ten feet directly behind your main gate and we'll join you."

Azerick heard the man issue a few orders before he opened a portal that let them step beyond the flames and into the town. Daebian crossed through behind him as he slid his sword back into its sheath.

"You tripped me," Daebian said flatly.

"Beg pardon?"

"You damn well should."

"I don't know what you're talking about."

Daebian spun on his father. "Are you seriously going to stand here and tell me you didn't trip me as we ran toward the town?"

Azerick looked around as if in search of something. "I don't see a chair, so I have little option but to stand."

Daebian opened his mouth to continue his rebuke but snapped it shut when a man approached them.

"Ho there," a middle-aged man called out as he approached.

The man wore a chain hauberk over leather armor. Numerous weapons clung to his body, all secured in a way that ensured they did not jangle about as he moved.

He stuck his hand out at Azerick first then Daebian, clasping each man's wrist in greeting. "The name's Rowen. I lead a pack of hunters in these parts. You came upon us just in time. Damn critters had made two paths across the flames and up the side of the earthen works with their bodies and were minutes from making a full-scale breach."

"Well met, Rowen," Azerick said. "I'm Azerick Giles."

The man's eyes widened. "The demon sorcerer Azerick Giles?"

Azerick grinned and wagged his head. "Just the latter half now."

Rowen let out a low whistle. "Well, I'll be the son of a whore spawn. I fought in the war. Watched you and the other wizards lay down hellfire upon these cursed critters."

Azerick arched his eyebrows as he took in the man. "You couldn't have been more than a boy then."

Rowen gave him a broad smile, showing off two rows of tobacco-stained teeth with a couple of gaps in them. "Twelve years old, gripping a short spear in trembling hands and wearing a chain shirt that hung off me like ship's sail draped over a scarecrow. Been killing these bastards ever since."

"I see. Do you belong to the town then?"

Rowen spat a gob of tobacco-tinged saliva onto the ground. "Naw. Me and a group of the meanest, ugliest bastards you ever met wander from town to town hunting these gods-be-damned spawn and killing 'em whenever we find 'em. We hire on to towns like this one when we get word of spawn activity in the area and help 'em shore up their defenses and provide additional protection until we clear 'em out in exchange for lodging and whatever coin, food, and booze they can spare."

He spat onto the ground before continuing. "There's been an increase in their numbers of late, and this town wasn't prepared to handle what we'd been seeing. We just got the trench dug deeper and wider and filled with wood for the fire about a day and half back. Good thing too, or you would'a come just in time to watch 'em feasting on our bones."

"An interesting vocation you've chosen. Are there many hunting bands like yours?" Azerick asked.

"More than a few. There's always been plenty of spawn needing killed, especially out here away from the cities where the soldiers don't seem inclined to go. Too far a walk I guess."

"And you all perform this crucial service for whatever the townsfolk can spare?"

Rowen's face lost its jovialness. "Most of us. There be a few who like to take more. We have words with 'em when we hear of it."

"And words are enough?"

"Sometimes. Sometimes not."

"What happens then?"

The hunter spat another gob of tobacco juice near his foot, close enough that it spattered the leather. "Well, they ain't no better'n spawn then, and we treat 'em accordingly." Rowen clapped Azerick on the back and nudged him toward the largest of the buildings within the town. "Looks like Norbert got the inn open. Let's go have that drink!"

"I'm Daebian Giles, by the way, if anyone cares," Daebian said as he followed them.

Rowen looked back over his shoulder and ducked his chin in the minimalist of acknowledgments.

"I don't know why I even try," Daebian huffed.

Azerick peered into globes of torch and lamplight and saw several groups tending to the wounded. It was clear even from a distance that some of them would never rise again.

They tromped up the two steps leading into the inn. Most of the tables sat empty, but Azerick figured they would fill up in short order as soon as the townsfolk finished tending to their wounded and ensured their defenses were in order. It was obvious few would return to their beds any time soon.

The innkeeper, Norbert, set three mugs down almost as soon as they seated themselves and filled them from a pitcher. He went back to work behind the bar without a word. Azerick took a sip of his beer and grunted in approval. It was a honey beer with hints of heather and yarrow, probably the inn's best brew.

"So, you back for good this time?" Rowen asked after taking a long pull from his tankard.

Azerick ducked his head. "That's the plan."

"You return to dark times, Azerick. We've been plagued by spawn since you left, and they've become even more of a nuisance of late."

The man did not bother with any honorifics, and Azerick's opinion of him grew. "That may have something to do with my return, but the spawn may be the least of our coming troubles."

"How's that then?"

"Have you heard word out of Southport of recent?"

Rowen shook his head. "Naw. We're off the main road, and it's been weeks since a caravan has come through from out that way."

"A foreign invader took the city, but Daebian and I and some other folks drove them out. Our success was short-lived as their main force arrived the very same day as our victory. They will spread across this land like a swarm of locusts."

Rowen grimaced. "Bad folk then?"

"Not so much as invaders go. They claim they are on a holy mission to purge the world of the spawn."

"Other than having to find new work, it sounds pretty good to me," the hunter said with a shrug.

"As long as you don't mind one in five able-bodied men being conscripted into their army to fight their many wars around the world. It gets worse if you wield magic. They don't seem to do much in the way of plunder or needless suffering though. If you don't have a problem with those first two things and adapting to their laws and culture and worshipping their rulers as gods, it might be an improvement over the current circumstances."

"So, what you're saying is there would be a fair bit of change."

"Quite a bit of change," Azerick affirmed. "They call themselves The Order, and they are zealous in living up to their name. There is no mercy for those who fail to toe the line. Gibbets will decorate most every town and city center for those who break an oath, a law, or even so much as speak a word against them."

"Hm, I'm not much for change or keeping my gob shut in the face of stupidity," Rowen rumbled into his cup before draining it. "You say there's a lot of 'em?"

"At least five thousand by my count, and their soldiers wield enchanted shields and weapons and are adept at defending themselves against magic. That's why Daebian and I are hastening to Brelland to warn the king so he can mount a defense before they get too entrenched."

"That's a lot of folk, and tough buggers from the sound of it. If Miles could rouse that many fighting men, we might not still be suffering this scourge of spawn. Maybe he'll be more inclined toward action now that his throne and the pasty arse it props up is threatened like his father did for the war."

"That's what I'm hoping as well," Azerick replied.

"What about us small folk? What are we to do should this Order come knocking?"

"Answer the door and welcome them in. Fighting them openly without significantly superior forces is pointless. Be warned, if you take an oath with them, breaking it is a death sentence. They hold true to their word with an iron grip and demand the same in kind."

Rowen held up his mug and Norbert hastened over to top them all off. The inn was beginning to fill up now. Many of the newcomers gave Azerick and Daebian a nod of thanks, but none spared the energy to engage them in conversation. They occupied the tables and bar and drank toasts to the victory and to fallen friends.

"Say you get Miles to sound the call to arms. What then?" Rowan asked.

"I suppose it depends on our enemy's disposition. With enough troops and wizards, we might be able to drive them out with a swift and powerful attack if they aren't set to meet our charge."

"And if they are or you don't get your army?"

Azerick took a deep breath and let it out. "Valeria is not a small kingdom, and they won't stop at our borders. They'll push into Sumara as well, and they have even more land to cover than we do."

"Good luck cracking that nut," Rowen chortled.

"Unless they double the number of troops, they won't try until they've pacified us sufficiently."

"Hm, me and mine aren't the sort to be pacified."

Azerick grinned. "Nor I. We'll have to do our best to avoid fighting until they've spread themselves out between the cities and towns. Then we hit them, cut them apart piece by piece until there's nothing left."

Rowen bobbed his head. "That'd be the best plan I can think of. Pick off the stragglers from the herd. Whittle down their numbers. What should those of us who don't take to being pacified do?"

"Avoid The Order. Keep hidden in the forests and meet up with other groups until you can, as you say, pick them off from the herd. Whatever you do, don't take their oath if you don't plan to hold to it. Without the oath, they'll treat you as an adversary. Break your word and you'll be a traitor."

"Good to know."

"Hunting The Order won't be much different than hunting spawn, only The Order is a lot smarter and a lot more dangerous. Bands like yours could be crucial should things go poorly for us. Meet with other hunting parties as quickly as you can and explain what I've told you here."

Rowen gave him a quick nod. "Sounds like the thing to do. Will you be moving on tonight?"

Azerick looked at Daebian who said, "I could use some sleep, and I don't relish the idea of sleeping out in the woods."

"Is there a place to bunk down for a few hours?" Azerick asked.

"My boys and I have all of Norbert's rooms taken, but I'll move a couple of 'em out to make space for you."

"I don't want to put anyone out."

Rowen waved off his offer. "Naw. We'll make space for 'em in the other rooms."

"We appreciate it."

Azerick and Daebian took the two cots Rowen's hunters vacated. They still had to share the room with three other men, but the accommodations were sufficient to catch a few hours of much needed sleep before they headed back out in the morning.

CHAPTER 3

The sun had barely risen before Azerick and Daebian set out on the road once again. Rowen and his band of hunters were already packing up their gear and preparing to leave while he and Daebian ate a quick breakfast and departed with nothing more than a brief farewell.

Azerick had unleashed a fair amount of magic during the battle, but he was confident The Order's arcanus were not looking this far afield for magic use. Even if they were, time was of the essence, so Azerick decided to open a series of portals to hasten their travel. A dizzying and exhausting nine hours later, Brelland's enormous walls hove into view the moment they stepped through the trees.

There was hardly a tree for a mile in any direction around the great city, but even at that distance, the walls were an impressive barrier and feat of engineering. They rose some thirty feet, and instead of ringing the town in a simple circle, the walls jutted out in several points like a star. This was new. New to Azerick anyway.

Azerick possessed a passing knowledge of engineering and saw how much more an effective barrier the unusual shape presented. Any army trying to storm the walls would be channeled between the points where archers and stone throwers could pelt them from two sides. Boulders hurled by catapults would likely strike at an angle, greatly reducing the missile's force of impact.

It also explained the expanded ring of deforestation around the city with trees having been harvested for building materials. Even if the wall's construction had taken the bulk of the two decades he'd been in the abyss, the manpower to complete them must have been extensive. Perhaps that was why Miles had too few soldiers to deal with the spawn in the more distant towns and villages.

It was getting dark, and lamplighters were out lighting the torches and lamps along the walls and within the city by the time Daebian and Azerick reached the gates and made their way inside. There were a fair number of soldiers and city watch patrolling the streets, but not as many as Azerick had expected.

Perhaps they were out patrolling the roads and protecting some of the nearby towns. Many of the men also appeared a bit rough around the edges, the kind more at ease chipping out stone with a pick or swinging an axe at trees than trained soldiers and watchmen.

Azerick dismissed his assessment of the men and reminded himself that the last twenty years had been difficult ones. If the spawn problem was as widespread as he had been told, then there was certainly some conscription used to bolster their ranks. Best to keep the trained soldiers out fighting the enemy and use the less skilled ones to chase the occasional thief or break up bar fights.

Azerick and Daebian kept the hoods of their cloaks pulled over their heads despite the likelihood of anyone recognizing them. No one bothered them until they reached the inner curtain wall surrounding the castle. As they approached the main gates, one of four heavily armed and armored guards held up a hand.

"Stop right there. Do you have business with the castle?"

Before Azerick could expel the words from his open mouth, Daebian said, "Business with the castle? How could a person would have business with a castle? A stonemason perhaps, but I can't imagine how such a conversation might go. No, we must speak with someone *inside* the castle."

Daebian said the last sentence in a slow drawl, as if speaking to a simpleton.

The soldier glared at Daebian, but he tempered his response. "Do you have a writ of passage or invitation declaring your business with someone *inside* the castle?"

"No," Azerick said, quickly biting off the word to prevent Daebian from speaking again. "We have urgent need to speak with King Miles regarding a matter of great importance."

"Without a pass or invitation, no one may enter the grounds after sunset. You may join the queue of petitioners in the morning. I suggest you come early as the king only has time for the first few."

"The matter cannot wait until morning, sir," Azerick said. "Please, send a runner to inform the king or his seneschal that Azerick and Daebian Giles must speak to him at once."

The soldier had probably not been more than a toddler during the Gods War, but the name Azerick Giles was spoken often enough as he grew up that he recognized it. He looked Azerick and Daebian up and down before jerking his head at one of his fellow guards. The man pounded on the sally gate and disappeared inside when it opened.

Azerick and Daebian waited patiently. There was not much other choice unless Azerick decided to set aside manners and niceties and simply gated them inside. He was certain Miles employed enough mages that such an action would not go unnoticed and raised an alarm, which would only delay them further.

He and the young king had also not departed on the best of terms last they met. Although he had played a crucial role in saving the entire kingdom and possibly the world, his nature and considerable power had presented a problem. One that only his death or banishment could rectify, and Miles had been ready to execute the former had Sharrellan not taken the demonic sorcerer back to the abyss.

The sally gate opened once more, and a profusely sweating guard beckoned them to enter. Given the man's sweating and heavy breathing, Azerick felt a bit better seeing their pronouncement had been taken seriously by someone of authority. Six more soldiers flanked them the moment they stepped through the gate.

Four soldiers, Azerick corrected himself as he took in their escort. Two of the men wore silver breastplates emblazoned with Solarian's holy symbol over their priestly garments. They wore swords Azerick recognized as the demon-slaying blades the church had provided Jarvin, Miles' deceased father and former king, with which to kill him immediately after the war. They had indeed accepted his identity at his word.

No one spoke as they marched down the wide boulevard leading up the hill to the castle proper. There were a few residences inside the inner curtain wall, mostly for the top court positions and ambassadorial residences. They passed a single patrol of half a dozen soldiers before traipsing up the steps and into the castle.

Whatever the exterior lacked in guards the interior made up for it. Pairs and quartets of guards stood at the entrance to every hallway, intersection, and stairway. All were alert, their eyes tracking Azerick and Daebian's procession until they disappeared around a corner where another squad took up the duty. They stopped before the large doors leading into the audience chamber.

One of the warrior priests turned and looked at Daebian's sword. "You will have to leave your weapon outside."

Azerick had left his staff in the woods since it would draw too much attention and he could summon it at any time.

Daebian bristled. "I don't think so."

"It is the king's law."

"The king will make an exception."

The warrior priest matched Daebian's glower a moment before pushing through the doors. Azerick heard a few muffled words of a terse conversation before the man returned and gestured for them to enter.

The audience hall was much as Azerick remembered it with a few changes in the decor and artwork. A few ranking court officials sat or stood near the walls as well as a score of armored guards and another pair of warrior priests armed with the demon-killing swords.

Miles sat upon his throne, alert with a sharp intelligence gleaming in his eyes. He was handsome like his father but a bit shorter and of lighter frame, but it was the person standing next to the king who drew Azerick's attention.

The man had the swarthy skin tone of a Sumaran. While he did not wear armor, he bore a heavy rapier belted around his waist. He was compact in size and lean. Aside from his nationality and proximity to the king, Azerick might have assumed him to be some sort of advisor and simply glanced over him. However, there was something in his eyes and hyper-focused bearing that made Azerick pause and consider him.

The smile Miles wore carried little welcome or warmth. "Lord Giles, so you have returned."

Azerick shifted his attention and performed a small bow. "I have, Your Highness, but it is just Azerick now. I claim no titles."

"None?" Miles asked with raised eyebrows.

"No official ones. Certainly none declaring nobility or station. I do hope I can still consider myself as a Friend to the King and Defender of the Kingdom."

Miles nodded. "Those are worthy titles indeed."

The fact the king did not affirm his statement was not lost on Azerick.

"You look well, Azerick. Your time away appears to have provided some benefits to your countenance," Miles continued.

"I feel well, Your Majesty. Better than I have in a great long while." Azerick pointedly directed his gaze to the priests bearing holy swords, which matched the one Miles also wore sheathed on his side. "So much so that your blessed weapons will have no more deleterious effect on me than a normal blade."

Daebian perked up at his father's words. "This is all conjecture, however. Feel free to test his theory if you wish. I admit, I am a bit curious myself."

Miles' lips twitched up just a bit. Daebian was not unknown to the king. He and his band of pirates had plundered more than a few of his ships over the years.

"I will take Azerick at his word," Miles replied.

"I hope you will also take what else I say at my word," Azerick said.

"Yes, you bring important information you feel I must know. Given the timing of your previous returns, I must assume they are foreboding."

"They are, Highness. A foreign invader calling themselves The Order had successfully occupied Southport until we were able to rouse forces sufficient to expel them."

Miles' face did not display a hint of surprise. "I am aware of this."

Azerick was not able to maintain the same steely facade. "You are?"

"I got word of the attack a few days ago, but of your success only very recently."

"You have some excellent sources of information then. I had not expected news to reach this far so fast."

"I have people who tell me much of what is happening in my kingdom. I only wish I could respond to every bit of trouble just as quickly."

"Then I hope my news arrives in time for you to respond to this trouble. A much larger force of five thousand Order soldiers, by my count, arrived shortly thereafter and have assuredly retaken the city by now. Likely without resistance."

Miles stroked his clean-shaven chin as he digested Azerick's information. "Five thousand is a significant force. My intelligence claims less than a thousand captured Southport with nary a drop of blood being spilled, until you returned, that is."

Azerick shifted his feet. "True, Highness. I was able to lead a smaller resistance, and through guile as much as force of arms, cast them out. I believe this larger contingent will be much more difficult to defeat by orders of magnitude. Guile is unlikely to take us nearly as far, and meeting them on open ground will be costly."

"What do you think of these invaders?" Miles asked.

Azerick blinked in confusion a few times before answering. "They are adept at defending against both mundane and magical attacks. They largely eschew using mages, what they call arcanus, for offensive purposes. Their soldiers are well-trained and disciplined. They all appear to be a professional fighting force as opposed to any sort of conscripts."

Miles held up a hand to forestall Azerick. "No. I mean what do you think of their character? Are they barbarians who will pillage and plunder the countryside before stripping it bare or getting bored and moving on? Are they heinous task masters who slaughter and oppress the citizenry in a display of dominance? What can I and my people expect from these invaders?"

"I see," Azerick replied, nodding, and looking down at his feet. "From what I have seen, they have a strong code of honor, and while maintaining strict and inflexible laws, are not given to wanton acts of violence. In fact, those who take their oath of allegiance are considered citizens of their empire with all rights and responsibility the moment they sign it."

"Is that why they have come, to envelope us into their empire? For what purpose, a broader base for taxation or simply to expand their rule?"

"Their agenda is greater than that. They have sworn an almost religious crusade to eradicate the spawn anywhere they can find it. To do so, they conquer every nation they come upon, conscript one of every five men of fighting age to continue their war, and demand that you worship their emperor and empress and renounce the very existence of any other gods but them. Their mantra is: There is only The Order and enemies of The Order."

"I see. Would you consider them an honorable people, honest and true to their word should we entreat with them?"

"Yes, zealously so. To break an oath is anathema to them, and doing so is a crime punished by death without mercy or exception. I believe they hold themselves equally accountable as well and not just those they conquer."

Miles nodded and his expression changed as if he had been pondering something of great importance and had just made a decision. "I am glad you brought me this information, Azerick. You have confirmed their claims almost point for point with virtually no discrepancy."

Azerick flicked a confused gaze at Daebian, who only glared at Miles, then back at the king. "Highness, I'm not sure what you mean."

Miles waved a hand over his shoulder, and a dark-skinned man dressed in shining silver plate armor with a small buckler strapped to each forearm stepped from a side passage and onto the dais.

"This is Imperator Aquila Martinus. He arrived yesterday on an amazing flying machine. He came alone, disclosed the number of his forces, their capabilities and disposition, and beseeched me to avoid the needless death of many good men who would be better served eradicating the spawn. His claims match your testimony, and this compels me to believe that he is being honest and is a man of his word."

Azerick's face clouded in anger. "Highness, to yield to The Order is to surrender everything that makes us who we are! They will shackle everyone capable of wielding magic to control their power, chain everyone else with their laws, and strip them of their customs, beliefs, and identity as a free people."

The king leaned forward on his throne. "Will they die? Will they suffer needlessly? Aside from the strictures on wizardry, will they be denied the freedom to live a decent life of their choosing?"

"Those conscripted into fighting their wars, yes!"

"We are already fighting a war with these accursed spawn. We've been fighting it for twenty years, and although we might not be losing, we are not winning either. And they have gotten only stronger since *you* returned." Miles jabbed a finger at Azerick to punctuate his words.

"Highness, you cannot yield without a fight," Azerick said, despising himself for the weakness in his voice.

"No, Azerick. It is precisely what I must do."

Miles stood up from his throne and knelt before Imperator Martinus. The man produced a rolled-up piece of paper from behind the buckler strapped to his left arm.

"King Miles Ollander, ruler of what was once the kingdom of Valeria, do you pledge your allegiance and loyalty to the emperor and empress of Syrna, Lords of The Order, and accept them as your divine lieges?" the imperator intoned in a deep baritone.

"I do so swear, knowing that to break my covenant is to surrender my life," Miles said pressing his thumb onto the paper.

"I accept your pledge and name you Harmost of the Valerian province. Let all know those who oppose you oppose The Order."

Miles stood and resumed his throne. Azerick flicked his eyes to look at Daebian. He could tell he was trying to determine the best way to reach Miles and strike off his head as well as that of the imperator. Azerick nudged his arm and gave him a slight shake of his head.

Imperator Martinus turned his attention to Azerick and Daebian. "I must applaud the both of you for your victory over Primus Ploutarch. Your courage and fighting skill are to be commended, but the time for fighting each other has come to an end. Let us end our hostilities and swear your fealty to the empire."

Azerick ignored the imperator. "Highness, you can't surrender our freedom so easily! You can't think I will."

Miles laid a baleful glare on the sorcerer. "There is The Order and enemies of The Order. Yield and swear your oath. What say you, Friend of the King?"

"I say, the king is dead. Long live the king."

Azerick summoned his staff, thrust it at Miles, and unleashed a powerful green ray of arcane energy that would reduce him to nothing but ash. Even as he channeled the power through his staff, he felt his connection to the Source vanish. Imperator Martinus swung an arm in front of Miles and summoned the magical shield the buckler produced. In the split second it took the beam to cross the distance between Azerick and Miles, it was so weak that even had the imperator not shielded the former king, the ray would have done little more than blister a patch of skin.

"Slay them!" Miles shouted to his guards and holy warriors.

Daebian's eyes flashed with a look of hatred at the men drawing weapons and charging at them. With forced resignation, he grabbed Azerick by the arm, sprinted for a shadow cast by a tall pillar near the side of the chamber, and leapt into it. Pure blackness enveloped them. Azerick heard Daebian's sword lashing out and striking flesh, eliciting snarls and hisses of pain and anger from the shadow spawn that sensed his presence and rushed in to attack him.

It would not take long for the creatures to realize Daebian was not one of them and ceased ignoring him. Azerick raised a strong ward and enveloped them both in its protective sphere. He expected them to burst back into the light at any moment, but Daebian continued running within the shadow plane. It was the longest trek through the lightless realm Azerick had ever experienced, and he found himself shivering, the tremors growing more intense the longer they stayed there.

Azerick had to force himself to concentrate on maintaining the ward that had so far protected them both from the onslaught of shadow spawn. The attacks grew more numerous and with increasing fervor the longer they ran. His ward was not invulnerable to the monsters' blades and claws, and he had to continually channel power into it to keep them from tearing it apart. It was only a matter of time before the spawn overwhelmed his defenses or he lost his concentration on maintaining the spell.

Just as he was about to tell Daebian of the precariousness of their current situation, Daebian thrust them back into the real world. Although nighttime, the moon's illumination was so bright compared to the darkness from which they had emerged, Azerick was forced to shield his eyes until they adjusted to the soft light.

"That miserable, cowardly, traitorous bastard!" Daebian railed as he hacked at some low-hanging boughs within his reach, imagining each of them was Miles' neck.

Azerick was too mentally and physically exhausted to properly vent his rage, so he chose to prop himself against the trunk of a tree.

"That was a very unpleasant transit," Azerick said once he caught his breath and Daebian ceased pruning the surrounding forest.

"It was a blind step, and I wanted to get as far from the castle as I could. I will return shortly and strike that knee-bending sonofabitch's head from his shoulders!"

Azerick shook his head. "No, not just now. He isn't important."

"He just presented himself like a bitch in heat and handed over the keys to the kingdom without so much as lifting a blade!"

"I know, but we need to plan. There was always the possibility we would have to fight this war without a traditional army."

Daebian hacked at another tree limb. "He still needs to die."

"He will. Just not right now. We need to reach the others and inform them of what has happened." Azerick looked around. "Do you know where we are?"

Daebian shook his head. "Not precisely. We should be in the Heartwood Forest midway between Brelland and Freehold. I cannot say exactly where. Since you don't like my plan, what's yours?"

"The first thing we need to do is inform Ellyssa, the Academy mages, and Marley's people that we won't be getting any help from Miles. I assume the same will hold true of Brightridge and Argoth to varying degrees."

"So we're going to battle an enemy that is both more powerful and larger than ours all on our own. Does that sum up your brilliant plan sufficiently?"

"Not quite. I still have some friends to call upon, but that will have to wait. Our trip through the shadow ways has left me disconcerted. Let's rest, at least a few hours, before moving on."

Daebian looked around. "There's a stream nearby. This is as good a place as any."

Azerick didn't move. He simply closed his eyes where he sat against the tree. He heard Daebian walk off, presumably toward the stream, before he fell asleep.

"Father," Azerick heard deep within his subconscious.

"Father!" the voice hissed a bit louder.

Azerick opened his eyes and found Daebian squatting next to him. "Someone approaches."

Azerick tightened his grip on his staff and turned his head in the direction Daebian was looking, but he did not stand up. Half a minute later, two figures pushed through the interlaced boughs of a pair of young evergreen trees. It was still dark out, and he was unable to make out their faces. Daebian had no such problem.

"Bastard!" Daebian snapped and rushed the pair with his sword held to deliver a killing blow.

The slightly shorter figure intercepted the sword aimed at the other man with a long, slender blade, batting Daebian's strike aside with seeming ease. The sword wielder's free hand delivered an open-palmed strike to Daebian's chest. There was a flash of light from the strike, and the blow lifted Daebian from his feet and sent him crashing into a nearby fir tree. The other figure took a few more steps toward Azerick.

"Azerick, it appears I must beg you once again to save my kingdom," Miles said.

CHAPTER 4

Azerick held up a hand to forestall Daebian's resumed assault. Even in the dark, he could tell his son desperately wished to make the other man answer for his swift and ignominious defeat. With great effort, and to Azerick's surprise, he did not renew his attack.

"What in the abyss are you talking about?" Azerick snapped.

"I apologize for the display I put on, but I saw no other option that would not result in innumerable deaths for my people and the inevitable destruction of their homes and lives."

"You lied to the imperator? You never had any intention of holding to your oath?"

Miles' face twisted into anger. "Of course not."

Azerick met the former king's gaze. "You know it will mean your immediate execution if The Order finds out you have broken faith with them."

"Any leader unwilling to die for his people is no king."

"It appears there is more of your father in you than I first thought."

Miles relaxed. "More than enough to spit in these invaders' faces when the time comes."

"How did you find us? And how did you get here so quickly?" Azerick asked.

"I have my ways." He gestured to the other man. "Radique is a man of many exceptional talents."

Azerick recognized him now as the assumed advisor who had stood next to Miles upon the dais.

"Come, we obviously need to talk, unfettered this time."

Miles and Radique took a seat on the ground next to a small fire Azerick made in the clearing. Daebian begrudgingly sheathed his sword, still desperate for a rematch, and sat across from them next to his father.

"Now that we can speak openly, I can tell you what kind of aid I can offer," Miles said. "The moment I heard that Southport had fallen to a superior enemy, I began gathering my forces and sent word to William and Paulina to do likewise in the event you and your people were unsuccessful. When Imperator Martinus arrived on his flying machine and told me of his arrival and the strength of his troops, I took him at his word."

Miles stared into the flames. "He knew you would be coming here, and while we waited, I began quietly moving the best of my army and replacing them with reserves and cheap hireswords. I instructed William and Paulina to do the same. Unfortunately, I have no easy communication with North Haven, but their army is too small to be of great consequence. I also knew you would probably have things well in hand up there anyway."

"What are we looking at in way of numbers?" Azerick asked, a great burden lifting from his mind.

"I managed to sneak about three hundred soldiers out of the city to join the nearly one thousand that are out hunting spawn and protecting the surrounding towns. William, having had a little more time, has a force of around two thousand hidden in the forest a few leagues from Brightridge. Paulina has the largest number of trained soldiers, nearly three thousand, as well as the entirety of the Hall of Inquisition."

Azerick nodded but did not smile. "Having the inquisitors in our ranks is a great boon, but we still barely outnumber The Order's forces once they all arrive, and I have no idea if there are more coming. They'll never make it to Southport in time. It will be more than a week to get William's men here, and three times as long for Paulina's."

"I know," Miles said, "but I don't think our best strategy is to face them on an open battlefield. Even with a larger army, from what I have heard, we still would not likely be victorious. I suggest we execute continuous harrying attacks. Whittle down their numbers and flee without ever committing ourselves to a larger battle. It could take years, but my hope is that they will eventually see that we are not worth the trouble and leave us be."

"That was exactly my thought as well," Azerick replied. He looked at Radique. "You're from Sumara, aren't you?"

The small man ducked his head.

"Is it possible for you to contact Devlin Sabaht? He's a sorcerer and an old friend of mine. Or anyone in the Sumaran hierarchy."

Radique grinned. "I know him well. He is my cousin and also the king."

Azerick's eyes widened in surprise. "He's the king? I thought his brother Yusuf was king?"

"Yusuf, may Solarian's holy light shine upon his soul, died years ago."

"Did Yusuf not have any children, any sons?"

"He has many sons from many wives and mistresses." Radique shook his head. "But that is not how succession works in my kingdom. Devlin is the son of our previous king and older and wiser than Yusuf's children, so he leads. In this way, we do not suffer from a young, foolish heir. It is a much better system. Your kingdom got lucky in both King Miles and Duke William despite them assuming their positions at such a young age."

If Miles took any offense, he did not show it. "Devlin is gathering an army as we speak, even reaching out to the independent nomad tribes. He has promised to aid us as best he can, but he will have to secure his own borders first. The Order will not find Sumara as unprepared as they did us. I need to get back to Brelland and play the obedient puppet. It is unlikely I will be able to leave again as my minders will arrive soon."

Azerick nodded at Radique. "What of him? They will discover he is a magic user and shackle him."

Radique grinned and shook his head. "I am adept at hiding every aspect of who and what I am. As long as I do not cast magic in their presence, even their arcanus will not know me as anything but a diplomat and advisor."

They all stood. Miles turned back around after he and Radique had walked a few paces away. "I believe I can do the most good from Brelland and will have to work very hard to maintain my ruse. No matter what I might say or seem to do, know that I am with you and Valeria unto death."

"I know that now, Highness. Forgive me for doubting your true intentions and nature."

Miles grinned. "That just meant I did a good job playing my part."

Radique pulled a handful of reddish sand from a pouch on his belt and sprinkled it in a circle around him and Miles. He drew in power from the Source, and a cyclonic wind whipped up, obscuring them from view. When the dust devil lifted from the ground and raced off into the darkness, both men were gone.

Azerick looked at the spot where Miles and Radique had stood. "I have got to get him to teach me that spell."

CHAPTER 5

Azerick watched the train of four skimmers, the hovering transport wagons The Order used to ferry their troops, race down the road toward the plume of black smoke billowing up into the sky near the farming community of Vargas. Twenty-five legionnaires, a full century in total, weighed down the skimmers.

In the past few weeks, Azerick and his people had become familiar with the invaders' movements and responses to attack. While rehearsed and excellently executed maneuvers made for a strong army, those same repetitive actions and reactions in guerilla warfare became a weakness. Azerick knew precisely how The Order contingent billeted in the nearby town of Wellin would react to an attack on their grain stores.

A century of legionnaires was more than capable of confronting most any force the rebels could bring to bear, as Duchess Paulina discovered to her dismay at the start of the insurgency. She had disregarded Azerick's warning, overconfident in her inquisitors' and soldiers' strength. Against most any other foe, her five-hundred strong assault force, which included nearly a hundred battle mages from the Hall of Inquisition, would have been more than sufficient to destroy an enemy they had outnumbered five to one. The Order was not any other enemy, as Azerick had repeatedly stressed in their limited correspondence.

While the century of Order soldiers lost half their numbers in her surprise attack, they routed Paulina's forces, destroying nearly a quarter of it and capturing dozens more. Paulina herself would have been captured had the handful of inquisitors who survived not whisked her from the battlefield. She had become far more respectful of their enemy's strength thereafter.

Azerick let the lead skimmer pass over the rune carved into the earth beneath the cobblestones. He activated the arcane trap as soon as the first vehicle passed it by. The arcanus aboard the second skimmer barked something Azerick could not hear from this distance, but it was too late. The rune exploded beneath the skimmer, sending a powerful shockwave, along with several cubic yards of earth and rock, through the vehicle and the soldiers it bore.

The third skimmer lurched off the road as cobblestones and gravel rained down upon them. The highway was one of the new roads the invaders seemed fond of building, employing a large number of the populace not conscripted into their army to construct it. Aside from killing spawn, it was The Order's greatest contribution to the kingdom in Azerick's eyes. However, the fancy roads were nowhere near equal in value to the theft of their freedom and identity.

The third skimmer's front dipped precariously as it left the roadway. Despite its limited maneuverability and clearance, it would have been able to recover had it not struck a tree stump jutting out of the ground. The skimmer caught the trunk at an angle and caused the vehicle to list with a loud crack and squeal of tortured metal. Legionnaires tumbled from the open bed, a few getting crushed beneath the vehicle's leading edge before the driver regained control.

The first and fourth skimmer glided to a stop, and the legionnaires hastened to deploy themselves into a concerted defense. Azerick was not going to give them the chance to form ranks. He, Ellyssa, and several mages from the Academy and Marley's band opened portals from where they lay in wait in the nearby trees. The hundred men, women, and handful of mages were still insufficient to take on the sixty or so legionnaires along with the few arcanus still battle-ready in a straight up fight, but that was not the kind of war they waged.

Azerick and the wizards led with fireballs, lightning, and other ranged destruction spells. Archers loosed arrows across the short expanse of open ground before those wielding swords and spears fell upon the legionnaires that had been thrown from the skimmers and struggled to get to their feet under the unflagging barrage.

When the two squads began double-time marching toward their fallen brethren and the attackers, their shields flaring with a nimbus of near-impenetrable magic, Azerick's people retreated with all haste toward the open portals still shimmering farther up the hill. The Order soldiers hastened their steps in an effort to engage the insurgents, but they leapt through the waiting portals and vanished.

Javelins flew, but the mages followed the footmen the moment the last ones made it through and disappeared before the magic-destroying lances plunked down and the portals winked out. A pair of gliders buzzed overhead, and their riders blew horns when they spied the fleeing ambushers within the forest.

The Order soldiers renewed their efforts and took up the pursuit. They were strong and conditioned. They were physically superior to most if not all the attackers, and they could eventually run them down even wearing armor. The steady cadence of churning legs ate up the distance between them and the insurgents. The slower, less fit amongst the rebel band hove into view as the legionnaires steadily gained on them.

If any of the pursuers considered the idea that they were being led into a trap or asked themselves why the attackers had not simply gated away again, the thought came too late. The squad's leading element caught the trip line across their ankles and released the log with numerous, sharpened stakes jutting out of it like a giant porcupine effigy suspended high in the trees.

The lethal pendulum dropped from the canopy and swung toward the double-time marching soldiers with little more than a rustling of branches and a sharp whoosh of air as it descended in an arc of death. Those with the reflexes, presence of mind, and situational awareness threw themselves to the ground or off the side of the trail, the former faring far better than the latter.

The legionnaires who "beat their faces" against the ground managed to avoid the worst the log had to offer, suffering little more than scrapes against the backs of their clamshell breastplates or swift kicks from some of the lower-hanging spikes. Those not quick enough to do either fared the worst, but only moderately so compared to the ones who leapt out of the log's path.

The legionnaires who chose to dive aside fell through the thin layer of dirt and detritus covering deep pits with iron spikes thrusting up from their bottoms. Not expecting the ground to give way beneath them, few had their shields erected to protect themselves and suffered gruesome wounds.

Arrows and spells struck at them from the twilit grove, eliciting more curses and cries as they raised their wards to fend off the vicious, cowardly attack. The other squad of legionnaires caught up to the one under attack and bolstered their ranks. Arcanus and archers from the backs of gliders loosed arrows and hurled magic blindly into the trees in the hope of giving the infantry time to collect themselves.

The sounds of the people they pursued vanished, leaving only the buzzing of gliders, cries of the wounded, and curses hanging in the air. The men who were still ambulatory helped those unable to walk on their own and carried away as many of their dead as they could manage. They would return for the rest when they could.

An orange glow through the tree line marred the otherwise black backdrop. When The Order soldiers emerged from the trees, they found that the glow was the burning wreckage of the remaining skimmers. The wounded from the initial attack they had left behind to pursue them were dead to a man. It was a long and somber march back to Vargas for the survivors. Their dead would have to wait a bit longer to receive a proper burial.

"Report," Imperator Martinus snapped, the order brusque and clipped.

He knew his aide-de-camp was unlikely to bear good news. For the last month, from the moment his advance legions came ashore, the dissidents had been striking their supply chains and depots and ambushing smaller units. The insurgent teams almost always had a few wizards amongst them to gate the ambusher away before his legionnaires could engage them. He did not have enough troops and scouts to track them down.

His aide, Optio Lazar Angelov, fingered the papers he held in nervous hands. "Imperator, I have received reports of another ambush.

It occurred midway between a farming village and a smaller garrison town called Vargas and Wellin respectively."

"Losses?"

Optio Angelov swallowed hard. "Fairly significant, sir." He laid out the details of the ambush. "In total, we lost twenty-three legionnaires with nearly a score severely wounded. The insurgents destroyed four skimmers and eight tons of grain and foodstuffs in Vargas. We believe the sorcerer Azerick Giles led that particular attack and heads the insurgency in those parts."

The imperator seethed inwardly, but his discipline prevented him from showing his anger in front of a subordinate. The insurgents had burned or looted several tons of foodstuffs earmarked for his legions, killed nearly two hundred legionnaires, and destroyed several gliders and skimmers. Other than a few early skirmishes, he had thus far been unable to manage an appropriate response. But that would soon change.

It was not unheard of for a newly assimilated nation to have its share of malcontents. People by nature resisted change, even when that change was for the better. The resistance did not usually last long, with a few exceptions. There was only one people who still battled against The Order as a whole. The savages in the primitive kingdom of Olmul had been fighting furiously against them for the past five years and showed no sign of submitting.

That was one reason why he and his legions were here. The emperor and empress wanted the Olmulians pacified soon, and to do that they needed more soldiers. Olmul was an enormous land, larger than any they had discovered in the past two decades of their crusade. Removing his three legions from that front would drastically slow down the occupation, but it was necessary for the well-being of both their people. They could not afford to get bogged down on a second front. There was still the land to the east and south to conquer, and his initial assessment was that it was going to be more of a challenge than this middling kingdom.

"How goes the progression on the arch?" he asked.

Optio Angelov squared his shoulders. "Excellently, Imperator. It is very nearly completed. Southport has little in the way of malcontents, and there has been no attempt to impede its construction."

Imperator Martinus let out a relieved sigh. "That is good news. Once it is completed and the rest of my legions arrive, I will have more than enough manpower to protect our resources and squash this petty insurgency. What of the other primary cities and their harmosts?"

"Mostly quiet. As you know, the former leaders of Brightridge and Argoth refused to bend the knee and now lead attacks around their respective cities. Brelland and North Haven, and here in Southport, as you surely know, have been quiet and compliant."

Imperator Martinus nodded as he turned his back to the optio and studied the enormous map spread out on the table in the middle of the room. He placed a small wooden icon on the map near the site of the latest ambush and compared it to other markers already positioned.

He drew a finger around a large swath of wilderness. "He and his band must be operating out of this forest. Have our scouts reported any activity within its boundaries?"

"It is a rather large tract of land, populated almost exclusively by hunters with nothing in the way of towns or villages. The dense trees make it impossible to properly survey by ground or aerial recon. We have scoured the areas around the attacks for miles without finding a trace of a campsite or even staging point."

The imperator grunted in acknowledgement. "Let them hide and think they are safe. We will send the dogs into their rat holes soon enough."

"Our wayward heroes have returned!" Marley crowed as Azerick and his weary band shuffled into Freehold.

Joah levied narrowed eyes at Azerick and growled, "Not all of 'em if I'm not missing my count."

Azerick ignored the surly man and returned Marley's grin. "We had several victories in this last outing."

"Tell that to the ones who didn't come back with you," Joah said, his voice icy and accusing.

Azerick turned to the man, allowing one insult to slide but not two. "No war is won without spilling blood on both sides. It is the price all who wish to live as free people are willing to pay."

"Easy to say when you're not the one paying it."

"I have paid more than you can imagine, Joah. I may not look it, but I am far older, seen more, suffered more, and sacrificed more than you ever will or can imagine. If you cannot be supportive of those who are willing to fight and die for their freedom, then at least be quiet."

Joah met the sorcerer's glare. "And if I don't?"

Azerick stepped toward him until he was inches from his face. "Then I'll rip your tongue from your throat and feed it to the pigs."

This was not the first harsh exchange between the two. Joah had always been a contentious sort since their first meeting, and he had not warmed in the least. Quite the opposite in fact. With every loss of life, no matter how great their victory, Joah went out of his way to make it as bitter as he could, and Azerick was tired of his constant sniping.

Marley interceded. "We all mourn those who gave their lives for the cause. Let's not tarnish their memory or sacrifice by bickering."

Azerick stared at Joah a moment longer before breaking his gaze and nodding. "You're right. We're all exhausted, hungry, and on edge. We'll all feel a bit better once we've eaten and rested."

Joah spun on his heel, stalked away, and muttered just loud enough for Azerick to hear. "Everyone who ain't already in their eternal rest."

"There's food in the dining hall," Marley said. "Why don't you all get some grub and some rest before we talk about what's next."

Daebian strode next to Azerick as he walked briskly toward the lodge that served as Freehold's communal dining area and dropped a length of cloth knotted at the ends over his head. "Here you go, Father. I made this for you."

Azerick lifted the small sheet draped over his shoulder like a sash. "A sling? There's nothing wrong with my arm."

"It's not for your arm."

"Then what's it for?"

"It's to help support the huge pair of balls you just whipped out in front of everyone," Daebian replied with a grin.

Azerick's shoulders shook and he wagged his head as he tried to stifle his chortling.

CHAPTER 6

Getting into the city was relatively simple by using Daebian's shadow walking ability. While he did not have line of sight to an exit shadow, he was familiar with the ones within Azerick's old lair. Travel was not instantaneous using what he called a blind step, but it was swift enough to avoid most of the shadow spawn, as long as the shadows at the destination did not change or vanish. Azerick and Vera had dedicated one of the small chambers to the task, ensuring that the light, and therefore the shadows, remained unchanged.

"Vera," Azerick said as he and Daebian approached the girl's laboratory.

Vera jumped at the unexpected voice, nearly dropping the two glass beakers half-filled with highly combustible liquids. "Gods on a goat, you nearly blew us all to the abyss!"

"Sorry," Azerick replied sheepishly.

"Need to put a freaking bell on you or something," the young alchemist muttered under her breath as she finished mixing the two agents.

She poured the fresh batch of demon fire into an empty wine bottle, corked it, and added it to a crate containing almost a dozen more incendiary projectiles.

Azerick looked from the filled crate to Vera. "Maybe you shouldn't keep the filled bottles in the laboratory while you're mixing."

Vera narrowed her eyes at the sorcerer. "I'm fine as long as people don't sneak up on me after working for days in a secret chamber beneath the city without so much as a rat fart to break the unending silence."

Daebian sniffed the air. "If it's not the rats then I assume the smell comes from you. Are you eating properly?"

She scowled at him, opened her mouth to issue a retort, but decided she did not want to engage in his acerbic banter. "I still don't like you."

Daebian twitched his shoulders as if he could not care less, which he did not. Vera lugged the crate to a room designed to house the volatile brew, stuffed it with straw, and gently nailed a lid onto it. Andrill had people with travel permits who would sneak the boxes out of the city in smuggler wagons and deposit them in the woods at a prearranged location. Marley's people would retrieve them and distribute the cases to the myriad resistance groups scattered around western and central Valeria.

Vera wiped the sweat from her brow and secured the room's heavy door. "Andrill wanted to talk to you as soon as you popped in for a visit."

"Has something happened?"

"Sort of. Not yet, but we're all pretty sure it will, and soon."

"You've been underground too long. Even your words are becoming cryptic," Daebian quipped.

Vera shot him a sidelong scowl but spoke to Azerick. "We know they're building something with a purpose, but we have yet to figure out what it is."

"I hope this doesn't come out as stupid as it sounds," Azerick said, "but what is it?"

"Swing and a miss. It is exactly as stupid as it sounds," Daebian said.

It was Azerick's turn to scowl at his son. "I mean, can you describe it?"

"Best to get you to Andrill and show you," Vera replied.

She led them to the hidden trap door that opened into a ramshackle building in the squatters' district. Travelling in the sewers was all but impossible since she and the others had used them so effectively in defeating The Order's advance cohort not long ago.

Engineers collapsed the tunnels not required to circulate wastewater and secured the ones needed to keep the system functional along with every entry they could find. It did not take long for the insurgents to discover that the arcanus had also created wards that alerted them to anything remotely human-sized passing through them.

Fortunately, the forged papers they had still worked. At least they did the last time she had walked the city streets. Azerick failed to see many soldiers in the decrepit ward, but he did identify numerous members of the reconstituted city watch. It looked to him like The Order used them to keep an eye on the poorer districts while their legionnaires patrolled the rest of the city.

One thing was certain; The Order certainly lived up to their name. No shadowy figures lurked on street corners or loomed in doorways. The streets were meticulously clean of both rubbish and vagrants. Azerick wondered what they had done to the city's homeless before recalling the new structures he had seen in the squatters' district they had passed through earlier. While still little more than shanties, most were constructed from fresh materials and built in orderly rows with proper thoroughfares.

The thought grated on his nerves. It was a lot easier to hate and kill a despotic invader than one who housed the homeless, cleaned up the streets, and nearly eliminated crime. For a brief instant, it made him doubt his cause, and the thought infuriated him. If he could see the benefit in welcoming The Order, even if only for an instant, how could he hope to continue to convince others to resist?

Azerick shoved the thought aside. A cage, no matter its gilding, is still a cage. He would not surrender himself and his power to The Order. Nor would he allow someone to use him as a weapon to oppress others who likewise fought to be left alone and sovereign.

Vera led them straight to a checkpoint. "It's best to look the dutiful citizen and not try to circumvent them. It could draw attention, and there are eyes everywhere. They reward people for reporting any sign of noncompliance."

"Let's hope our papers still work," Azerick said.

"They should. As far as we know, they haven't found out that we've managed to forge them. Andrill has several people tasked with doing nothing except listening for any word that they know about the forgeries or that they are making any kind of changes. He thinks even if they do find out, they won't be swift in going through all the trouble it would cause to replace everyone's papers unless there was a significant attack linked to the forgeries."

"Do you agree with him?"

Vera chewed her bottom lip. "These people have no qualms about inconveniencing the populace. They might not jump immediately upon finding out, but I don't think it would take much for them to act on it."

Azerick nodded in agreement. "How many people have forged papers now?"

"As many as we need to do business."

"Which is?"

Vera's head hung low. "Too damn many. I have created a device that will hopefully prevent the papers from falling into The Order's hands," she said, tapping a leather satchel hanging around her waist.

Azerick eyed the pouch. "What is it?"

"I call it a burn bag. Pull the cord at the top and it breaks a glass vial and ignites the contents. It burns hot and fast, destroying anything flammable in the bag almost instantly and goes out just as quickly."

"Smart."

"That's why they keep me around."

"It certainly isn't for your charming personality," Daebian piped in.

If his gibe insulted her, she did not show it. "I'm sure you're quite familiar with people tolerating an abrasive person's presence due to a useful skill or service they provide."

"Better to be needed than liked as the former is far more indispensable and difficult to replace."

Vera looked straight ahead and grunted. "Which is why I wish we could enlist your brother's aid. Then we would get both."

That barb struck a nerve, and Daebian's voice lost its levity. "I doubt you have ever met my brother."

One corner of Vera's mouth turned up. "No, but I've met you, and that's sufficient to make an assessment with a high probability for being factual."

Daebian had to bite off any retort he wished to issue as they approached the checkpoint.

The checkpoint commander shuffled the papers they handed over. "What is your purpose for entering the merchant district?"

"To buy things," Daebian replied in a tone that suggested he thought it an idiotic question before Vera could answer.

The decanus locked his eyes onto Daebian and peered beneath his hood. "Why do you wear those smoked spectacles?"

"My brother is blind," Azerick said as he took Daebian by the elbow. "His eyes, or what's left of them, is quite horrendous and he doesn't wish to frighten others with his hideous countenance."

"What?" Daebian shouted.

"He's also quite hard of hearing," Azerick added.

"Are we there yet?" Daebian's hand jutted forth and he began pawing at the legionnaire's face. "Is that Woodward? Woodward, the rash that whore gave me has returned and has spread to my hands because I can't stop scratching it. I need more ointment."

The decanus leapt back and spat when one of Daebian's questing fingers entered his mouth. He shoved all three sets of papers into Vera's hands. "Move along!"

Daebian pretended to stumble and stomped hard on the man's foot when Azerick swung him by the elbow. "Where are we going? Did you get my ointment already?"

"Nicely done," Azerick said with a snort as they hastened away.

"Finally, someone who appreciates my art," Daebian replied with a smile.

"You're lucky you didn't get arrested," Vera snapped, not nearly as amused as the two men.

"I'm sure they have better things to do than to bother with an infected blind man. I do need to stop by the chemist though. This living in the rough these past few weeks has done nothing good for my previously flawless skin. Especially around the groinal area if you know what I mean."

Vera slapped at his questing hand and lurched away. "Every time I think you can't be more repulsive; you go and outdo yourself."

"I always say, if you aren't continually outdoing yourself, you aren't trying hard enough."

"I would appreciate it if you tried a little less before you get us all arrested."

Daebian nudged Azerick with his elbow. "Clearly not a patron of the arts. Always trying to stifle another's imagination."

Azerick grinned at his son. "As much as I appreciate sticking it to The Order, particularly in such a literal manner, I agree with Vera that we should keep a low profile inside the city."

Daebian shrugged and flashed him a wan smile. "Sure, shouldn't be too hard. We did so well the last time we were here."

"This is a different kind of battle."

"I know precisely what kind of battle it is. I'm not sure you do," Daebian said, his tone devoid of its previous mirth.

Azerick let his eyes answer Daebian's challenge. Now was not the time to get into a verbal sparring match with him. Vera led them into a tavern patroned by hard-eyed men who looked to spend a lot of time in the establishment but did little drinking. They descended the stairs leading into the stock cellar and entered a room located behind a concealed door.

Andrill sat next to Braxis, who was slouched in a chair and snoozing as usual. Four other men stood or sat against a far wall, which was much too close for Azerick's comfort. Azerick wondered how much time Andrill spent in the cramped room as it was just about the only place he found the old thief since he had returned.

Andrill's face lit up when Azerick entered behind Vera. "Azerick, my boy, welcome back! I've heard of your successes out there in the wilds. You're becoming quite the notorious highwayman. You've certainly ruffled a few feathers amongst The Order."

"I'll be happy once we've plucked them clean," Azerick replied with a scowl.

Andrill winked at him. "Will you?"

"Vera says there's something going on in the city I should see but deferred to you when I asked what it was."

Andrill's smile grew even wider. "Ah, yes, there is indeed. Your arrival is quite fortuitous. I believe that whatever is going to happen is happening today. Probably in the next hour or so. Come, let us go for a walk. I need to see what all the fuss is about as well as the sunlight. I fear I may be turning into a vampire down here."

Braxis grumbled without looking up or opening his eyes, "You're certainly old enough to be one."

"Go back to sleep, you old goat!" Andrill snapped.

Azerick was not sure if the noise Braxis made in reply was a snore or a bleat. Either way, it was clear he did not intend to leave his chair. Andrill rushed up the stairs with the speed and grace of a much younger man, not pausing to see if his guests followed him or not. He looked up at the clear sky and blinked like a man just freed from prison.

"If it weren't for the lack of trash and reduced human stench, you could almost forget we're in an occupied city," Andrill beamed.

Azerick did not share his bliss. "A similar thought occurred to me upon entering the city as well. I am concerned it could influence our people's desire to continue resisting The Order, and not in a good way."

Andrill lost his smile and waved Azerick and the others to follow him as he walked briskly down the street. "It will and has."

He pointed at the merchant stands and storefronts. "The merchants are seeing a big upswing in sales and a decrease in crime. There are no more shakedowns or protection rackets anywhere in the city except maybe in the Squatters' District, and not much even there. What in the abyss do they have to take? The nobles and the wealthy are still wealthy and influential even after being stripped of titles and the heavy tax The Order levied on them."

"Is there anyone who will continue to support us?"

"The Order is collecting a third of all crop harvests to support their soldiers, and the farmers aren't compensated for it or are paid only a fraction of its worth. Same with blacksmiths, quarriers and most anyone in road construction, and other labor-based professions, and they aren't terribly happy working for less than market value. On the other hand, they are getting more work, so it's a mixed bag."

Azerick wore a grim expression and nodded. "So the only people we can really count on are those who disdain honest work like thieves, murderers, smugglers, and cutthroats. Not exactly the most reliable group of people on which to rest the fate of the kingdom. No offense."

"None taken," Andrill replied with a grin. "I'm quite familiar with all of them and wouldn't normally trust them to scrub my chamber pot. Unusual times make for strange bedfellows."

The streets started to become more congested the nearer they drew to the city's central plaza. By the time they reached the huge parade square, they had to shoulder their way through the crowd, which garnered many irate looks, but the offended parties voiced few complaints. It was still a city on edge, and most people did not want to attract the attention of their conquerors.

"Why are all these people here?" Azerick asked.

Andrill said, "Some were probably ordered to be here. Others most likely came for the show."

"What show?"

"That's what we're here to find out."

Azerick looked over the heads of the crowd, saw the stone structure arching overhead, and his blood ran cold. He fervently prayed he was not seeing what he thought he saw. His prayers went unanswered, and his worst fears were borne out when they finally reached the front of the crush of bodies being held back by phalanxes of Legionnaires.

Daebian took in the large stone archway. "That looks remarkably —"

"Like the gateway portals I built to evacuate the cities during the Gods War," Azerick finished.

"That was my assessment as well, but I had hoped I was wrong and it was just a monument of some kind," Andrill said.

Azerick gave the structure a slow shake of his head. "I thought their reinforcements would arrive by boat, that we had more time. They could bring entire legions through in less than an hour. We must destroy it."

Vera shook her head, breaking her usual silence. "We thought of that once we got an idea of what it could be. They have kept the plaza isolated from everyone but soldiers and workers. There are no sewers or tunnels intact beneath it, and the whole area is ringed by those magic nullifiers."

Azerick sent his senses out into the ether. "They don't seem to be active now."

"Do you think you can destroy it now that the nullifiers are down?" Vera asked.

Azerick's eyes took in the ranks of legionnaires and what must have been half the arcanus in the city all standing guard around the gate. "Maybe if the ground beneath it were not solid. It would likely be a suicide mission, but one I would take if it had a chance of succeeding. The arcanus have warded it and most of the plaza. I could probably break through their wards, especially if Daebian could shadow step and execute a number of their mages, but even then, I doubt I could overcome the defenses built into the gate itself before they cut me down."

"We have several wizards in the city," Andrill said.

"I don't think it would be enough even if we had time to gather them together and coordinate an attack. Like you said, it's obvious they plan on using it very soon."

As if on cue, a low drone sounded through the plaza, and the air inside the massive arch began to shimmer. The backdrop vanished, and blurry shapes and colors resolved into orderly ranks of legionnaires, their battle standards flapping in a breeze no one in the plaza felt. The region they could see within the portal looked a bit arid but nothing like a desert. It was fertile, and fine estates with manors of unusual design dotted the landscape.

A horn sounded; its clarion call slightly muted as it reverberated through the portal. The massive army, stretching as far as they could see, marched forward. Ranks upon ranks paraded into the plaza with masterful precision, not a single step out of thousands out of sync. Azerick ignored the oncoming legions, his eyes transfixed by a single figure leading the procession.

She was tall with a regal bearing. Although dressed in white silks and adorned with what must have been several pounds of gold and jewels, she exuded power and command. Her features were lean; her cheekbones high and prominent to buttress blue eyes so brilliant and contrasting with her dark skin that Azerick could make them out clearly even from this distance. The woman's pate was shorn clean, but it only accentuated her obvious strength and added to her mystique.

Her appearance managed to capture Daebian's gaze as well. "Uh, is that—"

"Sylvianne Attar, daughter of the emperor and empress of Syrna," Azerick answered in a hollow voice before Daebian could finish the question.

"Firstly, that's the second time you've cut me off mid-sentence, and it's getting damned annoying. Second, I was going to say the woman who kicked your spectral ass halfway across the sea."

Azerick could only nod. He was too focused on the woman beaming at her newest citizens, and what her presence portended, to muster even the desire to respond to his son. Sylvianne's piercing gaze seemed to settle on him, and he was certain she recognized who he was. He braced himself for an attack that never came.

The princess peeled off toward the castle with her retinue of senior officers and officials in tow while the bulk of her army marched toward the city gates. Even the gliders streaking through the portal and zipping overhead failed to distract Azerick as he stood transfixed until Sylvianne vanished from his sight.

"Well, this isn't good," Daebian quipped.

Azerick shook his head slowly. "No, this is bad. Very, very bad."

CHAPTER 7

Princess Sylvianne attar strode ahead of her entourage toward the castle amidst the waving and cheering crowd. She had no doubt that Imperator Martinus had commanded many, if not most, of them to witness the legions' arrival, but she was confident their cheers were not part of the script. Her regal yet daunting presence had that effect on most people.

Legionnaires knelt and bowed their heads at her approach. Those guarding the castle entrance sprang up as she drew near and pulled open the doors to admit her and her retinue of legion officers and court officials. After making a few inquiries, Sylvianne found the imperator in his war room with a handful of his senior officers. Someone had obviously run ahead and warned them of her arrival since they were facing the door and dropped to a knee with heads bowed the instant she entered.

"Rise," Sylvianne commanded. "There will be no more need of that inside these walls."

"Yes, Your Highness," Imperator Martinus said as he stood. "Your Highness, had I known you would be arriving with the legions, I would have prepared a proper greeting."

"I am sure you would have, which is why I chose not to announce it. I had no desire to suffer the delays it would have caused. I came because I read your reports, particularly the ones describing the resistance you have encountered."

Imperator Martinus' dark skin hid the blush heating his face. "It is a bit more than we expected. Not so much the size of the resistance but in their relative success in some of the skirmishes. Their greatest victories, while relatively small and few, have come under the direct command of a sorcerer of some renown in this land."

A smile tugged at the corners of Sylvianne's lips. "Yes, Azerick Giles. He was the one responsible for Primus Ploutarch's bitter defeat."

"Yes, Highness. The very same one."

"He was in the city when I arrived, watching from the crowd. Were you aware of that, Imperator?"

Imperator Martinus visibly swallowed and twitched his head. "No, Highness. You saw him?"

"I sensed his presence, but I'm certain he saw me."

"It is a shame you did not strike him down on the spot. It would have alleviated much of our troubles here."

Sylvianne arched her thin, perfectly groomed eyebrows. "And started a battle between two formidable sorcerers in the middle of a town square crowded with my newest subjects? How would their deaths, and possibly the destruction of the greater part of this city, been received by the rest of the kingdom?"

Chagrinned, Martinus cast his eyes to the floor. "Forgive me, Highness. I did not think before speaking."

"That is why I am here, to help you shoulder much of that burden. Tell me of the pacification efforts and the resistance you have met thus far."

Imperator Martinus nodded and directed the princess' attention to the map almost covering a large table. "Most of the citizens and local authorities have sworn the oath and appear to be keeping to it for the most part. As you likely noticed on your arrival, there are a few who failed to keep the covenant and paid the price."

"I did indeed. As of this moment, there will be no more public executions, and you will remove the criminals hanging in the streets. At this point, they only serve to undermine the benevolence of our rule."

"Yes, Highness." Martinus motioned to one of his officers, who left the room to carry out her orders.

"And the resistance?"

Martinus pointed to the map. "There are three main points of resistance. The sorcerer heads the ones centered on this city. His group is the smallest but also the most successful in terms of body count and disruptions. The second is between the two cities of Brightridge and Velaroth. That is the largest group, but they have the fewest number of arcanus, or mages as they call them. The former duke of Brightridge leads that group. We estimate their numbers to be around three to five thousand, broken down into smaller units spread across the region."

"What of the former king?" Sylvianne asked. "He has taken the oath. Is he abiding by it?"

Martinus ducked his head. "As best we can tell, Highness. He has provided names and helped familiarize our armies with the terrain. He has also been quite vocal about accepting The Order's rule. There is a rebel force in the area, but so far, they have done little more than raid food supplies and evade our legionnaires."

"Good. Transitions go far more smoothly if we have the cooperation of the previous rulers. What of the third group?"

Martinus pointed to southeast region of the map. "Argoth is their southeasternmost city and lies in this desert region bordering the kingdom of Sumara. We believe they are using the mountains and narrow passages to evade our scouts. Led by the former duchess of Argoth, her army numbers two to three thousand and has a significant number of mages, many of which specialize in combat. It's possible they are crossing over the border to strike at us before retreating back into Sumara."

Sylvianne pursed her lips. "Are they getting reinforcements from Sumara? We are not ready to expand into that nation and start a third front. Not until we have pacified Olmul, and our lack of progress in that war is why we are here."

The imperator nodded. "The emergence of the spawn more than twenty years ago created a common enemy and normalized relations between the two nations. We have sent glider scouts across the border, but none of them has reported any movement in our direction. However, they have been gathering their armies, likely in anticipation of our pending liberation."

"Tell me of this land. What can we expect once we decide to bring it into the empire?"

Martinus took a deep breath and let it out. "It is twice as vast as this kingdom, but the land is mostly desert and somewhat inhospitable. While they have several great cities, much of their populace reside in scattered tribes, much like Olmul, but they are not nearly as primitive. I expect its pacification to be a challenge in much the same way."

Sylvianne frowned and shook her head. "This is not welcome news. We had hoped to gather resources from both lands to hasten our conquest of Olmul. What you are telling me is we may need to pull even more legions from elsewhere in the empire if we wish to conquer Sumara. Otherwise, we ignore them, use our new legionnaires to push deeper into Olmul, and leave our newest acquisition nearly undefended and vulnerable to attack."

"I believe that is an accurate assessment, Your Highness."

"It appears to me that Azerick Giles is our biggest threat. He is a symbol for their people, a cause around which to rally. Remove him and you undermine the insurgents' reason to fight. Every death they suffer will sting that much more, and they will begin to question their cause."

"I can recall some of the deployed units to bolster the local ranks," Martinus said.

Sylvianne paused before answering. "No. Send most of our reinforcements to supplement the legions battling the other two fronts. I will take a personal hand in ending Azerick Giles."

"Your Highness, is it wise to place yourself on the front lines? You are too important to the empire to risk your safety in such a direct confrontation. I'm sure, with your council, my legions can bring this sorcerer to heel."

Sylvianne's expression lost its calm façade, and a storm raged in her glacial blue eyes. "Do you think this man is more powerful than I? Do you think my brother hides behind his legions' shields while they battle the Olmul?"

Martinus wilted beneath the princess' glare. "No, Highness, of course not! However, the sorcerer has shown himself to be a formidable opponent in both power and cunning. I only wish to serve the empire and preserve your family's righteous rule to the best of my ability."

Her stormy anger subsided as quickly as it had risen. "You are right, Imperator Martinus. Only a fool allows their pride to underestimate an enemy who has shown himself to be more than capable. I assure you; I am no fool, and I will take your words of caution seriously. Have someone show me to my rooms so I can locate Azerick Giles and deal with him accordingly."

Court officials raced ahead to evict the former duke and his wife from their rooms and prepare them for their princess' use. When Sylvianne arrived, her people were already putting the final changes on the rooms with practiced expertise. They bowed their heads and filed out moments later. Sylvianne located the solarium where her people had set up her arcanarium, a room dedicated to performing more ritualized magic.

She sensed the wards placed on the rooms by one or more of the stronger arcanus. They would suffice until she had time to create ones that were more powerful herself. Sylvianne suspected that Azerick would not tarry inside the city after witnessing her arrival, and her best hope of locating him was to catch him using magic to hasten his exit to report her presence to his people.

It was unlikely she could find him by sensing the residual magic of his arura as she had upon her arrival. It was sheer luck that she had gotten close enough to detect his presence in the plaza, and she was not about to go walking around the city in hopes of passing near enough to pick up his magical scent.

Sylvianne sat cross-legged upon a thin cushion placed on the floor, a large, shallow pan of pure elemental water resting before her. She concentrated upon the shimmering surface, and the reflection of her face and the ceiling changed to that of a bird's eye view of the city. She focused her will, and the image shrank to display the surrounding countryside.

For nearly an hour, Sylvianne sat unmoving, her focus unwavering in a trance-like state. The corners of her mouth curled up when a tiny ripple broke the surface of the water, as if a grain of sand had fallen into it, perhaps two miles from the city wall. Another ripple appeared in the same place a moment later, and then a third materialized what Sylvianne guessed to be perhaps a mile away from the previous one.

The sorcerer had clearly used a portal spell to speed his travel. She assumed it was Azerick. She could probably get a definitive identity, but doing so posed the risk of alerting him to her scrying if he had taken precautions against it. The odds of it being him was high enough that she did not feel the need to get confirmation. No matter who it was, their use of such magic was illegal, and she would deal with them regardless.

Several more ripples disturbed the water in short succession, each one forcing her to expand and shift her view so they did not appear outside her vision. They ran a fairly straight line, so it was not difficult to track them and estimate where the next one would appear. After waiting almost two hours without detecting any further use of magic, Sylvianne thought he might have reached his destination.

She was about to inform Imperator Martinus of her discovery when another ripple broke the surface, and this one appeared much farther away. Unless this sorcerer had an uncanny ability or power beyond even that of her own, conjuring a gate that far apart was impossible. That meant there was a fixed gate much like the ones her people used to travel vast distances. Her opinion of these people increased.

If he had used a fixed gate, she was certain Azerick had traveled home, or at least to a place of significant importance. This was good news. It meant she might be able to quell this resistance in very short order. Her parents would be pleased. Pacifying the region to which she was assigned while her brother still fought to conquer Olmul was just a bonus.

This was her first field command, so the pacification needed to be swift and flawless. If everything went according to plan, she could train and mobilize enough relief forces in this new land to spearhead a second front in Olmul. She smiled as she thought about riding to her brother Phaidros' rescue. He would be furious.

"Martinus!" Sylvianne called out.

In less than a minute, the imperator knocked on the door before letting himself in. "Highness."

Sylvianne stood and straightened her gown. "Prepare a company for an assault, and have someone prepare my armor. I will lead it myself."

Martinus looked about to argue before ducking his head and turning about. He barked orders as he stormed down the hall. Moments later, a team of attendants hurried in bearing her battle raiment. They strapped the form-fitting arcanum cuirass over a sleeveless gambeson. Bracers and greaves of the same silver metal protected her forearms and lower legs.

Sylvianne strode down the castle halls with her light helm tucked beneath one arm. A full company of elite legionnaires stood at attention in the courtyard. The princess slipped the helm onto her head and mounted her personal glider. She made the vehicle hover ten feet off the ground before the assembled soldiers.

"Legionnaires, we depart to assault what I believe to be an insurgent stronghold," Sylvianne shouted to her warriors. "Our primary objective is to capture the rebel sorcerer Azerick Giles or kill him should he leave us no other option. This is a precision strike, and I will not tolerate wanton slaughter. We are better than that. We are better than them, and we must prove that through our actions."

She turned to her commander. "Martinus, prepare your company to march."

Legionnaires began boarding the nearby skimmers at the imperator's orders while he and a handful of scouts and personal bodyguards surrounded their princess on gliders. In a few scant minutes, the company glided out of the city toward Freehold.

CHAPTER 8

Azerick and Daebian stepped out of the portal, each carrying a crate of Vera's explosive concoction. Although closely watched, no one challenged them as they made their way toward what was once the hidden village of rogues and dissidents. It now housed the Academy wizards and students that had managed to escape Southport, and those same rogues were now the kingdom's freedom fighters.

They handed their burdens off to the village's supply manager who stored them in a stone building. For some reason, Marley did not like the idea of keeping them in his meetinghouse. Kord stood sentry at his usual spot near the door, not bothering to hide his dislike of the father and son duo.

Azerick ignored him, and Daebian flashed a smile that conveyed nothing but sarcasm meant to goad the big man. Kord refused to take to the bait. Marley sat inside looking both disinterested and eager to hear of the latest news.

"What manner of tidings do you bring today?" Marley asked. "Bright ones I hope."

Azerick shook his head. "Only dark ones."

Marley frowned. "Depressingly predictable."

"We brought back two cases of Vera's fire bottles," Daebian said. "They'll brighten most anything."

Azerick gave his son a suffering look and said, "The Order's princess has arrived with another contingent of soldiers."

Marley's eyebrows shot up. "So, not only do we face a nearly unbeatable army, they have gotten reinforcements headed by what you have described as some sort of mortal demi-god."

"I never said she was a demi-god," Azerick replied.

"Although she was able to bitch slap him from halfway around the world," Daebian quipped.

Azerick sighed. "Her power appears to be significant, but I can't say how much of a danger she represents to us directly. It is unlikely she would risk herself by taking the field."

"But you are certain she is here?" Marley asked.

"Yes. We saw her emerge from a gate similar to the ones we used in the Gods War."

"Are you sure she did not see you?" Marley asked, pitching his voice louder.

Azerick shook his head. "It's very unlikely. We were in the crowd, and she was surrounded by retainers and soldiers."

The sounds of excited voices and pounding feet issued from beyond the door. A moment later, Kord stormed inside.

"Marley, our outer sentries report a company of Order soldiers headed directly toward us and moving fast on those flying machines and hovering wagons."

Marley's face twisted in anger and burned red. "You damn fool; you've brought them right to us!"

Azerick stared blankly. "There's no way they could have tracked us."

"You mean there's no way *you* could have tracked us," Daebian said. "Clearly someone isn't bound by your limitations."

"Damn it!" Azerick cursed and raced outside.

Marley was on his heels and shouting the moment he cleared the door. "Grab only what you need and get to the gates! Noncombatants first. The rest of us will guard our retreat."

At first glance, it appeared that everyone was in a panic, running about clutching a few possessions and dragging young children behind them by the hand. It took only a moment for Azerick to realize that while people raced through the village, there was order to their movements. Everyone had a job to do. Some loaded food and blankets into carts while others rounded up young children and counted them off before hurrying them toward one of the magical gates.

The sentries must have had a magical means of communication, because it took several minutes for the first gliders to hove into view.

The guards had said there was a company of soldiers coming, which meant the rest must have been riding skimmers hidden by the trees.

"Why aren't they advancing quicker?" Daebian asked.

Azerick looked around. "The veil they use to hide the village is still up. Their arcanus must not have pierced it yet."

"Maybe they'll fly by us?"

"Not likely. If someone was able to track us from the city, the illusion won't hide us for long."

As if on cue, the gliders lurched forward. Even wearing the silver helm, Azerick recognized Princess Sylvianne Attar astride the lead glider.

"Isn't that the princess?" Daebian asked.

"Yes," Azerick confirmed with a heavy sigh.

"Good gods, how many times were you wrong in the last few minutes? It must be some sort of record," Daebian chortled.

"Laugh it up."

"I am."

The gliders hovered about fifty feet overhead, and Sylvianne's magically amplified voice boomed out over the vale. "Surrender peacefully, and I will grant you mercy and protection as prisoners of war. Resist and you shall fall to our spears."

Kord jogged up to them with the crates of alchemical fire bottles. "Most of the noncombatants are away, but we need more time to get the rest through."

Daebian looked to Azerick. "Would you like to give her our answer?"

Azerick nodded. "Gladly."

The sorcerer thrust his staff skyward and unleashed a fireball that exploded an instant later. The fiery blast was so large it blocked all five gliders from view and sent a hot gust of wind blowing through the village. The conflagration winked out almost as fast as it had burst across the sky. The arcane assault appeared to have not touched any of the fliers.

"Well, crap," Azerick muttered.

"You will have to do better than that, sorcerer," Sylvianne said in a mirthful tone.

"Careful what you wish for!" Azerick called up to her.

A powerful gale tore through the treetops and hit the gliders with the force of a hurricane. The riders had to tighten their grips as the aerial vehicles pitched forward and were sent scattering like blown leaves across the sky. One rider lost his grip and dangled below the craft by a safety line. Sylvianne slashed the air with one hand and quelled the wind.

The sorceress glared down at her foes and sent a full flight of arcane arrows lancing toward them. Azerick raised a hasty ward to shield the three of them from the luminescent shafts. At least half a score of them slammed into his shield while twice as many struck and cratered the ground around them.

"By the gods' balls, if one of those things strikes these bottles, we'll go up like a...I don't even know—a volcano!" Kord exclaimed.

Daebian glanced at the explosive bottles. "Father, how good is your aim with those portals you open?"

"I can pretty much open them where I want. Why?"

Daebian picked up one of the bottles, flicked his eyes skyward, and smiled. Azerick caught on and matched it. He opened a gate in front of them.

"You won't escape me that way, Azerick Giles!" Sylvianne called down.

"Wasn't planning to," Azerick shouted back.

He sent half a dozen arcane orbs streaking toward three of the gliders while Daebian and Kord flung their bottles into the gate. As Azerick suspected, the wards or shields raised by the riders blocked the magical attack, but they were not as prepared for a physical assault from above.

Bottles fell through the portal exit and burst upon striking two of the flying machines. Liquid fire engulfed one's wing and immolated the other's front end. The pilots panicked and sped into motion, which only worsened their predicament.

The fire covering the glider's nose blew back into the pilot's face. The arcanus clawed and slapped at her face until she slammed into the ground in a flaming wreck. The other pilot managed a hard but controlled landing and vaulted from the vehicle.

Daebian was on him in an instant and plunged his sword through the arcanus' chest. Another bottle fell through the portal but missed its target and shattered against the ground. Flames erupted, and smoke quickly filled the air.

Small fires from the flaming liquid cast off by the two gliders dotted the clearing as well and began spreading. Azerick threw himself to the side in anticipation of another attack. The air exploded around him and tossed him more than double the length of his jump.

He opened a portal beneath him and transported himself across the vale. Azerick flung fire and lightning at the three remaining gliders with almost wild abandon, his intent to keep them too off balance to counterattack than to bring them down. Daebian pointed at one of the gliders, and Azerick opened a portal next to him the moment the rider stopped to unleash a spell.

Daebian leapt through the portal and fell onto the vehicle just behind the rider. Sparks flew as his sword pierced the ward surrounding the arcanus. He slashed through the rider's safety strap and hurled him from the glider.

The strange key attached to the arcanus' magical manacles pulled out of the vehicle's controls, and it plummeted toward the ground with Daebian still riding atop it. Daebian spied a shadow stretching across the ground and leapt toward it. He vanished into the patch of darkness and flew out of another nearby shadow.

Azerick and Daebian were not alone in their battle. Several Academy mages and archers struck at the skimmers laden with legionnaires when they broke through the tree line moments after the battle commenced.

One of the skimmers bucked wildly when a well-placed spell exploded beneath it and sent the contingent tumbling off it like water droplets from a shaking dog. The other soldiers dismounted with all haste and formed ranks. Spells, arrows, and bolts bounced off the legionnaires' shields from the physical and magical protection they provided.

Azerick grabbed Daebian by the arm. "We need to pull back. Help get the others to the gates. I'll distract and slow down the soldiers to give you the time you need."

At a nod from Azerick, Kord raised a horn to his lips and blew a single, long note. The mages and insurgent fighters turned and ran toward the gate hidden in the distant trees. Azerick sprinted in the opposite direction, hurling large, noisy fireballs at the ranks of soldiers to draw their attention toward him.

The earth beneath his feet churned and burst open as if a giant were clawing its way out of a grave. Azerick felt his feet leave the ground and began a slow arc that put them higher than his head. His ward protected him from most of the direct damage such a fall normally caused, but he could not ignore some of the other painful aspects of physics.

Azerick bounced and rolled several times before coming to a stop against the base of a large tree. He looked up and saw Sylvianne and her two flying escorts racing toward him. Azerick, still seated against the tree, slashed at the sky with his staff and opened a portal directly in front of all three of them.

The two gliders vanished into Azerick's gate spell, which spit them back out into the thick forest. One rider slammed headlong into an old oak tree and exploded in a spectacular ball of magical blue fire. Imperator Martinus pulled hard on the controls and avoided a direct collision, but one of the vehicle's stubby wings caught a stout branch, and he spun out of control before plowing into the ground.

Sylvianne, flying just behind her two escorts, reacted quickly. She leapt from the back of her glider and floated languidly down to the ground. Her aerial vehicle sped into the portal and back out the other end, nearly crashing into the unlucky imperator who just getting back to his feet.

The sorceress stalked toward Azerick with one of The Order's shimmering swords. She swept it before her and sent crescents of arcane energy streaking at him. Azerick rolled away from the tree. The magical spinning blades hued into the tree trunk, the third strike sending it crashing to the ground.

Azerick ran into the woods with the powerful sorceress and legionnaires dogging his heels. Getting an idea from Sylvianne's last attack, Azerick began lashing out with magic. Not at the soldiers but at the trees around him. Flames spread through the treetops, turning them into giant torches.

Smoke filled the air, and Azerick had to locate the enemy more by sound than sight. He began casting his stone spike spell around the base of the trees. The stone shards burst up through the ground, churning the hard earth and severing the roots holding the trees upright.

Azerick struck at the trees by conjuring powerful winds, gating, and hitting the large copse from different directions. Trees swayed violently in the howling gale and began toppling with ominous cracks and ground-shaking thumps.

Order soldiers began crying out as the flaming arboreal giants toppled and crushed or pinned them to the ground. They broke ranks and scattered, but the field of battle was too large and choked with felled timber and smoke to vacate quickly. Dozens of pained cries from soldiers pinned beneath trees and branches created a discordant chorus with the crashing and thumping sounds echoing through the forest.

The hairs on the back of Azerick's neck stood on end, and he hurled himself to the side. A green ray of light as big around as his thigh struck a tree trunk where he had been standing and bored a hole clean through it and several others beyond. The stricken trees began to topple. Azerick opened a gate parallel to the ground and in a falling tree's path.

The toppling giant passed through the portal and fell in two separate pieces to the ground. The ten-foot section that passed through the portal appeared above Sylvianne. The princess leapt out of its path and hued through it with her shimmering sword as if it were kindling.

The sorceress thrust out her free hand, and a cyclonic vortex of wind and arcane power slammed into Azerick. It lifted him from his feet and sent him hurtling through brush and saplings until gravity reasserted its control and pulled him painfully back to the ground.

Azerick started to rise, but a whip made of violet energy snapped at his head. It sheared through brush like a razor through beard stubble, leaving the shorn end smoldering. Sylvianne charged, her eldritch whip snaking out a dozen yards, slicing through everything in her path, including the troublesome sorcerer if he failed to avoid the deadly lash.

Azerick decided it was past time to vacate the field of battle and made an expeditious retreat. He opened a gate and jumped through it. He hit the ground on the far side and kept running, weaving in a drunken gait caused by the portal's disorienting effects.

Something struck him in the back with the force of a kick delivered by a draft horse. Azerick heard several ribs crack under the brutal blow and cried out as he tumbled across the ground. He kept rolling and put a large boulder between himself and the source of the attack.

"You're persistent," Azerick called out over his shoulder.

"And you are troublesome," Sylvianne replied with a hint of mirth in her voice.

"Yeah, I hear that a lot."

"If you don't surrender, I will kill you."

Azerick laughed. "I've heard that a lot too! A few people have even accomplished it, but it's never seemed to stick."

The princess chuckled. "So, it's true what they say?"

"That I'm handsome and charming? Guilty as charged."

"I hadn't heard that, but I'm willing to concede the point," Sylvianne said.

"I don't suppose you're willing to concede our fight as well."

"Hardly. You cannot defeat me, and even if you somehow miraculously managed the feat, you can never defeat The Order. You must concede that I am more powerful than you by a significant measure."

Azerick's shrug was not visible to her from where he sat, but he made it clear in his voice. "I won't argue with that."

"Really? It is rare for a person of considerable power to admit their inferiority. Particularly a man, and never to a woman."

"I lack the ego to deny the obvious, and I have known too many powerful women to underestimate them. Besides, I've achieved many of my victories not through raw magical power, but through its clever application."

Azerick opened a portal beneath a boulder next to him. Sylvianne moved at nearly the same time, avoiding the huge stone despite it appearing only a few feet over her head. Azerick unleashed a barrage of magical attacks and raised a field of stone spikes beneath her.

The sorceress' arcane shield blocked everything Azerick threw at her, and the stone shards crumbled to dust as quickly as they appeared for several feet all around her. She slashed her blazing sword downward and sent a spinning disc of energy back at him.

Azerick dashed away, and the disc split the boulder in twain. The earth began to quake, and massive fissures opened all around him. He tried to leap to solid ground, but the crevasses continued to spread, and an invisible force slammed into him. Azerick fell into the sundered ground's gaping black maw.

He conjured another gate as he fell and vanished an instant before the earthen jaws snapped shut around him. Azerick tumbled hard against the rocky ground upon which he found himself. Spray from a nearby waterfall felt refreshing as it spattered against his exposed skin.

Sylvianne's voice called out above the raging water's roar. "I have to say, I've never seen portal magic used in such an offensive manner. You are quite clever, but I can sense it the moment you begin your casting. You cannot escape me so easily. This close, I do not even need my scrying bowl to know where it goes. Now yield."

Azerick chuckled as he used his staff to help pull himself to his feet. "You think this is the end—a single battle? This is far from over."

Azerick flipped his staff around and drove the arcanum tip into the ground. A network of cracks spread out and raced toward Sylvianne. She grinned, shook her head, and escaped through her own gate. Azerick ripped open a portal at the same time. The full force of the waterfall jetting out of Azerick's portal met Sylvianne when she reappeared.

There are immutable laws of physics that not even magic can always break. Sylvianne raised her shield immediately, but thousands of gallons of water per second blasted into her and carried her away like a piece of flotsam.

"I can sense yours too, bitch," Azerick cursed under his breath and ported as far away as he could get before the sorceress could regain her bearings and track him.

CHAPTER 9

Azerick winced with every step as he limped as fast as he could through the forest. He dared not open a gate to hasten his travel even though it was unlikely the princess could track him this far away. She had probably only managed the feat because she must have seen him in the city and was able to detect his use of magic through close proximity.

He was not going to take the chance. The Order had found Freehold because of him. They had lost their main base of operation, and it was the nearest one to Southport. He would not risk exposing them once again, so he shambled cross-country for hours. The setting sun forced him to make camp for the night, not that the coming darkness required much effort to convince him to rest.

Azerick was exhausted, but the pain of his injuries prevented him from falling into a deep sleep the moment he stopped. The healing potion he had consumed earlier had repaired the worst of the damage, but he still felt enough of the abuse to delay his rest. He thought of building a platform up in a tree but discarded the idea. He simply lacked the energy and decided a simple ward would have to suffice.

The sorcerer strung invisible strands of magic throughout the area. Anything larger than a badger would alert him the moment it crossed the boundary. It should suffice for the night. It would have to.

Despite his pain, Azerick fell asleep soon after establishing camp. His mind continued to churn even after slipping into a dream state. His battle with the powerful sorceress played out over and over, refusing to let him rest even in sleep.

His discomfort may have saved his life. Azerick jerked awake the instant he felt something cross his wards. He hardened the air around himself and suffused it with magic just before something heavy crashed into it with shower of sparks. The scent of burnt flesh filled the air, and the spawn writhed on the ground, its hide smoking. Several more shapes leapt out of the darkness with talons extended in hopes of ripping him apart.

Azerick morphed the arcanum ball on his staff into a cleaver and slashed at the onrushing monsters. The blade cut through flesh and bone with only slight resistance. He could have reduced everything within a hundred feet to ash with his magic, but he feared The Order detecting such powerful spells even if the odds were low.

The handful of spawn balked at the bright light he conjured. Azerick took advantage of their momentary distraction and charged the tightest knot of creatures, hewing into them with his polearm and lashing out at others with targeted spells.

The fight lasted only a minute, but it felt longer to the sorcerer's exhausted mind and pained body. Azerick leaned on his staff and stared at the grisly scene. He estimated sunrise was still a good three hours away, but there was no going back to sleep now. With a heavy sigh, he forced his feet to resume the exhausting trek.

Azerick reached the camp after a thankfully uneventful day and night. Sentries noted his approach, and a large group of fighters and mages met his arrival.

"Took you long enough," Daebian said from the head of the welcoming party.

"I walked most of the way," Azerick replied.

Daebian gave him a lop-sided grin. "You look more like you were dragged most of the way."

Azerick tried to smile back, but he was too exhausted. "How is everyone?"

"Most of our people made it through the gates by the time our fighters retreated. Those who stayed back to defend the gates suffered a few casualties, but your distraction worked long enough for most of them to get away as well. We have a handful of missing people who probably failed to reach the gates before they closed. Joah is among the missing."

Azerick nodded. Joah was one of Marley's lieutenants and deeply opposed to their involvement in the resistance. While he would not miss the man's presence and constant arguing, it was a loss they could not afford. Joah had been a capable fighter and leader despite his prickly nature.

"Are we secure here?" Azerick asked.

Daebian nodded as he led the way into camp. "We're twenty miles from the nearest Order occupation. The mages have screened us from both mundane and magical view as best they can. We will be roughing it for a while until we can build some proper structures. Food is our most urgent concern."

Azerick nodded. They would only have as much as the people had thought to carry with them through the portal and the small stash they had created when they had established their fallback position.

"What about Marley?" Azerick asked.

The corner of Daebian's mouth quirked up. "Complaining as usual, but he's done a good job getting everyone organized building shelters, defenses, foraging, and setting up sentries. What do you want to do now?"

Azerick let out a long breath. "Sleep for a couple of days."

Daebian nodded. "I figured you would. I have tent set up for us over here."

Daebian led Azerick to a tent replete with cot and bedroll. Azerick did not bother to ask which bed was his. He picked one at random and fell onto it face first.

"Tell everyone if they wake me up, I will make them regret it," Azerick said into the thin pillow.

"Even Marley?"

"Especially Marley."

Azerick plunged into the blackness of deep sleep. Whatever nightmares sought to plague him were little more than a backdrop his mind ignored as it focused on rest. When next he opened his eyes, light streamed through the narrow opening in the tent flap at a steep angle. Since the tent opening faced to the east, it must have been late morning the next day. He hoped it had been only one day.

Azerick found Marley seated in a chair just outside his tent. The sour look on his face said he was not there to wish him a good morning.

"I have been waiting for you to awake for some time now," Marley grumbled.

Azerick stretched his arms over his head. "You can wait a little longer unless you want to watch me piss."

Marley appeared to consider the option a moment. "I'll meet you at the cooking fire."

Azerick finished his business and found the cauldron suspended over a fire in the center of camp. He helped himself to a bowl, filled it to the brim with stew, and sat on a nearby crate to eat his repast.

Marley loomed next to him. "I hope you enjoy your meal. You've taken two rations worth.

Azerick shrugged and spoke past the lump of potato in his mouth. "I have been walking nearly three days, battled a god-like sorceress, and fought off a pack of spawn. I think I've earned it."

"I wonder if Joah and the other missing or dead think so."

"I couldn't say, but I bet the survivors might agree with me. Did you want something, or are you just here to complain?"

Marley clenched his jaw and spoke through gritted teeth. "What I want is for my people to be free. What I want is to push these invaders out of my land and back whence they came, but the only ones I see being pushed out is us."

Azerick tipped the bowl to his lips and poured the remnants down his throat. He stood and met Marley's eyes. "I told you this would be a protracted conflict, and likely a costly one. The sorceress' arrival has only added to the challenges we all face."

Marley took a deep breath. "Do you have a plan to counter this newest threat?"

"I do, but I may be gone for a couple of days. You will need to send some people into the nearest town to get some food and supplies. I recommend you don't engage in any offensives until I return."

Marley glared at the sorcerer. "I have already taken actions to see to my people's needs. Do not think you are in charge here, unless you want to get bogged down in logistics and mundane administration."

Azerick clapped him on the shoulder. "Not in the slightest. You're doing an admirable job. Keep up the good work."

Marley muttered a string of expletives as he stormed away.

Daebian appeared at Azerick's side, wiping the remaining contents of his bowl out with a piece of bread. "And people ask where I get my charming personality."

It was a subtle yet stinging rebuke.

"Yeah, well, I don't like him much," Azerick replied, a bit chagrined. "Besides, I'm still sore; bodily and emotionally."

"You did just eat. Maybe you need burped." Daebian tried to put his arms around his father, but Azerick shoved him away. "Fine, but don't come complaining to me when you get a tummy ache or need your diaper changed. So, do you have any brilliant plans you want to share? Preferably ones that don't end in brutal defeat."

Azerick pulled a plain-looking stone from his pocket. "I thought I would seek some help that might even the playing field a bit."

Daebian's eyebrows shot up, and his eyes sparkled. "Oh, family reunion! Can I come? Please!"

"Are you going to behave?"

Daebian gave Azerick a crooked smile. "What do you think?"

Azerick stared at him a moment before shrugging. "Sure, why not, but if you get your ass kicked, don't say I didn't warn you."

"I'll say I learned that from my father too."

Azerick scowled at him. "I got in the last punch!"

"And how many did she get in before that?"

"Shut up," Azerick snapped and began drawing a circle in the dirt.

He drew several carefully crafted runes along the circle's border. Azerick then took a chunk of grey stone from his bag and set it in the center. The stone was roughly square and had several straight lines giving it the appearance of a cobblestone. It was in fact a piece from his old tower that once stood outside of North Haven but now existed in another plane of existence.

Azerick crouched next to the stone and laid a hand upon it. "I need you to touch me."

Daebian's eyebrows rose. "Beg pardon?"

"If you want to come, you'll have to touch me."

"I'm sorry, I couldn't hear you over my mind shouting, *phrasing*."

Azerick gave him a flat stare. "Must you always be like this?"

Daebian shrugged. "If history is any indication, but who knows what the future might bring? Don't look at me like that. You've spent more than half your life surrounded by demons and things of nightmares. The gods only know what that might do to a man's predilections."

"Just put your damn hand on my shoulder or stay your ass here!" Azerick snapped.

"All right, all right." Daebian laid his hand on Azerick's shoulder and began kneading the muscle. "You're so tense and knotted up. Would like me try to *rub it out*?"

Azerick snarled several words of magic, and the world turned into a twisting kaleidoscope of colors. The two fell through the swirling vortex for a handful of seconds that felt like several torturous minutes.

Daebian tumbled onto solid ground cushioned with grass. "Did you intentionally make that transition as awful as possible?"

Azerick lay on his back and stared at the sky. "Do you think I would deliberately torture myself just to punish you?"

Daebian turned his head to look at him. "That's rhetorical, right?"

"I think we both know the answer already."

Daebian sniffed and crinkled his nose. "Good gods, what is that horrible smell? It's like someone put out a fire at a tannery with raw sewage—only worse." He turned his head and grinned. "Oh, it's just you. Hello, Brother."

Raijaun towered eight feet over Daebian's prone form. A pair of black horns swept back from his hairless, grey head. His chiseled jaw came to a narrow point below his serpent-like eyes. Black draconic wings sprouted from his broad, muscular back.

"I carry no discernable odor. At least none your weak senses could detect," Raijaun rumbled.

"You also carry no discernable sense of humor. At least none I can detect."

"I would say is good to see you, but I am incapable of lying."

Daebian sat up, grinning. "I lie all the time, but I can say with complete honesty it is never good to see you. You know, on account of you being so ugly."

Raijaun extended his hand to Azerick. "It is good to see you, Father. You look well."

Azerick took his huge hand and pulled himself to his feet. "I feel well, mostly. It's good to see you too, Son. I just wish it were under better circumstances. You appear to have expected us."

Raijaun ducked his head. "I did. Let us speak in the tower. I have tea on."

Daebian called out as the two turned away. "What, no help up for your big brother? You are supposed to be the polite one."

Raijaun turned around, clasped Daebian's' outstretched hand, and flung him twenty feet into the nearby pond.

Daebian came up sputtering. "Looks like you found a sense of humor after all. I'm not a big fan of pratfall. I find it rather boorish, but you do the best you can with what you have to work with."

"Is that what you tell Ellyssa in the bedroom?" Raijaun asked.

"Nice one. How long have had that arrow knocked and waiting to loose?"

"Seven years, forty-three days, and eleven hours, give or take," Raijaun replied.

Daebian stood on the shore and ceased wringing out his shirttail. "Wow. I don't know what's sadder, holding onto that little gem for so long or having a life so dull you kept track of its age like it was your only child."

"It's really no effort."

"How about expending a little effort to dry me off."

Raijaun flashed him a smile. "Of course, dear Brother. You'll want to hold onto something."

Daebian grabbed onto a low-hanging tree limb like a man overboard clutched a piece of flotsam. "Now wait just one—!"

A powerful gust carrying the heat of a desert wind blasted into Daebian. It blew with such ferocity that it peeled his lips back and made his cheeks flap like flags in the wind. He fought to keep his hold on the branch and his feet on the ground.

Daebian gasped in air when the gale abruptly ceased. "Well, that was certainly effective if a bit extreme," he said as he ran his hands over his dry clothing.

"I thought you might appreciate such a measure since it matches your own approach at most everything you do," Raijaun replied.

Daebian jogged to catch up with his brother and father. "Keep behaving like that and I might one day find you tolerable company."

"Enough, Daebian," Azerick said. "We have important matters to discuss and no time for your antics."

"My antics? He's the one who flung me into the water and blasted me with forge-heated wind."

"Enough, I said! You are both behaving like children."

"Apologies, Father," Raijaun rumbled.

Daebian crossed his arms and sulked. "Don't look at me like that. You know better than to think I'm going to apologize."

"Ignore him, Father. Some people are incapable of emotional growth," Raijaun said.

"I got your emotional growth," Daebian grumbled.

The trio entered the tower. Azerick found it much the way he had left it more than two decades before. Raijaun disappeared into the kitchen and returned with a tea set on a wooden tray. He set the tray on the table and poured them all a cup of tea.

Azerick spoke over the rim of his teacup. "You were expecting our arrival, so I assume you know why we are here."

Raijaun nodded as he sipped from a cup that looked ridiculously small in his huge hands. "I do, and I cannot give you the help you desire."

"Why not?" Daebian snapped. "Are you too much of a coward or simply lazy?"

Azerick raised a hand to forestall Daebian's ire. "Raijaun, these invaders have conquered their way across the world and now want to put their boots upon our necks as well. They have access to powerful magic that is difficult to counter to say the least. I fought one of their rulers, and she handily beat me—twice. Without someone of equal power to challenge them, we are almost certain to lose."

"I agree," Raijaun said. "If your approach is to defeat them with strength, you are likely to lose this war. However, I cannot be your weapon. This is a mortal concern, and I was created to protect the world from immortal threats."

"Their rulers want to become gods! They call our gods betrayers and seek to replace them."

"Should that come to pass, I may then have to intervene, but not in this."

"Raijaun!" Azerick exclaimed.

The Guardian raised a hand. "What you ask me to do is take a side in a mortal cause, a political battle. I cannot do that. It is the very reason the gods forced you to return to the abyss. We, as immortal creatures of power, cannot choose or direct the course of history."

"But they're destroying every civilization around the world!" Azerick insisted.

Raijaun's hairless brow crinkled in what approximated raising his eyebrows. "Are they? How many cities have they destroyed? How many homes burned to the ground and fields salted? How many leaders have they executed out of hand? I understand Miles yet sits his throne as does every leader upon their seat of power who has chosen not to fight."

"But they're...!"

"What? Foreigners? Would it be different were it were someone seeking to usurp King Miles from within Valeria? The Order represents change, and people are naturally resistant to change of any kind, particularly when it comes through force by a foreign entity."

Raijaun set his empty cup onto the table. "I have been watching the goings on, and I do not see The Order as some sort of evil that blackens and destroys all it touches. They build roads, schools, and bring technology that would improve the lives of a great many. They are not like the scourge of undead or spawn we helped destroy. They are simply agents of change."

Azerick took several deep breaths. He had not expected Raijaun to rebuff him so thoroughly. "They will destroy our culture and way of life. We will no longer be Valerians, just another part of The Order. A great, boring, mindlessly loyal homogenous body. There is nothing but The Order, to quote their mantra."

Raijaun nodded. "That is so."

"You think we shouldn't fight them?" Azerick asked, his voice soft and hollow.

"That is something every man and woman must choose for themselves. I do not fight because I cannot. I am bound by the gods and the nature of my creation."

"Would you yield to them?" Daebian asked, breaking his silence.

Raijaun thought a moment before replying. "My identity and power are all I can call my own. It is the essence of who and what I am, and I would not surrender it willingly."

Azerick nodded. "He's right. We must fight if we wish to maintain our identity. Raijaun cannot help us, so we must find other help."

"But from whom?" Daebian asked.

"The Order does not threaten only Valeria," Raijaun said. "They are a threat to everyone not yet under their control, and many who already are may not wish to be so."

Azerick thought a moment. "That is true. The Order is a threat to everyone. If we are to drive them out and keep them from returning, we must band together once again just as we did against the old gods."

Daebian said, "Speaking of the old gods; is it possible they are not as bound as we thought? Could their prison not be keeping them contained?"

"Why do you ask?" Raijaun asked.

"There are creatures in the shadow ways that should not be there. I am certain they are spawn, and it seems the spawn are increasing in number despite the hunting squads."

Raijaun nodded. "The old gods agreed to be bound as they once were, but they are not without influence in the world. Their power cannot be fully contained, and they yet work behind their prison walls to sow chaos."

"Why don't the gods do something about it?" Daebian demanded. "That was the whole purpose of binding them!"

"No. The Scions agreed to a truce not outright surrender. To stop their machinations totally, the gods would have to fight them once again, and that is something they do not wish to do. The cost is simply too high."

Daebian nodded his understanding though it still irked him. When someone was a problem, his response was to excise the threat in its entirety. The Scions had managed to kill Serron, the god of the sea, during their battle. Daebian had evened the score by slaying one of the Scions with his soul-stealing sword, which he no longer possessed.

Another of the old gods was trapped in the mind of a half-mad elf, who was the descendent of a former Guardian like Raijaun. While down by two, renewing a fight between gods could have catastrophic consequences.

"Raijaun, may I use the Source pool?" Azerick asked. "It's the easiest way to communicate with those I wish to speak to."

Raijaun ducked his head. "You may."

"I'm going to stay here and catch up with my little brother," Daebian said.

Raijaun rolled his eyes. "Oh, joy."

CHAPTER 10

Azerick descended the stairs into the tower's sublevel. He found his old laboratory much as he had left it. Raijaun had added some equipment and replaced others, but it was largely the same as he remembered. The gleaming silver Source pool occupied the middle of the room like a table-sized mirror.

The pool appeared liquid, but it was solid now. Azerick knelt next to it and took a few seconds to appreciate its beauty and awesome power. His mind traveled back to its creation. He and so many others had sacrificed so much to defeat the old gods, yet here he was once again.

With a resigned sigh, he touched the tip of his staff to the Source pool and spoke a name with his face fixed firmly in his mind. "Duncan Runecarver."

A ripple undulated across the pool where he touched it with his staff. When the rippling ceased and the pool was solid once more, a broad face nearly hidden behind a black beard with a few more streaks of grey than Azerick remembered replaced his reflection.

The dwarf's bushy eyebrows knitted together as he stared into something above the workbench at which he worked. "Azerick, is that you, boy?"

Azerick beamed at the rune carver. "It is, Duncan. It's good to see you."

"You look...normal. Young! Are ya back then?"

Azerick nodded. "I am, and demon free. I'm my old self once again. Or new self, depending on how you look at it."

Duncan slapped the workbench with a thick, calloused hand and sent several tools and instruments clattering about. "I knew ye'd get out of that hellish place one day!" He sighed and his face grew somber. "Ya aren't here just to chat about the good times, are ya?"

Azerick frowned and shook his head. "There is another threat to all of Valeria and beyond. An army from far away has landed on our shores and has all but conquered my kingdom just as they have done many others."

"And you want ta ask for our help in repelling 'em." Duncan sighed and shook his head. "We might not have lost as many folks as others in that blasted gods war, but we're a slow bunch when it comes to recovering from our losses. The elves are much the same way, and if ya haven't already contacted 'em, I wager they'll tell ya the same thing."

"Duncan, these people threaten more than just us. They will not stop until all kneel to their emperor and empress." Azerick fixed his gaze on the old dwarf's eyes. "I have seen thousands of their soldiers, and they were all human. Maybe there aren't dwarves and elves and other people outside of Valeria, or at least in the lands they've conquered, but I get the feeling they will not treat nonhumans kindly."

The corners of Duncan's mouth turned down. "That has often been the way of humans. It is why we, the elves, and ogres hid ourselves from the eyes of man. You're a friend and I mean no offense, but you're a fickle lot, and your memories are even shorter than your lifespans. I will bring this information and your request to the council, but I would not make any plans that require our involvement were I you."

Azerick nodded solemnly. "That is all I can ask and will respect whatever decision your people make."

The dwarf looked away in an attempt to hide the shame in his eyes. "I'm glad ya made it back. The world is a better place with ya in it. I just wish ya had returned to the world you deserve."

The Source pool shimmered, and his own reflection returned. He touched the pool with his staff once more. Moments later, a snow-white face with large eyes that were almost all pupil appeared. She was beautiful despite her foreign countenance, but it in no way masked the power she possessed.

Her look of angry confusion vanished in the space of a breath. "Sorcerer, I should have known not even the abyss could hold you forever. Does it still exist, or did you manage to destroy it and our goddess as well?"

Azerick shuddered at the reminder of the genocide he had wrought in his escape from the psyling city. It had been an accident, and he did not mourn the vile masters of that place, but countless innocents, at least one he had called a friend, perished as well.

"Teraneshala, I am glad to see you well," Azerick said.

The abyssal elf smiled. "It is not for lack of my enemies' attempts to see it otherwise, but I am still here, and their skulls decorate my walls. So, what portent of doom brings you to my mirror?"

Azerick gave her a sheepish grin. "Am I really that predictable?"

"I am an abyssal elf. No one calls upon us for purely social reasons. Particularly human sorcerers with a certain reputation."

"Fair enough. Humans from a faraway land invade Valeria." Azerick detailed the invasion and everything he knew of The Order. "I do not think they will stop until all people serve them, no matter where they reside."

"I will be blunt. The war created a power vacuum that we are still trying to resolve. We are a contentious race at the best of times and will likely not set foot in the cursed light again for several of your generations." An evil smile played across the elf's face. "Should these humans choose to step into the darkness, we will welcome them to the deeps where even the gods fear to tread."

Azerick sighed and nodded. "I understand."

Teraneshala gave him a pouty frown. "I will give your problem some thought. If I come up with something that may aid you, I will contact you."

"Thank you, Teraneshala."

Her smile returned. "You don't have to thank me, only repay me in kind." The abyssal elf turned her head in the direction of an agonized scream. "It appears I must go. A lady's work is never done."

The elf's image vanished, and Azerick looked upon nothing but the gleaming silver surface. It was clear he was unlikely to get any help outside of his own people. Duncan's odds of convincing the dwarves to help were slim at best.

He walked with leaden steps back up the stairs and paused when he reached the top. In the small living area, Raijaun held Daebian aloft by one foot, his arm outstretched. Daebian was trying to punch his brother, but his arms were too short to reach anything, including the floor. Both brothers looked at Azerick when he cleared his throat.

"He was being himself," Raijaun said in explanation.

"Daebian?" Azerick said.

Daebian shrugged. "He's not lying."

Azerick shook his head and sighed. "Please put him down."

Raijaun opened his hand, but Daebian's incredible agility allowed him to land in a crouch.

He stood up and brushed himself off. "So, I assume they told you to go sit on your staff?"

"More or less," Azerick replied. "Raijaun, could I speak with Tarth?"

The Guardian nodded. "I think he would like that. I can open a gate to his home if you like."

"I would." Azerick looked at Daebian. "You should stay here."

Daebian touched his hand to his chest and said in mock innocence, "Why ever for?"

"Exactly."

Raijaun gestured at the door. "I'll open it outside."

The three of them walked outside, and Raijaun opened a gate. The scene on the other side showed a lush forest surrounded by snow. Azerick stepped through the shimmering rift and shivered at the abrupt temperature change.

His feet crunched in the snow as he made his way toward the woods. The temperature made a sudden shift to a more temperate level as he crossed over the invisible boundary separating the harsh northern climate with that of the elven homeland.

It was not the actual homeland but a near perfect copy, just like the rest of this world, but without people. Birds chirped overhead and a deer bounded away at his approach. He had seen but not taken notice of the wildlife around Raijaun's tower, which was something the world had lacked the last time he had been here.

His stroll through the tranquil forest helped calm his nerves. He knew he had nothing to fear here. No Order or spawn lurked nearby waiting to spring an ambush. He walked for about half an hour before he heard voices up ahead.

Azerick slowed his steps and continued forward, tense and alert once more. He saw shapes flitting between breaks in the trees and foliage, dashes of color disrupting the expanse of verdant green and earthy brown.

The path opened up, and the back of a tall figure with black hair streaked with green flowing over a silk gown of emerald, blue, and gold stood before him. The elf looked over his shoulder at him and smiled.

"Welcome, Azerick. You look positively human this time," Tarth said in greeting.

Azerick rolled his shoulders. "I feel positively human in every bone, joint, and muscle in my body."

"And you are actually here?"

"I am."

Tarth turned his attention back to the city. "Beautiful, is it not?"

Azerick stepped beside him and traveled his eyes around the elven city. There were a few buildings made of stone and marble, but most structures were trees whose trunks spiraled around each other scores of feet high to create large, hollow cores.

He saw stairs through an opening at the base of one such structure that appeared to grow naturally and climb the interior. Azerick had once seen such an elven home inside Tarth's broken mind on a mental journey to that tortured place. It was far more beautiful to see in person.

"It is," Azerick replied. "Tarth, who are all these people?"

The elf beamed. "They're my people, of course."

"You brought them from our world?"

Tarth shook his head. "No, of course not. They are *my* people. I made them."

Azerick stared at the multitude walking, talking, and going about what must have constituted normal daily activities for their kind. "They're illusions?"

Tarth made a slightly pursed frown, although not enough to cause wrinkles, as he thought a moment. "They are more like a memory infused with the world around us and a tiny bit of my essence to give them the imitation of life and sentience."

Azerick shook his head. "I'm not even going to pretend to understand more than fraction of what you just said."

Tarth smiled. "Do not blame yourself. I likely would not understand it entirely without the aid of a mad god living within my mind. In its more lucid moments, it can be quite useful."

Azerick gulped and shuddered at the thought. "That's one of the reasons I'm here. Is it possible for me to speak with it? There are things happening in our world, and I think it and its ilk have something to do with it."

Tarth gave him another wrinkle-free grimace. "They have been particularly active these last few years."

"Is it possible they are still able to influence our world and send their creatures to attack us?"

"Possible? It is a certainty. The gods were able to contain the Scions but not their power. Not in totality at any rate. It was a mutual agreement to return to the former status quo to prevent more death and destruction."

"And yet we still die," Azerick snarled.

Tarth nodded. "I meant the gods' death and the destruction they might otherwise cause."

"Of course," Azerick responded dryly. "Is it a problem for you to let me speak to it? Could it harm you?"

Tarth thought a moment and shook his head. "I do not think so. It has become somewhat docile over the years."

"Then I would speak with it, if I may."

Tarth inclined his head and closed his eyes. His eyelids snapped open, showing nothing but the white sclera. Despite his obvious blindness, Tarth settled his gaze on Azerick.

"You have returned, sire of the Guardian," the creature, no longer Tarth, said in a multitoned voice. "You return weak, frail, and mortal."

Azerick stiffened his spine and shoved down his fear. "I was far weaker when I destroyed your favored children."

"An imbecilic accident. Do not place yourself higher than your station lest we feel the need to knock you down into the filth where you belong."

"As the gods did to you?" Azerick said with a smile.

Tarth's mouth curled into a sneer. "Hardly. It was our choice to return to our prison."

Azerick shrugged. "Well, three out of five of you."

Tarth's face contorted in rage. "We know why you seek us out! Speak your words and be gone."

"Your creatures still invade our world. Why? How?"

"The same way they always have and for the same reason. Do not waste our time with inane questions to which you already know the answer," the Scion snapped.

Azerick snorted. "Why, you have somewhere to go?"

"Ask your question!"

"Where does The Order get its power? Why do they seek to conquer the known world? Can we stop them?"

Tarth's sinister smile returned. "Three questions asked, and three we shall answer. Then bother us no more, mortal. They get their power the same as you. They believe the only way to destroy our pets and put an end to our machinations is by uniting all humanity under one banner. They are mortal, and all mortal things can be destroyed be it a wizard, monster, or empire."

The smile vanished. "Three questions we have answered, but you may be better served by asking and answering one yourself."

"What question is that?"

The smile returned. "Why do you seek to defeat them?"

Azerick shook his head at the absurdity of the question. "To be free! For self-determination of our future and way life."

"Ah, yes. Pride wears many faces, but that is one of its favorites."

"It's not pride."

"Isn't it? You face a binary problem yet you insist upon a third option that will result in the failure of them both."

Azerick shook his head. "I don't understand."

"Of course you don't. You are too prideful and pig-headed to consider it. You face two foes, but you can only defeat one. Choosing which to fight ensures the victory of the other."

"I refuse to accept that."

"You can refuse to accept the laws of gravity, but it won't prevent you from falling no matter how stubborn and righteous you are in your belief."

Azerick clenched his jaw and wagged his head. Could that be true? If he continued to fight The Order, and if he was able to defeat them, would it allow the Scions to win at whatever game they are playing? Is the only way to defeat the old gods is to join The Order? They are bent on destroying the spawn and ensuring the Scions never touch this world again. They also seek to supplant the gods with their emperor and empress, thus giving them power he could scarcely imagine.

The church had sought to create something of a theocracy just as The Order has done, and it had nearly allowed a scourge of undead to rampage across the kingdom and beyond. He could never allow them to ascend to godhood. Mortal born are simply not able to wield so much power with wisdom and benevolence.

"No! Physical laws may not lie, but you do. However, they can be manipulated, and that is what you're trying to do to me."

Tarth shrugged. "Perhaps. Perhaps not. The most you can accomplish is to squash our entertainment. For a time. We will enjoy watching you regardless of your choice."

"You must enjoy watching your own failure then," Azerick replied. "I thought such a thing would leave a sour taste in your mouths. You know, after what happened last time and all."

The old god let out a sinister chuckle. "We shall see, mortal. We shall see."

"I am done with you. Be gone!" Azerick commanded.

Tarth's eyelids fluttered, and his eyes rolled back down to reveal the golden irises once more. Azerick opened his mouth to speak, but the elf's hand shot out and clamped around his throat. His toes scraped against the earth as Tarth drove him back.

Azerick dropped his staff out of reflex and tried to pry Tarth's hands off his throat, but he may as well have been trying to remove shoes from a horse with his bare hands.

"Tarth!" Azerick choked out as he beat upon the elf's forearms.

Tarth's perfect, white teeth flashed. "You have done this to me, mortal! You are why I live in darkness with only flashes of madness to light my way. I will make you know my suffering. Before all is done, you will be a slave, stripped of power and free will until you too succumb to insanity so great you will gladly destroy all you love to be free of it. This I promise you!"

"Been there, done that," Azerick gasped out.

Tarth opened his hand, and Azerick fell to the ground. The elf looked down at him and blinked in confusion.

"I...apologize," Tarth said. "It had not acted out in such a way for over a decade. I had thought it more tractable. Are you all right?"

Azerick rubbed at his throat with one hand and let Tarth help him up with the other. "I'll make it. Not your fault."

"Did you find what you sought?"

Azerick shrugged his shoulders. "I confirmed much of what I assumed. I had hoped to find some help against an implacable foe, but it appears I am on my own."

Tarth gave him a sympathetic nod. "Guardians are forbidden to interfere in the ways of mortals. Do not think it is an easy mandate for your son to obey."

Azerick let out a breath and nodded. "I know. The Scions said I must choose one path or the other. If I fight The Order, they will win. Am I wrong for resisting these invaders? Do you think I am dooming humanity by not conceding to their rule?"

Tarth stared out across the plaza and let out a long breath. "My people nearly destroyed themselves trying to resist change and what they saw as human encroachment. It was only my sacrifice that prevented our destruction."

"You're saying I should yield then?"

"I am saying the Scions are liars and manipulators. No one, not even the gods, old or new, can foretell the future with any amount of certainty. The future, destiny, it is not immutable. Humans are creatures of chaos, and all it takes is one person willing to sacrifice anything, including themselves, to alter the course of history."

Azerick sighed and looked down at his feet. "I'm tired of sacrificing myself. Or being sacrificed. My entire life has been nothing but loss and conflict, and I am exhausted. I thought when I came back, I might finally know some peace."

Tarth's mouth quirked up. "What in the world ever gave you that idea?"

Azerick tilted his head back and chuckled hard at the sky. "Those who fail to learn from their past..."

Tarth laid a hand on the sorcerer's shoulder. "You will know what to do when the time comes to do it. If your history is any indication, then I see some uncertain, and possibly upsetting, futures for anyone who stands against you be they implacable mortals or all-powerful gods."

Azerick returned the gesture and smiled. "Thank you, Tarth." He looked around the elven city. "Do you have a way back to the tower? It's a rather long walk."

CHAPTER II

Azerick stepped through the portal Tarth created and stood before his old tower once again. He could have opened a gate himself just as he had back in his world, but Tarth was able to manage it far easier. It was a shame he no longer had the arcanum door handle he had made that allowed him to travel between the two dimensions as easily as stepping into another room of his house.

He frowned as he realized he no longer had a house. If he managed to evict The Order from Valeria, he could return to his old haunts beneath Southport. Azerick assumed Vera would likely return home once the war was over. The thought of living underground once again was not appealing.

Azerick shook his head to clear his wayward thoughts and looked for his sons. He heard shouting through the trees and followed the sound of their voices. The shouts grew louder until he located a clearing not far from the tower. It was not quite a clearing as there were a few trees populating the small glade.

He found Raijaun and Daebian kicking a ball around the clearing, each trying to drive it toward opposite ends of the glade. Raijaun's greater size gave him an advantage in strength and raw speed, which he put to use by kicking the ball, and Daebian's legs, out from under his brother.

Raijaun lengthened his considerable stride and raced for the far end of the clearing. What Daebian lacked in strength he made up for in quickness and was back on his feet in an instant. Unfortunately, Raijaun was already ahead of him, and there was no way Daebian was going to catch up with him now. Unless he cheated, which he did.

Daebian leapt into a shadow cast by one of the trees. He emerged from Raijaun's own shadow, feet first, and kicked him hard in the left shin. Raijaun went toppling with a short cry that ended in a loud whoomph of expelled air when he struck the ground.

"Too slow, Bro!" Daebian cackled as he raced for the opposite end of the field, kicking the ball ahead of him.

Raijaun sprang to his feet and sprinted after his brother. He beat his wings to achieve even greater speed, and it was apparent he would catch Daebian before he reached the imaginary goal line. Daebian looked over his shoulder and altered his course toward one of the trees. More specifically, its shadow.

Raijaun knew what he was about to do and conjured a bright light just before Daebian leapt into the shadow ways. The light obliterated the shadow, and Daebian smashed headlong into the tree trunk. It was Raijaun's turn to go running across the field laughing before heaving back one large foot and kicking the ball across the clearing and into the woods.

He returned to where Daebian still lay on his back. "Looks like I won."

"You cheated," Daebian gasped.

"You cheated first."

Daebian shook his head. "We said no magic. My shadow walking is an innate ability, not magic."

Raijaun shrugged. "It is semantics. Besides, you're the one who said all is fair in love and kickball."

A grin spread across Daebian's face. "You're right, I did."

Arching his back for maximum reach, Daebian's foot flashed up and kicked Raijaun between his tree trunk-like legs. Raijaun grunted and took a step back. He recovered quickly and reached down for Daebian's skinny neck.

Daebian fell into the tree's shadow and immediately dropped from the darkened canopy onto Raijaun's head. He managed to grab onto his horns without impaling himself and began kicking and slapping him on the side of his head.

Raijaun tossed his head and roared his outrage. Daebian reached up with one hand and grabbed a fistful of leaves from the tree limb just above his head. He leaned forward and jammed them into Raijaun's open mouth.

"Aw, the demon cow sounds hungry," Daebian quipped and nearly lost several fingers for the sake of his joke.

Raijaun lowered his head and tried to crush his brother into the tree trunk. The impact shook the tree and caused a cascade of leaves to fall. Unaffected by the blow that would have knocked a human unconscious, he spun around and smashed his shoulder blades against the trunk as Daebian scampered around his back like a squirrel being chased by a dog.

Daebian climbed lower and punched his brother in the back of his thigh. Raijaun let his legs go slack and plopped to the ground, trapping his brother beneath him. A sudden exhalation of air and Daebian's muffled cries issued from beneath Raijaun's kilt.

Azerick cleared his throat. "It gladdens me to see you two getting along so well, but if you don't mind, I'd like to get back to the business at hand."

Raijaun chose to roll off Daebian instead of standing up, which elicited another groan from his brother.

Daebian sprang to his feet, scrubbing at his face and sputtering. "Ugh! Why are they so warm? It was like have two hard boiled eggs fresh from the pot resting on my face!"

"Actually, it's three," Raijaun replied offhandedly.

"Wait, what? Three? What exactly are we counting here?"

Raijaun just winked in reply.

Azerick's staff vibrated in his hand and tugged slightly toward the tower. "You boys work it out."

Azerick quickened his step and hastened back to the Source pool. He touched the tip of his staff to the shimmering surface, and Duncan's solemn face appeared.

"Ah, there you are. I wasn't sure if I could make this work," the rune carver said. "I'm afraid my concerns were quite prophetic. The council wants no truck in what they see as human affairs."

Azerick bowed his head a shook it. "This will expand beyond human affairs. I'm sure of it."

"We'll be preparing for any incursion. I'm sorry, lad. I argued for ya, but I'm but one of a dozen voices. I know it's not what you wanted to hear, and I hate to have to voice it."

"I understand. I think they're making a mistake, but I can appreciate their lack of desire to enter into another war."

"I wish ya luck, lad. If I come up with anything that might help your cause, I'll try to get word to you."

Azerick ducked his head. "Thank you, Duncan. I understand your council's decision. A war was the last thing I wanted when I returned, but there is no avoiding it for me—unless I choose to capitulate."

"You, capitulate?" Duncan scoffed. "I'm more likely to shave my beard than you are to yield to anyone."

"Yeah, well, I do have a reputation to uphold."

Duncan nodded. "That ya do. Be careful. It'd be a shame to waste this second chance at life."

Azerick bobbed his head from side to side. "It's probably more like a third or fourth, but yeah, I agree. I doubt I'll get another one. Take care, Duncan."

Azerick dismissed the image and shuffled back up the stairs. He could not tell if his sons' bruises were new or a result of their previous scuffle, but they both now reclined in chairs in the tower's sitting room.

"We need to get back," Azerick said as he topped the stairs. "Raijaun, can you open a way back for us?"

Raijaun ducked his head. "Of course. Do you wish to return whence you came?"

Azerick thought a moment and nodded. "Yes. Things are in a bit of disarray, and the best thing I can do right now is to help secure our position."

"It was good seeing you again, Father. I hope you return soon. I am sorry I cannot help you more."

"What about me?" Daebian asked.

Raijaun turned his head toward his brother. "It was good seeing you again as well. I look forward to your next visit."

"Maybe I'll bring you a present on your birthday. Or is hatch day a better term? Whatever. I'll be sure to bring you something inappropriate."

"No need to hurry back. Every twenty years is quite sufficient."

Raijaun opened a gate with a simple wave of his hand. Azerick and Daebian stepped through and emerged at almost the exact spot where Azerick had opened his gate.

Raijaun's voice followed them through an instant before the portal shut. "The source of their power is also their weakness!"

Daebian spun around and glared at the empty air where the portal had spit them out. "Did he seriously just spew some bullshit cryptic parting words? Open the portal again so I can go kick his big, grey, cliché-spouting ass!"

"You didn't look like you were doing all that well earlier," Azerick said.

Daebian crossed his arms over his chest. "I was taking it easy on him."

Azerick nudged him toward camp. "Come, we have more important things to attend to."

"But…"

Azerick took him by the arm. "I'm sure it will prove helpful in time."

Daebian looked over his shoulder and whined, "But it's so stupid. I'll only stab him a little bit, I promise."

"It isn't stupid. It means our enemy has a central point of power. If I can find it and disrupt it or destroy it, I might be able to end this war."

"Then I can stab him?"

Azerick paused before answering. "No."

Daebian stuck out his lower lip. "You never let me do anything fun."

The refugee camp was beginning to look a lot more like a military camp. Several tents, some large enough to house a score of people without having them packed shoulder to shoulder, now stood beneath the forest's thick canopy. Azerick could not see it, but he felt an illusion further concealing them from both physical and magical sight.

A mess tent with proper stoves replaced the open campfires. The distant sounds of chopping axes and the occasional falling tree carried through the camp. Most of the people Azerick saw were families, still mostly huddled close, the fear caused by the attack and their retreat still coursing through their veins.

Azerick found Marley's tent not far from the mess hall. Kord stood sentry outside and held the flap open at his approach. Marley, Headmaster Florent, and Chancellor Barret McGill leaned over a map spread across a table. All three heads turned his direction as he and Daebian entered the room.

"Ah, our self-appointed savior has returned," Marley said.

"You're more than welcome to take up the mantle," Azerick replied.

Marley flashed his teeth. "I'm afraid I lack the requisite hero complex for such a position. Besides, you're doing such a bang-up job."

Headmaster Florent silenced Marley with a scowl and said, "What news do you bring?"

Azerick's shoulders slumped and he sighed. "I'm afraid we're on our own."

Chancellor McGill grunted. "Can't say as I'm surprised. It was a miracle they joined with us in the Second Gods War."

"Their lives are not sufficiently threatened as of yet," Headmaster Florent said, "but their time will come should we fail."

Azerick nodded. "I think you have the right of it on both accounts, Headmaster. What is our situation here?"

Chancellor McGill spoke. "We have sufficient shelter for the time being. Our greatest problem is food. We recovered the hidden supply cache, but it will keep us a week at most, and that is with stretching them. Winter is fast approaching. If we do not stock an ample larder before then, this war ends as so many others have in the past—on empty stomachs."

"What are our options?" Azerick asked.

Marley stabbed a finger onto the map. "There's a gate a day's march from here. It connects to another gate half a day's walk from a farming hamlet called Orrinshire."

"A hamlet?" Azerick asked. "Is it big enough to supply us without creating a food shortage for them?"

"For a normal hamlet, no, but Orrinshire has some of the largest wheat and grain fields in the kingdom. While small in population, they grow more grain than the next three farming communities put together."

"It sounds to me like a place The Order would heavily defend," Azerick said.

Marley nodded. "Especially since it's harvest time. We haven't had eyes on it in weeks. There was a heavy platoon guarding the place the last we knew. My guess is that it has been reinforced since then."

Azerick looked to the archmage. "Headmaster, can you scry the location and give us a better idea of what we will face?"

Maureen shook her head. "I tried. It is protected from every form of farseeing I can manage."

Azerick frowned. "That means they have a significant arcanus presence as well. Are there any other viable locations that aren't so heavily defended?"

Marley shook his head. "There are two we could reach in time if just barely, but they aren't likely to have enough to see us through winter. Not without leaving them in dire straits. The Order has already confiscated their first harvest, and it would be a race to get to the second."

"How's our army looking?"

"Fourteen missing, a dozen wounded, and three dead," Marley said without hesitation. "Of the missing, I have reliable reports that at least six of the fourteen are dead—killed during the attack. Joah and Sybil are among the missing."

Sybil was also a key asset and one of Marley's mages. While their losses were light overall, losing the two officers was a hard blow.

"Sybil was tasked with destroying the gates around the camp if the Academy, now The Order, ever found us," Marley continued.

"So, she might still be making her way here?" Azerick asked.

Marley nodded. "If we're lucky, but I wouldn't want to place any bets on it. Those soldiers were all over the place, but they're both resourceful people. I wouldn't count either of them out just yet."

"Maybe we should dispatch a search party," Azerick suggested.

Marley shook his head. "No sense in it. They both know how to find us, and sending people out after them is likely to do nothing but draw attention and increase the chance of them capturing more of our people. Only a handful of our officers know about our fallback locations, and they have a geas cast on them to forget it if captured or questioned."

Azerick detested the thought of leaving anyone behind, but Marley was right. If The Order had caught them already, they would not be able to free them without sending a significant force. If the sorceress was with them, even going after them with their strongest people would be suicide.

Azerick conceded with a resigned sigh. "What's our next move?"

General McGill cleared his throat. "The way I see it, we have two tasks to complete before launching any kind sortie. We need to reconnoiter our target location, or locations if we choose more than one, to get an exact count of enemy forces, positions, and capabilities."

"Daebian and I should be able to do that," Azerick said.

Daebian looked at his father. "How kind of you to volunteer me."

"What else?" Azerick asked, ignoring his son.

General McGill straightened his back and shifted his focus from the map to Azerick. "Do you know what the key element is to a successful war?"

Azerick shrugged. "A superior fighting force?"

The chancellor shook his head. "Logistics. They say an army marches on its stomach, but without logistics, those bellies remain empty and the army goes nowhere. Being able to move troops and supplies is the linchpin of warfare. You can have the most powerful military in the world, but if you can't get them to the battle, they're useless."

"Sounds just like Raijaun," Daebian quipped. "Supremely powerful, but you can't get him to move his lazy, grey ass."

"Raijaun's unwillingness to join the fight has nothing to do with laziness, and you know it," Azerick snapped.

Daebian shrugged. "All I know is that I've been conscripted while he's back at his tower probably abusing himself whilst looking at self-sketched pornography."

"He's not—would you prefer to stay here in camp, maybe help with the cooking or dig latrines? Perhaps you would rather get back on your boat and sail away?"

Daebian crinkled his brow. "And miss out on stabbing more of those impertinent, imbecilic invaders? Not a chance."

"Then quit your bitching."

"Not a chance."

General McGill cleared his throat again.

"Sorry, please go on," Azerick said.

"As I was saying," the chancellor continued, "the gates Marley's people created are a significant logistical advantage for us. We can move large forces hundreds of miles with only a short bit of walking. Our weakness is the span we must cross on foot to reach them or the battle. That is where The Order and their infernal vehicles surpass us hands down."

Azerick nodded. "We have always been able to slow them enough to break off our engagement in the past. Besides, except for their aerial vehicles, they tend not to fight from the backs of them. Once dismounted, they are no faster than we are. Not significantly so."

"That was during skirmishes. This time we will be trying to transport a few tons of grain," General McGill countered.

"And the gates are too narrow to allow passage of a wagon," Marley added. "We built them small on purpose. Not only are they easier to conceal, but the energy required to power them increases exponentially with size. Even had the evacuation gates not been destroyed in the war, it would be nearly impossible to power them without access to the Source pool."

Azerick rubbed his chin as he thought. "And the small gates are barely large enough to accommodate a hand cart."

"Or a very narrow wagon, which would be unstable, particularly over the broken ground we'll be traversing," Marley concurred with a nod.

Azerick paced the room a moment before stopping in his tracks. "I need one of their troop transports."

Headmaster Florent frowned. "I'm not sure we could use it without abducting one of their arcanus to operate it, and they're as big as a heavy cargo wagon and won't fit through the gates. I suppose we could unload it at the gate, but that would risk our enemy discovering it."

Azerick shook his head. "I don't want to use the skimmer. I want to figure out how it works."

Marley smiled a wolfish grin. "To make our own."

"Exactly."

Headmaster Florent slowly wagged her head. "You're talking about reverse-engineering an unknown magic and using it to rebuild a similar vehicle better suited to our needs. I don't know that we have that kind of time even if we are able to manage it."

Azerick held up a finger. "I am certain that their armor, weapons, and vehicles are based on rune magic. Rune magic is the only way to store arcane energy efficiently enough to create these effects without the prohibitive expense and effort required to make permanent enchantments."

The headmaster let out a breath. "I don't know. I admit that I know little of rune magic. Few people other than the dwarves and some of the primitive races do."

"I'm far from being a master, but I'm no novice," Azerick said. "Rune magic has some universal principals in order to function. It's like mathematics. No matter what the numbers are called in any given language, two plus two always equals four. I think rune magic is the same."

"You think?" the headmaster asked with a raised eyebrow.

"I'm fairly certain. Rune magic has its foundation in geometry whereas wizard magic is much more like grammar. The rules governing the latter vary widely across the languages, but those guiding the former do not. They can't. A square is a square no matter what you call it."

General McGill took in a deep breath and let it out. "So, you think you can decipher these runes and make wagons like theirs but are narrow enough to fit through the gates? And do it before our enemy steals the last harvest for itself?"

Azerick paused only a second before nodding. "I do. I built hundreds of battle constructs for the war using similar rune magic. I think I can adapt it to suit our purpose once I understand the principals used in the runes that allow their skimmers to levitate off the ground and propel itself."

"Will they require mages to operate them?" Headmaster Florent asked.

"Absolutely. They will be the source of power for the runes to work just as my students were for the constructs."

Marley clapped his hands together. "Sounds like we have a plan. I'll send a couple of my more experienced woodsmen and hunters to help guide you through the woods."

"Daebian and I can move faster on our own," Azerick said.

Marley shrugged his shoulders. "It's up to you. My men know the area and the people there. You don't have to bring them into the town with you, but it might be smart to have someone along who can at least return and inform us if you run into any problems."

Azerick glanced at Daebian, who gave a disinterested shrug. "Two people. One of them needs to be able to use the gates in case I'm not there to do it."

"You got it."

"I guess that's where we're going then," Azerick said. "Daebian, you up for some infiltration?"

Daebian raised his eyebrows. "The two of us against an entire Order contingent?" He shrugged his shoulders. "Seems like overkill, but why not?"

"We'll try to get in and out without them knowing we were even there."

"Sounds like Mother's description of my conception," Daebian replied with a grin.

General McGill covered his mouth with his hand and coughed loudly as he turned away.

Azerick gave his son a flat stare. "Are you ready to go now, or do you need to rest and maybe wash up after Raijaun used your face for a stool?"

Daebian jutted his chin upward. "I let him win. It's what a big brother does for his sad, ugly little brother to make him feel better about himself."

Azerick gave him a wry grin. "Uh huh. Let's get to it then. No sense in wasting daylight."

CHAPTER 12

Azerick and Daebian used the fixed gate to take them as close to Orrinshire as they could get. An experienced huntress named Daniil and a young hedge mage named Jepson accompanied them. Daniil carried a short blade and an assortment of knives along with a worn self bow. Her eyes were furtive and attentive, constantly taking in their surroundings.

Jepson Boon was a gaunt man, and the creases in his face made him look older than the mid-twenty-something he was. Another of Marley's people, he looked more like a dockworker than a wizard. His eyes also constantly darted about in their sockets, but Azerick sensed it was more from nervousness than vigilance.

Repeated casting of Azerick's portal spell brought them to within an hour's walk of the town. He dared not cast any closer in case The Order contingent had an arcanus on alert for errant use of magic. Given Orrinshire's strategic importance, it was almost certain they did. Probably more than one. They made camp to rest and wait out the remainder of the day.

"What do you think Raijaun meant when he said the source of their power was also their weakness?" Daebian asked from where he sat near the small fire.

Across from him, Azerick sighed and stared up at grey sky, his breath coming out in a fog in the chill air. "I think it means that whatever they are using to harness and channel so much power is a double-edged sword. Something capable of giving them the ability to do what they do often is. The more power you seek, the greater the cost. Fail to pay that cost…"

Daebian rolled onto his side to look at his father. "How much power are we talking about?"

"More than I have ever been able to wield. A lot more. Even in Klaraxis' body and his access to abyssal magic I couldn't manage what they do."

"What about Raijaun?"

Azerick thought a moment and shook his head. "No. Not even with the Source pool at his disposal. We're talking about an empire-wide control and distribution of power. Something like that is simply unfathomable. The closest thing I can think of is the divine magic of Chosen clerics."

Daebian nodded. "We know the gods aren't giving it to them since they want to usurp them. Not our gods anyway."

Azerick turned his head toward Daebian. "You think the Scions are acting as their divine conduit?"

"Possibly. Unwittingly, of course, since The Order wants to destroy them too."

"It doesn't stretch credulity much, although I'm not sure they can manage the feat from within their prison."

"They're still sending spawn through, so there's obviously cracks in the walls," Daebian said.

Azerick nodded slowly. "It's possible. The Scions care nothing for their spawn. They give these power-hungry sorcerers the ability to control vast amounts of power, shackle all those able to freely wield magic, and then cut them off once they've conquered most of the world. There would be little to stand in their way once that happens. Especially if the emperor and empress are able to remove the new gods."

Daebian rolled onto his back. "I know one thing for sure."

"What's that?"

"That my shit heel brother knows more than he's telling us."

Azerick sighed. "Very true."

Daebian turned back toward his father. "Which part, withholding knowledge or being a shit heel?"

Azerick pursed his lips. "Maybe both."

Daebian grinned. "Well, well, well. Look who's becoming disillusioned with his precious baby boy."

Azerick rolled away from him. "Don't get too excited. You're still my second favorite."

"Yeah, but I'm closing the gap!" Daebian crowed.

"You just slipped to a distant third."

Azerick and Daebian gazed upon Orrinshire from the cover of trees three hundred yards from walls made of logs. Scores of torches and braziers flickered with orange light in preparation for the impending sunset.

It looked as though The Order had reinforced the wall with a berm, dry moat, and palisade. The only visible break in the defenses was a narrow stretch just wide enough to admit a wagon. It was a common defense for smaller villages that had chosen to defend their homes from the spawn instead of moving to the larger, better-defended towns and cities.

"Looks like they really batten down the hatches at night," Daebian said.

Azerick nodded. "There's probably a second gate on the far side. Only fools would trap themselves in a corner with no method of retreat. We can sidle around back and check, but I doubt any other point of access is any less defended. Can you shadow step us inside?"

Daebian shrugged. "I can, but without being able to see where we're going, and having never been here, we'll be stumbling around in the dark. The shadow spawn are starting to wise up to my camouflage trick too, and we'll likely find ourselves in a fight before I can find the way out."

Azerick flicked his eyes toward the farmers harvesting the grain. "I guess we'll just have to blend in and go through the front door."

Daebian stowed his dark spectacles and wrapped a strip of cloth around his head. "Great. I've gone from god slayer to pirate lord and now farmer. If this downward social spiral continues, next I'll be...well...you."

Azerick clapped him on the shoulder. "No matter how high you shoot your arrow, it will always strike the ground eventually."

"That is the most depressing bit of wisdom I've ever heard."

Donned in peasant attire, Azerick left his staff in the woods with their escorts, and Daebian kept a short sword concealed beneath his rough woolens. They insinuated themselves into the workforce, picking up sheaves of wheat stalks and lugging them to the nearest wagon.

A bell tolled, and the workers deposited their last bundles into the wagons and trudged toward the village. Azerick and Daebian followed behind one of the wagons as it trundled toward the gates.

"I don't recognize you lads," an older man said from behind them.

Azerick glanced over his shoulder. "We're new hires passing through. Just trying to earn a bit of coin before continuing on our way."

The farmer bobbed his head. "Ah, Willard must'a hired you then."

Azerick nodded. "That's right."

"Odd though."

"Why's that?" Azerick asked.

The farmer's grin revealed several missing teeth. "Because I'm Willard, and I still don't recognize you."

Daebian snapped his head around and glared at him. "Think you would recognize your guts if I spilled them on the ground?"

Azerick hissed a warning at Daebian, but Willard's gap-toothed grin only widened.

"Don't get your knickers in a twist," the farmer said. "I ain't gonna out ya to the invaders no matter what your purpose here is."

"We're just trying to earn a little coin before moving on," Azerick repeated.

"If'n ya say so," Willard replied with a wink.

Daebian looked about to issue another biting reply, but an elbow from Azerick silenced him as they approached the guarded gate. A pair of legionnaires began prodding the stacked bundles of wheat with short spears and allowed the wagon to proceed only when they were satisfied there was no one hiding within.

One of the legionnaires lowered his spear to bar the way. "I don't recognize you two."

"This one's my wife's cousin and his son," Willard said before Azerick or Daebian could reply. "They've come up from Duncaster. They stopped to make a bit of coin before moving on for Valecroft."

The guard stared at the two new faces. "You don't look old enough to be this one's father," he said to Daebian.

Daebian pointed to the strip of cloth he had lowered over his eyes. "I wouldn't know. Maybe I've aged well—or he aged poorly."

"How do you work if you're blind?"

"I lift with my hands, not my eyes," Daebian replied.

The guard scowled at him. "I need to see your papers."

Azerick glanced around as Daebian made a show of looking for his papers. Thinking quickly, he sent a small tendril of magic toward the lit brazier nearest the departing wagon. There was a loud pop, and an ember leapt from the brazier to the dry wheat stalks in the wagon.

With a little arcane encouragement, the chaff combusted with a whoosh of air. People began screaming "fire!" and ran about, some slapping at the flames with coats and cloaks while others went off in search of water.

Willard pointed at the chaotic scene and added his own cries of dismay to the growing chorus. He grabbed Azerick and Daebian by the arm and pushed them forward through the gate. "Come on, I know where the water buckets are!"

The legionnaires at the gate did not attempt to stop them as they ran at the wagon, stripping off their cloaks to aid in extinguishing the fire. Willard led Daebian and Azerick to a hand pump next to a watering trough where someone was already working the handle to keep the trough full while people scooped out the water with buckets.

They made a show of filling buckets and pots and handing them off for a couple of minutes before Willard ushered them down a nearby alley. The old man rested his hands on his knees as he fought to catch his breath.

"You fellas should keep your heads down for a bit if you plan on staying in town," Willard said as he straightened up.

Azerick nodded and clapped him on the shoulder. "We won't be here long. Thanks for your help."

"Do us a favor and try not to get them too riled up, assuming you're here to cause some sort of trouble. They ain't necessarily a cruel bunch as conquerors go, but they are damned intolerant of disobedience."

"We've seen how swift and brutal their justice is," Azerick said. "Don't worry. We should be gone without anyone knowing we were here."

The corners of Willard's mouth turned down and he bobbed his head. "Good. You lads give them hell—just not here."

A look of concern crossed Azerick's face. He opened his mouth to speak, but a sharp glare from Daebian made him hold what he was about to say.

"Good luck," Azerick said.

"To you as well," Willard replied as he walked away.

Daebian still wore his scowl. "You were going to warn him about the pending raid, weren't you?"

Azerick furrowed his brow. "I was just going to—"

"Say something stupid that could jeopardize the entire mission and get people killed just for the sake of your sentimentality."

Azerick wanted to argue, but there was no refuting the truth of the matter. "Come on, it's getting dark. We should look around while we can still see."

CHAPTER 13

Azerick and Daebian joined the flow of pedestrians returning home from work or were on their way to their favorite inns and taverns. The foot traffic was dense for a town this size. It appeared that few, if any, citizens lived outside the town's protective walls and garrison.

Not for the first time, Azerick wondered if he was putting too high a value on self-determination. While The Order was strict, it was not cruel, and the protection they offered was the difference between life and death for some.

He spied an older woman in simple, homespun robes wearing the shackles of a fettered mage and knew the answer. She likely possessed a minor talent like making subtle changes to local weather to improve harvest yields, and yet she was chained like a criminal. Azerick's blood boiled at the sight.

They found four barracks buildings housing the garrison along with the unit's headquarters and a large structure that had once been a warehouse of some kind near the center of town. Columns of soldiers marched in different directions, probably on their way to relieve those on duty.

Azerick nudged Daebian and gave the large barn a pointed look. Daebian nodded, and they took a roundabout path toward the structure. The front of the building was open, and Daebian nodded to his father when he was able to see the gliders and skimmers inside it. They walked around the entire building but found only the single entrance, which was guarded by a pair of sentries.

Azerick stared into the gloom from shadows beneath the awning of a building across the street. "Think you can get us inside?"

Daebian's inhuman eyes pierced the darkened interior with ease. "Yeah. Should only take a second. Of course, we're assuming there's no one guarding the inside. I guess we can cut that bridge's throat when we get to it."

Azerick turned his head to look at his son. "Your use of idioms is disturbing."

Daebian shrugged, unconcerned, and took Azerick by the arm. "Ready?"

Azerick took a deep breath. "Ready."

Absolute darkness enveloped them as Daebian leapt into the shadow ways. The feeling of jumping into icy water filled with man-eating creatures washed over Azerick. He gasped and found himself in the warehouse's dim interior seconds later.

"Well, that was easy," Azerick said as he got his bearings.

Daebian wiped black ichor from his sword. "Easy enough, I guess."

"They didn't waste any time, did they?"

Daebian shook his head. "I'm going to have to find better camouflage, especially when I'm dragging around outsiders like bait on a hook."

Azerick shuddered at the mental image and looked around. "There are the vehicles. I should be able to copy the important runes off one of them. Keep an eye out."

The two walked over to the farthermost skimmer, putting the others between them and anyone who might enter the building. Azerick examined the runes he could see.

"I think this is what I need. I'm fairly sure they wouldn't put them on the bottom where they could get marred.

"Good thing," Daebian replied. "We'd have a hell of a time lifting it up."

"They're engraved too." Azerick pulled out several large pieces of paper and a dark block of wax. "I can copy them with rubbings. This will be a lot faster than I had feared."

Azerick began rubbing the wax block over the paper he pressed against the arcanum-filigreed runes.

"Could you make more noise?" Daebian hissed. "You sound like you're scraping barnacles off a hull!"

"Would you rather we spend an hour in here while I copy them by hand?" Azerick retorted as he laid the next piece of paper over another section of runes.

"Shut up!" Daebian hissed.

Azerick glared up at his son from where he lay on the ground. "Listen, you little turd, I am still your father and I will not tolerate—"

He stopped talking as his ears picked up a droning sound that was getting louder by the second. Daebian scrambled behind the skimmer and hunkered down next to Azerick just before a glider buzzed through the open doors and touched down.

The legionnaire swung himself off the glider as if dismounting a horse. He took a few steps toward the open doors before stopping and turning around. The scout cocked an ear and traveled his eyes around the barn's gloomy interior, slowly stalking toward the shadows in which Azerick and Daebian hid.

At a look from Azerick, Daebian slipped into the shadow ways. He reappeared for an instant, clamping one hand over the soldier's mouth and pressing a dagger to his throat with other, before pulling him into the shadow ways.

Daebian reemerged next to Azerick, wiping his dagger off with a cloth. "See, my bridge idiom was perfectly appropriate."

Azerick started at his sudden appearance. "Do you have to do that?"

Daebian pursed his lips. "Have to? No. Like to? Yes. Will continue doing? Also yes."

"One of these days you're going to startle the wrong person."

"Already did. Ellyssa whilst using the privy. She hit me with a shock so strong I fouled myself."

"Was it worth it?"

Daebian grinned. "Totally."

Azerick sighed and returned to his rubbings. "I'm nearly done. Just keep an eye on the entrance."

"There's movement near the door," Daebian hissed minutes later.

"I need one more minute," Azerick insisted.

Two figures stood framed by the large doorway. "Sestos, is there a problem?" one called out.

Both sentries took cautious steps into the building.

"We don't have a minute," Daebian whispered.

Azerick redoubled his rubbing efforts, which had the effect of increasing the sound he was making.

"What's going on over there?" one of the sentries demanded.

Receiving no answer, the guards stalked toward the odd sound. They circled around each side of the skimmer, their spears leveled and shields raised. With perfect coordination, they sprang around the skimmer's front and back, ready to engage whatever foe lay lurking behind it. The shimmering light their shields emitted revealed nothing but dust and a discarded piece of dark wax.

Azerick and Daebian emerged from the shadows of the building across the street from the warehouse. Daebian's sword dripped black ichor, and Azerick bled from a shallow cut across his left forearm.

"We're going to have to leave town the old-fashioned way," Daebian said. "The shadow spawn know where we're at and are waiting for us the instant we enter their realm."

Azerick grimaced. "We have a problem."

"How so?"

Azerick pressed a hand against the wound on his arm. "I dropped one of the rubbings."

Daebian narrowed his eyes. "Where?"

"In the shadow ways," Azerick replied, chagrined.

"Are you freaking serious?" Daebian railed.

Azerick flashed his son a wide grin. "No. Come on, we need to find a way over the wall."

"You suck so bad, you know that?" Daebian said as he hastened after Azerick.

Both men hunkered down next to the wall between a grain silo and a small building that likely contained tools. It was close to the midway point between two braziers illuminating the area around them.

They waited for a roving guard to pass by before Daebian wrapped himself in shadows, leapt high enough to grab the top of the wall, and heaved himself up. He dangled his arm over the side, grasped Azerick's wrist, and pulled him up before they both dropped over the far side.

Azerick nearly lost his footing on the narrow ledge between the wall and the dry moat filled with sharpened stakes. Daebian kept hold of the shadows, pulling them along as he and Azerick slid down into the moat and climbed back out the other side.

Daebian held Azerick's arm as they crouched next to the edge. A legionnaire standing on the wall stared at the spot of blackness in which they hid for several seconds before moving on. Only then did they jog away in a hunched crouch until they blended in with the surrounding darkness.

"Do you see our guides?" Azerick asked once they reached the distant tree line on the far side of the expansive grain fields.

Daebian cast his gaze around the dark forest. "Nothing. They may be deeper in the woods. Let's make our way toward the gate."

The two of them moved briskly through the forest until Daebian stopped and knelt on the ground. "There are footprints here."

"Our foresters?"

Daebian shook his head. "If it is, they aren't alone."

"How many are there?"

Daebian scowled up at Azerick. "How in the abyss should I know? I'm a pirate, not a damned ranger!"

"But you're sure it's more than two?"

"More than two less than a hundred."

Azerick sighed. "Can you narrow it down a little?"

Daebian grunted as he stood up. "Two others. Could be three or even four if one or more of them made half an attempt to conceal their tracks."

Azerick nodded. "So not a squad of legionnaires."

"Certainly not ones in uniform. None of these were made by their heavy boots."

"Can you follow them?"

Daebian tapped a finger against his chest. "Pi-rate. I was lucky to see these. Had they walked a foot to either side I never would have noticed them."

Azerick sighed again. "OK. Should we look around for them, or make camp?"

"Hell no. We told them to wait and they chose to leave. The spawn can take them for all I care. What's important is getting those tracing back to camp and doing something with them so we can poke the dragon again."

Azerick looked around at the darkness. "I don't like the idea of leaving them out here."

"Do you like the idea of everyone starving?" Daebian asked. "Because that's what's going to happen if we can't raid that town for their food stores. Besides, they're both accomplished woodsmen. They'll make it back on their own."

"You're right," Azerick conceded.

"Pretty much always am. That's the beauty of being a true pragmatist."

"Or a person lacking in conscience and moral decency."

"You use your word, I'll use mine. Let's go."

Azerick did his best to match Daebian's brutal pace, but while his body was young, it lacked the conditioning of a person accustomed to physical activity. While much improved over the weeks following the invasion and his resurrection, Azerick still lacked his previous physical strength and endurance, even when he had just been a human.

Azerick stopped and braced his hands on his knees while he fought to catch his breath. Daebian pulled up short and turned around, giving his father a snide look as he walked back to where Azerick rested.

"Shall I carry you over my shoulder like an invalid or sack of potatoes?" Daebian asked.

Azerick lacked the breath to form words, so he responded with a raised middle finger. He finally took a deep breath and stood up straight.

"We should be far enough away for me use my gate spell."

Daebian quirked one corner of his mouth up. "You just don't want to run anymore."

Azerick narrowed his eyes. "We need to get these runes back to camp where I can study them and make carts capable of hauling the food we need through the gates...and I don't want to run anymore."

"You're getting lazy in your old age. Have at it then."

Azerick spun the magical weaving with practiced ease, and a portal opened before him. He and Daebian leapt through and jogged until Azerick had to stop to rest before opening another. Their loping portal hopping whittled hours of travel down to tens of minutes.

In a little over an hour, Azerick stopped and gulped in air after their most recent transit. "Look around. We should be near the gate."

Daebian searched the dark forest as he made a slow circuit around the area. He returned a couple of minutes later. "I have some good news and bad news."

Azerick stood with one hand bracing himself against a tree. "Why am I not surprised?"

"Because I'm awesome and you're a bad luck magnet," Daebian replied helpfully.

Azerick made a rolling motion with his free hand and Daebian continued. "The good news is I found the gate about fifty yards over there. The bad news is we are not alone."

Azerick pinched the bridge of his nose. "Not our companions?"

Daebian grinned and shook his head. "Not our companions."

Azerick took in a deep breath and slowly let it out. "Spawn?"

"Lots of them."

"Shit," Azerick swore.

"Shit indeed. Deep, and we stepped right into it. Hope you're wearing high boots."

"Can we get to the portal before them?"

Daebian shrugged. "If we move quickly and they sluggishly, we might beat them there."

Azerick sucked in a deep breath. "Then let's move quickly."

The two of them raced toward the stone arch. Azerick spied it between the trees just seconds before they reached it. He slid to a halt next to the gate, his magic tingling in his fingertips as he laid a hand against the stone. Nothing happened.

"Uh, Father, the spawn are coming," Daebian said as he whipped his head around. "You want to activate that thing so we can leave?"

"It's locked!" Azerick exclaimed.

"What in the abyss do you mean it's locked?"

"I mean someone locked it!"

"Well, can you unlock it?"

Azerick studied the ward barring him from activating the gate. "Yes, but I need a minute."

"Stop saying you need a minute for everything! We don't have a minute. We never have a minute!"

"And yet you are able to find one."

Daebian looked out at the approaching spawn, drew his sword, and muttered, "Goddammit."

Daebian's shouts of challenge rang out over the sound of snapping brush and savage snarls as he did his best to lead the murderous creatures away. Azerick tried to push aside the sounds of combat and Daebian's frequent cursing as he worked to unravel the ward preventing him from using the gate. It was well crafted, but it appeared to have been cast in haste.

A tingling on the back of his neck was all the warning Azerick got before the creatures leapt at him. He raised his staff and made a swirling motion over the top of his head. Stone spikes erupted from the ground, ringing him and the archway.

Several spawn impaled themselves upon the spikes as they closed to form a spiny dome over him. The construct looked something akin to a massive, stone sea urchin in the middle of the forest. Azerick staggered and fell to one knee. His vision swam as he tried to force his mind to work past the crippling fatigue.

Able to focus once more, Azerick returned to the task of removing the ward. He plucked a string of power from one invisible nexus and attached it to another. The entire arcane form shimmered in his mage sight before vanishing.

Azerick slapped a hand to the gate and sent a trickle of power barely strong enough to activate the runes carved into it. He breathed a sigh of relief when the inside of the archway shimmered.

"Daebian, it's op—!"

Daebian flew out of a shadow before Azerick could dispel his spiny dome and crashed headlong into him. The impact drove them both through the gateway to go rolling across the ground on the far side.

"Shut it!" Daebian cried.

Azerick oriented himself and crawled on his hands and knees back to the gate. He saw a massive spawn shatter the stone spikes barring them from their prey. It lurched forward, reaching out with a claw-tipped hand. Azerick touched the cold stone and blocked the energy powering it. The portal closed, shearing off the huge, clawed hand cleaner than any blade could have managed, and it dropped next to his head.

Daebian sat propped up on his hands, his clothes shredded and his flesh torn in numerous places, and glared at his father. "I am no longer having fun."

CHAPTER 14

Azerick and Daebian both lay on the ground for several minutes before finding the strength to sit up. Azerick fetched up against the stone arch while Daebian propped his back against a nearby tree trunk.

"Someone is going to answer for this," Azerick said.

"For our missing companions, the conveniently located spawn horde, or the locked portal?" Daebian asked.

"All three."

Daebian wiped his gore-covered blade off on the grass. "Good. That means I get to stab them three times."

Azerick looked at Daebian's wounds. "Are you OK?"

Daebian looked down at himself. "Well, my clothes are as tattered as my patience, but none of my injuries are life-threatening, barring infection, which I believe I am immune to."

"You did well distracting that mob."

"I did bloody fantastic. Honestly, I cannot understand your insatiable desire to play hero. The constant ass-kickings are beyond intolerable."

Azerick grinned. "It's all about that warm feeling you get when you've helped someone."

Daebian snorted. "I'm sure that's just the infection spreading. Unless the warm feeling is a sexual reference, then I completely understand."

Azerick shook his head and chuckled as he climbed to his feet. "No, neither of those things are what I speak of, although the latter is an occasional perk."

Daebian finished tying off the last of more than half a dozen hastily applied bandages and stood as well. "I believe the correct word is rare rather than occasional in your case. You strike me as a bit of a prude."

"I'll have you know—"

"No, you will not," Daebian interrupted. "I have no desire to hear of your sexual prowess or proclivities. I like to think even my conception was by way of some magical or intangible implanting."

"Now who's a prude?"

"That is propriety and a desire not to vomit, not prudishness."

Azerick chuckled as he walked away. "You can dwell on it while we walk. We need to get back to camp."

Daebian followed his father. "Right behind you. Looking forward to kicking someone's ass always makes me feel better."

It was nearly noon the next day when Azerick and Daebian made it back to camp. They had both needed to rest several hours before making the last leg of their journey. Azerick had exhausted himself opening so many gates in succession, and Daebian's injuries needed time to heal even with the healing potions he had quaffed. They also wanted to be prepared for a fight should it come down to one.

Little had changed in their short absence. People went about the daily tasks of maintaining and improving the camp's living conditions and keeping the army and their families fed. The only notable change was a tension in the air Azerick could feel like a storm rolling in. He saw worried looks in people's eyes that came not from general fear but his and Daebian's arrival.

"You feel that?" Daebian asked even as Azerick's mind formed the thought.

Azerick nodded. "They know the fur is about to fly, which means at least some of them know why."

Kord appeared a few paces in front of them. "Marley needs you in the command building."

"We'll deal with Marley in a minute," Daebian growled. "Where in the abyss are those two idiots he sent with us?"

"Command building," Kord said again and spun on his heel.

Azerick lengthened his stride to keep up with the big man. "Are those two there?"

Kord remained silent as he led the two of them to the log building that was the command center. Kord held the door open and fell in behind them when they entered.

"Marley, where are the two you sent with us, and who in the abyss locked the gate?" Azerick demanded the moment he crossed the threshold.

A woman's voice cut through the air. "They are here in camp, and I sealed the gate."

Azerick turned his head toward the speaker and almost gasped in surprise. "Sibyl? You made it back."

"As did I, thanks to her," Joah said as he stepped beside her. "Try not to look so pleased to see me. People might get the wrong impression about our relationship."

"What happened to you two, and what does it have to do with sealing the gate and nearly getting the two of us killed?" Azerick demanded.

Sibyl took a deep breath and straightened her back. She looked as haggard and exhausted as he and Daebian. "The Order captured Joah and handful of others during the attack on Freehold. I was able to remain at large and followed them until they made camp. Both sides had wounded needing attended to before marching back to Southport. The princess left on one of their flying machines, and I knew if I was going to free anyone, I would have to do it that night."

"You managed to free Joah but not the others?" Azerick asked.

Sibyl shook her head. "They kept Joah apart for interrogation. Even if I had been able to get to the others, which was unlikely, few if any of them were in any condition to escape. As an officer with significant knowledge of our people and operations, I felt it most important to get Joah out."

"It would have been less risky just to kill him," Daebian said. "That's what I would have done."

Sibyl fixed Daebian with a steely gaze. "And that is what I would have done were I unable to abscond with him. Fortunately, his guards gave me an opportunity to extract him with an acceptable chance of success. We've been on the run ever since."

"That doesn't explain the gate or our two guides," Azerick said.

"The nearest gate relative to our position was likely guarded. The one you used to reach Orrinshire was the next closest and our best bet of making it back. We had just managed to elude the soldiers chasing us when a group of spawn picked up our scent. They hounded us all the way to Orrinshire, and that's when we ran into Daniil and Jepson."

"Technically, they ran into us," Joah said. "They heard us crashing through the brush and nearly did the spawn's work for them."

"Damn pity that'd have been," Daebian snorted.

Sibyl rolled her eyes. "The four of us were able to beat back the nearest spawn, but we knew there were more closing in on us. I ordered Jepson and Daniil to follow us to the portal. By the time we reached it, we were near to being overrun. We barely managed to make it through before I was able to seal the gate behind us."

"But why lock it? You had to have known we were going to use it!" Azerick snapped.

Sibyl met his glare without flinching. "Because I don't know what those things are capable of other than killing us! There are new ones coming out every time we face them. If they can ignore magical wards, then who can say if another one might be able to activate the gate? I had more confidence in you two being able to get past them than them not being able to open the portal. It appears I was at least partially correct, and I won't apologize for ensuring the safety of my people and this camp."

Daebian exposed a few inches of his sword blade. "What if I stab you in a few of your more sensitive areas? Would you feel like apologizing then?"

"Daebian," Azerick said in warning.

"Don't Daebian me! I look like a damned scratching post for lions!"

"And yet you're still here to complain about it," Sibyl snarled. "Some might call that a win."

"Winning is when I make others bleed," Daebian retorted.

Azerick raised a hand. "She's right. The fact we are all still here means she probably made the right call. That's a win in any book."

Daebian crossed his arms. "Must be a children's book."

"Were you able to copy the runes?" Headmaster Florent asked.

Azerick pulled the rolled-up rubbings from his extradimensional bag. "I did. I'll need to study them a bit, but I think I can decipher them in short order."

"What about the actual construction?" Marley asked. "Are we going to need any exotic materials? Our resources are quite limited."

Azerick shook his head. "Just find some people who can build a cart without wheels to the desired specification. We only need them to work once, so simplicity works best for us. If you can do that, I'll begin deciphering the runes immediately."

Daebian followed Azerick out of the cabin. "Do you believe that crap Sibyl said about rescuing that prick Joah and hotfooting it across the countryside to the same gate we needed to use to get back?"

Azerick pressed his lips together. "It stretches credulity on several points. I still don't know the location of all the gates they've made across the kingdom, but that one is one of the closer ones. The timing sure is suspect. Also, legionnaires letting their guard slip on a high-value prisoner like Joah enough to allow Sibyl to snatch him away *and* avoid recapture…"

Daebian nodded along with Azerick's assessment. "That begs the question of which one might be a traitor? Did The Order allow Joah out or Sibyl in? Both? Neither?"

Azerick shook his head and sighed. "I don't know. I need to return to the tower to work on these runes. Stay here and keep an eye out for any suspicious behavior. If we're compromised, none of this is going to mean a damn thing in the end."

"Sure, there's only about two-hundred people in this camp. Shouldn't be too hard to watch them all."

"Just focus on key leaders."

Daebian nodded. "Like Sibyl and Joah."

"And Marley, the headmaster, Chancellor McGill, and anyone else privy to inside information. Right now, the only person in this camp I trust explicitly is you."

Daebian snorted. "That's damned short-sighted of you, but I appreciate the vote of confidence all the same."

Azerick flashed him a grin. "Believe me, in most any other situation you would be near the top of my list. I trust in your desire for avenging the humiliation and pain they inflicted upon you to be sufficient to keep you steadfast at my side. For once, your ego is an asset."

"It has indeed served me well all these years."

Azerick returned to the same spot where he had created the doorway to his old tower. He refreshed and verified the runes before channeling power into them and crossing into the parallel realm.

Raijaun stood in the tower's doorway, ducking his head a bit to keep his horns from scraping the upper jam. "Father, you have returned—and alone. I hope my brother is well."

Azerick nodded. "He is. I needed him to stay behind to keep an eye on certain matters."

"It is good. One visit every ten years or so is quite sufficient."

Azerick chuckled. "Yes, a little bit of Daebian goes a long way."

"He is being useful to you though?"

"While difficult, he has been indispensable. He is one of the few people around me I can trust."

Raijaun furrowed his brow. "Things must be dire indeed. Daebian is not one I would want to rely upon to watch my back lest I wish a dagger in it."

Azerick pursed his lips as he sought a reply. "I think despite his talk and ruthless practicality, he tries to do the right thing even if it is not the decent thing to do."

"Perhaps Ellyssa has had a positive influence on him after all."

"I think she has."

"What is it that has brought you back?" Raijaun asked. "I still cannot actively assist you in your mortal war."

"I need to use the Source pool again to contact some people. May I?"

Raijaun ducked his head and stepped back into the tower, clearing the doorway. "You may. I consider such an action benign enough not to interfere. However, depending upon circumstances, such may not continue to be the case."

"I understand. Thank you—again."

Azerick descended the stairs into the tower's sublevels once more and knelt before the silver disc set in the floor. He fixed Duncan's image in his mind until the brilliantly reflective metal showed the dwarf's bearded face.

"Gads, boy, you seem determined to give an old dwarf a heart attack," Duncan grumbled. "This ain't one of your tower of wizards who likely get this kind of summons every day."

Azerick smiled at him. "Sorry, Duncan. I have some rune questions, and you're the best rune master I know. If anyone can make sense of them it's you."

Duncan's bushy eyebrows leapt up higher on his forehead. "A rune conundrum you say? If it has you stymied it must be a real puzzler."

"To be honest, I haven't studied them much, but I'm in a hurry and don't want to waste any time with it. They're foreign, and I'm hoping together we can translate them into something I can use."

Impossibly, Duncan's eyebrows crawled even higher. "Foreign you say? Well, I wouldn't be much of a rune master if I passed on the opportunity to study new glyphs. Did I teach you the transcribe rune form?"

Azerick shook his head. "No, but I saw a mage cast a spell that copied the contents of one book to several books with blank pages in them once."

"Aye, it's much the same from the sound of it, except if you get it wrong the books won't come to life or the contents spring out in an embodied form and try to murder you like that unreliable wizardry might."

Azerick chuckled. "I don't think that could happen. At least I've never heard of such a thing occurring."

"Maybe because no one lived through the experience to tell of it."

"Maybe," Azerick conceded. "How does it work?"

"I'm going to draw a rune form on some vellum and show it to you. You can see me, right?"

Azerick nodded.

"Good. You just copy the rune form exactly onto whatever you've transcribed your runes upon. Anything written or carved on your page or tablet will show up on mine."

"Got it."

"All right. Give me a minute."

Duncan hunched over a sheet of vellum and began drawing linked sigils onto the material to create the rune form. In just over a minute, he held the sheet up to the polished silver mirror displaying Azerick's face.

"Can you make it out?" he asked.

Azerick nodded. "I can. Yeah, I should be able to do that."

"It must be exact, and make sure it's not reversed, what with the mirror nonsense and such."

"Got it."

Azerick took a quill and enchanted ink from his bag and began drawing the rune form. It took him three times as long as it had Duncan, but the moment he finished it, smoke began billowing in front of the dwarf.

Duncan leapt off his stool and began waving his hands at the smoke. "Gads, boy! What have you drawn?" He leaned in toward the smoking vellum. "Is this from a rubbing?"

"Yeah, sorry," Azerick replied, chagrined.

"That explains it. The transcription burns what's written onto the vellum. Since it's a rubbing, it's covered in what the rune sees as writing."

"Sorry about that," Azerick said again.

Duncan waved a hand in dismissal. He moved about his workroom and returned with what looked like a small windmill. The rune master activated a rune etched into its base, and the blades began spinning, blowing the smoke out of the window set above his workbench.

"That's better," Duncan said. "How many of these things you got?"

Azerick hunched his shoulders and looked askance. "Four more pages."

Duncan sighed. "Not a problem. Copy the same rune form onto the other pages, only you'll end each one with successive numbers. You do remember your dwarven numbers don't ya?"

"I remember," Azerick assured his former tutor.

"Good. You humans tend to be a forgetful bunch. We'll start with the number two and work on from there."

Azerick went to work creating the rune forms. He did not have to see how Duncan made his numerals as there was only one way to write dwarven script. Each letter and number were as exacting as any blueprint detailing precise measurements for the most complicated of constructions. As in construction, there was no deviation from the blueprints no matter who was reading or writing them.

More smoke began filling the room as Azerick finished inscribing each page until he could no longer see Duncan within the obscuring haze.

"Duncan, you set something alight in there?" a gruff voice called up from somewhere in the distance. "Do ya need the fire brigade?"

Through the smoke, Azerick saw Duncan's silhouette move toward the open window. "No fire. Just transcribing some rubbings!"

Duncan's answer must have sufficed, as there was no more discussion about the smoke billowing out of the window. Dwarves might be a stubborn people, but they handled most anything out of the ordinary with aplomb. As long as whatever was happening was being dealt with, they went on with their business as though nothing was amiss.

"Is this the last of them coming through now?" Duncan asked minutes later."

"It is," Azerick replied.

The smoke cleared quickly, and Duncan sat hunched over the sheets on his workbench. "Do ya know what the runes do?"

Azerick nodded. "They're locomotion runes for the most part. When powered, they cause a wagon-like vehicle to hover a few feet above the ground and propel it at speeds near a horse's gallop."

Duncan traced a rune form with one stubby finger. "Ah, yes. This must be the locomotion runes here. Not overly complicated. Much like the ones we use on our ore carts. Just foreign. I'm surprised humans came up with them. If you hadn't told me otherwise, I would have thought them dwarven or possibly elvish given the unnecessary flourishes. These others though, they're complex. You say these carts hover above the ground?"

"Yes. They have smaller vehicles that can actually fly. I've seen them up as high as one or two-hundred feet."

Duncan scratched at the blocky chin covered with thick, black and silver hair. "Gotta be inverse gravimetric runes then. Can't be anything else. If that's true, then you've got one heck of a find here, my boy."

"Inverse gravimetric runes?" Azerick asked, shaking his head.

"Aye. It flips the effect of gravity, more or less, around an object. When equalized, you get a floating effect as the downward and upward force cancel each other out. Increase one or the other and you get vertical motion. Same with shifting the force to either side to get lateral movement."

"Can you replicate it?"

Duncan sputtered his lips as he let out a long breath. "Gravimetric rune scribing is entirely theoretical. Well, it used to be. It has been the pursuit of just about every master rune carver in our history, including mine. We got as far as basic locomotion but no further. The power and precision needed to invert gravity is, well…significant does not begin to describe it. All these rune forms here, better than eighty-percent of them, are dedicated to the inversion."

Azerick sighed and nodded. "That must be why they require a mage to continually channel arcane energy into them. The power draw is simply too great for them to be self-sustaining."

"Exactly right. I suppose you could use an artifact containing significant energy to power them, but it would exhaust the stored energy soon enough. In fact, unless I miss my guess, this rune form on the first page is some sort of conduit to channel power from an outside source."

"The mage controlling the craft," Azerick supplied.

Duncan wagged his head. "No, I don't think so. Not by itself anyway. Look at the third sheet. The rune form in the center is also a conduit, and while it is tied to the other, it also draws from a source I can't discern."

Azerick studied the runes Duncan referenced. "Ambient magical energy perhaps?"

"Hm, that would be my guess as well, but I don't see how it could draw nearly the requisite amount, and no way could a mage channel the kind of power needed to do what you describe by themselves for long. You with your staff or maybe an archmage of significant strength could power it for a couple of hours but not much longer, especially at anything approaching its maximum speed."

Azerick rested his chin in his palm and wracked his brain for an answer. "The order binds everyone able to use magic in shackles that allow them to channel only as much power as their rulers allot. They claim to be gods and dole out their magic much like clerical deities. Could the energy conduit be connecting to that source of power?"

Duncan furrowed is brow. "Yes…yes, I think that might be the right of it, but I can't imagine anyone other than a god being able to transmit that kind of power across vast distances like that."

Azerick's shoulders slumped. "Then not only am I battling gods once more, I've set myself upon an impossible task."

Duncan frowned, the concept of an impossibility, particularly when rune crafting was involved, irked his dwarven stubbornness. "What exactly do you need this vehicle of yours to do?"

"Our camp needs food. Our plan is to raid a grain store and cart it off with these wagons able to traverse rough ground faster than a horse-drawn one could. A normal wagon is too wide and the terrain too rough and broken between the portal gates hidden in the forest."

"How far do ya have to move them, particularly under load?"

"The longest stretch is maybe twelve miles, but I can open portals to carve large chunks of that off. Say two or three stretches of five or six miles each. That's assuming I don't have to use most of my energy in battle. The Order has also shown an ability to track mages opening dimensional gates, so I want to use them as little as possible, especially when anywhere near their arcanus."

Duncan ran his fingers through his beard. "Ya got any other mages ya can bring?"

Azerick bobbed his head. "A dozen with at least a middling ability."

"Hm… might be you can muster the power needed if you all switch off, assuming I can translate and reproduce this gravimetric inversion rune form."

A surge of hope coursed through Azerick. "Do you think you can do it?"

Duncan scowled at him. "Son, you're looking at the preeminent rune carver in all dwarven kind. I'll bet my beard I can decipher this human-made gibberish. How much time can ya give me?"

"They'll ship most of the grain off within the next two weeks. I'll have the carts built before then. Say ten days at most? That should give me enough time to inscribe the runes, instruct the mages on how to channel power into them, and get to the town before they ship out the grain."

Duncan sputtered his lips once more. "You're asking me to solve a riddle we dwarves have been trying to decipher for centuries in just a handful of days." His blocky teeth flashed white against his dark beard. "But they didn't have a piece of the code! You go and inscribe that transcription rune form I showed ya onto several blank sheets. You'll know when or if I've cracked it. Just keep them away from anything flammable. They burn a might hot."

"I will, Duncan. Thank you. If there's anything I can ever do to repay you, you need only ask."

"Are you kidding? If I can crack this, I'll be a legendary rune caster in me own time. The world best be ready for flying dwarves!"

Azerick laughed deeply as he pictured it in his mind. Duncan's grinning visage vanished as he let go of the scrying spell. He knew deep in his bones Duncan would come through. He had to. Whether he did or not, Azerick knew it would not be enough to win this war. He took a deep breath as he channeled the power for another scrying spell.

CHAPTER 15

Azerick knelt next to the glimmering disc of arcanum and pondered his next move. Part of him wanted to return to camp and work with Headmaster Florent on deciphering the runes. Perhaps she or one of her fellow wizards had more experience in rune crafting than he did, but he doubted it.

If Duncan could not unravel them, it was unlikely he or anyone else would have more success. No, what he needed to do was focus on defeating The Order. He had been thinking too small, and The Order had them on the defensive. They needed to attack and in a way that mattered.

They were a small band and little more than a nuisance, like an insect buzzing around the head and was more likely to be swatted than deliver a fatal sting. They needed to consolidate and go on the offensive. Until they controlled territory, no matter how small, they would always be defending. It was time to change the game.

Azerick focused his will and channeled power into the Source pool once more. A powerful wave of pressure shoved against his will. Every hair on his body stood on end and felt as though they were moments from erupting into flame.

He ignored the pain and fought against the wards until his consciousness burst through the barrier as if he had fallen through thick ice over a frozen pond. Azerick gasped as the wave of cold washed over him so frigid it felt as though his flesh burned. When he opened his eyes, the face he had imagined in his mind stared back at him with a rueful smile.

"You are lucky I have not yet become forgetful in my old age and recognized your unique arcane signature. You do realize you just broke into my home like a burglar or assassin? My sorcerer guards and I were about to incinerate your mind."

Azerick smiled back at the man who looked almost exactly as he remembered with the exception of a little more grey in his jet black goatee and hair. "Master Devlin, I apologize for the intrusion. Or should I call you Your Majesty?"

Devlin Sabaht, Azerick's former instructor and now king of Sumara, gave him a genuine smile. "For you, it is just Devlin. I may be king by standing, but you are so much more by deed. We are at the very least equals and friends. At least I hope so."

Azerick nodded. "Of course, and always. It is why I have so rudely intruded into your home—or wherever you are. I had to scry you out by image and desire. Such magic cares nothing for location."

"Indeed, it does not," Devlin said with a chuckle. "What causes you to risk contacting me in such a way?"

Azerick took in a deep breath. "I know King Miles has contacted you through your cousin Radique and warned you of what is coming."

Devlin nodded; his face grim. "He has. It did not sound as though things were going well in his last report."

"That's what I wanted to discuss with you."

Devlin held up a hand before Azerick could continue. "I know what you are going to ask of me. If I were to commit my armies now, it could prove disastrous for my kingdom and would avail you nothing if we failed."

"I'm not asking for an army. Not all of them anyway. Devlin, if we fall, they will come for you, and they will bring in more legions when they are able to augment their other war with conscripted valerians. This is not a rival kingdom but an empire that may well span most of the known world. Even if you prove to be a greater challenge than we presented them, which I am certain you will, they have countless forces they can bring to bear."

Devlin raised his hands. "Then what can I possibly do to help if things are as dire as you say?"

"That strength is also their weakness. The reason they are here is because this is not their only war. They came to gather more soldiers to fight a larger front elsewhere. What we have to do is create a strong, fortified position within Valeria from which we can advance in force.

If we can control territory, disrupt their supply lines, and most importantly destroy the gate they use to bring in reinforcements, then we can defeat them. I thought our insurgent tactics would prove too costly for them to stay, but I was wrong. We have to join forces and fight as a whole if we are to have any chance of pushing them back."

Devlin dropped his gaze and sighed. "I understand the logic in your thinking, but I have to put the welfare of my people ahead of all else. Storming across the border before we are ready is simply not an option."

"I don't need your entire army. Well, I do, but that's not what I'm asking for. Duchess Paulina and her cadre of inquisitors are the only ones holding their own right now. If you could spare a strong, mobile force and join up with them, my people and I could create enough of a ruckus here to allow Miles and William's forces to reach them."

Devlin nodded along. "They could create a lodgment strong enough to withstand all but an all-out assault. It is unlikely they would or could commit a large enough force to oust them, especially with you and your people constantly striking at their flanks and rear."

"Exactly!" Azerick exclaimed. "From there, they could take back territory and increase their numbers. Once we can hold Brightridge and Argoth, you could have the rest of your army ready to strike at them from the east and south. With any luck, my people will have destroyed their gate in Southport, denying them reinforcements. Then, it is just a matter of hitting them until they retreat on their ships or surrender."

"It is a sound plan worthy of the most seasoned general."

Azerick grinned. "I've had some experience defending against larger and even scarier forces than these invaders."

Devlin smiled back at him. "All right. There is a narrow pass only a couple of days ride from a town called Sandusk. It is mostly a smuggler path, but I can get a couple hundred soldiers and sorcerers through it within a fortnight. Paulina's main contingent is not far from there. As long as The Order does not get between us and them, we should be able to reconnoiter with the duchess soon after."

"Are you able to contact William and Miles?"

Devlin nodded. "I am in frequent contact with Radique who is able to relay messages to William. It will take a few days for him to get to the duke, but it will happen."

Azerick ducked his head. "Good. I have something to work on over the next week that should help secure my position here. Once that is done, we can then focus on our harassment and distraction campaign."

"Very well. If there is a change in our position, I will ensure Radique keeps you apprised."

Azerick held up a finger. "Speaking of Radique, do you think he would be willing to teach me that sand travel spell of his?"

Devlin tilted his head back and laughed. "He won't even share his secret with me! Perhaps when this is over, he might be more forthcoming."

"I've learned some neat tricks of my own. Maybe he'll be willing to trade knowledge."

"Mayhap. Fare thee well, Azerick. I look forward to seeing you in person again. We have much to discuss."

Azerick smiled back at his former master. "We certainly do."

He let go of the spell and sat back on his heels. He took several deep breaths and wiped the sweat from his brow. Forcing his way past Devlin's wards had been taxing, but the excitement he felt from finally having a proper plan in place energized him.

Azerick glanced around the room as he knelt next to the Source pool before touching the tip of his staff to the arcanum disc. The solid surface rippled like water, and tendrils of the shining metal crawled up into the arcanum sphere atop it. His staff absorbed the liquefied arcanum like a sponge, storing it away without a trace.

He felt like a thief, but Azerick could not risk Raijaun rejecting his request had he asked. He would not directly defy his son, but in this circumstance, it was better to beg forgiveness than ask permission. The stakes were simply too high.

"Did you get all you needed," Raijaun asked as Azerick crested the stairs.

The question stopped Azerick in his tracks and caused him to stumble over his words. "Huh…what?"

"Were you able to get the information you required?" Raijaun reiterated.

"Uh…yeah. For the most part. Duncan is working on translating the rune forms I brought him, and Devlin has agreed to send a contingent of soldiers into Argoth in hopes of solidifying Duchess Paulina's position."

"That is good."

The two walked in silence back to the crossover gate Azerick had created to enter this realm.

"I am gladdened to have you back, Father," Raijaun said as Azerick reached out to open the doorway. He looked pointedly at Azerick's staff. "However, I fear this is the last time I can be of assistance in this matter. I hope you understand."

Azerick grimaced, and his face flushed like a child caught with his hand in the cookie jar. "I am glad to be back and to see you again. I also hope this is the last time I must avail myself of anything but your company from here on, at least as it pertains to this fiasco."

Raijaun ducked his large, horned head. "I have faith that you will resolve this situation with the best possible outcome for everyone involved."

"I certainly hope so," Azerick replied with a sigh. "Every day I do not, people die."

"It is the way of mortals and their unending conflicts. When one is resolved, another soon replaces it."

Azerick grinned at him. "You have become quite the optimist."

"It is reality. Optimism and pessimism are merely different lenses used to make life appear less chaotic."

"Farewell, Raijaun. When I return next, I hope it is for naught but your company."

"And you, Father," Raijaun replied with a nod.

Azerick stepped through the doorway and reeled from the sudden assault of differing senses. The dimension in which Raijaun dwelled was an almost sterile environment even with his introduction of wildlife. The contrasts, particularly in regards to smell, were overwhelming when not introduced gradually.

He followed his nose back to camp, the smell of unwashed bodies and waste providing a sense of direction as accurate as any worn path or shining star. He found Daebian sitting on a stump whittling a piece of wood near the edge of camp.

"Good visit?" Daebian asked before Azerick appeared in his line of sight.

"I think so," Azerick replied. "See anything unusual or suspicious?"

The corner of Daebian's mouth quirked up. "I'm suspicious of everything, but nothing out of the ordinary. Joah and Sibyl have been sleeping since the meeting broke up. Headmaster Florent and Chancellor McGill spoke a bit after you left. Marley wanders around camp chatting people up when he isn't locked away in the command building brooding about one thing or another. Beyond that, nothing."

Azerick frowned and nodded. "Do you think I'm just being paranoid?"

"I think you would be stupid not to be paranoid, but I haven't seen or sensed anything to support evidence of betrayal."

"All right," Azerick said with a sigh. "Maybe I'm just jumping at shadows."

"Speaking from experience, the shadows these days can be quite dangerous."

Azerick woke to the sound of men cutting and planing down boards for the carts they needed to construct. He washed in a basin, the near-freezing water doing more to energize him than the night's sleep had, and crossed through the camp to the command building.

Kord loomed outside the door as always. The large man scowled when Azerick asked him to fetch the other leaders but stomped off to do as he was bade. Azerick found Marley inside scraping the remaining contents of his breakfast out of a bowl and shoveling it into his mouth. The man looked up at him but immediately returned to his meager meal without a word of acknowledgement.

Joah sat nearby, chewing on a piece of bread that was days past being fresh. He took the time to sneer at Azerick before tearing out another chunk of stale bread with his teeth. Chancellor McGill was the first to arrive, followed by Headmaster Florent and a hollow-eyed Sibyl a few minutes later.

Marley dropped his empty bowl on the table with a clatter. "Well, looks like we're all here. What brilliant plans are you bringing us today?"

Azerick ignored the man's acerbic tone and bent over the map rolled out across the table. "I've enlisted help translating the rune forms we need for our carts. I also contacted King Devlin Sebat of Sumara in hopes of acquiring additional forces."

General McGill's eyes widened in surprise. "Were you successful? It was my understanding he was reinforcing his own cities and would spare none for Valeria."

Azerick ducked his head. "I was able to convince him that his best defense was our success in pushing these invaders out of our kingdom, or at least away from his borders."

"How many is he sending?" Headmaster Florent asked in a voice strained with hope.

"Around two-hundred," Azerick replied.

Marley tossed back his head and laughed. "Two-hundred? You expect another ten-score of men to turn the tide of this war? We have nearly two-hundred here, and we've barely raised a welt on the Order's perpetually clenched backside."

"Not immediately, no. I've decided we cannot hope to defeat them or even cause a retreat with our current tactics."

Joah scoffed. "You've decided."

Azerick ignored him and continued. "Devlin's people are going to sneak through a hidden pass near Sandusk where they will rendezvous with Duchess Paulina's forces. Duke William's people, and those from Brelland if they are able, will join them to create a single, united front. This should enable them to establish a secure territory from which to launch strikes against The Order's widespread forces."

"Ah, then they would have the strength to push them out of the nearest towns and take back territory," Chancellor McGill said.

"What's to keep The Order from doing the same?" Marley asked. "The fact is they still field more soldiers, each one worth between three and five of our own."

"We are," Azerick said with certainty. "Just as the Academy and local forces had you and your people outnumbered, you outmaneuvered them by hitting and retreating, always staying just beyond their reach but not striking so hard as to warrant full-scale retaliation. We keep prodding their rear echelons to ensure enough of them stay put that they can't bring their full might to bear against our main force."

Azerick caught everyone in the room with his icy gaze. "As long as we have the gates, we can harry them all across the region. They will never know where we'll strike next, so they will have to maintain sizable garrisons. As far as their numerical and tactical superiority goes, we're learning how to counter them."

Headmaster Florent looked up from the map. "What of their gate in Southport? They are also able to move armies across vast distances to reinforce their positions."

"Or moving in behind our advancing army to strike at their rear," Joah added. "Won't Paulina and William's people also have to garrison soldiers in their towns and guard supply lines as they advance?"

Azerick nodded. "Both are valid issues. I believe Devlin will commit more of his army to our cause once we show that we can drive back The Order. As far as the gate goes…we'll destroy it."

"Easier said than done," Marley replied. "You're talking about their most valuable asset. I imagine they keep it guarded like it's the princess herself."

"It is," Azerick conceded. "It will take a lot of coordination and inside information. We'll have to communicate with the people we have in the city to get consistent and current updates regarding the garrison forces and their disposition while we harass them afield and our combined southern front pushes toward us."

"More moving parts means more places for it to break down," Marley grumbled.

Chancellor McGill bristled. "War is neither easy nor without great risk. If either is too much for you, you should stand aside."

The rogue met the former general's challenging glare with equal measure. "I didn't back down from The Academy's threats, nor was I able to hide behind high walls and ranks of soldiers like some lordling and his generals commanding an army from a distant hilltop."

"Enough," Azerick said with quiet finality. "The fact we are here is proof of everyone's courage and tenacity. If we start fighting amongst ourselves, we are doing The Order's work for them. We have a plan. It is time to execute it."

"I don't recall voting on any plans, only you telling us what we're going to do," Marley sniped.

Azerick cocked his head to one side. "Do you have a better idea? Anyone? I'm open to any suggestions anyone has to make."

"Sure you are," Joah snorted.

"I'll take that as a no," Azerick said. "While I'm working on deciphering the rune forms and how to bend them to our purpose, I suggest the rest of you work on securing our position and food supplies."

"My hunters found the tracks of an elk herd that passed through not far from here," Marley said. "They're tracking it down now. If they're able to catch up to it, they should be able to bring a few hundred pounds of meat back to camp in the next couple of days," Marley said.

Azerick ducked his head. "Good. Unless anyone has any other business they would like to bring up, we should all get to our duties."

Daebian detached himself from the shadows and walked with Azerick back to the tent they shared.

"Did you sense anything wrong at the meeting?" Azerick asked.

Daebian shook his head. "Nothing out of the ordinary. If anyone in there is working against us, they are masters at hiding it. I didn't catch so much as a shifty look."

Azerick sighed as he parted the flap and pushed into the tent. "I suppose we can take that as good news. If we do have a collaborator in the camp, particularly among the war council, we're screwed from the get go."

"What do you want me to do now?"

Azerick began rolling out the sheets of rubbings as well as the blank sheets he had prepared to receive Duncan's findings should he succeed in deciphering them before he did. "Just keep watch as you have been. I'll be in here staring endlessly at these incomprehensible runes."

Azerick cast a contemptuous glare at the stack of papers containing his numerous failed attempts at recreating The Order's rune forms. Four days of intensive study had failed to produce any measurable understanding of the runes' operation and function.

Even knowing their function, an artificer or rune scribe had to understand how they worked and channeled mana in order for them to function properly. Without understanding them, they were nothing more than decorative designs.

At least his stomach was full. The hunters had returned late last night with half a dozen elk carcasses, which the camp cooks had turned into a hearty stew. Compared to the last several days, it was practically a holiday feast.

Azerick started when Daebian bolted upright from where he slumbered on his cot. "What is it?"

Daebian's head twisted from side to side, willing his eyes and other senses to see beyond the walls of canvas. "Something is coming—fast."

Azerick was already standing, knowing better than to ignore his son's intuition and danger sense. "What is it? The Order?"

Daebian's eyes flicked nervously in their sockets. "Spawn. A lot of them."

Neither men made it out of the tent before screams tore through camp, human and otherwise. Azerick stopped and stared in horror just a few paces beyond the tent. Inhuman monstrosities leapt over the trenches and spike barricades and tore into the scrambling humans desperately trying to mount a defense on the other side.

Other spawn slammed into invisible walls raised by the mages with enough skill and composure to react quickly, some monsters falling and impaling themselves onto the sharpened stakes lining the trenches. Daebian's sword flashed by Azerick's ear, stabbing straight into the maw of a spawn leaping at his face.

"Focus!" Daebian shouted as he muscled the creature aside enough to drive it to the ground near Azerick's feet.

Azerick cursed his slow reaction and forced his brain into action. "Mages, avoid flashy spells! Focus on ice and earth. These things die to spear and sword as easily as magical spells. Work to bind them so the soldiers can hack them to pieces."

"Lancers and shield bearers, form ranks!" Chancellor McGill bellowed over the din of terror and battle, his voice adopting the tone and volume of his former commanding general persona.

Azerick waded to the fore, his spear-headed staff darting out to skewer any spawn within reach while his free hand sent shards of stone and rock-hard icicles streaking through the air like volleys of arrows. The loud shrieks of several voices caught his attention, and he spun toward the sound.

A host of creatures was bearing down on a knot of mostly women and children, and only Kord and Sibyl stood between them and the command building in which they hoped to find protection. Azerick made a clawed, upthrusting gesture with his free hand, raising a field of stone spikes in the creatures' path.

Several of the monsters managed to leap high into the air only to slam into an invisible barrier Sibyl fought to maintain. Kord descended upon them with his axe in a berserker's fury, hacking off limbs and heads before they could regain their feet.

Marley appeared from the darkness and pushed the noncombatants through the log cabin's open doorway. More people with weapons in hand created a picket to keep the path clear so others could seek shelter inside the building.

White-hot pain flared across Azerick's back. He stumbled forward beneath the heavy impact and felt warm blood streaming down his flesh. He spun in a circle, hoping to dislodge the creature that had pierced his wards, but the spawn clung to him with great tenacity. With no sign of immediate help, Azerick raised a small patch of stone spikes, put his back to them, and threw himself to the ground.

The blue-skinned creature yowled in pain as the spikes pierced its flesh and organs. Azerick wriggled from side to side and bucked up and down until the spawn ceased its squalling and writhing. He rolled off the monster now pinned to the ground, climbed unsteadily to his feet, and incinerated the corpse with fire along with a string of expletives.

Azerick's tirade did little to extinguish his fury. He unleashed barrage after barrage of stone and ice missiles into the largest knots of spawn he could find. His spear sought out individual monsters, his magically empowered thrusts exploding their organs and sending them spraying across the battlefield.

Like many battles of this nature, it was short but fierce, the fifteen or so minutes feeling like an eternity. For some, it lasted the rest of their lives. Daebian found his way to Azerick's side, who was on his feet mostly due to his staff propping him upright.

Daebian wiped the gore from his blade but seemed unperturbed by the black ichor nearly covering him from head to toe. "Looks like they followed the blood trail the hunters left when they brought in their kills."

Azerick hung his head in weary frustration. "At least Kord, Marley, and Sibyl got all the women and children into the building."

"Not all," came a low growl.

Azerick looked up into Marley's face, which was twisted in anger and disgust. He cast his gaze around the camp and found parents weeping over a child in their arms or lying on the ground and children wailing for parents that did not appear. A shudder wracked his form, and his stomach heaved, but he dared not let the carnage control him.

"How many?" Azerick managed to croak out.

"Seven children under the age of maturity, fifteen parents, and nine others," Marley spat. "That's the dead count so far. We're still getting a proper tally, and the wounded at least twice that. Both those numbers are certain to increase in the next few days."

Azerick did not need to ask what he meant. Spawn attacked with an insatiable desire to kill and rarely relented until either it or its victim were dead. Not only were the wounds they inflicted particularly gruesome, they became septic within hours. His own gashes down his back were already inflamed and throbbing.

"I'll get with the mages," Azerick said, his tone flat and weary. "We should be able to set up an alchemical station and brew something to help ward off the infections. I have a few healing draughts to give to the most severely wounded."

Marley merely grunted in reply and stormed away.

"We're setting a heavy perimeter guard," Daebian said. "I'll go and make sure there are not any spawn still lurking about."

Azerick nodded, too exhausted to waste the energy to speak, and plodded toward his tent. He had not been able to put much together in way of supplies, particularly the glassware needed for making alchemic concoctions, but he had a mortar and pestle and a few reagents. Headmaster Florent and the other mages should have a better supply since many of their castings required such things.

Leaden footsteps carried him into the tent. He found the pack containing most if his few worldly possessions and began rummaging for the pouches and bottles of ingredients within. Orange firelight and smoke filled the tent with the sound of sizzling bacon.

Azerick grabbed his staff and spun around in a crouch, prepared to deal with whatever sudden attack beset him. His eyes snapped to the table where he had several pieces of vellum rolled out onto its surface. Smoke and fire flared from the pages, leaving behind blackened rune forms.

The sorcerer summoned a light breeze to blow the smoke through the open doorway and gazed at the rune forms burned into the white material. Azerick sighed as he gazed upon the sigils, his mind translating their forms into purpose. The parts he had been unable to decipher were obvious to him now and it made him feel foolish.

"Thank you, Duncan," Azerick whispered to the empty tent. "Maybe we aren't doomed after all."

CHAPTER 16

Thanks to the alchemists' efforts, only three more people died from their wounds over the next few days, and the rest were likely to recover given time. As the only rune carver in camp, it was up to Azerick to inscribe the half-dozen carts himself.

It was a laborious undertaking. Each cart required hours of meticulous inscription. The tiniest flaw undermined the entire rune form's function, if not make it useless. The few times Azerick had made a mistake, he was able to replace a single board on the cart's frame and remake the rune, but even that small correction cost him at least an hour or more.

Azerick gave the chisel one final soft tap before he straightened up and examined his work. Deciding the rune form was functional, he touched the arcanum tip of his staff to the engraving just as he had done five times previously over the last few days. The silver metal trickled from his staff and inlaid the engravings with the precious, magical element he had taken from Raijaun's Source pool.

"That's the last one, correct?" Headmaster Florent asked over his shoulder.

Azerick turned and nodded. "That's it."

The archmage knelt and traced the arcanum-inlaid runes. "You've probably built the most expensive cart in the kingdom at the very least."

Azerick chuckled. "The inlay is extremely thin—barely thicker than gold leaf, but you're probably not far off."

"It would not have worked without it?"

"It would have, but not as efficiently. Given the load they must bear, we would have had to swap out mages several times given the energy draw required. Getting them all back in one haul will be a challenge, and that is assuming we can get in and out without expending much magic in battle. It also ties the carts to my staff, which can act as a secondary source of power should the need arise."

Headmaster Florent stood up with a grunt of effort. "When are we leaving?"

"I'll go and coordinate with Marley now. I expect early morning. Have as many of your mages practice operating them as you can. Even with all my additional efforts, they will have to rotate out at least once. How The Order is able to make their vehicles operate so efficiently or supply enough power is beyond me."

The headmaster ducked her head. "A few of my people have been practicing with the ones already completed. They are simple enough to operate, and the children certainly enjoy riding in them. I'll see that the others understand their operation as well."

The two powerful spellcasters set off in opposite directions. Azerick found Marley outside of the command building talking with Chancellor McGill.

"Ah, our fearless leader graces us with his presence," Marley declared at Azerick's approach.

Azerick clenched his fists and took a deep breath before speaking. He refused to let Marley goad him. "I've finished the last cart. Headmaster Florent says her people will be ready by morning."

Chancellor McGill nodded. "Ours as well. We were just discussing readiness and tactics. We've decided upon creating a stir in a village about an hour's journey for their skimmers to the east. This should draw at least half their garrison away from Orrinshire and give us time to overwhelm any defenders and make off with all the food stores we can carry before they're able to return."

"Do you expect any resistance from the citizens?" Azerick asked.

Marley shook his head. "My scouts say there's no love for The Order regardless of the oaths they were forced to make. While most won't help us, I don't think any will cause a hindrance. Either we take the grain or The Order does. They're going to lose it one way or the other, so there is no gain for them interfering."

"What about the man I spoke to you about, the one Daebian and I met when we infiltrated the town?" Azerick asked.

"Yes, we've made contact. He has a few rabble-rousers who have been subtly taking measure of the townsfolk and sowing the seeds of nonresistance should anyone attack the hamlet."

"You're taking a risk dropping those kinds of hints," Azerick said. "If even one person they talk to reports it to The Order, they could be waiting for us."

Marley shook his head. "Doubtful. They're careful who they talk to and what they say. Like I said, it's all been very subtle, and Willard knows who he can talk to and how much he can say to the townsfolk. I wouldn't worry."

Azerick nodded. "OK. When do you want to set out?"

Chancellor McGill scratched at the stubble just a handful of days from becoming a beard. "We discussed a night operation. That would give us the most cover and element of surprise, but navigating the forest, even with floating carts, is a challenge. We've agreed a dawn attack is best. It makes timing our distraction much easier while still catching most of them before they've readied themselves for the day."

"One thing we liked to do when…collecting our toll…was to blanket a patch of roadway in fog," Marley said. "With the number of wizards we have at our disposal, we could cover the entire area in and around the hamlet in mist. We'd be at the gates before they ever knew we were there."

Azerick considered the idea. "Fog is a minor casting. Unless an arcanus is near the casters, it is unlikely they would detect its magical creation. Same with a breeze to spread it out. I'll talk to Headmaster Florent, but I think it's a good idea."

The old general nodded. "I will have my troops ready to march at first light. We and our distraction forces should be in position by daybreak the next morning."

A low fog blanketed the expansive fields while Orrinshire's walls seemingly held the miasma at bay like a dike against a rising sea. A glider swooped down from the sky and dropped behind the walls. Several minutes later, the gates swung open, and three skimmers loaded with legionnaires raced away, parting the mists like ships' prows through water.

"There they go," Chancellor McGill said as he peered through a spyglass, barely able to make out their shadowed forms from his position above the gathering fog.

Azerick inclined his head. "Headmaster."

Headmaster Florent waved her hand, giving the mages the signal to increase the fog. The cloying mists thickened, and a light breeze carried it across the fields and into the sleepy hamlet just beginning to rouse from its evening slumbers.

Half an hour passed before Azerick gave the command to proceed. "OK, people, let's go. Keep as silent as you can."

Wizards pushed the half-dozen carts, now loaded down with people, out of the woods and across the field of hewn wheat. Azerick winced with every crunching footstep, clunk, and clank of a scabbard against a thigh or rattle of armor that had not been properly muffled with cloth and leather.

Azerick ordered the group to halt with a whispered command less than fifty yards from the hamlet's defensive fortifications. Even this close, the walls were barely visible as a slightly darker shape against the white backdrop.

Nearly a hundred souls held their collective breaths in anticipation of the slaughter to come. With any luck, the battle would be a short one. Shouts erupted from within the walled town. Azerick and Headmaster Florent tore open dimensional gates, and their small army flooded unimpeded into Orrinshire.

Bodies already littered the ground thanks to Daebian's earlier infiltration. The rebels stormed through the dimensional gate and leapt from the carts. They stumbled a moment from the slight disorientation traveling through the portals caused before forming ranks and marching toward the grain silos and warehouses.

By Azerick's estimation, there was less than a score of Order defenders left in the hamlet. Daebian had cut down several already, and the rest had hastily organized into a few uncoordinated groups. Their shields flared brightly, and overcoming their powerful defenses was no easy task even so taken by surprise, but their attackers were many and supported by powerful magic.

Azerick's people overwhelmed them with the knowledge of how to break through their defenses and by shear numerical superiority. The pair of arcanus left in the garrison tried their best to support the legionnaires with bolstered wards and offensive magics, but the battle's conclusion was inevitable.

When the fighting subsided, Azerick spied faces looking on through doorways or from groups of people huddled together but standing back so as not to impede them or become collateral damage.

"Go! Get the carts in here and stack the sacks and barrels as high as you can!" Azerick ordered from the warehouse's large, open doorway.

Mages guided their floating carts inside, and scores of hands passed sacks of grain and dried corn like a bucket brigade. Azerick could feel the increased demand on the carts' runes and the magic they drew from their drivers with every burlap sack stacked upon them.

"That's it, people!" Azerick shouted. "Strap it down and let's get moving."

Azerick opened a portal in the mouth of the warehouse. Mages and warriors alike helped push the carts laden with nearly a ton and half of food each through the gate. They emerged halfway across the field and disappeared into the forest within minutes with no one in Orrinshire knowing from what direction they had come or departed.

It was not long before exhausted mages had to pass their burdens onto their fellow wizards as the army pushed hard toward the hidden archway.

"What are our casualties?" Azerick asked, his breath slightly labored.

"Two dead, seven injured," Chancellor McGill said, his greater fatigue showing with every word and step. "Four are ambulatory. The other three are riding atop the carts."

"I'm sure we can manage a cart for you as well, General," Azerick said, noting the older man's heavy footsteps and labored breath.

The chancellor's mustache bristled in contempt. "I've been marching from the day I was able to wield a toy sword. Don't you worry about me, boy. My muscles know better than to disobey my orders and break ranks."

Azerick grinned. "Yes, sir."

Chancellor McGill's mustache drooped in response. "That being said, I would not countermand any recommendation to take a ten-minute respite."

Azerick chuckled as he watched the mages powering the carts hand off their burdens to another group. He could feel the carts' runes drawing power from his staff as well. It was a small trickle now, but they had a long way to go before they reached the gate and nearly the same distance to cover once they passed through it.

Darkness descended on the forest. The shift from day to night happened swiftly and with little warning, but they were almost to the gate. The forced march was brutal and exhausting, but they needed to put as much distance between themselves and Orrinshire as they could.

To make matters worse, an evening fog had come down from the higher mountains and blanketed the forest floor in thick mist. Their footing was even more treacherous as darkness and miasma swallowed the narrow path they followed.

"We should be nearing the gate," Sibyl whispered.

Azerick nodded. "That is my estimation as well. Can you sense its location?"

Sibyl closed her eyes and craned her head around as if trying to pick up a scent. "Not yet. Tell everyone to hold up while I go out and search. I need to be close to detect the gate's ambient energy, and the carts are throwing me off."

Azerick passed the order to stop the caravan and waited while Sibyl went in search of the gate. The minutes ticked by in eerie silence with only a few hushed voices disturbing the relative tranquility. Daebian sat on a log next to Azerick, absently flipping twigs with the tip of his sword before his head snapped up and his eyes went wide.

"Someone is trying to sneak up on us!" he hissed.

Azerick leapt to his feet. "What direction?"

Daebian stood and spun a slow circle. "All of them. They're boxing us in."

Azerick swallowed the growing lump in his throat. "Spawn?"

"No. Men."

A voice cut through the dissipating fog less than a hundred yards away. "A grand idea to conjure mists to conceal your approach. So good I thought to employ it myself."

"Who are you?" Azerick demanded.

"I am Primus Andronikos Antigonus, commander of The Order's ninth expeditionary cohort. We have you surrounded and outnumbered. I have no desire to crush you, but do not doubt that I have the capacity to do so if you leave me no other option."

"What do you want?"

"Your surrender, of course. Give me the sorcerer Azerick Giles and his warlock son, surrender your weapons, take the oath of compliance, and the rest of you are free to go. We will of course shackle any of you capable of wielding magic, but I will release them once I have secured their power and their oath. This is the most generous terms I will offer. Refuse any of them, and I will order my legionnaires to cut you down to a man."

Headmaster Florent and Chancellor McGill appeared by Azerick's side.

"How in the blazes did they manage to sneak up on us with an entire battalion?" the old general asked.

"With magic," the headmaster replied. "I detect a feint trace of magic in both the fog and the spell they used to silence their approach."

"If they approached at all," Azerick said. "They were here already, directly in our path."

"We've been betrayed!" the chancellor snarled.

"What do we do?" Headmaster Florent asked.

Chancellor McGill turned his furious gaze to the archmage. "Do you fancy being shackled and magically neutered?"

Headmaster Florent scowled. "I do not."

"Then we tell him to stick his terms up his perpetually clenched arse!"

"Great plan, but we're going to need a strategy," Daebian said.

"General?" Azerick inquired.

The chancellor's handlebar mustache quivered. "We push toward our best guess as to the gate's location. I recommend the Headmaster's wizards form a bulwark at our rear to create a delaying action. With The Order soldiers' ability to counter magic, I think that to be our best use of their waning strength. The rest of us will do our best to punch through their defenses and open the gate."

"I agree," Headmaster Florent said. "Powering those carts has sapped most of our energy. What we have left is best put to use in a defensive manner. Are we under any restrictions?"

Azerick shook his head. "None. They know we're here. There's no reason for subtlety now. Daebian, you feel like giving yourself over?"

Daebian caught Azerick's wink and waved his arm with flourish, "After you, Father."

Azerick turned and stalked toward the direction from which the voice had emanated. The fog was dispersing, and even Azerick could now make out the vague outline of legionnaire ranks and their commander ahead of him.

"Surrender your weapon," Primus Antigonus said.

Azerick glanced at his staff, shrugged, and flung it at the man like a spear. Shields and armor rattled and clanked as the soldiers braced themselves. Even Primus Antigonus raised his arm and ducked behind the shimmering disc surrounding the buckler strapped to his left arm.

When the anticipated destruction failed to materialize, the legionnaires relaxed their stance, and the primus lowered his guard as he took cautious steps toward the artifact sticking out of the ground a few yards away. He reached his hand out to take hold of the staff. He met Azerick's gaze, and even at this distance, recognized the feral gleam in the sorcerer's eyes.

Primus Antigonus brought his shield around and snapped his head toward his men to bark an order, but it was too late. Azerick extended his fist and splayed his fingers. Raw power exploded from his staff and sent the primus flying and knocking down the first two ranks of legionnaires.

Ragged battle cries cut through the fog as Azerick's people fell upon the momentarily stunned enemy ranks. The air surged with magic as the mages raised walls of earth, ice, and fire in an attempt to hold back the units flanking them.

"I have to find the gate," Azerick shouted over the din. "I'll send up a signal when I locate it."

Daebian nodded and leapt into battle. Azerick focused on sensing the gate's magical emanation, but the spells the wizards were hurling with wild abandon made detecting the subtle energy even more difficult. While the fog had thinned, the sun had fully set, and visibility was still only a handful of yards.

Azerick opened a portal in hopes of getting past the platoon of legionnaires in his path only to land amid another group preparing to reinforce the one he had sent reeling.

"Hello, boys," Azerick said with a grin at the startled faces staring back at him.

The sorcerer slammed the butt of his staff against the ground and sent a pulse of arcane power blasting out in a ring around him. Order soldiers reeled and fell. Some of them had the reflexes and presence of mind to set their shields and absorbed enough of the blast to stay on their feet, but their reprieve was short-lived.

Azerick waded into the nearest group, his staff looking more like a halberd, and cleaved into shields and armor. He carved a path of destruction and sowed fear through the enemy ranks until breaking free and opening another gate.

In a rare show of offensive magic, a fireball exploded behind Azerick and propelled him through the rift he had opened. He landed a hundred yards away, his back burning and smoking like a meteor. He continued his tumble, smothering the flames and closing his gate before coming to a stop.

Ignoring the searing pain across the backside of his entire body, Azerick set his senses to locating the archway. His minimal familiarity with area coupled with the looming darkness and lingering fog made finding it a challenge. Unless he could spot a landmark he recognized and was able to get his bearings, locating a camouflaged stone arch only slightly larger than a household doorway was going to be difficult.

Azerick chased a barely visible trail until spotting a fallen tree and boulder he recognized from his previous trips through the gate. He knew the archway lie a bit west of north, but which way was north? Azerick balanced his staff on the back of his hand and sent a small tendril of magic into it. The staff began a slow rotation a few degrees counterclockwise before stopping.

He darted off a little to the left of the direction his staff pointed. Azerick tried to block out the sound of battle and the knowledge that people, his people, were dying, and every minute it took him to find the gate, more of them perished. He was close. He knew it, could feel it! There!

Subtle vibrations of magic raised goosebumps on Azerick's flesh. He raced in the direction from which the magic emanated like a draft or faint smell that got stronger as he neared the source. There, between two trees and almost entirely obscured by branches and clinging plants stood the gate.

Azerick cupped his hands around his mouth and shouted. "Daebian! This way!"

Realizing even Daebian's acute senses might not be able to pick his voice out of the chaotic din, Azerick sprinted back the way he had come, taking note of the path so as not to lose it again. Approaching from a flanking position, he found Daebian in a desperate battle with Primus Antigonus, who looked only a little worse for wear after Azerick's sneak attack.

Azerick pointed his staff at Antigonus' back and channeled his arcane power. At least he tried to, only to find that the Source was beyond his reach. The Order had laid down an anti-magic field, rendering him and any mage caught within its boundary useless.

While the magical dead zone rendered his magic inert, he would show these invaders he was still a dangerous opponent. Azerick threw himself at the squad of legionnaires standing between him and the primus, his staff's arcanum tip thrusting at the gaps between their shields.

More legionnaires closed in and forced him back. Pressed on all sides, Order soldiers corralled Azerick's people in an encircling shield wall. The air grew quiet as most of the fighting died down, The Order content to hold their ground while the insurgents gripped their weapons and cast uncertain looks at one another, knowing they had lost the battle.

Primus Antigonus pushed through his ranks of soldiers and stood before Azerick, his armor dented and breached in several places. "You are defeated, sorcerer. Yield and save your people more needless death."

Azerick gritted his teeth. "Where is my son?"

"He had the wisdom to quit the battlefield. I suggest you do the same. Her Imperial Highness wishes me to capture you alive if possible but has given me leave to end you should you give me no other option."

Azerick looked around and spotted Headmaster Florent surrounded by a group of mages. There was no sign of Chancellor McGill.

A solitary howl echoed through the forest to the north. A chorus of howls answered to the south. Everyone shifted uneasily. The wolf pack was close by, and it was huge given the number of lupine voices adding to the chorus. All eyes turned south save Azerick's, who focused on the lone howl to the north. There was something very familiar about it.

The air came alive with the sound of arrows slamming into unprotected backs and sides. The legionnaires, every one of them professional soldiers, pivoted in place and faced outward. Another volley of arrows whistled through the air, but most shafts shattered and reflected off the raised shields.

A third volley clattered against Order shields and breastplates, masking the soft pattering of scores of paws before it was too late to react. Dozens of furred shapes leapt atop the surprised legionnaires, rode them to the ground, and sank fangs into exposed throats, arms, and thighs.

To make matters worse, arrows began streaking down from above. Whenever a legionnaire raised his shield to protect himself from the treetop sniper, half a dozen or more arrows struck him from the sides and back, nearly every shaft finding a vulnerable spot unprotected by armor.

Azerick felt his connection to the Source return. Their saviors must have destroyed the nullification generators. He opened a rift with his dwindling power and amplified his voice.

"Get through the portal and find the gate!" Azerick ordered.

He raised his staff overhead barely in time to intercept Primus Antigonus' furious overhand chop. Azerick backpedaled, driven back by the force of the blow. The primus hacked at him with wild abandon, forgoing any finesse, determined to slay him through shear brutality.

Daebian appeared at the legion commander's back and drove his blade through flesh until the tip of his sword exited through the man's breastplate.

"I told you I'd be back," Daebian hissed in the dying man's ear before retracting his sword and kicking the primus to the ground.

Azerick shook himself from his momentary daze. "Was that Wolf I heard?"

Daebian flashed him a feral grin. "Him and a couple hundred others."

Lightning and shards of ice blasted into a group of Legionnaires as a powerful wind blinded them with airborne detritus.

"That would be Ellyssa." Daebian said. A fireball like a miniature sun lit up the forest. "And Rusty."

Azerick stared open-mouthed for just a moment before resuming command. "Get to the carts! Get them through the portal! Daebian, stay with the carts and make sure everyone gets through. I'm going ahead to mark the archway."

Daebian nodded and dashed off to round up the ambush survivors and direct them to the way out. Azerick stepped through the gate he opened, found the archway once more, and activated it. Weary fighters staggered through his gate first, many helping wounded who were unable to walk on their own. He breathed a sigh of relief when the first cart laden with foodstuffs appeared.

Traveling through two portals in succession was going to be brutal, particularly for the uninitiated, but it was vastly superior to fighting and dying in these cursed woods. Azerick subconsciously counted the number of people passing through the portal and felt buoyed by the numbers until realizing that many of them were not part of their original force.

Azerick started when Wolf and Ghost, his lupin friend in the form a huge, black wolf, appeared soundlessly by his side. "Looks like you saved me once again. Thank you."

The handsome half-elf beamed his signature toothy smile. "Remind me how many times I've had to this? I keep losing count."

Azerick clapped him on the shoulder. "Far too many. How's the fight going?"

Wolf glanced over his shoulder. "They've gone turtle behind those spears they stick in the ground to block magic. My people are bouncing arrows off them to hold them in place until everyone escapes."

"What are you doing here? How did you know where to find us?"

"Rusty and Ellyssa. Rusty showed up and told us what was happening. As you predicted, The Order moved into North Haven and demanded obedience. Duchess Melina, Miranda, and most everyone did as you said and took the oath. Most of those at the school who are fighters and mages headed into the woods."

Wolf sighed and hung his head. "My people joined them, figuring whatever The Order had in store for them wasn't going to be any more friendly than how they treat the humans."

Azerick wagged his head. "I think you're right. I haven't seen a non-human among them. Unless they come from lands exclusive to humans, I don't want to think about what happened to the other races."

Wolf crinkled his nose. "Whole kingdoms with nothing but humans? Sounds awful. As far as how we found you, we've been moving toward you for days. Ellyssa was able to scry your location this morning and thought you had moved your camp again, so we headed this way. Our timing was mostly dumb luck."

Azerick watched another group he did not recognize pass through the archway. "How many dead have you seen?"

Wolf's smile fell. "Quite a few. There's more enemy down than yours now, but they had a lot more to begin with. Still do. It's a good thing you guys killed their leader. If they realize how precarious our position is and went on the offensive, my people wouldn't be able to hold them back."

Azerick sighed and nodded. "There is almost no way they could have known where we would be without someone having told them."

"I think you're right. Even Ellyssa was only able to find you through her connection with Daebian."

"This does not bode well for our future and chance of success. Will you be joining us?"

Wolf shook his head. "We'll melt back into the woods once you're safe. Don't worry. We won't be far away when you need us again."

Azerick gave him a wan smile. "I understand. I would not be here either if I had any other option."

"What are you going to do about the spy?"

Azerick sighed and hung his head. "I don't know. I have to determine if there even is a collaborator in my camp first. Then...I just don't know."

Ghost curled his lips to show his gleaming white fangs, telling them exactly what he would do. Headmaster Florent, Daebian, Ellyssa, and Rusty stepped through the portal Azerick had conjured, followed by a gaggle of humans and one of the last carts.

"Is this the last of us?" Azerick asked as he hugged Ellyssa and clasped hands with Rusty.

Headmaster Florent nodded. "We've carried away all the wounded we could find. We…don't have the time or resources to bring the fallen with us."

Azerick nodded his understanding. "Chancellor McGill?"

Headmaster Florent shook her head. "Fought to the last. We lost one of the carts as well, but we managed to carry almost half of its load away with us."

Azerick cursed under his breath, but he knew it could have been much worse. Ghost cocked his head and flicked his ears.

"Ghost says we have to go," Wolf translated.

Azerick nodded. "Thank you. All of you."

Wolf clasped wrists with Azerick before he and Ghost bounded off into the dark forest with barely a whisper of sound.

"We should disable the gate behind us," Headmaster Florent advised.

"I'll see to it," Azerick said and planted his staff next to the archway before stepping through.

Once on the other side, he took up a position behind a stout tree and motioned the others to catch up with the main body. Azerick waited patiently, slowly recovering a small fraction of the energy, both body and magic, he had expended during this nearly disastrous campaign.

Only a handful of minutes later, he spotted the first Order soldiers approaching the gate. They called out their find, and soon more than a full company converged on the area, their shields held out before them, their weapons poised to strike.

Azerick waited until the nearest legionnaire was almost close enough to touch the stone arch before releasing his staff's pent up, awful power. The explosive blast was short, dying on his side of the portal with the gate's destruction in an instant. Those on the other side were not so fortunate.

His staff, totally depleted of power now, slapped into his waiting palm. With a heavy sigh, the burden of more than a score of deaths weighing on his shoulders, Azerick fought to catch up to the others. It was nearly a full day of marching to reach the camp, everyone was exhausted, and now they had close to another hundred mouths to feed.

Azerick did not know what was worse, that someone they trusted had betrayed them, the deaths that lay at his feet and the knowledge that there would be more blood staining his hands long before this ended, or the self-perpetuating cycle of death and violence that was the beast of war. Was victory even possible, and what would be the final cost? Who would pay it, and would the prize come anywhere near being worth it?

CHAPTER 17

Azerick pushed his body to its physical limits trying to catch up with the rest of his people. Long past the point of exhaustion, anger and a familiar desire to strike out at those who wronged him fueled his charge. He found Sybil somewhere in the middle of the caravan plodding toward their camp despite everyone's fatigue.

Finally reaching her, Azerick grabbed her by the shoulder and spun her roughly around. Sybil's eyes flared in anger, and she lashed out with a lightning-shrouded fist. The blow struck Azerick in his chest, and he reeled back a couple of steps, but being equally exhausted, both her physical and arcane strike lacked any appreciable strength.

She reached deep for more power to follow up her attack, but Daebian's sword settled on her shoulder, its razor-sharp blade kissing her neck.

"No need for anyone to lose their head. Not yet anyway," Daebian practically purred.

"What in the abyss do you want?" Sybil snapped.

Azerick kept his hands clenched into fists by his side, fighting to keep from lashing out. "Where were you?"

Her questioning reply died on her lips as she comprehended what he was asking. "They caught me. I couldn't see a damned thing through that fog. I was so focused on finding the gate I didn't realize I was surrounded and in a null magic zone until it was too late. I tried to call out a warning but...gods-be-damned arcanus," she spat.

"Sounds a bit convenient, doesn't it, Father?" Daebian said.

Azerick nodded. "Much like her story about rescuing Joah and escaping from all those soldiers."

Sybil's face twisted in anger before melting in resignation. "I knew how this looked. It's why I didn't seek you out during or after the battle, but damn it, it happened!"

"Which one?" Daebian asked.

"Both!" Sybil snapped.

"You see how we have a problem believing you?"

The mage spun on Daebian but levied her glare on both men. "I don't give a damn what you think about me as long as you don't try to stop me from fighting these bastards! I didn't risk my life throwing my lot in with Marley so the Academy couldn't tell me what to do and how I have to practice my craft just to surrender to a bunch of sonsabitches who would strip it from me entirely."

Daebian arched his eyebrows at Azerick. "Gosh, she almost sounds convincing, doesn't she?"

"She does," Azerick replied with a nod.

"Look," Sybil said, letting out a long breath, "I knew how getting caught and escaping once again looked and the suspicion it would cast on me, so why would I return to the group if I had set them up?"

Azerick shrugged. "Maybe you thought your acting skills were good enough to convince us you were telling the truth and could betray us again to make up for your failure."

Sybil sighed, shook her head, and stared at the ground. "I understand why you think I had something to do with this. If I were you, I would too. All I can tell you is that it's not me, but damn it, I think someone might be. If you have to put me under guard or restrain me, do it if it will help find the real traitor, but promise to let me fight The Order if they attack us again. I will not allow them to shackle me. I'd rather die."

Azerick looked to Daebian. "She sounds sincere. What do you think?"

Daebian shrugged. "We both know what I would do and that you would oppose such a drastic response. It just depends on how many people you're willing to let die before taking unpleasant but necessary action."

Azerick stared daggers at Sybil before shaking his head in disgust. "Just go. I'm not in the proper state of mind to make rational decisions. Just know that we will be watching you closely."

Sybil looked as though she were about issue a retort but wisely chose to remain silent and stalked away.

"That looked a little intense," Ellyssa said as she and Rusty approached.

Azerick stepped toward her and embraced his former apprentice before passing her off to Daebian. He noted the mutual adoration in their eyes when they looked at each other and held hands. It was possibly the first time he had seen his son openly display his love for anything other than himself and his desires.

Azerick nodded. "We're concerned that someone in our camp might be collaborating with the enemy."

"And you think it's her?" Ellyssa asked.

"We don't know who it is, if that's actually what is happening," Azerick explained. "It sure as hell was not coincidence that allowed them to ambush us. It is possible one of their arcanus, or more likely the princess herself, was able to scry our location. She is exceptionally powerful."

"Sybil also went missing only to reappear after the last time The Order launched a coordinated attack," Daebian said.

"Azerick, if there is a traitor in your camp, then we're all in danger," Rusty said. "We fled North Haven to avoid The Order and marched for days so we could continue to fight them with some chance of victory, even if it were only a small chance. If your camp is compromised, we just led them to their doom."

Azerick cursed and slammed the butt of his staff against the ground. "I know, Rusty!"

Ellyssa laid a calming hand on Azerick's arm. "What do we do? How do we find out if someone is betraying us and who it is?"

Azerick shook his head. "I don't know yet, but I will damn sure find out. For now, we keep our eyes open and restrict information sharing to a minimum."

"It would most likely be someone with access to our plans at some level," Daebian agreed.

"That's right," Rusty concurred. "How many people outside of your command element or officers had specific information about what you were going to do and when and where you were going to do it?"

"Exactly right," Azerick said. "They were waiting for us just a few hundred yards from the gate."

Daebian nodded. "Waiting until the last minute to spring the trap knowing we would be exhausted by that point."

"That narrows down our list of suspects significantly," Azerick said. "Many people knew what we were going to do since we had to train them on operating the carts, but only a few knew exactly when we were going to launch our attack and even fewer who knew the location of the gate."

"Unless someone was able to scry you and overhear your plans," Ellyssa said.

"There is that," Azerick agreed. "Headmaster Florent herself established our defenses against scrying, but that does not mean they are unbeatable."

"Is she beyond reproach?" Rusty asked.

Ellyssa wagged her head. "Given how The Order treats its spellcasters, the odds of it being a mage seems rather slim to me."

"And even slimmer almost to the point of impossibility of it being the headmaster," Azerick said with a nod. "They attacked her school, shackled them, and took many of her fellow mages and students away. That is not something she would soon forgive."

Ellyssa, the one caster amongst them who knew how it felt to be captured and forced to use their power at another's whim said, "What if The Order agreed to release all the students they had taken?"

"And put all the ones we had rescued in danger?" Azerick asked. "Not likely. Besides, most of the mages The Order was able to ship off surrendered of their own volition out of fear for either themselves or their families. No, I trust the headmaster almost as much as any of you."

"We should still keep as much information among ourselves as we can," Daebian said. "Personally, I don't trust anyone one-hundred percent except Ellyssa and Father's inability to not play the hero."

Azerick chuckled. "It's agreed then. We discuss nothing with anyone outside of this circle."

The expedition party and newcomers rested only a handful of hours before pushing on toward the camp. Headmaster Florent and Ellyssa layered multiple wards against scrying. If anyone in The Order could break past the defenses they laid down, there was little if anything anyone could do about it. If that were the case, they probably knew where their base was already.

They reached camp in the early afternoon. The people welcomed the expedition's return and the food stores they brought with them, but the mood turned somber when friends and family noticed the missing faces as well as the many new ones that seemed to have replaced them.

Azerick stalked straight for his tent, but Kord jogged ahead and cut him off. "Marley wants to talk to you about all these new folks you brought back."

Azerick glared daggers at the man. "I'll speak with him later. I have something important to do first."

Kord crossed his thick arms. "Marley said not to take no for an answer."

Azerick smiled and turned to Daebian. "I'm going to be in my tent. If *anyone* comes asking for me, tell them I'm indisposed. If they won't take no for an answer, deal with them however you see fit."

Daebian's return smile was feral as he rested a hand on his sword hilt. "It would be my pleasure."

Kord's face burned scarlet, but he spun around and stormed off, likely to inform Marley of Azerick's reply. Azerick threw back the tent flap, grabbed a mirror, and sat cross-legged on the floor.

"Azerick, thank the gods you returned," Devlin said, his anxious features reflected in the mirror. "I've been trying to reach you for the past day. Do you know of the ambush?"

Azerick sighed and nodded. "All too well I'm afraid. How did you hear of it?"

Devlin flashed him a quizzical look. "One of my men informed me hours after the battle of course."

A chill ran up Azerick's spine. "Wait, I think we're talking about two different things here."

Devlin clamped his eyes closed. "You were attacked as well. I feared as much. That removes any doubt in my mind that you have an informant amongst you."

"The reinforcements you sent were ambushed also?"

The elder sorcerer nodded. "Within the pass leading into Valeria. It was a massacre and perfectly timed. Our losses were heavy but thankfully not total. I do not think they expected the amount of power a unit that size could bring to bear. Still, I lost nearly half my fighting force. I'm afraid this poses a significant problem in terms of coming to your aid."

Azerick trembled with rage and was barely able to contain his fury enough to keep from unleashing his anger on the tent. "I'm sorry I brought this upon you and your people."

Devlin gave him a stern shake of his head. "I am king. They were doing my bidding, and I do not place any blame upon you. It is war."

"Not your war though," Azerick sighed.

"Do you think the invaders will be content to leave my kingdom be?"

"Not a chance."

"Then it is my war as well," Devlin said with finality. "I will still come to your aid when asked, but not until you are certain no one will betray you. I am not a king to squander the lives of his people."

"Nor should you. I will contact you again when I have dealt with our traitor. Again, I'm sorry for this."

Devlin held up a hand. "Focus on your people. I will manage mine."

Azerick dismissed the magic and sat for several long minutes before jumping to his feet. He stormed out of the tent and went in search of Sybil. He found her talking to Marley and Joah outside of the command building.

Marley stiffened at Azerick's approach. "I do not appreciate being dismissed like a common servant."

"And I do not appreciate being summoned like one. I guess we'll both just have to get over it," Azerick snapped and proceeded to ignore the man. "Sybil, I need you to show me the location of every gate still in operation. Can you do that?"

"I—I can, yes, but…" she stammered.

"Then do it," Azerick demanded and pushed open the cabin door.

Marley followed on Azerick's heels. "See here! Who are all these people you brought back?"

"They're the only reason any of us returned at all, and that's all you need concern yourself with," Azerick replied. "Sybil, mark the gates on the map."

Sybil looked to Marley before stepping up to the large map rolled out across the table. She began placing markers at more than a dozen locations across Valeria and even one in Sumara.

Azerick's anger spiked once more. "You have a gate in Sumara and didn't tell me?"

Marley crossed his arms in defiance. "It is a state secret."

"You are not a state. We aren't even a kingdom anymore! People died coming to our defense because of your secret."

"And how many would die if The Order found our gates?" Marley countered. "They work both ways you know. Are you so certain they are incapable of figuring out how to remove the protections we've put on them and how to operate them? I sure as hell am not."

Azerick took a deep breath and let it out. "You're right. We cannot even trust everyone in our camp much less whoever might learn of the gate in Sumara."

"What is that supposed to mean?" Joah asked.

"It means someone betrayed us," Azerick replied. "The Order ambushed us and the Sumaran expeditionary force. They knew exactly when and where to strike. There's only one likely explanation."

Marley shook his head. "That does not mean it came from someone in our camp."

"Doesn't it? Who else knew of our plans?"

"Whom did you tell?" Marley said. "We know the Sumarans knew when and where they would cross into Valeria. Did you mention, even offhand, of our need to raid Orrinshire for food or risk starving this winter?"

Azerick thought about it and nodded. "I mentioned it to King Devlin when we discussed coordinating the joining of their forces with ours."

"Ah," Marley said with a knowing nod. "Are you certain he did not mention it to whomever he spoke to when coordinating with Duchess Paulina, Duke William, or King Miles? Sounds to me like the source of the leak may well have been you, unintentional to be sure, but leaked just the same."

Azerick shook his head. "The timing and location of the ambush near the gate though..."

"All they needed to know was the most basic of information regarding where we might be. They could have been scrying the area for days, or maybe one of their scouts on their flying machines spotted you from the sky. I would not jump to conclusions and start launching inquisitions just yet."

Azerick sighed. "You're right. From here on, nothing spoken in this hall leaves this room. Not to trusted companions, friends, or allies. I have a plan to salvage something from this mess. I just need a few hours to contact the other leaders."

Marley quirked a wry grin. "That certainly worked out well last time."

Azerick scowled but could not blame the man's lack of confidence. "We will control the information this time, and I will assume all the risk myself. I will not lead another group into an ambush."

"Let us hope not," Marley replied.

"You also got a plan to feed all these people you returned with?" Joah asked. "The food you brought back was barely enough to sustain the numbers we had before their arrival. Now, we'll be lucky to make it through till spring even on starvation rations."

Azerick met Joah's challenging gaze. "It won't be a problem."

Azerick left the meeting and sought out Ellyssa. He found her with the newcomers who were erecting tents and crude shelters in a small clearing a short distance from the main camp. With a gesture, Azerick led her far out of earshot of anyone who might be listening. He stuck his staff in the ground and enveloped them in a sphere of impenetrable silence.

"I need your help with a spell," he said without preamble.

Ellyssa leaned back on her heels. "You need *my* help?"

"It's a spell I don't know and don't have time to make from scratch. Wizards are better at that sort of thing. Can you do it, and can you have it prepared within the next couple of days?"

Ellyssa shrugged. "Depends on the spell."

Azerick explained what he needed her to do.

Ellyssa considered his request and nodded. "It's a simple visual and auditory illusion. The way you want me to employ it is going to be a bit complicated, but I'm sure I can come up with something."

Azerick laid a hand on her slender shoulder. "Our entire future might well depend on it. It has to be discreet. Not even Headmaster Florent can know it is in effect."

"That will require significant subtlety. You know subtlety is not my strong suit. I'm more of a reduce everything to rubble sort of mage."

"Can you do it?"

Ellyssa gave him a firm nod. "I'll make it happen. How soon do you need it?"

"As soon as possible. Preferably within the next day or so. Sooner is better."

"Can I ask Rusty for help?"

Azerick nodded. "But only him, and make sure you two protect yourselves from scrying or eavesdropping by every means."

"Consider it done."

Azerick returned to his tent and waved Daebian over. "I'm going to be gone for a bit. Keep your eyes and ears open. If the traitor is in our camp, they might make contact with The Order to report on our new arrivals."

"Sure. What are you going to be doing?"

"I'm going to try to salvage our plan. If Devlin can't reinforce our consolidated forces, then we will. We're too exposed out here and lack the logistics and support required for a protracted insurgency. The Order is just too damn mobile, and our minimal resources are stretched too thin."

Daebian stared at Azerick. "You're not telling me something."

"I'm not telling something to anyone."

"I thought you trusted me?"

Azerick laid a hand on Daebian's shoulder. "I do. I just want it to be a surprise."

Daebian smiled back at him. "I normally despise surprises, but since yours often result in death and mayhem, I'm looking forward to it."

"I'll try not to disappoint."

"That in itself would be a surprise."

Azerick grinned and shook his head as he strode toward the gate.

CHAPTER 18

A zerick returned late the next day. It was early evening, and he found Ellyssa in the chow line, so he sidled up next to her with a curt apology for cutting in.

"You're back. Are you finished with what you needed to do already?" Ellyssa asked as she ladled stew into her bowl.

Azerick took the offered ladle from her and did likewise. "I am. Let's talk away from the crowd."

Ellyssa followed Azerick to a secluded part of the camp. She cast a warding of silence without prompting and sat on a crate across from him.

"I know it's earlier than expected, but were you able to create the spell?" Azerick asked around a mouthful of stew.

Ellyssa nodded. "With Rusty's help it was rather simple. It would have taken me another day to figure out on my own. The subtlety was a challenge for me. I'm surprised Rusty was able to provide as much insight given that his preferred spells typically revolve around explosive balls of fire."

"I imagine his years working in Southport's government forced him to change his focus. Officials and nobles speak in whispers more often than not."

"That's almost exactly what he said. When will you call a meeting?" Ellyssa asked.

"As soon as I inhale a second bowl of stew," Azerick replied. "I haven't eaten since I left and I'm famished."

Ellyssa grinned at him. "Two bowls violates the ration policy."

"Piss on the policy. Benefits of being in charge and making sure no one else dies because of a traitorous weasel," Azerick snapped.

"You're sounding more and more like a leader every day," Ellyssa chuckled.

"Not for much longer. If all goes well, I will have schemed myself out of a job."

Ellyssa cocked her head. "What do you mean?"

Azerick shook his head. "Nothing. I'm hungry and surly, that's all. Still, if my plan works, there are others better suited to leading this army than I and in a better position to do it. Then I'll be free to do what I do best."

"Being a huge pain in someone's ass?"

Azerick pointed at her with his spoon. "Exactly."

It took fifteen minutes to gather everyone Azerick wanted in the meeting after he had called it. He, Daebian, Ellyssa, Kord, Joah, Sybil, Marley, and Headmaster Florent stood around the table in the center of the room. Chancellor McGill's absence was a heavy gloom weighing on the shoulders of those in attendance. At least for some of them.

"I assume you're finally going to let us in on your secret escapades of late?" Marley asked.

"I am," Azerick replied. "Ellyssa, could you please ward the room?"

Ellyssa nodded and cast her privacy ward.

"Yesterday, I scouted the area around several of the gates in order to determine the best location to set up a face-to-face meeting with Brelland, Brightridge, and Argoth's resistance leaders." Azerick placed a marker near one of the gates Sibyl had marked on the map. "I've chosen this location since the terrain is favorable and it is far from any road, aerial route, or garrison."

"What's the purpose of such a meeting?" Joah asked.

"After our latest debacle, it is clear to me that we lack the resources and manpower to maintain an effective insurgency. The Order is simply too strong, numerous, and mobile for us to fight on our own."

"What of the reinforcements from North Haven?" Headmaster Florent asked. "They have doubled our fighters and include several talented mages from your school."

Azerick nodded. "Their numbers have indeed bolstered our strength, but as Joah pointed out, it comes at a cost. We simply don't have the resources to house and feed them. Our last excursion to gather food nearly got us all killed or captured. All it takes is for The Order to get lucky one time to all but end us."

"You want to combine forces with one of the other resistance groups," Marley said.

Azerick shook his head. "Not one. All of them. My original plan was for reinforcements from Sumara to augment Duchess Paulina's forces and ultimately combine all three armies to capture territory on the border and have the strength to hold it. That would allow more of King Devlin's army to join us with minimal risk."

"But that failed," Sybil said. "The Order caught the Sumarans trying to cross into Valeria."

"Which is why we need to control territory on the border," Azerick replied and set a stone marker on the map. "The day after tomorrow, here at first light, I am going to meet with the three resistance leaders and a handful of their senior officers to discuss the safest way to move our people and hopefully convince them to consolidate forces."

Marley frowned. "That sounds dangerous. Why take the risk of a face-to-face meeting?"

"The risks are minimal," Azerick said. "Up until now, I have had to use go-betweens to get messages to them. This reduces the possibility of someone intercepting those messages. Also, no one outside of this room knows about it."

"Except whoever delivered your request for a meeting, the leaders you contacted, and whatever officers they're bringing with them," Joah said. "That's the best-case scenario. Who knows if those officers spoke to anyone else, like a family member or ordered a valet to pack a bag? That's the problem with nobles and officers. They can't wipe their own arses without a decree or committee."

Azerick nodded. "It is not without risks, but we are all taking precautions. That is one of the reasons I'm meeting with them alone. I will also scout the area before moving our people through the gate to ensure there is no ambush waiting for us."

"It's still damned risky," Kord said, breaking his usual silence. "I think you're right though. We're essentially fighting a war of attrition, and we don't have the numbers to come close to winning one. Where do you plan to have us all join forces?"

Azerick gave the big man a sidelong glance. "I'm not ready to disclose that just yet."

Kord raised his hands. "We're going to need a place with access to water and enough food to feed an army of several thousand. That's the only reason I ask."

"Wherever we decide to consolidate, it will provide what we need."

"And this is what you have decided for us all?" Marley asked.

Azerick spread his arms. "I'm open to any viable alternatives. I think this is our best chance at long-term survival."

"I got one," Joah grumbled. "We scatter into the woods and do what we'd been doing successfully for years before you and this damned Order showed up."

Azerick flashed him a humorless grin. "But we are here now, and this is the reality we all have to deal with. Anyone else have any suggestions?"

When no one spoke up, Azerick retreated to his tent. The next day and a half was possibly the longest of his life. He was either going to uncover the traitor or look like the world's biggest ass. If he was wrong, it was unlikely anyone but his closest friends would ever listen to him again.

Azerick's stomach fluttered with unease as he made his way to the meeting hall. He found everyone was already there, and several of the faces staring back at him held little warmth.

"Good, Daebian got you all here," Azerick said as he entered and closed the door. "Before we begin, has anyone spoken a word about our last meeting to anyone, anyone at all? This is very important. Even an offhanded remark to someone close to you?"

Everyone was emphatic in their denials.

"Is there a problem?" Headmaster Florent asked.

Azerick shook his head. "As long as no one mentioned anything from our last meeting there's no problem at all."

"What in the abyss is going on?" Joah snapped. "I thought you were supposed to be gone to your bigwig conclave, not here calling more damned meetings to discuss the last damn meeting!"

Azerick gave everyone a sheepish grin. "Yeah...I'm afraid I lied about that."

"What are you talking about?" Headmaster Florent asked with a scowl. "There's no meeting? Then what was this all about?"

"Oh, there's going to be a meeting. Just not with the other leaders. Not today anyway."

"I've had it with your gods-be-damned games!" Marley snapped and stepped toward the door.

Daebian was before him in an instant, his sword out and hovering inches from the man's throat. "Return to the table until the meeting is over."

Kord and Joah drew blades as well and stood behind Marley. Sybil did not draw on the Source, but Azerick could tell she was prepared to do so in an instant. Headmaster Florent must have also sensed it as she too kept her arcane power near her fingertips.

"Let's all remain calm," Azerick said. "I'm not playing any games. Far from it. This is all necessary for our continued survival. Everything will become clear in a few minutes. I just need you to indulge me a little while longer."

Marley glared at him and Daebian but returned to his spot around the table.

Kord pointed at Daebian with his long dagger. "You and me are going to have words after this meeting and settle some things once and for all."

Daebian grinned at him. "You won't like where that discussion leads, trust me. But if you insist, you should bring your little friend with you. At least make it interesting," he said, pointing his chin at Joah.

"Is this an open debate?" Sybil asked.

Daebian shrugged. "The more the merrier."

"Will everyone just calm the fuck down?" Headmaster Florent shouted, surprising everyone into silence at both her volume and vernacular. "Azerick, you had best start making sense, or we all might be forced to reconsider your continued roll in the current chain of command."

Azerick ducked his head and began setting a single agate of varying colors on the table before everyone in the room.

"What in the abyss is this?" Marley asked as he studied the stone in front of him and the rune etched onto its surface.

"Those of us on the supply raid might recall a number of half-elves and rather odd wolves that came to our aid along with the people from North Haven," Azerick said.

"What of them?" Sybil demanded.

"While not terribly social, they make excellent scouts. The other day, I posted a couple of them at the meeting spots I told you all about and gave them a matching stone to the ones before you. When Ellyssa cast her ward on the room, it did more than simply shield us from scrying or eavesdropping. It created a visual and auditory illusion that made each of you see and hear me give a different spot for the meeting."

Headmaster Florent frowned. "I thought I sensed something odd with her ward. I dismissed it as inefficiency from lack of experience."

"To what end?" Sybil snapped, clearly not liking having been tricked, particularly by magic.

Azerick beamed a bright smile. "Each stone before you represents the spot you heard me say and saw me mark on the map. If my scouts see The Order preparing an ambush, they will activate the stone I gave them, which will cause the matching stone before you to glow."

Headmaster Florent smiled at his cleverness. "Which would indicate which of us informed them with little question."

"Exactly," Azerick replied with a small bow.

"Unless, as I said, one of the other leaders, officers, or someone in their camp informed them," Joah snapped.

Azerick cast a devilish grin at everyone in the room. "Oh, I lied about that too. I haven't spoken to them, and since you all just affirmed that you have not spoken to anyone either, the possibility of any betrayal originating from outside this room are very slim."

Joah pressed his lips together in consternation but stood quietly behind his stone. The minutes crawled by in palpable silence. The air practically thrummed with tension as eyes flicked from colored stones to faces in a mechanical fashion, like gears within gears, each one driving the next in a silent tick tock marking the time.

Joah, unsurprisingly, was the first to lose his patience. "This is ridiculous! I have better things to do than stand around here looking at you lot and your pretty rocks."

Daebian's sword made it only halfway out of its sheath, his command dying on his lips, when Joah stopped in his tracks and turned his head toward the soft orange glow reflecting off the faces bearing a myriad of expressions. Surprise, anger, confusion, and disgust met Azerick's smirk of satisfaction mixed with disappointment.

Joah was the first to break the heavy silence. "Marley, say it ain't so. He's wrong ain't he?"

Marley cast Joah a look of regret tinged with shame before giving Azerick a flat stare that failed to hide the disgust and disdain he held for the sorcerer.

"You're responsible for the ambush?" Joah croaked. "You sold us out?"

"Those were our people you got killed!" Sybil screeched, fighting her desire to incinerate the man where he stood.

"It was a necessary sacrifice," Marley said, his tone devoid of emotion. "The plan was to capture the raiding party, harming as few people as possible."

Azerick nodded, now understanding why The Order had seemed to hold back when they could have overrun them given their superior numbers and strength.

"Why?" Joah asked in a strained whisper.

"Because we never had a chance of winning this war!" Marley railed and pointed a trembling finger at Azerick. "He was going to get us all killed, and for what? What does it matter upon whose head the crown rests? At least The Order would see our lands purged of the spawn. That's a damn sight more than Miles has done."

"And all it would cost was your freedom, your identity," Azerick said.

"Freedom? What freedom?" Marley turned pleading eyes to Joah and Sybil. "We all had this idealized notion of freedom when we chose to strike out on our own, to thumb our noses at Miles and the Academy who did nothing to help us. What did it get us? Living like bandits, skulking around in the forest just waiting for the day they decided hunting a few spawn outside of their precious towns and cities wasn't worth the annoyance and put a stop to us?"

"They tried on a few occasions to take us, and we beat them every time," Sybil replied, her voice trembling with a mix of emotions.

Marley's mouth twisted into a sneer. "You think we beat them? We weren't worth the effort needed to remove us. Are you really so deluded you thought they were afraid of us? We were a nuisance, and every once in a while, they had to make a showing of doing something to placate the merchants who didn't like paying our tolls. Ask her. Ask her how big a threat the Academy and the king and the dukes and duchesses thought we were."

Sybil and Joah both turned their eyes to Headmaster Florent.

The archmage dropped her gaze to the table. "We knew where Freehold was and the strength of your forces as well as the location of some of the gates you built. We could have shattered you in an instant. You are a competent wizard, Sybil, but you lack the formal training to comprehend the power a conclave of archmages can bring to bear when working in concert."

"Then why didn't you?" Sybil asked in quiet, tired voice.

Headmaster Florent shrugged. "You and your people provided a service. While the merchants complained, they knew in their hearts that we lacked the ability to patrol the distant stretches of roads between the cities. You filled a niche. It was not a perfect solution, but until King Miles and the city rulers were able to bring more stability to the land, it was all we had."

"And The Order defeated them in a single night," Marley rumbled. "The night the spawn came and killed so many of us, I knew we could not fight them and The Order. So I picked a side to save as many of our people as I could, and I damn well won't apologize for it."

"Then you can die for it," Kord said as he turned and thrust his big hunting knife into Marley's guts. "No matter how noble you thought your intentions, you betrayed us, made decisions for us that weren't yours to make that affected our lives"

Everyone stared at Kord standing calmly over Marley as the life left his eyes.

"Aw man, I wanted to kill him," Daebian said, breaking the silence. "Can I still stab Joah?"

"I didn't know anything about it!" Joah insisted.

"Yeah, but you're still a huge dick," Daebian retorted.

"You're one to talk," Sybil said.

Daebian flashed her a roguish grin. "Yeah, but I'm charming in my own way."

"Charming like a snake."

"Some people find snakes quite charming," Daebian countered and batted his eyes at Ellyssa.

"Don't look at me. She's got you pegged," Ellyssa said.

"You love it and you know it."

"Eh..." Ellyssa replied, bobbing her head from side to side.

"Where do we go from here?" Headmaster Florent asked.

"I have left instructions for our camp to meet up with the other war leaders. They have agreed that we need to unite and take back territory we can hold. Once you have all secured an area near the border, King Devlin has agreed to revisit the possibility of providing additional support," Azerick said as he called his staff to hand and made for the door.

"I thought you said you hadn't spoken to the other leaders?" Headmaster Florent asked.

"Only about the meeting," Azerick replied. "They'll be contacting you soon to work out the details."

He ignored the barrage of questions launched at his back as he strode out of the room. Daebian, Ellyssa, and Rusty chased after him.

"Where are you going now?" Ellyssa asked.

"My bet is to do something heroically stupid," Daebian said.

"I'm going to cut the head off this snake," Azerick said.

Daebian elbowed Rusty and quipped, "Nailed it."

"How?" Ellyssa asked.

"After her people failed to capture us after our raid, there's no way she won't take a direct hand in capturing me and the other leaders. I know right where she is," Azerick replied.

"Perhaps the four of us could take her down, but won't she have a large number of soldiers with her?" Rusty asked.

Azerick shook his head. "You three aren't going with me."

Daebian cleared his throat. "Father, while I have often mocked your prowess these last months, what with your demonic neutering and all, I am sincere in my asking if you think you can defeat her on your own? I seem to recall her having kicked your ass on more than one occasion."

Azerick chuckled. "Regardless of the outcome, with any luck, she will no longer be taking a direct hand in the campaign here. She'll probably think she doesn't have to once I'm no longer a threat."

"My, someone thinks highly of themselves," Daebian said.

Azerick nodded. "I just hope she does as well. Once she has vacated the field, one way or another, my recommendation is for the newly united forces to make slow, cautious advances until the right moment to hit them hard."

"When will that be?" Ellyssa asked.

Azerick furrowed his brow and shook his head. "I can't say, but I think you will know when you see it. Whatever happens to me, stay with our people and help see them to victory."

Rusty grabbed Azerick by the arm and pulled him to a stop. "Azerick, do not throw your life away in some foolish attempt at saving everyone once again. You are far more valuable here as a symbol of strength and defiance."

Azerick laid a hand on his shoulder. "You know as well as anyone that I don't sell my life cheaply."

"Just often," Daebian said. "You're like Grandmother's blanket of martyrdom, handed down once every generation."

Azerick chuckled. "I have no intention of dying, but I won't lie. This is a big risk and more likely to fail than succeed."

"Just…" Ellyssa began, wringing her hands before sweeping him up into a hug. "Just try your hardest not to die. I'm not ready to lose you again."

Azerick returned her embrace. "Whether I win or lose, the princess, and hopefully her entire damned Order, is going to come to regret ever stepping foot in Valeria."

"Please come back," Ellyssa whispered.

Azerick smiled at her. "I plan to."

CHAPTER 19

Princess Sylvianne Attar stood at the head of her full contingent of legionnaires. Nearly a thousand strong, it was the largest force she had fielded in this primitive land whose mission was not to capture a major city. Just a gaggle of insurgents and one sorcerer who has proven to be a thorn in her side from the start of The Order's latest conquest.

"Highness, it is well past the expected time of contact," Legate Demetrius Duilius, the second highest-ranking officer on the continent, said. "I am concerned that we may have been misled, or our informant has been found out. Please allow me to send my glider scouts to reconnoiter the gate."

Sylvianne stood stock still with her hands clasped behind her back. "You lack patience, Demetrius. These are a crude people, and this bunch, with a few exceptions, are the lowest of them. Rabble and bandits are not known for their punctuality or discipline. Getting so many of them to move in concert is likely akin to herding feral cats."

The legate made a small bow. "As you say, Highness."

"I do say, therefore it is fact."

Her teeth flashed brightly when a lone figure stood atop the rise behind which her forces lay in wait. Legate Duilius' eldritch sword sprang from the arcanum disc strapped to his right arm, and he raised it skyward, his mouth opening to bellow a command.

Sylvianne touched her hand to his wrist and guided his arm back down. "Hold, Legate. I do appreciate a trap expertly sprung. It is unfortunate it was we who walked into it. There will be no battle this day, Legate. Not for you and your men anyway."

The officer looked at his Lady in confusion. "Highness?"

"I believe you were correct in your assumption regarding our informant."

Demetrius scowled at the man looking down at them. "At least we can take this one. The arcanus we have in hiding around the gate to disable it—"

"Are likely no longer in play," Sylvianne said, her smile never fading. "This is a personal challenge. I shall deal with the sorcerer myself."

The legate's face widened in shock. "Highness, I cannot in good conscience allow—"

The princess' smile fell, and an icy glare took its place. "You cannot do what? Allow? Me?"

Demetrius stumbled back under her displeasure. "Highness, forgive my impudence! I only mean that it is my highest duty and honor to ensure your safety."

Her scowl softened only slightly. "I do not know what I find more insulting, Legate Duilius. Your presumption or lack of confidence in my ability to defeat this man—any mortal man."

"Highness, I never meant to question—"

"Of course you didn't. Perhaps your impudence was born of a flaw in your courage," the sorceress continued her beratement. "Do you lack such courage, Legate? If so, I shall have to review your ability to command my legionnaires. They deserve nothing less the finest officers in the world. I had thought you among those prestigious members. Was I mistaken?"

Duilius fell to his knees. "No, Highness! I misspoke out of my duty and loyalty to you and the empire. I simply thought the man too far beneath your station with whom to bother yourself."

"Then you are mistaken about a great many things today." Sylvianne rolled her eyes. "Off your knees, Legate. It is unbecoming. Order your forces to stand down and hold their position. You may deal with anyone else who takes the field as you see fit. I shall return with the sorcerer in shackles shortly."

She opened a portal and appeared a few yards from where Azerick stood. "I assume our friend Marley has met his end?"

Azerick ducked his head. "He has."

"Did you slay him with your own hand?"

"No. One of his men took his betrayal quite personally. My son was none too happy of being deprived of the pleasure."

Sylvianne smiled and looked around the large clearing. "Will the warlock be joining us as well?"

Azerick shook his head. "Just me."

Sylvianne gave him a mock frown. "A pity. He would have made our battle interesting."

"I will do my best not to disappoint you."

Her mouth turned up into a smile. "I certainly hope so. I do loathe being disappointed. Shall we begin?"

Azerick vanished, as well as did a large portion of the hillside. Sylvianne stood in the air as dozens of hidden runes flares with eldritch fire and the ground flowed out from beneath her in a massive mudslide. She watched almost dispassionately as the mud wall washed over and carried away more than half her contingent of legionnaires.

With a tsk and shake of her head, the sorceress opened her own portal and gave chase. A barrage of flaming meteors met her the instant she stepped out of her dimensional gate. With a flick of her fingers, she whisked the portal in front of her. The rift swallowed the streaking orbs and spat them back out atop Azerick's head.

Azerick flung himself aside, lacking the time to escape through another portal. His own spell pummeled the ground and exploded around him. A dozen small shockwaves and flying earth and stone crashed against his wards and propelled him several extra yards through the air.

He continued to roll as spears of ice and arcane force slammed into the ground until he reached the bottom of a small knoll out of Sylvianne's direct line of sight.

"I want to thank you for teaching me about the offensive possibilities of portal magic," she called out.

Azerick did not bother wasting time to stand up. He dropped through another gate and landed on his feet several hundred yards away. It was clear the sorceress was able to track his portals as she appeared not far away almost immediately.

"And I wanted to thank you for teaching me about making magic nullification zones," Azerick said as he charged at her with his staff poised to strike.

The smile vanished from Sylvianne's face when more rune forms flared all around her and she found herself unable to call upon her magic. The princess wore the same arcanum discs, almost too small to be called bucklers, as her senior officers did, but they required magic to form the arcane shields and swords—magic now denied her.

Instead of turning and sprinting toward the nullification zone's boundary as Azerick had thought she would, the princess drew a pair of ornate long daggers from the belt around her narrow waist. With deft movements, she used the daggers and under-sized bucklers to deflect Azerick's flurry of thrusts.

Azerick had hoped that as a practitioner of magic, she would lack appreciable martial skills. As more and more of her blade strikes began chipping at his wards, it was clear such was not the case. Azerick soon found himself on the defensive, his staff twirling and cutting through the air to parry the wild flurry of dagger strikes.

He tried to disengage and put some distance between them so he could take advantage of his superior reach, but Sylvianne drove forward and kept the battle in tight. One of her elegant blades slipped under his guard and punched through his ward enough to score a deep furrow across his stomach.

Azerick threw himself backward out of reflex and pressed a hand against his bleeding wound. Sylvianne surprised him once more by also taking a few steps back instead of pressing forward. When Azerick saw her smile and followed her gaze to the stone by her foot, he understood why.

The sorceress raised her foot and brought it crashing down onto the rune stone. Azerick reacted immediately, hurling a wall of force at her the moment his anti-magic barrier fell. Sylvianne acted just as quickly, and their two opposing spells met in the middle with a dramatic explosion that slammed them both to the ground.

Azerick staggered to his feet, ripped open a portal, and leapt through. He barely had time to set his feet when the air shimmered just a few yards away and Sylvianne appeared. She lashed out even before her entire body made it through the rift, blasting Azerick with an arcane strike that hurled him through another portal he had just opened.

He flew through the gate and hit the ground in a tumble. Azerick did not bother trying to stand. He slashed at the air with his staff, tearing through the fabric of reality, and rolled through the dimensional gate. Another portal opened a short distance from him through which Sylvianne strode with an air of confident elegance.

"You cannot run from me this time," she said. "I have your signature and can track you to the ends of this world. Submit."

Azerick wiped away a bit of blood from the corner of his mouth with the back of his hand. "I have never, and will never, submit to you or anyone. You can ask all those before you who have demanded the same of me—assuming you can commune with the dead."

Sylvianne opened her mouth to retort, but Azerick did not give her the chance. He touched the rune-carved stone at his feet with the tip of his staff. A ray of white light streaked across the ground toward the sorceress. She raised her shield to block the impending attack, but the light forked around her and activated the rune carvings hidden beneath the grass.

Needle-sharp stone spires the size of buildings erupted from the ground, their tips stabbing through the air like massive, interlaced fingers steepling toward the sky. The fingers of stone exploded in a massive shower of rock, but Azerick was already escaping through another portal.

Sylvianne appeared moments later, her armor pierced and blood trickling from several fresh wounds. She glared at Azerick with newly found vitriol.

"We are no longer amused," she snarled.

Azerick flashed her a grin. "I used to share my brain space with a demon, and even then, I never referred to myself as we. You might need some help."

The princesses' face contorted with more fury than Azerick expected from the verbal jab. "I need no help from anyone! I am Sylvianne Attar, princess of The Order and master sorceress!"

Azerick feigned rocking back on his heels and widening his eyes before smiling. "If you didn't like that last bit, you're really going to hate this."

He thrust his staff above his head then whipped it forward. The ocean pounding the cliff face behind him roared, and a massive wave of seawater broke over his head and crashed down upon Sylvianne. With a sharp command, runes flared on Azerick's staff, and the freak breaker froze solid into a towering icy archway with the princess caught inside like an insect trapped in amber.

Azerick was no fool, and he did not trust that his frozen wave would contain the sorceress long. He pointed his staff at the silhouette, but before he could trigger another spell, the ice exploded with violent fury. Chunks of rock-hard ice battered his wards, and the glacial arch crumbled atop him.

Sylvianne's rage was palpable, and her voice no longer held a hint of amusement. "I am done playing with you. Submit or die."

Azerick heaved himself off the ground, dislodging several blocks of ice as he stood. "I will never submit."

He aimed his staff at her once more, but an invisible fist, or possibly a mountain, struck him from above. The impact drove him back to the ground and reduced the ice around him to snow.

Sylvianne strode toward him, her fist raised. "Submit."

"Eat shit," Azerick said, his voice quavering as he raised a shaky hand.

Another mountain of force struck him hard enough to concave the ground beneath him several inches.

"Submit."

Azerick tried to climb to his feet but fell before he could lock his knees. Kneeling on the ground, he clung to his staff for support.

"No."

A third strike crushed the last vestiges of his ward along with several ribs, leaving him lying in a crater deep enough to provide him a shallow grave.

"Submit."

Azerick tried to speak, but his mouth filled with blood, and he lacked the air with which to form words. He settled for raising his hand a few inches off the ground and flashing her a rude gesture.

Sylvianne stood at the lip of the crater and smiled down at him. "You amuse me once again." She tossed a pair of shackles by his prostrated body. "Put those on of your own volition and I will treat you as a special guest of the empire. Make me come down there and do it for you and I will toss you with the rest of the peasant rabble where you can languish in useless obscurity."

Azerick looked at the shackles then down at his battered body and the shallow crater in which he lay. He took in Sylvianne's composed stance and detected only slightly increased breathing and a few trickles of sweat running down her flawless dark face. He knew then that she had not unleashed her full potential and had still beaten him soundly.

With trembling hands, Azerick picked up the shackles. He gazed down at them for several seconds before clamping his eyes closed and snapping them around his wrists.

"Good," Sylvianne purred. "Now, bring me your staff. Such an impressive weapon will make a fine trophy."

Azerick picked up his staff, summoned the last bit of his remaining power, and sent it sailing over the cliff and into the pounding sea. "I'm your trophy. Be content with that."

The sorceress directed a frown toward the cliff before smiling at Azerick. "Still defiant, I see. Good. I feared I had broken you and would have soon become bored."

Azerick crawled out of the depression, dragging himself with his one good arm, and looked up at her. "Let's get one thing very clear. You may have beaten me, but you will never break me."

Sylvianne pursed her lips in amusement. "You also said you would never submit, yet here you are prostrate at my feet. I do hope lying is not common with you. I do detest lies. Fear not, I have no desire to break you."

"Then what do you want with me?" Azerick said with a pained grunt as he managed to rise to his knees.

Sylvianne reached down and stroked the side of his bloody face. "I want to correct you. You are terribly misguided in your ideas about The Order and what we stand for, the good we can bring, and the suffering we can end."

"You have brought nothing but suffering!" Azerick snarled.

Sylvianne knelt and gazed into his eyes. "You are the cause of suffering in this land. You and your desire to fight that which is inevitable instead of submitting. We have rebuilt your roads and ensured they are safe for travelers. Reports of spawn have diminished despite having to commit valuable resources to deal with you. Your children now receive a far better education than what little they were afforded before our arrival."

Azerick curled his lip in disgust. "You mistake education for indoctrination."

Sylvianne huffed through her nose and shook her head. "Come. You will understand when you see the true face of The Order."

She reached down and helped Azerick stand with surprising strength. The sorceress pulled a small, metal vial from a pouch at her waist and gave it to Azerick. "Drink this. You look like a wheel with several broken spokes."

Azerick studied the vial for just a moment, sniffed its contents, and drank it down. Warmth suffused his body followed by sharp pain that dulled until it became nothing more than irritating itches. His deeper wounds still throbbed, but he was ambulatory.

"What now?" Azerick asked as he pressed a hand against his aching ribs.

Sylvianne smiled, leaned in close, and stroked his cheek. "What all girls do when they capture a boy who interests them. I take you home to meet my family."

CHAPTER 20

A zerick found flying on the back of Sylvianne's glider more than a little disconcerting, but he kept his complaints to himself. He refused to show any semblance of fear. He held his head high as they walked down Southport's streets to the looming archway constructed in a plaza near the city center.

A platoon of soldiers and a handful of arcanus stood watch over the gate, and Azerick knew there was at least a full company billeted nearby. Sylvianne strode up to the arch amidst bowing legionnaires and pressed her hand against the stone.

The empty space within shimmered and resolved into a landscape that appeared warm but was neither tropical nor desert. Sylvianne beckoned Azerick to follow and stepped through. She breathed in the sea air and smiled.

"It is good to be home," she said as she basked in the warm sun. "Your land is too cold and damp for my taste."

Azerick ignored her and turned in a circle to take in his new surroundings. He stood outside a large fort built of thick stone with a surrounding wall twenty feet high and nearly as thick. While he spotted a few civilian laborers and people selling goods out of stalls set up near the walls, the vast majority were soldiers, most of them the same dark hue as Sylvianne.

One of them strode toward them, an officer given the look of his armor, clapped a fist to his chest, and bowed at the waist. "Highness, forgive our lack of reception. I was not informed to expect your arrival."

"That is because I had not decided to return until now, Primus," Sylvianne said. "I will require the use of a glider in which to return to the mainland."

The primus ducked his head. "Of course, Highness. Would you like me to have my chefs prepare a meal or attend to any other needs you may have before you depart?"

"No. I shall leave immediately."

"As you wish, Highness."

The man hastened away, barking orders at his subordinates. Everyone who had been sitting idle suddenly found the need appear busy polishing armor, drilling, sharpening swords, or attentively standing guard. An arcanus arrived astride a glider and touched down nearby.

"Your glider, Highness," the woman said before bowing and backing away.

Sylvianne mounted the glider and patted the seat behind her. "Come, Azerick, and behold the most glorious civilization humanity has ever built."

Azerick was unable to prevent his exaggerated eye roll, not that he tried very hard. Once aboard the flying craft, they lifted into the air and sped away. It took him only a moment of travel and a few hundred feet of elevation to see that they were on a peninsula surrounded by the bluest sea he had ever seen.

The vast ocean was the color of a sapphire, its gem-like surface glittering in a vast expanse. Mountains peeked above the horizon ahead of them, and the mainland showed itself just moments later. The land was warm and rocky, covered mainly in shrubs and scrub brush with orchards of smaller, leafy trees and vineyards coloring much of the rolling hillside.

Sailing ships with triangular sails dotted the ocean below, and houses made of stone and white stucco topped by red clay tiles populated the land. Cobble and flagstone roads wound their way through the towns and across the countryside, connecting even the smallest settlements to the larger towns and cities.

Azerick studied the people he saw below as best he could from his aerial vantage point. He saw no sign of war or the pervasive fear of spawn attacks in the people going about their daily routines. Other than a handful of what he assumed were the town watch, there were no soldiers marching down the streets or looming over the populace.

The tranquility filled Azerick with both envy and anger. How dare these people enjoy such freedom and happiness when they brought nothing but death and subjugation to his own? Sylvianne's words surfaced in his memories about how it was they who had chosen to fight. Chosen to die.

He shook the thought from his mind. No! Peace and freedom of choice were not mutually exclusive concepts. One should not be forced into subjugation to have it. That was not peace but a blind acceptance of servitude and obedience. He would never accept it.

A look ahead brought an enormous city into view. It rose high into the sky and spread across more land than any two cities Azerick had ever seen combined. The population must be in the hundreds of thousands! No, more than that.

An enormous palace and a few other buildings adorned with tall, fluted columns stood atop a high hill in the very center of the sprawling city. The only curtain walls Azerick spied surrounded the hill upon which the palace and temples stood, and a much older one, by Azerick's estimation, perhaps half a mile beyond it. The engineering and materials that would have been required to ring the entire city were beyond his meager engineering skill and imagination.

Sylvianne surprised Azerick by setting the glider down outside some kind of constabulary a good mile from the city center. She slid off the craft and beckoned to a uniformed man.

"Ensure this gets back to Homegate."

The man clapped a fist to his chest. "Yes, Highness!"

"Come, Azerick. I thought we would walk the rest of the way so you can see a bit of my home from the ground."

Azerick dutifully, if grudgingly, fell into step beside her. He traveled his eyes all around, taking in the people, sights, sounds, and smells. His gaze settled upon a creature that appeared to be a cross between a gnome and a goblin. It and a handful of its brethren were sweeping the street and picking up what little refuse contaminated the otherwise pristine paths through the city.

"I had wondered about other races within your empire," Azerick said. "Are they all relegated to menial labor?"

Sylvianne flicked her eyes toward the odd people. "The verdung are a special case if not unique. They are a primitive people whose skills have not evolved beyond simple labor or servitude."

"Servitude," Azerick replied. "That is what your precious Order brings, and you call it beneficence."

"Everyone contributes what they can for the betterment of society. This is their contribution. They are quite good at it, and our cities and towns are better for it."

"You say they are not unique. Does that mean there are other races in your empire? I've only seen humans in your army."

Sylvianne nodded. "We have dwarves, elves, and other races with which you may or may not be familiar. No, very few peoples outside humans are allowed to join our legions as soldiers."

Azerick quirked an eyebrow. "Why not?"

Sylvianne furrowed her brow as she thought how best to respond. "Arming and training people with significant racial and social dissimilarity is dangerous. We find humans, even from different lands, assimilate far better into our society than other races."

"What do you do with those you don't assimilate?"

"We reserve large tracts of land where they can live much as they always have without interference or outside social pressure."

Azerick nodded as he processed what she was saying. "What happens if some of them are not content staying within this land reservation?"

The princess took a deep breath. "There has, on occasion, been a people that required stricter boundaries than simple lines drawn on a map and reinforced by legionnaires."

"What kind of boundaries?"

Sylvianne debated on how much she should share with this sorcerer but decided the best way to earn his trust and fealty was through honesty. "When Castracene betrayed our alliance and fell to our might, we created a reservation within a large valley inside their former borders. We then sent that valley to a parallel plane of existence where they could no longer cause us harm. You are familiar with extra-planar and dimensional travel, yes?"

Azerick thought about how the elves had attempted something similar long ago with catastrophic results and how he had accomplished precisely that with his old tower. He wondered if it were the same plane? It did not matter. He was not about to tell his captor.

"Not particularly," Azerick replied. "Beyond my dimensional gates and a few trips to the abyss, I haven't had much experience with extra-planer space or travel."

Sylvianne cocked her head. "You still claim to have resided in the abyss?"

"It's not a claim. It is a fact. A very unpleasant one at that."

"Some say you were possessed by a demon lord. Others say you possessed the demon. Which one was it?" she asked, one corner of her mouth turning up.

"Both," Azerick replied with a shrug.

Her grin turned into a fully formed smile that reached her eyes. "You are serious, aren't you? You must tell me how that came about."

Azerick looked up and took a deep breath. An odd bunch of carriages coupled together raced along what he had thought was an aqueduct like those he had seen in Sumara.

"What in the abyss is that?" Azerick asked in awe as the conveyance stopped at a platform and disgorged dozens of passengers.

Sylvianne beamed. "We call it a skyrail. Isn't it marvelous? It operates similarly to our skimmers but can move scores, even hundreds, of people to the farthest reaches of the mainland within hours. The internal line can take you across the city in minutes."

She locked eyes with Azerick. "This is but one of the amazing things we bring to those who join The Order. It expands commerce and labor to levels undreamed of. People can live and work on separate sides of the city or even an outlying town without losing precious hours to travel time."

"It connects to all your towns? The labor involved must have been extraordinary."

"It is, and so far, it only reaches the primary cities and any towns that lay along its path, but someday it will be available to almost everyone. Fortunately, The Order does not lack for laborers."

"Like the verdung," Azerick said, not bothering to hide the scorn in his voice.

If Sylvianne noted or cared for his tone, she did not show any reaction to it. "Yes, like the verdung, although they are not involved in any of the actual construction. It takes some skill and engineering to build, which the verdung simply are not capable of achieving."

Azerick spotted a short man standing near one of the tall, arching support structures. While not as wide and brawny as Duncan's people, he was clearly a dwarf. His skin was darker than the somewhat pale, short folk of his homeland, but it was lighter than that of Sylvianne's people. His beard was shorter, the wiry hairs tightly coiled and groomed with the precision of a topiary. The man pressed an ear to the stone pillar when the skyrail sped past, nodded, and wrote something down on a sheet of paper.

"So, you do have dwarves here," Azerick said.

"Indeed, although they are known as dvergr," Sylvianne explained. "Unlike the verdung, dvergr are masterful engineers. Our people have learned a great deal from them."

"The runes you use to enchant your weapons, armor, and vehicles, those are all of dvergr design," Azerick stated.

Sylvianne smiled and nodded. "They are for the most part, but it was our people who were able to work them into the designs you see now."

"And are they also relegated to these reservations of yours?"

"Not everyone is willing or able to assimilate. Those who are can do quite well for themselves."

"You mean the ones you allow," Azerick replied in a flat tone.

Sylvianne shook her head. "You insist upon seeing us as villains. You will understand your erroneous thinking once you see everything we are doing to save this world from the spawn scourge as well as the inherent chaotic mindset of unenlightened civilizations."

Azerick bobbed his head. "Bringing order to chaos, hence the name of your empire."

"Precisely!"

"Whether they want it or not."

Sylvianne's beaming smile fell. "People are afraid of change, even when it is for the better. It is yet another flaw of the unenlightened mind."

Azerick said nothing more as they walked through the city. People bowed and smiled when they saw their ruler stroll past. Sylvianne acknowledged them with warmth convincing enough that Azerick had a hard time denying her feelings toward her people were genuine.

Everywhere he looked, he saw citizens going about their business with a seemingly happy and carefree attitude. Children ran about laughing and playing, merchants hawked their wares from tables and stalls, and workers bent to whatever task was at hand.

The only thing that surprised Azerick more than what he saw was what was missing. The rank smell of waste and unwashed bodies he thought was normal for city life was all but absent. He saw no beggars or people wearing clothes that were little more than tattered rags held together by thread. Homes and businesses were clean and in good repair.

The poorest sections of most any city was always those nearest the outskirts, which they had flown over before landing. Azerick would need to find a way to visit those to see if this level of quality continued. If it did, was this only true in the capital, or did all the empire's towns and cities fare so well?

If so, it was indeed a remarkable achievement, and all it cost was some people's freedom, culture, and way of life. He saw how many people might see this as a bargain depending on what they surrendered and gained. He also saw how such homogeny could destroy entire civilizations without drawing a single drop of blood.

It was then that Azerick noticed something else was missing. He and Sylvianne stepped aside to allow a carriage to roll past. While wheeled like the carts and carriages he was accustomed to seeing, a shackled arcanus sat in the driver's seat, often next to a more ordinary passenger.

Azerick looked around and noted that none of the carts and carriages he saw had a draft animal to pull them. "Are all conveyances rune powered and driven by arcanus?"

Sylvianne nodded. "Within the city, yes. Unless going to slaughter, animals are not allowed upon the streets. Farmers and merchants who require carts and wagons either employ or temporarily hire an arcanus to ferry them through the city. Those of less means also rent a wagon capable of being powered and piloted by an arcanus. Outside of warfare, it is the primary means of employment for those gifted with magical talent."

190 / Brock E. Deskins

"I think cursed is a more appropriate term if you are not royalty," Azerick replied.

"It can be a burden for some, but the alternative is far too dangerous. Uncontrolled magic breeds chaos. It is its nature and the nature of those who wield it without constraint."

Azerick remained silent as they made their way across the city. His magic was so infused into his very identity that he could not imagine living without it. Sylvianne stopped at a columned building with a pair of legionnaires guarding the entrance. It appeared to be some sort of government office building.

Much bowing and scraping commenced the moment they entered. A rotund man in splendid regalia appeared, his feet propelling him toward the princess as fast as they could go without breaking into a jog. He dabbed a silk kerchief to his sweating, bald head as he bowed deeply.

"Highness, we are pleased beyond words for gracing us with your presence. How may I serve you?"

"I require a carriage to take myself and my newest acquisition to the palace," Sylvianne said.

"At once, Highness." The functionary snapped his fingers several times in quick succession. A younger man darted forward without attempting to conceal his undignified haste. "Bring a carriage around, and don't dawdle."

"Yes, sir!" the boy squeaked, performed a swift bow, and raced away.

"May I be of any further service, Highness?" the official asked.

"No, thank you. I shall see myself out," Sylvianne said before spinning on her heel and marching back the way they had come.

The carriage, a floating one this time and more opulent than any Azerick had seen thus far, awaited them outside. An arcanus sat in the driver's seat while a footman stood next to it holding open the carriage door. Sylvianne declined the man's offered hand and climbed inside. Azerick lifted his arm and bent his wrist toward the footman, but apparently the man was not going to extend such courtesies to a prisoner of war.

Sylvianne matched Azerick's grin. "I'm glad to see you are enjoying yourself despite your circumstances."

Azerick's lips turned up even farther. "I'm just finding amusement where I can. You'll know when I am truly enjoying myself."

The princess quirked one, thin, dark eyebrow. "Oh? And how is that?"

Azerick's beaming smile became feral. "There will be a lot more fire."

Sylvianne tilted her head back laughed, not mockingly but in genuine amusement. "You are quite confident; I grant you that."

"Not without good cause," Azerick replied with a quick shrug.

Azerick stared out of the carriage's window as they passed through the formidable gates allowing access through the towering walls. Lawns, hedges, and flower gardens broke up the white stone pathways traversing the expansive grounds. Fountains spurted water into pools, and the central piece nearest the enormous palace sprayed a geyser thirty feet high.

Azerick felt the mist touch his face through the open window as they passed by the fountain before reaching the front doors. The palace walls shone brilliantly in the sun. Nearly every surface was made of marble, as was the gravel used to make the many roads and pathways. The stone must be truly abundant in this land for them to use it so liberally.

Soldiers lined the long, wide steps leading up to the palace proper, which was built so high up Azerick had to crane his neck to take in the entire structure. The legionnaires snapped to attention, clasping a fist over their chest hard enough to make their breastplates ring like bells.

Attendants rushed them the moment they stepped through the large doors pulled open by the guards. Azerick gawked at the scene inside. If the outside was majestic, the interior was positively celestial. Sharrellan herself would feel at home in such a place. It was not the ostentation of gold and art that so captivated him, although there was plenty of both, it was the absolute perfection those things achieved.

The most common decorations were marble carved so masterfully that the people, plants, and animals they represented looked more as if they had once been living things turned to stone rather than manmade. The placement and theming created a sense of perfect harmony and symmetry—or order.

"Highness, welcome home," an older woman flanked by a squad of younger women said. "Would you like me to draw a bath?"

"Two please," Sylvianne said with a pointed look at Azerick.

Azerick flashed her a devilish grin. "Separate, please. We are not yet so familiar as to bathe together."

The handmaidens all shared scandalous looks, but Sylvianne matched his impish smile. "Yet? What makes you think we ever could be?"

"I am told I can be quite charming when I want to be. Some might even say irresistible."

"Well, do let me know when you choose to put forth the effort. I would hate to miss it."

Azerick narrowed his eyes, his grin widening. "Oh, you'll know when it happens."

Sylvianne cocked her head. "More fire?"

"Of a sort," Azerick said with a wink.

Sylvianne's attendants looked ready to faint, but the princess merely chuckled and left him in their capable hands. Once Sylvianne was out of view, a couple of the women fought to suppress grins of their own, but the older woman's scowl sobered them with the surety of ice water. They led Azerick away at the needle-sharp point of the matronly woman's stern gaze.

CHAPTER 21

A zerick woke when the morning light streaming through the open window reached his face. He felt the soft mattress beneath him and the crisp sheets caressing his skin as he made a lazy attempt to roll out of bed. A pang of guilt for experiencing such simple pleasure ran through him as he thought about his friends and family back home.

He pushed the feeling aside. This was an infiltration not a vacation despite the decadence all around him. Still, it was nice, and that recognition caused his guilt to spike again. Azerick repressed the feeling once more. He had been living on the ground, in tents, and without proper food since his "rebirth."

Even as the lord of the Fifth Circle of the abyss and Sharrellan's consort, his existence had been far from luxurious. While the goddess' realm was palatial and lacked for nothing, the overwhelming pressure of being in her presence, not to mention the inescapable gloom permeating the hellish realm, prevented him from ever being able to appreciate it.

He could worry about all of that later. He had an empire to destroy. All he needed to do was figure out how to do it, assuming it was possible at all. Azerick was confident it was. Anyone, be it a person or a nation, that came into this much power so quickly did so through means not entirely their own.

This source of power was their linchpin, and all he needed to do was to find it and pull it out to make the entire thing come tumbling down. He certainly hoped that was the case. If he was wrong, he had just locked himself in a lion's cage, and his people were likely doomed.

Azerick rolled out of bed and was so startled by the verdung standing right in front of him and bearing a stack of clothes that he fell back onto the bed with a less than manly yelp of surprise. The verdung pushed the folded articles toward him. Azerick snatched the clothing from the odd creature's hands and slammed them down onto to his lap to cover his nakedness.

If the servant took any notice of Azerick's state of undress he did not show it. The verdung pointed at the clothes and held his hands up, bobbing them up and down slightly.

Azerick watched the pantomime a moment. "Ah, no thank you. I can manage them myself."

The creature made a slight bow from the waist and moved to the open bedroom door. It did not appear that he was going to leave anytime soon, so Azerick stood back up and donned the garments. While not silken finery, no one would mistake him for a peasant or laborer.

The clothes were made of sturdy linen, well-tailored and bleached to present a fashionable and respectable appearance. The sleeves were open along their entire length to accommodate his shackles and buttoned closed. The tunic was long, ending just above his knees, and belted at the waist.

Instead of shoes or boots, a pair of leather sandals with long laces lay at his feet. Azerick picked one up and studied it a moment before setting it back down on the floor. He turned enough to catch sight of his verdung attendant.

"Excuse me," Azerick said.

The verdung turned to face him.

"You seem to have forgotten the trousers."

The creature cocked its head and gave him a quizzical look.

Azerick stood and gestured at his legs. "Trousers. I need trousers to cover my legs and…bits."

When the verdung failed to reply or give any indication that he understood him, Azerick sighed and laced on his sandals. He recalled having seen a good many people wearing a similar style of dress, mostly in and around the palace and almost exclusively men. Women appeared to prefer a longer gown with a loose, sleeveless top draped over one shoulder.

The verdung appeared satisfied with Azerick's attire and motioned for him to follow. Azerick walked behind the short man and took in his surroundings as they navigated the maze-like palace halls. The attendant led him to a flagstone patio with a small table and benches made of carved marble.

Sylvianne sat upon one of the short benches and motioned for the verdung to leave. Azerick took in her appearance as he sat down across from her. She had discarded her armor and wore garb similar to his own. Her garment was made of the same quality linen, but hers had exotic, and possibly magical, designs sewn into it with gold thread.

She still wore the arcanum bracers and circlet but little other jewelry. Azerick knew they were magical and suspected they played a part in how she and her family were able to channel so much arcane power. He was confident that this was their lynchpin, and if he could find and pull it, it may well be the key to toppling their empire.

"You are staring again," Sylvianne said with a brilliant smile.

Azerick cleared his throat and dropped his gaze from her circlet to the low-cut V in her chiton that exposed a gracious amount of cleavage. While she did not have large, prominent breasts, they were shapely and taut, like the rest of her body.

Even if he had not fought her, Azerick could tell by her appearance and bearing that she had been forged as a weapon from the day of her birth, heated in the fires of combat and repeatedly hammered to remove any trace of flaw or weakness.

Azerick returned her smile. "It's hard not to. Your style of clothing leaves little to the imagination."

"You do not care for it?"

"Well, it's certainly airy and refreshing, but I'm more accustomed to having something a bit more substantial between my flesh and the outside air." Azerick squirmed on his bench. "And the cold, stone bench."

Sylvianne tossed her head back and let out a melodious laugh. She gestured in the air with one hand, and a team of verdung appeared bearing trays of fresh fruit, cheese, and bread.

"Eat. We have a long day ahead of us," she said and helped herself to the food.

Azerick followed her example and ate with gusto. Food in the camps had been tightly rationed and bland with very little in the way of fruits and vegetables. He particularly enjoyed the soft, sweet cheese spread upon a piece of bread and topped with fruit, several of which were unknown to him but pleasing all the same.

"What am I doing here?" Azerick finally asked once satiated enough to talk between bites. "Why have you not simply tossed me into one of your training units and shipped me off to fight in one of your wars?"

Sylvianne dabbed a napkin to the corner of her mouth before answering. "Because I think you would be wasted in such a capacity. You are clever and powerful, but with your shackles on, you are no stronger than any other arcanus in our legions, and you will wear them for the rest of your days."

Her expression turned serious and hard. "You are special. Your experiences, if even half of which are true, are extraordinary. You possess knowledge beyond some of the most learned scholars. Your people also see you as a symbol, a hero, even among those who might not think of you in a positive light."

Azerick grinned. "For good or ill, I certainly tend to make an impression on those around me."

Sylvianne nodded. "You do, and I am no exception. You even claim to have caught the attention of a god."

"A few of them actually," Azerick quipped.

"As you have said, and I am inclined to believe you. Either way, your people follow your lead. It is my hope that once you see what we are fighting for, how just our laws and decent our society, you will help me convince your countrymen it is best to fight with us and not against us. Most kingdoms prosper under our rule, and all are much safer now than they ever have been."

Azerick glanced toward the verdung standing a polite distance away. "Most kingdoms, but not all."

Sylvianne sighed. "No verdung is mistreated in any way. Those who do face legal reprisal. The spawn would have destroyed them had we not saved them. They had no defense against an enemy even half as deadly as those foul creatures. That is all we want for all the races."

"Safety?"

Sylvianne nodded. "And order."

"But not freedom."

"Freedom without order is anarchy. It is chaos. We bring order to all, and in so doing, a level of freedom some have never before experienced."

Azerick waved a hand at his surroundings. "And you think this will convince me?"

Sylvianne chuckled. "Hardly. I think I understand you well enough to know you are not a man impressed with luxury. No, I will show you our true enemy, what we are fighting against, what we are trying to protect others from, and the scale of what you, what we all, face. Once you see it in its totality, I think even someone as stubborn as you will understand."

"I don't know. I'm not sure there's ever been a tool invented that can crack through this," Azerick said and rapped himself on the head with his knuckles.

Sylvianne held a hand to her mouth and chuckled. "It is a truly formidable barrier. Were we able to lock the warlocks and their monstrosities behind such an impenetrable wall I think we would all sleep easier."

Azerick picked the purple seed kernels out of a piece of fruit with a rind like that of an orange. "So, will I get to meet your emperor and empress? Having met a few gods in my time, I look forward to seeing the claims with my own eyes."

"In time. I want you to witness the greater scope of our mission before I inflict them upon you. Being in their presence tends to be a bit…intense."

Azerick cocked his head. "You speak of them with some trepidation. Is your relationship with your parents not a loving one?"

Sylvianne thought a moment before answering. "Of course I love my parents, and I respect them beyond measure."

"But you don't adore them?"

"You claim to have been Sharrellan's consort. Did you adore her?"

"That's hardly an equal comparison," Azerick scoffed.

"But a comparison none the less. You did not hate her, correct?"

"No…"

"But you cared for her without adoring her. A person adores a puppy, kitten, or child because they are soft, loving, and largely harmless. One cannot attach such emotion to a being capable of shattering a mountain with a thought no matter how close they may be or familiar a bond they might share."

Azerick held her gaze. "You truly believe your parents are gods?"

Sylvianne dropped her eyes to the table. "Not yet, but they do possess extraordinary power. Once they are able to shift their focus from the wars and we are all safe from the evil around us, I believe they will ascend and replace the gods who abandoned us."

Azerick reached across the table and laid a hand on her forearm. "They did not abandon us."

He felt her flinch beneath his touch but did not pull away. The rebuke he saw form on her lips dropped as quickly as it had arisen.

"So you say." Sylvianne sprang from her seat and stormed away. "Come! It is time for you to see."

Azerick hastened after her. Neither of them spoke as they made their way across the palace grounds until they reached an enormous building within an expansive military training ground. Legionnaires marched to and fro and practiced with weapons ranging from swords and spears to ballistae and catapults.

Officers snapped to attention and saluted with fists slammed to chests as they passed. The front of the building had huge sliding doors behind which lay dozens of gliders and skimmers. Sylvianne made her way to a handful of gliders clearly set apart from the others.

"Do you think you can operate one on your own, or must you cling to my back like a baby monkey?"

Azerick smirked. "As enjoyable as it might be, it could become awkward for both of us given my outfit's minimal covering and lack of support. I think I can manage my own."

Azerick slotted the small arcanum tab hanging from his shackles into the glider's receptacle. He felt a slight surge of power course through the chains, but he was unable to harness any of it for his own use when he attempted to do so.

The glider lifted off the ground at his mental urging, and he floated out of the building behind Sylvianne. They sped across the countryside, passing over smaller towns and villages. People looked up and often waved. Azerick had to admit that their people looked happy, but his anger resurged at the sight of their serenity when they brought such turmoil to his own land.

They flew for nearly an hour before Sylvianne guided her craft to the ground atop the peak of a high hill. Azerick lifted and flexed his legs to work out the kinks and return proper blood flow to them as he stepped beside the princess.

Sylvianne pointed to the crescent coastline below. "Tell me what you see."

Azerick stared at the remains of what had once been a large city lost to some destructive calamity and decay. "A ruined city."

"It was once our capital. Now it is a graveyard for nearly a million souls. Tell me, does that look like a place not abandoned by the gods?"

Azerick stared and tried to imagine so many people and what catastrophe could have befallen them. "This was from the Castracene betrayal?"

Sylvianne gave him a slow nod. "They sent a plague upon us first. Do you see the blackness marring the stones? We call it the creeping doom. There was almost nothing we could do to stop it, and it did not kill quickly. The last few hours of a victim's life were spent in unimaginable suffering. Try to imagine the tortured cries of hundreds of thousands of dying voices and being powerless to do anything but grant them a swifter death."

Tears formed in her eyes and clung tenaciously to her long lashes. "Once sufficiently culled, the Castracene sent their abominations in to kill off any survivors. We had already begun to set fire to the city in hopes of slowing the spread, but it was too late. Those who were able, fled into the countryside. My parents were young but powerful sorcerers. They and the strongest among our people went in search of a way to save us from eradication. And they found it."

She turned to face Azerick. "What would you have done to protect your people from such a scourge? What would you do to ensure it never happened again?"

Azerick stared down at the scene below him. "Anything."

"Then you must understand why we have taken upon ourselves this crusade—as well as the restraint and mercy we have shown. Do not think for a moment that we could not crush your nation to dust should that be our desire. It is not. Our goal is to ensure no one suffers as we did anywhere on this world."

"But your methods only change the type of suffering, not prevent it," Azerick said with far less conviction than he had before.

"Setting a broken bone causes pain as well, but it is necessary in order for a person to regain proper use of it once it has healed," Sylvianne countered. "Come, this is only the first stop. We have much ground to cover."

As Azerick flew beside and just behind Sylvianne, he pondered her words and could not form a strong argument against them. Those he did come up with felt like weak things, words of justification more than genuine counterpoints. He thought about what he had done in response to those who had hurt him or those he loved, and the hypocrisy was not lost on him. Still, there was a line between understanding and agreeing. One he was not yet ready to cross.

He was a stubborn man, prideful and tenacious when it came to defending himself, his people, and his freedom. It was not something he would relinquish without a fight no matter how logical his opponent's argument. Marley had defied the Academy and kingdom at large to live his view of freedom until The Order convinced him of the logic of their argument.

They would not sway Azerick so easily. His entire existence had been one of conflict and pain. His scars ran deep and covered him body and soul. They were an armor not easily defeated. Not by swords, spears, or spells, and certainly not by mere words.

They were moving north as fast as the gliders could go. Azerick could not help but marvel at their speed. So much of what he had seen of The Order's technology amazed him. He thought about how much it could improve the lives of so many people. Their rail system could move people and goods from Southport to North Haven or Brelland in hours or days instead of days and weeks.

So much potential good wasted on warfare, on destruction. His people could have it, or so Sylvianne said. All they had to do was submit. Just thinking the word caused the bile in Azerick's stomach to rise into his throat.

The land changed the farther they headed north. The small, leafy trees became tall conifers. Rolling hills grew into more mountainous land, and the towns and villages grew smaller, fewer, and farther between.

The decay started gradually but quickly became pronounced. Once tall and proud, trees became twisted, gnarled things sticking up from the ground like desiccated skeletons. Moss clung to those arboreal bones instead of leaves and green needles.

An enormous wall capped the end of a large valley between two mountain ranges. Watchtowers manned by legionnaires dotted the peaks at regular intervals, standing watch over some unseen enemy. Sylvianne slowed and dropped lower to the ground. She motioned Azerick to move close to her.

"This is where we banished the Castracene," Sylvianne explained when Azerick pulled up next to her.

"Seems like a lot of guards even for a prison," Azerick remarked.

"It is a fool who underestimates their enemy no matter how powerful they believe themselves. Even behind the veil, the Castracene's vile magic takes its toll on the land. Sometimes, even more substantial things find their way through. The soldiers are here to ensure they do not leave this valley when they do."

Azerick nodded. "Much like how the old gods manage to send the spawn through even though they are supposed to be safely locked away."

"Very much so," Sylvianne confirmed. "There are too many similarities for us to think they are not somehow related."

Azerick narrowed his eyes. "You think they're colluding in some way?"

She thought and slowly wagged her head. "We have no direct evidence, but our enemy, both of them, have shown they have no reservations about making dark deals, no matter how black and evil they may be, in order to gain power over others."

Azerick nodded. "It makes one wonder what deal your parents made to attain theirs."

Sylvianne glared at him and opened her mouth to issue a rebuke, but an unseen force struck them. The two riders held fast to their machines as they began to fall from the sky. Azerick tried to force more power into his glider, but his efforts were fruitless. A glance at Sylvianne showed she was having only slightly more success.

"Jump onto my glider!" she ordered Azerick, her eyes wide with controlled fright.

Azerick stood upon his glider with shaky legs as Sylvianne fought to maneuver her craft closer to him. With the glider lying dead beneath him, the ward that surrounded it vanished. The wind howled in his ears and tore at his clothing. The gnarled treetops rose toward him at frightening speed, and he leapt toward Sylvianne's glider seconds before the two met in a catastrophic fashion.

"Hold tight!" Sylvianne ordered when Azerick landed on the seat behind her.

Azerick felt the magic Sylvianne tried to force into her glider, but the runes engraved upon the machines surface glowed so faintly that he could barely make them out.

"Hold on!" Sylvianne shouted again as the trees reached up for them like gnarled fingers.

Giving up on the glider, Sylvianne enveloped them both in a resilient ward. They careened off the tree trunks and larger limbs, snapping the smaller ones with loud cracks as they plummeted through them before striking the ground with a dull thump.

Azerick felt the breath blasted from his lungs when they hit, but his body felt mostly intact. He rolled onto his back, stared up through the broken, dead limbs at the grey sky, and groaned.

"What…what happened?" he finally managed to utter as his breath came back to him.

Sylvianne struggled to a sitting position. "I am not sure. Something interfered with the runes powering the gliders, and I was not able to channel enough magic to charge them directly."

Azerick began looking around. "It sounds to me like an attack."

Sylvianne rolled her eyes. "Do not be ridiculous. The Castracene might be capable of causing such interference with their magic, but not from behind the veil. The only other thing I know of that can block the Source from such a distance is—"

A sound like a hundred horns blasting the same note blared not far away. The ground trembled and trees began snapping and falling in the distance as if an avalanche was bearing down upon them.

"Dear gods above…" Sylvianne gasped.

"What in the five hells is that?" Azerick asked, unable to keep the panic from his voice.

Sylvianne swallowed the expanding lump in her throat. "Void drake."

The enormous creature's clarion call sounded once more and shook Azerick to his core. "What do we do?"

Sylvianne grabbed him by the arm and pulled. "We run!"

The two sprinted toward the mountain chain's rocky slope. Trees crashed down behind them, and the source of destruction and certain death rapidly closed the distance. In moments, Azerick caught a glimpse of the creature when he glanced over his shoulder.

The enormous reptile was similar to a dragon but with a short neck, broad head, and lacked wings. It appeared slow and ponderous, but when each step propelled it some thirty feet, it did not have to move quickly. It bellowed again, and Azerick felt its hot, fetid breath wash over his back.

"There!" he shouted and pointed at a cleft in the rocks.

Sylvianne shifted her course slightly and oriented on what they both hoped was safety. Azerick shoved her in the back, propelling her through the opening ahead of him. The void drake slammed into the stone with enough force to send a shower of rocks pelting into Azerick's back.

He and Sylvianne rolled onto their backs and crab-walked deeper into the cleft as the void drake began clawing at the stone barring it from its meal. Each swipe of its sword-length claws widened the cleft as it ripped out chunks of rock the size of Azerick's head.

"Don't just stand there, kill the damn thing!" Azerick demanded.

Sylvianne cast him a furious glare. "I can't! It is a void drake, you nitwit!"

"Pretend like I have no idea what you're talking about other than a giant lizard is going to eat us."

"A void drake can project a burst of power that nullifies most sources of magical energy. That is how it disabled our gliders and prevented me from channeling enough power into it to keep it aloft. Any magical attack only hastens its ability to create another void burst, and its scales are nearly impervious to any physical or magical attack we have ever been able to muster."

Azerick let out a deep breath. "Great. I suppose there's a reason you can't just portal us out as well?"

Sylvianne shook her head. "We designed the area to suppress any sort of planar travel as an added safeguard."

Azerick pressed his back against the chasm wall as the colossal drake dug its way toward them. "Remove my shackles."

Sylvianne snapped her head toward him. "Why?"

"So I can kill the damn thing!"

"How? Even with your magic, which we both must agree is inferior to my own, you can't possibly break through its defenses."

"I've never encountered something I can't kill," Azerick said, his tone as hard and cold as the stone around them. "What do you have to lose?"

Sylvianne took a deep breath. "Your word, if we do get out of this, you will not flee or fight me. You will agree to don your shackles once more the moment we are out of danger."

Azerick narrowed his eyes at her and gave her a curt nod. "Agreed. I'll shackle myself once we're out of danger, but I will remain as defiant and resistant to your Order as I was before."

The void drake tore a chunk of stone out of the cleft the size of a small wagon.

"Fine, but I have no idea what you think you can do to change our situation," Sylvianne said in a heavy, defeated tone.

She touched Azerick's shackles, and they fell to the ground with a clatter. He turned and faced the horror digging its way toward them and just stared at it.

"Do you have some mind power of which I am not aware?" Sylvian asked. "It does not appear to be effective."

Azerick smirked at her over his shoulder. He then thrust his hand upward and raised several sharp, stone shards beneath the drake's chin. The stone spears shattered against the beast's scales, barely scratching the diamond-hard plates.

"You see!" Sylvianne shouted to be heard over the bellowing roar Azerick's pitiful attack elicited from the drake. "I told you—"

Sylvianne's words died in her throat when Azerick sprinted forward and leapt into the creature's gaping maw. She stared dumbfounded, unable to comprehend the idea that he had chosen suicide in such a horrific manner.

Azerick's ward pressed against the soft tissue of the void drake's gullet as he pulled his way deeper inside. The drake involuntarily swallowed the unexpected morsel, hastening its meal's passage into its stomach.

Just outside Azerick's protective bubble, he could hear the wet squelching of the creature's innards above the muffled clawing and grunting it made as it fought to reach Sylvianne. Once again able to access his formidable magic, Azerick tried to summon his staff to hand. He felt a pull of resistance, as if drawing it through mud, but it heeded his command.

The staff's runes flared with power, illuminating the drake's slimy innards and his own feral grin. He unleashed arcane fury inside the drake's vulnerable interior, scorching and rupturing every bit of tissue and organ in his path.

The drake roared in pain, and Azerick could feel its attempt to capture his magic to fuel another void burst. The drake fell abruptly silent when Azerick's cleansing fire and lightning destroyed its lungs and finally its heart before it was able to create its anti-magic pulse. The creature bucked and writhed in its death throes, tossing Azerick around, before falling still, never to rise again.

Azerick dropped his staff where he lay inside the beast, figuring it was a good a spot as any to leave it. He crawled toward what he hoped was the giant drake's mouth. Reinforcing and expanding his ward, he forced open the creature's jaws, rolled out of the drake's charred interior onto the ground near Sylvianne's feet, and stood up.

"If you thought that thing smelled bad on the outside…" Azerick said, leaving his words hanging in the air as he dusted himself off.

Sylvianne stared at him, mouth agape. "How…what in the world ever possessed you to throw yourself into a monster's open maw?"

Azerick picked the shackles up from where they lay on the ground, turned, and walked toward the beast. "In my many travels and extraordinary conflicts, I have found that when an opponent's power and defenses are too strong to penetrate with spell or blade, the only way to defeat them is from the inside."

He strode past the drake's corpse to the outside of the small cave as he snapped the shackles onto his wrists. "Coming?"

A chill ran down Sylvianne's spine. Was he merely referring to the void drake, or were his words directed at her? Had she unwittingly invited a fox into her henhouse? No, The Order was eternal and unassailable. There is only The Order, she told herself. If she noticed her words lacked some of the conviction they once held, she chose to ignore it.

CHAPTER 22

Azerick stared at the twisted wreckage that had been Sylvianne's glider. "Well, this isn't going to ever fly again. Looks like we're walking out of here." He looked down at his feet and wriggled his exposed toes. "Wish I had more sensible shoes. My wand isn't the only thing feeling a bit exposed."

"Wand? What wand?" Sylvianne snapped and stared him up and down in search of a potential weapon.

Azerick grinned and waggled his hips.

"Must you be crude?" she demanded and stalked away.

Azerick hastened after her, chuckling not just at his joke but at the sight of the quivering corners of the princesses' lips fighting to keep from turning up into a smile.

A thick fog crawled across the ground until it filled the valley and obscured anything that lay beyond a handful of yards away. Sylvianne stopped and dug her knuckles into her hips.

"Great! This is all we needed," she said bitterly.

Azerick looked around but saw nothing other than fog and the gnarly silhouettes of dead trees. "We should look for the other glider."

Sylvianne spun toward him. "What good will that do us? It's likely in worse shape than the other one."

"We were traveling in a relatively straight line even after they lost power. Mine went down first. If we can find it, we can draw a line from yours to it and know the direction to the valley wall."

"How do you propose we find it? I can barely see my hand in front of my face!"

"Unless your arm is ten or twenty feet long, you can see it just fine. Azerick said. "If you remove my shackles, I should be able to pick up the magical emanations from the runes on it if there's any power in them at all and I get close enough."

Sylvianne thought for only a moment. "No. You stay with my glider and I will find the other. I will call out when I locate it."

Azerick bent at the waist and made a sweeping flourish with his arm. "As you wish, Highness."

Sylvianne narrowed her eyes at him and huffed through her nose before spinning about and storming away. The thick miasma swallowed her almost as quickly and thoroughly as the drake had Azerick. He waited patiently for several minutes before he heard her call out for him.

Azerick oriented on the sound of her voice and took note of the direction from which it came. Picking up a broken, slightly misshapen piece of metal the length of his arm, he dragged it in the coarse, dry soil behind him.

A shadow flitted through the fog in Azerick's peripheral vision. He turned his head but saw nothing other than the floating mists gently swirling in the breeze. Azerick spun toward the sound of a snapping twig just in time to see another dark, barely discernible shape disappear into the miasma.

"Sylvianne?" Azerick called out in a loud whisper.

His feet churned the earth beneath him as he twisted sharply toward the movement he caught out of the corner of his eye. A shuffling step to his rear had him leaping a half-circle to face whatever was out there just beyond his view.

"I'm guessing *not* Sylvianne then," Azerick said to the fog in a breathy voice.

Whatever was out there, it was more than one. Several dark shapes darted about in the fog. Their footsteps were swift and quiet, barely rustling the detritus and loose stone littering the ground of what had once been a verdant forest.

There was another sound behind him, but Azerick kept his gaze focused on the flitting shadows ahead of him. He spun around, swinging the length of metal in a sweeping arc. A fang-filled mouth hissed its displeasure an instant before Azerick's makeshift weapon struck it in the side of its pasty, bat-eared face.

The creature was goblinoid in appearance but slightly taller and had skin the color of a corpse. Azerick had no time for further analysis as a heavy weight struck him in the back and clung to his shoulders. He bent swiftly at the waist and flung the creature over his head.

He felt warm blood trickle down his cheek where the foul being had raked him with its fingernails. The monsters abandoned subtlety and charged out of the fog as a horde, screeching shrill battle cries as they slavered and waved crude weapons over their bald heads.

Azerick met their challenge with a roar and sprinted forward, taking the focus of his charge by surprise. Three of the creature's faltered in their charge, and Azerick waded into them with wild abandon, swinging his length of metal without thought or tactic other than to overwhelm his foes with pure savagery.

This was not the first time Azerick had to fight without the use of his magic, but it was still something that left him deeply disconcerted. It was like fighting with a missing arm. It made him feel vulnerable and off-balance. His mind continuously attempted to latch onto the Source and use it to strike down his enemies, but he knew only failure lay down that course of action.

Azerick cried out and took a stumbling step when something struck him in the lower back. He fought to maintain his footing, but a pair of bodies leapt onto him and drove him forward.

"Get off me!" Azerick screamed and spun wildly.

The two clinging creatures' legs extended outward from the centrifugal force and clubbed their fellows as they tried to press in to attack. One of the creatures lost its grip, went flying away, and struck another, sending them both tumbling across the ground.

Azerick's victory was short-lived. There were simply too many of them, and his weapon was grossly inferior to the task. Even as he clubbed another attacker in the head with his length of metal, three more rushed in, one grabbing him around the waist, another around the knees, and a third trapped his ankles with its spindly arms.

Azerick went tumbling to the ground. The remaining creatures charged in and battered him with fists, clubs, and stones. His only saving grace was with three of them still clinging to his form, they limited the exposed bits of his body for them to land a clean blow.

They struck their brethren as often as they did Azerick, who used his arms to ward off blows to his head as best he could. He knew he was in a precarious situation, and had his attackers been stronger or equipped with sharp weapons, he likely would have already succumbed to their assault. As it was, his doom was not far off unless his situation changed for the better and rather quickly.

A club found its way past his meager defenses and struck him hard enough to bring stars to his eyes. More blows found tender flesh as he teetered on the edge of consciousness. He felt the weight lift from his body and thought he had succumbed to oblivion's inexorable pull, but the creatures' snarling and hissing only intensified in his ears before turning into cries of pain.

Hard thumps of bodies hitting the ground and the sharp cracking of snapping limbs, possibly both bodily and arboreal, filled the air. Azerick opened his eyes while still curled into a fetal position and saw pale bodies falling from the sky, raising clouds of dust with their meteoric impacts.

Sylvianne appeared out of the fog like a goddess of retribution. With a snarl on her lips, she crushed and flayed the pasty flesh from the creatures' bodies. The monsters tried to flee in the face of this new and implacable threat, but for Sylvianne, retreat was not an option.

She stretched a hand out toward a fleeing creature's back and pulled. The monster's feet left the ground, and its body reversed direction with twice the momentum. Sylvianne's other hand shot forward, pierced the creature's ribcage, and reemerged grasping a blackened heart.

The princess tossed the organ beside the body, raised both hands above her head, then dropped them, spreading her arms. A burst of power expanded out from around her as fast and loud as a thunderclap and as sharp as a sword. The invisible ring burst outward and cleaved through everything in its path.

Azerick had no idea how far it continued to travel, but he heard trees toppling over well in the distance. Despite her having beaten him rather soundly, he shuddered to think she had been pulling her punches in both their encounters. She certainly held nothing back now. At least so he hoped.

"Are you all right?" Sylvianne asked, only slightly winded.

Azerick rolled onto his hands and knees and held the pose a moment before climbing to his feet. "A bit battered and bruised but otherwise intact."

Her look of concern vanished in an instant, replaced once again by dispassionate resolve. "Good. Are you able to chart our course out of this accursed valley?"

Azerick looked around. "Where is the other glider?"

"A score of yards that direction," she replied and pointed back in the direction from which she had appeared. "Where is the wreck?"

Azerick found the line he had drawn on the ground and pointed. "That way."

"Good. Let us be gone from this place. I will let you set our pace."

"How very kind of you," Azerick said as he set off, a slight hitch in his step.

Sylvianne flashed him a crooked smile. "It is, isn't it?"

"Thank you for coming to my aid back there," Azerick said after a couple of minutes of walking in silence.

Sylvianne made a soft grunting sound. "I took you into my charge. It is my responsibility to look after your welfare. To do less would be dishonorable."

"Honor is important to your people."

Sylvianne raised her delicate eyebrows. "Is it not to yours?"

Azerick shrugged. "To an extent. To some more than others, but it is not what I would consider the foundation of our society."

She wrinkled her nose as if having gotten a whiff of a foul smell. "It is everything for our people. What we do and who we are is built around and upon our honor. It is why we take such an unforgiving stance regarding oath breakers. We consider it a higher crime than murder."

"I guess I understand that. I have certainly killed more people than I have broken oaths."

"Of course you do. You are a man of logic, mostly, as well as strong character, so you see the right of it. If you were not, I would not be wasting my time on you."

Azerick smiled over his shoulder at her. "So that's what you're doing—trying to get me to see the logic of your actions, not break me so I capitulate."

"That also would be a waste of my time. As a person of unbreakable spirit myself, I recognize the trait in others—in you. It would be futile for me to try just as it would be useless for you to attempt were our roles reversed. I hope you see that as well."

Azerick nodded. "That's why I'm here. As a person of logic and strong character, I hope to convince you of the right of my position, that freedom and allies create a stronger bond than subjugation."

"You are here because I bested you and put you in shackles."

Azerick shrugged. "I guess you could see it that way as well."

Sylvianne snorted. "It is the only way to see it since it is fact."

"Maybe."

"There is no maybe in reality!" Sylvianne snapped.

Azerick hid his expanding grin by keeping his face pointed forward, but he did not attempt to hide the amusement in his voice. "Maybe."

Sylvianne let out a low growl but said nothing further. Traveling in a straight line with limited visibility was a challenge, but since their target was the mouth of a valley over a mile wide, Azerick was confident in his meager navigation skills. Were it something like a house or even a small town, his confidence would certainly have taken a hit.

They had been traveling for nearly an hour when Sylvianne stopped and raised a hand for silence. Azerick cocked an ear and heard something in the distance. A muted voice called out followed by a long blast from a horn. Sylvianne flicked a finger, and a blinding ball of light sped skyward for a second before bursting in an even brighter flash.

The horn sounded three short notes, and within minutes, the sound of many booted feet and the clanging of armor drew near. An entire company of legionnaires appeared out of the fog. Their commander stopped in front of Sylvianne and dropped to one knee as his men formed a defensive ring around them.

"Highness, thank the illustrious ones we located you," the officer said.

"Rise, Optio," Sylvianne ordered. "We appreciate your coming to escort us away from this place. I was unsure if our mishap had gone unnoticed or not."

The optio stood but bowed his head as he spoke. "Yes, Highness. A spotter on one of the watchtowers saw your gliders go down. We sent out search parties immediately."

"Well done, Optio. I will see you commended for your swift action. I must speak to your Primus immediately upon our return. I do not like the increased activity within the valley."

"Yes, Highness. We encountered several groups of hostiles in our search, but most fled into the fog after our first engagement," the officer replied.

Sylvianne nodded. "We also encountered a void drake. It is dead now, but be prepared to deal with such a threat should there be more. I do not have to remind you of the damage those creatures can do should they manage to escape the valley."

The man's eyes went wide and a look of awe spread across his visage. "Yes, Highness! The power of our illustrious leaders never ceases to amaze."

Azerick looked between Sylvianne and the subordinate, wondering if the princess would correct the man's erroneous assumption. While she did not claim to have committed the deed herself, neither did she clarify what had happened and that it was Azerick who had brought about the powerful creature's demise. He chose not to set the record straight and fell into step behind Sylvianne and the optio.

CHAPTER 23

Azerick woke once more in a bed more comfortable than any he had ever known except for Sharrellan's. However, one could hardly compare any mortal construction with something of divine creation. He opened his eyes and found his verdung attendant standing near the bed with a stack of clothing in his hands once more.

"I'm up," Azerick said when the verdung appeared ready to clear his throat a second time.

Azerick was pleased to find his ensemble included a pair of linen trousers dyed olive green with a dark brown shirt that felt two sizes too big. Sylvianne had even included a pair of soft leather shoes. He hastened to don his clothes as the verdung seemed even more agitated than usual.

When Azerick followed him out of the room he saw why. Sylvianne stood outside his door waiting for him. While her clothes were not much different than what he had seen her wear previously, there was something more formal about them. Perhaps it was simply her bearing that made them appear so.

She turned and stalked down the hallway, snapping her fingers over her shoulder. "Come, we have been summoned to break our fast with my parents."

Azerick broke into a jog to catch up with her. "Meeting your parents already? It all seems so sudden. Perhaps we should slow down a bit, get to know each other better before taking such a big step forward in our relationship."

Sylvianne flicked her eyes toward Azerick. "You seem to enjoy using levity when you are uncomfortable. I suggest you refrain. It is not as charming as you believe, and my parents' sense of humor is far less than my own."

"I'm not sure what surprises me more, that you don't find me charming or that you have a sense of humor."

"Those who know me find me quite droll," Sylvianne replied.

Azerick's eyebrows arched upward. "Do let me know when you decide to be droll. I would hate to miss it."

"Trust me, you will know."

"Will there be fire?" Azerick asked with a smirk.

Sylvianne gave him a crooked grin. "Of a sort."

It took them several minutes of swift walking before they reached their destination. They crossed through a luxuriously appointed dining room and exited onto a veranda much like the one he had supped at yesterday morning only larger and grander.

The presence of the emperor and empress eclipsed all other ornamentation and drew one's full attention to them like an inescapable current. Leontius Attar was a large man, broad with defined muscles that looked as though he was carved from the trunk of a walnut tree. His head was shaved, but a wavy black beard draped down to the bottom of his neck and barely caressed his sternum.

It was clear that Sylvianne favored her mother. Noela Attar was statuesque, possibly even taller than her husband. Her wavy, ebony locks cascaded down her back to just above her waist. There was no mistaking the physical strength in her lean form or the arcane power she radiated in a way Azerick had only felt when in the presence of the gods.

"We have been waiting for you, Daughter," Leontius said in a rumbling baritone.

"Forgive me," Sylvianne said. "I am recovering from a trying day yesterday and did not rise as early as I normally do."

"That is one reason we wished you join us this morning," Noela said as she took a sip of fruit juice. "Sit."

Sylvianne took a seat next to her mother, and Azerick sat beside her when she gestured for him to do so.

"What were you doing in the void?" Leontius asked.

Sylvianne spoke as she gathered food onto a plate. "I had been showing Azerick around the empire. I wanted to educate him and show him we are just in our cause and why it is best to submit. Today, I plan to take him to Olmul."

"I hope you do not expect to impress your brother with your newest…acquisition. I fear you will both be rather disappointed," Noela said.

"Azerick is far more than he appears," Sylvianne said.

Leontius frowned his disapproval. "He would have to be. He certainly does not look like much."

Sylvianne fought to control her tone and the glare creeping onto her face. "It was Azerick who slew the void drake yesterday."

Noela's thin eyebrows rose. "Is that right? How did he manage that?"

"A better question is why could you not?" Leontius asked. "You are our daughter, your power second to none outside our family."

"You know full well the creature's ability to suppress certain magic, particularly our connection to—"

Leontius silenced his daughter with a look. "Again, I ask, how was he able to do what you could not, particularly in light of him being shackled?"

Sylvianne took a calming breath. "Upon his word of obedience, I removed his shackles."

"That was foolish of you," Noela said. "You know his people lack honor and place little value on oaths."

"Azerick is different!"

Noela shrugged her shoulders. "So you say, Daughter."

"He leapt into the beast's mouth and slew it from the inside," Sylvianne said, her voice taut with suppressed ire. "It was the most remarkably courageous act I have ever seen."

"You should spend more time in your brother's presence so you might gain a broader sense of the word and be able evaluate such actions in better context," her father said.

Sylvianne clenched her hands into fists. "You read the reports. Azerick was consort to the failed god, Sharrellan. He spent decades as master of the Fifth Circle of the abyss. He led the battle against the old gods and helped return them to their prison."

Noela gave her a dismissive wave of her hand. "Fanciful stories created by peasants in dire need of a hero."

"I also juggle," Azerick said, interrupting the family squabble.

All eyes turned toward Azerick, who had thus far been in attendance in name only.

"He speaks unbidden," Leontius said, his voice low and rumbling.

"I do," Azerick replied. "The real trick is getting me to shut up."

"Silence!" Sylvianne hissed.

The power behind the emperor and empress's simple emotion of displeasure struck him like a wave and threatened to knock him off his seat. It vanished as quickly as it had arisen.

"No, he is your guest. Let him speak," Leontius said. "Tell us, now that you have seen the heart of our empire, what do you think?"

"It is quite remarkable. Your technology, education, and social order are truly enviable," Azerick said in all honesty.

"And yet you refuse to bend the knee and accept us as your masters?" Noela asked.

"Well, the fact that you use the term masters strikes at the heart of my resistance. It carries a connotation of being subservient, oppressively so. I also do not care for how you marginalize nonhuman races in your empire. That sort of thinking often leads to atrocities through the actions of self-righteous types convinced of their own superiority. It is our differences, when accepted and even celebrated, that make us stronger. Without them, we become…inbred."

The glare Noela gave Azerick showed he had struck a nerve. "If you refuse to yield and convince your people to accept us as their rulers, then what do you hope to gain by being here? Surely a man as powerful as you claim to be could have, at the very least, forced my daughter to give you an honorable death through combat."

Azerick spread soft cheese onto a piece of flatbread and topped it with a piece of fruit. "Oh, that's easy. I plan to do what I do best."

"And what is that?" Noela asked.

"Abolish the fallacy of you being gods, destroy your hopes and dreams, and bring your empire crumbling down around you."

Noela's lips were taut as they fought indecision to become a frown or amused smile. "And how do you plan on doing that?"

Azerick furrowed his brow. "I haven't quite figured that part out yet."

Laughter erupted around the table. Only Sylvianne remained silent, shooting daggers at Azerick with her eyes. He had made her look like a fool, and she was not pleased by it.

Leontius wiped a tear from the corner of his eye. "Daughter, are you certain this man is a sorcerer and not a jester? He tells the most splendid jokes!"

"Don't forget about the juggling." Azerick smiled at Sylvianne. "And you said your parents had a terrible sense of humor." He looked back to the emperor and empress. "Would you like to hear another one?"

"By all means!" Leontius crowed.

"Knock, knock."

"Ah, we have these jokes as well, but they are usually told by children," Leontius said. "Very well, who is there?"

"The man."

"The man who?"

Azerick locked eyes with the emperor. "The man who committed his first murder when he was but a child the night someone killed his mother. The man who was still a boy when he slew his mother's killer with his own hands. The man who burned to death an entire thieves' guild for murdering his adopted family. The man given to a demon lord in sacrifice who then refused to submit and in turn commanded the demon and its power. The man who forced the most powerful duke in his kingdom to commit suicide in front of his subjects in a most gruesome manner for having murdered his father."

Azerick's voice grew colder yet more intense. "The man who stood before the elder gods without wavering and forced them back into exile. The man who eradicated those very same gods' entire civilization of generals when they killed his wife and child!" He lowered his voice to a barely audible whisper. "The man whose family and loved ones you threatened when you started this unprovoked and unjust war. The man who is going to bury you beneath the awesome weight of your own hubris."

Silence reigned. No one spoke a word. Azerick was unsure if they were even breathing.

He took a bite from the layered food in his hand and gave it an appreciable nod. "This is really good. What do you call it?"

CHAPTER 24

Sylvianne's furious wake buffeted Azerick with a storm made of anger, humiliation, and possibly a little fear as he trailed behind her.

"I cannot believe you would speak so brazenly, to my parents of all people!" she railed, breaking the silence. "Were they half the monsters your foolish words portrayed them as, they would have reduced you to ash where you sat, and they very nearly did."

"Then I'd have been right, wouldn't I?" Azerick replied without a hint of shame.

Sylvianne stopped in her tracks and spun around to face him. "You play a very dangerous game."

Azerick's eyes crossed to focus on the finger she pointed in his face. "It's the one with which I am most familiar. Thus far, I have always come out on top in the end no matter how poorly I appear to be performing in the moment. I am an endgame focused sort of person."

Sylvianne narrowed her eyes at him. "I will warn you this one time. My parents may have felt a small amount of appreciation for your boldness. My brother will not. His ego is as large as it is frail, and he will not hesitate to strike you down if you offend him in the slightest."

"Surely you wouldn't let him break one of your toys."

The anger in her face relaxed, but her expression remained serious. "My ego is made of sterner stuff, so I have no problem admitting that I might not be able to stop him were he intent on doing so. Your life is in your hands. You should treat it with care."

"I wouldn't have to had your people not invaded my kingdom."

"That may be so, but we did, and in a couple of hours you will finally understand why."

"I think I understand why," Azerick said as he hastened to keep up with her. "I simply don't agree with your reasons."

Sylvianne shook her head. "You may understand at an academic level, but witnessing it with your own eyes is something far greater and impactful. It is why this excursion is so important. I would not inflict my brother upon you otherwise."

"Can't you show me without making formal introductions?"

"No. I brought you here as an honored guest and ambassador to your kingdom. Not introducing you upon our arrival would be seen as a grave insult, and as I mentioned, my brother does not take well to insults."

Azerick nodded his understanding. "I take it you and your brother do not get along well?"

Sylvianne took in a deep breath and let it out slowly. "I know how you likely view me. I appear cold and dispassionate in your eyes because it is the image I choose to project. Openly displaying kindness and compassion is considered a weakness, so I keep such emotions hidden from view. My brother does not show them because he does not possess them. For him, conquest and victory in battle is everything. He is the son of the most powerful man and woman to have ever existed in our empire and possibly the world."

"I see," Azerick said. "Being powerful in your own right yet still living in the shadow of your parents or master can be a difficult thing for some people. It makes them desperate to prove themselves."

"You do understand."

Azerick ducked his head. "My son, Daebian, is driven by similar emotions."

"The warlock?" Sylvianne asked. "He fights beside you. I thought you were allies."

"Only in this cause. He also says only he has the right to kill me and opposes anyone who attempts to take that away from him."

"Do you believe him sincere in his desire?"

Azerick shrugged. "Perhaps less now than before. He did run me through once and nearly succeeded."

"He stabbed you? Not even my brother would think of striking our father."

"He had insisted it was for the greater good. The sword was a powerful artifact, and he used it to pull out the demon soul cohabiting my body so that he might wield it as an extension of his own power. He even slayed one of the old gods with it and fed its soul to the demon he kept trapped within the blade."

Sylvianne arched her eyebrows. "Indeed? It sounds as though we may have underestimated his power and ability in this conflict."

"Many have. None have survived to tell of it. The world at large is fortunate that his desire for rule and conquest is somewhat narrow in scope. Were he similar in mind to you and your people…" Azerick wagged his head. "I fear to think of it."

"Let us be grateful for small favors then."

"My former apprentice, daughter in many ways, has proven to be a great counterweight to his darker desires and instincts." Azerick met Sylvianne's eyes. "Were he to lose her, it would bode ill for more than just those he held responsible. My tenacity and penchant for revenge is nothing compared to his. Like your brother, he lacks any social or moral boundaries that might interfere with his goals."

Sylvianne nodded. "I will take your words to heart and instruct my commanders accordingly. The last thing any of us want is to make these troubling matters worse than they already are."

Azerick once again found himself zipping through the air astride a glider. For all his hatred toward The Order, he had become enamored with their ability to travel such vast distances so quickly and easily. It was not worth sacrificing his freedom for, but it was something he could and would take home from his ordeal.

He and Sylvianne flew over the arid yet abundant land and arrived at the Homegate fort. Sylvianne led him through the massive archway after issuing a brief command to the arcanus in charge of the portal.

Warm air, even hotter than the balmy climes he was leaving, washed over Azerick as he guided his glider through the gate. The land was dryer, mostly flat, and covered with tall, dry grass. Trees with wide, flat canopies dotted the expansive savannah outside the garrison in which he now found himself.

The Order camp was a bit rough but well-established. A quick count put the population at around a legion of soldiers plus hundreds of noncombatants. The portal stood just outside the tall earthen berm surrounding the encampment. It was clear to Azerick that they did not expect any concerted attack given the bulwark's meager protection.

Sylvianne did not acknowledge the legionnaires stationed around the portal and immediately guided her craft over the berm. She and Azerick landed before a large tent erected in the garrison's center. An officer, a primus if Azerick properly identified his rank, emerged from the tent before Sylvianne could push past the sentries guarding the entrance.

"Highness, we are blessed with your presence. Primus Horatius Ariston at your service," the man said as he struck his fist to his chest and knelt before his liege lady.

"The empire appreciates your diligent service, Primus Ariston. You may rise," Sylvianne replied.

The primus stood at attention. "How may I serve you?"

"I would know where my brother is. I assume he is leading one of the next battles himself."

Primus Ariston nodded once. "He is, as always. Prince Phaidros spearheads the western assault this very morning."

"Perfect. I will find him there."

"Will Her Highness require an escort?" the Primus asked.

Sylvianne shook her head. "I will not disrupt your duties here. I assume the way is pacified?"

"Of course, Highness. There may be a few small bands of Olmul between us and the front, but they are almost entirely civilians and pose no threat."

Sylvianne straddled her glider once more. "Excellent, we shall depart straight away. I see no need to distract Phaidros by sending notice of my pending arrival."

The primus bowed. "As you wish, Highness."

They flew over the ground at an altitude roughly twice the height of the tallest tree Azerick saw. The vast savannah stretched out unbroken for as far as he could see. It made Valeria's Habberback

Plains look like a small dune within a great desert in comparison. If the land sported any mountains, they were far beyond his vision even at this elevation.

Azerick marveled at the strange creatures below. Enormous herds of antelope and smaller packs of impossibly tall creatures with long, gangly legs and snaking necks bolted at their approach. Huge cats looked up at them with golden eyes, unimpressed by their presence.

Grey, thick-skinned animals the size of wagons and sporting a long horn from their snouts grazed impassively on the dry grass. He spotted even bigger creatures similar in appearance but with tusks the size of jousting lances jutting out on each side of a prehensile proboscis that nearly dragged the ground. They gathered around their young in a defensive posture at the sound of their approach.

Azerick had heard of these elephant creatures in one of his more obscure books, but he had never thought to see one or even believed they were little more than myth. However, there was no doubting his own eyes.

They passed over a small village of huts made from bundles of dry grass. People emerged from their homes and stared up at them. They wore skins, loose, colorful wraps, or nothing at all save a loincloth. Their skin was even darker than that of Sylvianne's people, and their hair was short and tightly coiled.

The few men in the village and several young boys stabbed at the aerial intruders with primitive-looking spears. They hurled what Azerick assumed were grave insults but took no other actions against them. The village made two things quite clear to Azerick: The Order was not welcome here, and men of fighting age were almost nonexistent. At least so it was in this instance.

Azerick was certain it was this way in a great many villages across this land. The Order was like a plague of locusts, spreading across kingdom after kingdom, devouring everything in its path. Whatever doubt might have wormed its way into his head vanished in that moment. Azerick knew then that there was nothing he would not do to put an end to The Order no matter how far he had to descend into chaos.

Sylvianne began to slow her craft as they neared a long swell in the otherwise flat plain below. Azerick spotted tents, legionnaires, and pennants snapping in the breeze atop the rise. What lay on the other side of the hill so caught him by surprise he nearly lost control of his glider. He wrestled the controls and brought it swooping back around in a lazy arc where Sylvianne had landed near a large tent.

Azerick stared down at the largest army he had ever seen. Order soldiers formed ranks three legions deep and almost as far as he could see to each side. The forces arrayed before him was easily as large as the army he had managed to cobble together from nearly every man and woman of fighting age of every sentient race in Valeria and Sumara.

While almost every legionnaire Azerick had seen in his homeland had clearly been from Syrna, Sylvianne's homeland, most of those he saw below were from other lands. This was likely where people went after The Order conscripted them into their army. Now he understood why.

Across an open field half a mile wide stood an enemy horde that numbered perhaps two to three times that of the legionnaires they faced. It was difficult for Azerick to make a proper estimate of their numbers since they lacked the legions' ordered ranks and were spread out as far as he could see.

Sylvianne stepped up next to Azerick where he stood atop his glider. She made a square with the thumbs and forefingers of each hand and drew them apart. The scene within the invisible borders she created enlarged until Azerick could make out the finer details of what he saw.

"I would not want you to miss anything," Sylvianne said with a smile. "I've allowed a tiny trickle of power to flow through your shackles so you can move the scrying window where you wish."

Azerick raised a hand and felt the static in the air as the two magics came into contact. He slowly panned the scrying window over the horde. Like those he had seen in the villages they flew over, the men and women possessed exceptionally dark skin and curly, black hair. They wielded spears and clubs with sharpened pieces of stone attached to them. A few appeared to have bronze tips, but they were in the minority.

Those in the front did not appear to have weapons at all and wore nothing but animal skins on their backs like cloaks. Intricate tattoos depicting some of the animals Azerick had seen were indelibly inked into their flesh. Others appeared to be covered in scars that were too uniform to have all been from combat.

Azerick felt like a fool for ever having thought he could defeat these people through standard warfare. If The Order deployed even half of the troops he saw on the battlefield to his homeland, they would swarm over Valeria and even Sumara, and nothing could stop them. While the realization of how small he really was struck a painful blow, it reaffirmed the actions required to break their hold from the inside.

"You now understand the futility of fighting us," Sylvianne said as if reading his mind.

"I never imagined there could be so many people in one place set upon killing each other," Azerick said.

Sylvianne nodded. "The land the Olmul claim is enormous. While there are only a handful of true cities dotting the continent, there are thousands upon thousands of tribes. You see now why The Order must recruit its legionnaires from across the world. We never expected this level of concerted resistance from such a primitive and fractured people."

"Few things bring people together like having a common enemy. Particularly one that seeks to destroy their way of life."

Sylvianne cast him a sidelong glance. "People once lived in caves like animals and foraged to survive. Did the advent of engineering and agriculture destroy their way of life, or lift it to new levels?"

"I don't see that as an equal comparison."

"That is why you are here, so that we might start seeing the same thing," Sylvianne replied.

Horns rang out from The Order legions. The Olmul tribes responded by banging their spears and clubs against shields made of sticks, stretched hides, and bones and took up a uniform chant that drowned out the horns. The foreign, melodious tone sang by hundreds of thousands of voices was nothing short of awe inspiring.

The Olmul charged across the open expanse straight at the legion ranks. Azerick fixated on those leading the charge, the ones without weapons, and steeled himself for the inevitable slaughter to come. He wondered how the Olmul were able to recruit such a large number of fodder. Were they heroic volunteers, or were they forced to sacrifice their lives on the orders of others?

The tiny amount of magic Sylvianne allotted him allowed Azerick to see a faint glimmer of power highlight the tattoos inked into the warriors' flesh. Their bodies contorted and transformed. The unarmed men and women that had appeared about to sacrifice their lives onto legion spears became huge cats, apes twice the size of a man, dog-like creatures, the big, horned animal Azerick had seen, and other creatures he did not recognize as they bore down on the enemy ranks.

"Skin walkers, they call themselves," Sylvianne said, answering Azerick's unasked question. "One of the most dangerous magics the Olmul possess. We had to create special enchantments for our legionnaires' weapons just to kill them. Even so, they do not die easily."

Azerick had heard of druids able to shift from human to animal form, but his magical instincts told him this was something different and more powerful. The once human horned beasts, rhinos Sylvianne told him when he asked, lead the charge and struck the legions' front ranks with a resounding crash.

Spears plunged into their grey hides, snapping the hafts of many of them, but the damage they inflicted was not enough to bring them down. Not all of them anyway. A few rhino skin walkers fell, but most plunged deep into the enemy ranks, crushing and scattering the legionnaires in their path until the press of bodies finally brought them to a standstill.

Ape and cat skin walkers leapt high into the air to strike even deeper into enemy territory. While The wards built into The Order's armor mitigated much of the damage, it was insufficient to negate it entirely. The wards flashed and shattered beneath the unrelenting attack. The Olmul wielding weapons rushed into the openings the skin walkers created and used their armaments to slay the legionnaires whose protections had failed.

The rear legions rushed forward to hold the line as their front ranks collapsed. With reinforcements bolstering their ranks and sweeping around the flanks, The Order began to regain lost ground and pushed the Olmul back. The legionnaires shoved forward with spear and shield and took perfectly timed steps with a cadenced chant.

Azerick felt a buildup of magic somewhere in the distance that raised the hairs on his arms. The wind began to blow and created dust devils across the open savannah. The small vortices kicked up dust and chaff until it obscured the battle from sight. Horns blasted through the air, and Azerick saw the legions' arcanus take the field although well behind the rearmost ranks.

The mages worked in concert, and Azerick could feel them trying to unravel whatever magic bound the dust storm together. Azerick heard what he thought to be the rumble of thunder in the distance, but it only increased in volume instead of abating. He felt the ground beneath his feet begin to tremble until it felt like a small earthquake.

"This likely signals the climax of the battle," Sylvianne said.

"What's happening?" Azerick asked.

Sylvianne nodded toward the field. "Keep watching."

The arcanus finally overcame the magically-driven dust storm's arcane bindings. Huge, dark blobs burst through the obscuring haze. Scores of elephants the size of small homes smashed into the legion ranks with devastating force. Tusks stabbed and slashed, and trunks capped with spiked balls smashed into men and sent them flying in all directions. It was some of the most brutal warfare Azerick had ever witnessed, and he was certainly no stranger to violence.

Sylvianne lifted a hand and directed the screen toward an impressive figure wearing The Order's piecemeal armor, sans helmet, but it was meticulously crafted out of what Azerick was certain was pure arcanum. The man favored Sylvianne's father but with a slightly more economical form.

He was tall and powerfully muscled like Leontius but sleeker and without an ounce of extraneous flesh. An arcanum circlet a bit heavier than the one Sylvianne wore crowned his shorn head. His posture and the razor-sharp analytical look in his eyes spoke of a man of unshakable purpose.

"That is my brother Phaidros," Sylvianne said.

"I assume his taking the field is what marks the battle's peak you spoke of?" Azerick replied.

Sylvianne ducked her head. "And its conclusion."

Azerick focused his attention on the scryed image. Legion horns blared, signaling the legionnaires to fall back and regroup. Seeing so many soldiers retreat with such order and precision impressed Azerick. It was clear it was a defensive maneuver and not a result of the enemy beating them back.

Phaidros opened a portal before him and leapt through, his twin eldritch blades flaring from his forearms like violet fire. He appeared just ahead of The Order's front lines and fell atop one of the gargantuan elephant's broad head. He thrust his shimmering arcane swords through the creature's skull and into its brain with no more effort than a knife through soft cheese.

Even as the beast began to fall, the prince threw himself at the men riding in a basket on the elephant's back and hewed them down. Spears and arrows flew toward him. A few glanced off his ward, but the rest passed harmlessly through the air when he vanished through another conjured portal.

Phaidros appeared on another elephant's back where he proceeded to cut down the riders before severing the beast's spine just behind its massive head. He rode the dying animal to the ground where he leapt off its back and began cutting the legs out from beneath the titanic cavalry.

Sharp thwacks resounded through the air as legionnaires let loose with their huge ballistae. It often took several of the enormous spears to bring down a single elephant, but between those and the devastation Phaidros wrought, it was sufficient to shatter their momentum.

The tide of battle shifted once more as legionnaires began driving back the Olmul, reclaiming lost ground and advancing deeper into enemy territory. The battle had been raging for the better part of two hours, and Azerick thought it might have continued for several hours more had Phaidros not taken the field.

The air hummed with power as Phaidros gathered more and more arcane energy and unleashed it against his enemies. He flung arcs of devasting magic that cut through dozens of warriors at a time in wide swathes. Phaidros reached a hand over his head and brought it down in a slow wave.

Pinpoints of fire filled the sky. The flickering motes of flame enlarged as they plummeted toward the ground. The fiery meteors struck with devastating force, starting at one end of the miles long battlefield and raining down in an advancing cascade of death until it reached the far end.

The insurmountable arcane attack was too much for the Olmul. They began to retreat en masse, sprinting deeper into territory they still claimed as their own. The dust storm resumed, obscuring the retreating enemy from view. The Order did not attempt to pursue them, instead reformed their ranks to hold the few hundred yards of ground they had won for the small price of tens of thousands of lives.

Azerick stared at the carnage below, unable to speak. He had seen death of this magnitude during the Second Gods War, but the experience had done nothing to dull its effect. He looked over at Sylvianne and saw she wore a grim expression.

It heartened him just a bit to see she did not bask in the glory of their supposed victory as many of the legionnaires did. A ruler who enjoyed the savagery of conquest was nothing but a tyrant. It meant there might still be a chance of winning this war without requiring The Order's complete destruction.

CHAPTER 25

Azerick watched in silence as legionnaires gathered their dead and herded prisoners into enclosures after shackling them regardless of whether or not they possessed magical abilities. He was no stranger to death and had seen his own people die by the tens of thousands during the Second Gods War, but for whatever reason, he felt more detached then than he did now.

Watching the innumerable bodies being laid out and wrapped in burial cloths left a bitter pit in his stomach. Azerick turned his gaze back to the blood-soaked battlefield.

"What about the Olmul dead?" he asked, traveling his gaze over the lifeless forms still littering the scene.

"They will collect their dead once they recover from the battle and we have cleared the field," Sylvianne replied. "Likely tonight after the sun sets. Today was a particularly brutal fight, so it might take them a day or two."

"And you'll give them the time?"

"Most likely. I can never say what my brother will do with a hundred percent certainty, but that is our custom."

Azerick issued a quiet grunt. "That's surprisingly accommodating of you."

Sylvian shrugged. "Leaving the dead to rot does no one any good. It is best to clear the field before resuming hostilities." She stiffened slightly when she spotted Phaidros striding toward them. "I warn you once more to watch your tongue. My brother does not tolerate fools."

Azerick arched an eyebrow and grinned. "You think I'm a fool?"

"I think you like making people think you are a fool, particularly with your words. This is not the time to test your enemy."

Phaidros flashed a beaming smile showing brilliant white teeth. Drying blood painted a large portion of his body and armor. Since he gripped a damp towel in his hands and only began cleaning away the gore once he was certain his sister and her guest had seen him, Azerick surmised the display was intentional.

"Little Sister, come to see what victory looks like? I hope you paid attention. Perhaps you can now conquer that tiny, primitive land that has caused you so much consternation."

Sylvian kept her voice neutral with practiced expertise. "I have the conquest of Valeria well in hand, Brother. You field thousands of new legionnaires thanks to my successful conscription. The vast majority of that kingdom is in our control with the exception of a handful of insurgents who are too ignorant to see the benefit of submitting to our rule, but they will soon see the light."

Phaidros tucked his chin to his chest and raised his eyebrows. "Really? I received a report just this morning stating that not only have these insurgents managed to steal and duplicate our skimmer vehicles, they have begun lading them with some kind of alchemical concoctions and crashing them into your formations."

Azerick failed to stifle a chuckle as Vera's young face sprang to mind. It appeared she had decided to take the field against her father's urgings.

Phaidros turned narrowed eyes onto Azerick. "I see you brought back a prisoner, or is it another pet you seem keen upon collecting?"

Azerick opened his mouth to reply, but Sylvianne stepped in front of him and spoke. "I consider him more of an ambassador than a prisoner. You recall the reports of the sorcerer Azerick Giles? This is he."

The prince looked Azerick up and down. "He certainly does not look like much. I assumed the stories sent back were just that, fanciful tales of a primitive people easily awed by even a basic display of magical power."

"On the contrary, Azerick is exceptionally accomplished in the arcane arts, and his deeds are legendary among his people. It is why I brought him here, to show him that continued fighting is foolish so that he might then convince his people to cease their pointless resistance."

Phaidros' smile returned. "Ah, and the best way to do that was to bring him here, to see firsthand the might of our empire."

Sylvianne nodded. "Very much so, Brother, among other things."

Phaidros traveled his eyes up and down Sylvianne's form "Yes, those other things are quite well known."

Sylvianne's anger flared like oil tossed on a fire, and Azerick swore he could feel the heat of her fury against his flesh. "Watch your perfidious words, Brother, or I will rip that slanderous tongue from your mouth!"

Phaidros flashed her an unconcerned smile in the face of her threat. "What can I say, dear Sister, you have something of a reputation."

"Only because people assume we are of similar disposition by nature of our shared bloodline."

Phaidros shrugged. "Men are expected to display a certain amount of sexual prowess, particularly those of power and importance."

"Whereas women must be chaste and deny our own sexuality?" Sylvianne snapped.

"I do not make the rules. I simply enjoy their many benefits." He turned his gaze to Azerick. "I am sure Azerick knows of what I speak. I hear you bedded the goddess, Sharrellan. Is that true or just another fanciful tale?"

"I was her consort for a time,' Azerick confirmed.

Phaidros gave him a mocking frown. "Seems my sister is a lateral move at best for you then, and that is being quite generous of me I think."

"Her Highness has been nothing but an icon of grace and nobility," Azerick replied. "You could take a lesson from her in that regard, and a good many others I'd wager."

Phaidros' expression hardened. "So, you are the best your sad little nation can spawn?"

Azerick shrugged. "I'm sure such a claim is relative and deeply debatable."

"Care to test your mettle against me?"

"I would love to, but..." Azerick raised his shackled hands and gave his chains a shake.

"I'm sure Sylvianne would unfetter you for the short time it would take me to teach you your place."

Sylvianne stepped in front of Azerick. "I brought him here to show him the wisdom of yielding to the empire, not be battered into submission by a petulant egomaniac desperate to prove himself."

Phaidros looked about to strike his sister, but he plastered on a smile and chuckled. "I see. You do not want me to break your new toy before you have gotten a chance to play with him. Very well, I will wait until you become bored with him as you have so many others."

"Azerick is not a toy," Sylvianne said, her tone low and strained. "He slew a void drake with relative ease despite never having heard of their existence until then."

Phaidros gave her a condescending sneer. "Yes, that is almost as impressive as you being so incredibly foolish as to have been cornered by one in the first place. As usual, I have grown weary of our conversation. I have a nation to conquer that requires my attention. That is something you would do well to learn, little Sister."

Sylvianne glared daggers at his back as he walked away. "Please, do not think my brother's awful demeanor represents the empire as a whole or even part."

"No, he's just the one who will inherit most of the world when your parents ascend," Azerick replied.

Sylvianne's shoulders slumped. "The notion has kept me awake many a night. Unfortunately, there is nothing to be done about it other than pray he falls in battle."

Azerick arched his brow. "Pray to whom, exactly? The gods or your parents? The former can't be bothered and the latter are surely unwilling."

She sighed and shook her head. "It is a paradox not lost on me."

"What do you think will happen when he runs out of nations to conquer? It is my experience that those kinds of rulers then find enemies closer to home—particularly those who might one day oppose them."

Sylvian stood unmoving for a moment before turning away. "Come, we must find accommodations. It is too late to return home tonight. I hope what you have seen today makes your only wise path much clearer."

Azerick looked toward Phaidros' command tent and at the vast army he commanded. "It certainly has."

"I would like to walk about the camp," Azerick said.

Sylvianne cocked her head and gave him a dubious look. "For what purpose?"

Azerick twitched his shoulders. "You said I need to understand The Order and why is does what it does. Speaking with those most deeply involved, on both sides, seems to me to be a good way to go about it."

"I assume you wish to do so on your own."

"Your presence would certainly impact what people might be willing to share. It would taint my research."

The princess narrowed her eyes but quirked up one corner of her mouth. "You think me a taint now?"

Azerick pressed an open hand to his chest and annunciated in a dramatic tone. "Your beauty and power have the strength to shift the ocean's tide. Your presence would sweep away a mortal man like a grain of sand in the surf, his words lost to your roaring waves."

Sylvianne threw back her head and laughed. "This must be the charm you spoke of. It may be more formidable than I had given it credit. Very well. Speak to whomever you wish, but know I can find you no matter how fast or far you might run."

"I have no intention of attempting escape. Such is not my plan."

Sylvianne grew serious once more. "And what exactly is your plan? If you attempt to sow dissent or even speak improperly, Phaidros will kill you without a second thought, and there is nothing I could do to stop him."

Azerick shook his head. "I merely intend to understand those who fight for and against you. Nothing else."

Sylvianne held Azerick's gaze for several long moments. "Go with my blessing, but tread lightly."

Azerick ducked his head and threaded his body through the luxurious tent's door flaps. Night had fallen, but the almost full moon cast a blue light over the savannah well enough he could easily navigate the camp. A ring of open ground several strides deep surrounded the tent he shared with Sylvianne before a sea of canvas and legionnaires swallowed the land once more.

Small campfires dotted the landscape like sparse, orange stars flickering against the black backdrop. The land was warm even at night, so their purpose was more for illumination and heating water for cups of tea, coffee, or a light repast for those discontented with whatever the chow halls served or simply found insufficient.

The camp was orderly, the tents pitched in perfect squares to provide straight thoroughfares without risk of tripping over guide ropes. Azerick had traveled a good distance in mere minutes before a voice called out to him.

"Lord Giles, is that you?"

Azerick stopped and turned toward the voice. A man shuffled out of the deeper darkness toward him, his white teeth flashing when he smiled.

"It is you!" The man knelt and clutched Azerick's hand. "Have you come to bring us home?"

Azerick gazed down at the man who must have been near the maximum age of conscription for The Order. "You're Valerian? What is your name?"

"Amos, Sir! I was but a boy living in North Haven when you led us away from the monsters during the Gods War." Amos' eyes latched onto the shackles around Azerick's wrists and sadness stole away his excitement. "I thought perhaps you had come to lead us to safety once more, but I now see mayhap I was mistaken."

Azerick laid a hand on the man's shoulder. "Do not despair. I am captured but far from defeated. For as long as I draw breath, I aim to return you and everyone else to their families."

A twinkle returned to Amos' eyes and he smiled. "Ah, they think they've caught you, but they've no idea. They think they've hooked a mackerel. I can't wait to see the looks on their faces when they discover they've pulled a shark into their boat!"

Azerick knelt and whispered, "And find that they haven't set the hook nearly as well as they thought." He clapped Amos on the shoulder and stood back up. "Stay safe, Amos, and keep your friends safe. We will all return home soon. I swear it."

Amos' excited whispers faded away as Azerick cut a path through the sprawling camp. He noted the faces of men from several foreign nations illuminated by the campfires around which they sat and talked.

The translation magic etched into his shackles turned their words into something he understood, but there was a marked difference in tone and cadence that often set each one apart.

The Order wisely formed their legions from men of several different nations. Not only did this help prevent any organized rebellion within individual units, it meant having to fight one's own countrymen should they seek to overthrow the empire.

Azerick had not been walking long despite having taken a circuitous route to his destination. The prisoner pens were located near the center of the camp. Although it put them near the command tents, it meant any escapees or infiltrators had to make their way past thousands of legionnaires to escape.

The pens themselves were not terribly secure, nor did they need be. Scores of alert legionnaires stood sentry over the prisoners, and there were thousands more between them and even the hope of freedom should they attempt to escape.

A lower ranking officer stopped Azerick as he approached. "Hold. The prisoner pens are off limits."

"I am here at the behest of Princess Sylvianne Attar," Azerick said.

"I need to see your orders," the optio replied.

Azerick wagged his head. "I don't have any. I am an ambassador for the Valeria campaign. Her Highness wishes me to speak with the prisoners so I may better understand The Order's mission and capabilities to help her convince my people to submit. You can send a runner to confirm, but she is likely asleep now, and I am unsure how she might respond to being woken."

The optio stared at Azerick for several seconds before nodding. "You may speak to whomever you wish, but if you provide any material aid or speak words of insurrection or dissent, Prince Phaidros will have your head along with anyone else who disturbs the order of his camp. Do you understand?"

Azerick nodded. "I do. My only purpose is to understand who and what we are fighting over so that I can facilitate peace."

The optio motioned for his men to open the gate and for Azerick to enter. Azerick felt every eye locked onto him as he walked into the pen, those of the legionnaires as well as the dark-skinned prisoners. One man near the center, his body covered in paint, tattoos, and blood, stood up and met Azerick with a challenging gaze.

Azerick picked his way past scores of men and several women who glared at him, but they made no move to impede or accost him. He stopped a couple of paces away from the Olmulish man who stood with his arms crossed, highlighting his already impressive musculature.

"You are chained but came of your own free will," the man said. "Are you a prisoner or an ally of these invaders?"

His voice was deep and heavily accented, which indicated the translation runes in both their shackles were struggling to make sense of the language, which included clicks and short whistles.

"I am a prisoner but with a bit more freedom," Azerick replied. "The Order has invaded my land as well. A few of us still fight, but already some of them are here fighting your people, though they wish for nothing other than to go home to their families."

The big man lifted his chin in what passed for a nod. "That is the way of these people. They take everything and use what they steal to take even more from others, especially fighters. Why do you come to us this night? Are you merely curious about what you see as strange people with black, painted skin?"

"I'm here to learn," Azerick replied. "I need to understand The Order and those who resist them. From what I understand, you are their greatest, and perhaps last, remaining foe. My people are all but defeated and our neighbors will likely fall as well, even if not quite as quickly."

The ebony man straightened. "I am First Claw K'tar, son of Cha'lan and Bateem of the Owani tribe, and lion fang brother."

Azerick ducked his head. "I am sorcerer Azerick Giles, son of Darius and Celeste. Lord of North Haven and…a bunch of other things."

K'tar nodded. "Well met, Azerick of North Haven. What you say is true. You and anyone who opposes The Order will likely fall. Even all the mighty tribes of Olmul together are unable to drive them from our lands. Their numbers seem endless. It is as if we are fighting the whole world. Seeing so many different peoples flying their banner, I suppose we are."

"You appear to be holding your own," Azerick said. "The Order made little progress this last battle."

K'tar stared off into the darkness in the direction of his people. "What you see is the last true battle we can bring, and we will lose. There are no more Olmul to call upon. They are all here, both the dead and the living."

"Then why continue to fight a battle you know you will lose?"

K'tar cocked his head and gave Azerick a questioning look, as if the translation magic had failed. "We fight because we still can. Because this is our home, our blood. Without it, we are worse than dead. We are bound to this land in body and spirit. If we lose it, we lose ourselves. Better to die and return to the soil."

Azerick nodded. "I understand. Do you know why The Order is here?"

"They wish to be our masters so they can use our might against the tainted beasts. Look around, Azerick of North Haven. There are no tainted ones here. We killed them all and kill all that foolishly return. The invaders, they do not understand that once we are gone, the tainted beasts will return and there will be no Olmul to kill them."

"You hate The Order then?"

"Hate?" K'tar asked, seemingly not understanding the word.

"You find them intolerable. You have a profound dislike of them and want to hurt them."

"We wish only for them to leave. They are our enemy only because they have chosen to be so. If they leave, then they are no longer our enemy."

It was Azerick's turn to give the powerful man a quizzical look. "You would not seek revenge?"

"Re—venge?" K'tar asked, struggling to form the word with his tongue.

"Yes, revenge. Make them suffer for the suffering they have caused you."

K'tar shook his head. "Why would we wish to cause another to suffer? To make more suffering does not ease pain. To act in such a way would only result in a world that knows nothing but suffering. No, we would not seek this revenge. We want them to return to their home so we may return to ours."

Azerick slowly wagged his head as he tried to come to terms with their two conflicting ideologies. He had known nothing but revenge for so long it was the core of his being. At least it once had been. Like K'tar, all he truly wanted was to go home, to return everyone to their families. Still there existed a small but insistent part of him that demanded he teach The Order a painful lesson for the destruction they had wrought.

Azerick extended his hand. "Thank you, K'tar. You have helped me understand a great deal."

The tattooed man stared at Azerick's hand, unsure what was expected of him. He mimicked the gesture and started slightly when the white man grabbed it.

K'tar looked at his palm when Azerick released him. "What will you do now that you know something of the Olmul?"

"I'm going to make The Order go home, but I may need a favor from you and your people after I do."

K'tar frowned. "I cannot speak for all of the tribes, but if you can make them leave our lands for good, we will all be in your debt."

Azerick smiled. "Good. I expect to collect on it very soon."

"You are a very strange man, Azerick of North Haven. Even for your pale kind."

Azerick grinned and shook his head. "You don't know the half of it, my friend."

CHAPTER 26

The sound of a bustling camp woke Azerick from his slumber. While his narrow bed was only a slight step up from the typical army cot, it was still better than he had become accustomed to over the last several months. Traveling with a princess certainly had its privileges.

"You slept well," Sylvianne said, already dressed and sipping a cup of aromatic coffee.

Azerick rolled out of bed with great reluctance and stretched. "I did. Is the camp preparing for another battle?"

Sylvianne shook her head. "Not likely. Both sides will continue to sort their dead today and probably tomorrow as well. The Olmul are willing to wait for my brother to decide the timing of their next engagement."

"I see. Will we be returning to Syrna today?"

"Are you satisfied with what you have seen?"

Azerick nodded. "I am. Seeing the scope of what lies before us, I know now what the most logical course of action is."

"That is good. I hope you can convince your compatriots of the wisdom of your choice."

"As do I," Azerick agreed. "I hold no official power within the kingdom. Not much anyway, so I will need a couple of days to prepare. I hope you will allow me the comfort of the palace in which to do so."

Sylvianne inclined her head. "Of course, but do not tarry. The dead continue to pile up with every moment you delay."

The tent flap flew open and Phaidros barged in. "Ah, you are awake, Sister. I know how much you like to sleep in and was unsure in what state I might find you. I would invite you and the *ambassador* to break your fast with me, but alas I shared my morning meal with the rising sun as I am wont to do. I hope you will forgive me."

Sylvianne returned his painted smile. "And I hope you can forgive my abrupt departure. I have shown Azerick the futility of continuing to fight the inevitable and the wisdom of convincing his people to lay down their arms."

Phaidros' manicured eyebrows rose toward his shaven pate. "Have you now? Well, it is a good thing for you both. I just received a report from your bedraggled front, and it does not appear that things are improving for you. In matter of fact, this alchemist seems to be giving your legion quite a battering. The insurgents have even stolen or produced their own glider and have taken to dropping explosive concoctions down upon their heads."

The prince turned to look at Azerick. "Do you perchance know of this alchemist?"

Azerick grinned. "That would be the youngest daughter of a friend of mine. One of the cleverest people I have had the good fortune to meet despite her having barely reached the age of majority. She reminds me a good deal of myself."

Phaidros smiled back at him. "Clearly not a man of modesty. Good on you. I find it tedious when coming from someone of power and import. Anyway, this aerial bomber did significant damage before the arcanus were given leave to use their magic to drive it away. It is a sorry state when one must resort to mages to achieve victory."

Azerick cocked his head. "Isn't that pretty much the backbone of your empire? From what I understand, it was magic that allowed you to drive out the Castracene, imprison them, and create defenses and weapons powerful enough to conquer so many nations."

Phaidros' expression turned dark and dangerous. "Everything has its place, and magic is no exception. However, strength of arm, courage, and a man's will be the true measure of his worth, not simply bending otherworldly forces to do that which he cannot."

Azerick shrugged. "That is an interesting take on it. Still, it's a good thing you have all that magical power your mommy and daddy dole out to fall back upon should you find those other personal qualities insufficient."

"Sister, I suggest you and your pet be your way sooner better than later," Phaidros said through gritted teeth before storming out of the tent.

Azerick watched the prince depart. "Seems I struck a nerve."

"You did, and you are lucky he did not strike your head from your shoulders, you damned fool!" Sylvianne snapped. "Were he not in such high spirits from achieving a great victory yesterday, I am certain he would have."

Azerick frowned. "Gee, I hope I didn't take away his joy of spending the lives of his soldiers to slaughter all those people in their own homes. Perhaps I should go apologize."

"You will do no such thing. Gather your belongings and let us be away while my brother still allows you to draw breath."

"It must rankle you to no end having to kowtow to your brother," Azerick said as he hastened to keep up with Sylvianne.

Sylvianne glared at him over her shoulder. "I do not kowtow to anyone. I am simply smart enough not to start a fight I might not be able to win. My brother knows there are lines he would do well not to cross with me as well. Do not mistake wisdom for subservience. It is beneath you."

"Does he though?"

"Does he what?"

"Know there are lines he should not cross?"

Sylvianne frowned as she stared at the path beneath her feet. "He had damn well better."

The trip back to the palace in Arkala was much as the journey to the frontlines had been. He saw more animals and a handful of Olmul in their small villages dart about as they flew over them. Sylvianne wasted no time with formalities or pleasantries as they traveled through the gate back to Syrna.

"Azerick, I must see to these latest developments on the Valerian Front," Sylvianne said once they reached the palace. "Is there anything you need so you may work on your people's surrender?"

"Just some ink, parchment, and maybe a bit of food and wine brought to my room," Azerick answered.

"I will see to it." She turned back around and spoke before Azerick disappeared into his room. "You should not leave your quarters. If you must, ensure you do so with an escort. Your servant can arrange one for you, but it should not be necessary."

"I can't think of any reason why I would require one, but thank you for your consideration. I think I should be able to resolve our conflict very soon."

The smile Sylvianne gave him was genuine. "I am very glad to hear it."

Only minutes passed before the verdung servant brough the writing implements Azerick required.

"I have some very important work to do and do not wish to be disturbed for any reason," Azerick said as he dipped the quill into the inkwell.

"Yes, Master," the squat man replied and moved to the corner of the room.

Azerick sighed and said, "I tend to pace about the room when I think, and seeing you lurking in the corner is likely to drive me to distraction. Can you please wait outside?"

The servant looked from Azerick to the door several times before ducking his head. "I be outside if need. Very close."

"Perfect. Remember, I do not want to be disturbed if I can avoid it. I have food, drink, a chamber pot, and everything I need until morning."

"Yes, Master."

Azerick waited until the Verdung closed the door behind him before sitting down and setting ink to parchment.

Sylvianne stormed down the palace halls. Her meeting with her parents and military advisors had taken the remining hours of the day and much of the night. This girl alchemist had indeed presented a problem for her forces, and the insurgents even managed to secure one of their larger outposts near the Sumaran border.

News from other fronts, while not nearly as stinging, were not proceeding as well as she had hoped either. It was a good thing Azerick had finally agreed to get his people to stand down, or this war would become a quagmire.

While not as great as the one her brother had been fighting the last few years, she would have to ask him for another legion or two if she had any hope of fully conquering Valeria within the next few months. Longer if the neighboring kingdom continued to sneak more of their soldiers and sorcerers across the border.

The Verdung tasked with serving Azerick stood between the guards in front of his door and did not immediately move aside. "Not want disturbed."

"Get out of my way, you little cretin!" she snapped and forced herself not to grab the little man by the front of his tunic and fling him bodily across the hall.

The servant nearly tripped over his own feet as he darted out of Sylvianne's way. Sylvianne peered through the gloom at the lump upon the bed. She conjured a light and stepped into the room.

Azerick pulled the covers off his face and sat up a little. "Is something wrong?"

Sylvianne let out the breath she had not realized she had been holding. "No, everything is fine. I hope your evening was more productive than mine was."

"Yeah. I'm tired though. Lots more to do tomorrow," Azerick said and pulled the blanket back over his head.

Sylvianne glanced at the scattered parchments on the table, closed the door, and began walking back to her rooms. She was glad he had heeded her words and appeared to be working diligently as he had promised. Then why could she not shake this uneasy feeling that seemed to squeeze her heart with icy fingers?

A sudden jolt ran up Sylvianne's spine and froze her in place. She spun on her heel and sprinted back toward Azerick's room, snapping at the servant and guards standing in the way. She threw open the door and lit the room with magical light.

Azerick sat up in his bed once more. "Is something wrong?"

Sylvianne stood in the doorway, unsure how to answer. "I...don't know. I just got this feeling something was amiss. Are you all right?"

"Yeah. I'm tired though. Lots more to do tomorrow."

Sylvianne watched him pull the covers over his head as he had done previously. *Exactly* as he had done before. Even his words were identical. A sense of dread followed her into the room. She looked at the writings on the table then turned around and traced a finger along the doorframe.

There! The tingle of magic was subtle but clear. She crossed the room and tore the blankets off Azerick's sleeping form. Only it was not him in the bed but a garment mannequin with a piece of parchment tacked to its chest. Sylvianne looked at the runes scrawled upon the page. The illusion magic they created was obvious. It was shoddy work by most any decent magic practitioner's standards but effective enough for its task.

The tingle she had felt before returned like a lightning bolt. The sensation was nearly strong enough to drive her to her knees.

Dear gods, no! Sylvianne shouted within her mind.

With firm resolve, she collected herself and tore down the hall. It simply was not possible! It must be something else. When she saw her parents barge into the hall wearing nothing but their nightclothes and looks of fear, confusion, and anger, she knew without a doubt the impossible was coming to pass.

CHAPTER 27

Azerick stood before a pair of enormous, ornate doors covered in carved runes inlaid with arcanum. He had already dismantled or bypassed half a dozen potent warning and defensive wards on his way here, and it was clear these were the last line of defense. At least so he hoped. It would take all his skill and knowledge to get past them, and the likelihood of doing so without detection was slim at best.

He decided it did not really matter. If his goal did indeed lie just beyond these doors, then the need for subtlety was long past. The entire empire would know something horrible had transpired even if only the royal family knew precisely what it was.

It had not been difficult to trace the magic in the shackles back to its source. The same invisible tethers linked Sylvianne and Phaidros to their parents, but the emperor and empress' arcane umbilical cords connected to whatever lay beyond these doors, and he had a good idea as to what that something was.

Azerick took a deep breath and began unraveling the first of dozens of powerful wards. The first glyph was masterfully crafted, and it was the simplest. They only became more complex from there. He was perhaps halfway through the arduous task when he knew the precise moment he made his first mistake.

Azerick took a step back and sighed. "Screw it."

The sorcerer stood away from the doors, drew in his arcane power, and struck the barrier a mighty blow. The doors blew inward with a clap of thunder Azerick felt in his bones. Even that sharp boom of destruction likely went unheard by most of those dwelling some thirty feet over his head.

Azerick had long suspected what he would find, but he still stared in amazement as he walked past the smoldering, ruined doors and into the arcanarium beyond. Before him lay a silvery mirrored disc in the floor that looked liquid but he knew was solid. They had made a Source pool, only one far larger than the one he himself had created so many years ago.

If his had been a pond, this was a small lake. Stretching some twenty feet across and an unknown depth, it was at least five times as large as Azerick's pool, now in the safe keeping of his son Raijaun. That was assuming an equal relative depth, and he suspected it went even deeper. He had a sinking feeling the power it produced scaled even greater than that.

Runes of both protection and manipulation ringed the stone rim all around it. He saw in an instant how the royal couple had tied it to themselves and were able to divvy out power, or choke it off, to those of their choosing. The shackles allowed the latter while Sylvianne and Phaidros' adornments permitted the former. As if his thoughts were a summoning spell, Sylvianne and her parents burst into the chamber using a portal spell.

"Azerick, what have you done?" Sylvianne shouted.

"I have uncovered your little secret, although I suspected as much for quite some time," Azerick replied, his response nonchalant.

Instead of being angry, as her parents clearly were, Sylvianne dropped her eyes to the floor and slowly shook her head. "You never had any intention of suing for peace between our people."

"Peace?" Azerick scoffed. "I practically begged you for peace, but you, in your arrogance and need for total control, would accept nothing but absolute servitude! I told you I would never surrender. I even warned you how I would go about it. What happens now is on your heads."

"And what happens now, boy?" Leontius boomed. "So, you know the source of our power. It changes nothing, even if we allowed you to leave here alive, which we will not."

"There's one thing I can do," Azerick replied with a smirk.

"And what is that?" Noela challenged.

"I can tell on you."

Leontius' expression became incredulous. "You can what?"

"I can tell on you," Azerick repeated. "Sylvianne told me you two had nearly died, and several other gave their lives, acquiring the power to defeat the warlocks. When I sought to make my Source pool, those denizens who so jealously guard the material nearly killed me as well. Even then I only acquired it through convincing them it was in everyone's best interest, and it was a fraction the size of yours. You people clearly lack such diplomacy, so I doubt you came into possession of it rightfully. I'm sure those from whom you stole it would love to take it back."

Noela snorted. "Even if you had the ability to summon those creatures here, you can't do it while you wear the shackles. They are bound to the pool, and the pool is bound to us, you little fool."

"You mean these little things?" Azerick raised his hands, gave them a shake, and the shackles clattered to the ground.

Sylvianne stared, her mouth agape. "How…No one can remove the shackles other than us."

Azerick held up a finger. "Correction. No one can remove *your* shackles but you. Those aren't yours. I made those counterfeits myself and put them on after you so graciously removed yours so that I could deal with the void drake."

"But I watched you put them back on!"

"Did you though? I may have downplayed my knowledge of extradimensional magic. I made a tiny pocket dimension in my belly button where I kept them hidden until I got the chance to switch them out." Azerick flashed her a grin. "Good thing I'm an innie and not an outie or I might have had to make it in a most embarrassing and uncomfortable place."

Sylvianne shook her head, dejected. "You have lied repeatedly to me this entire time."

Azerick shook his head forcefully. "No, I have not. Recall my words and actions and you will see I have always been honest if not overly forthcoming with you."

Sylvianne opened her mouth to argue, but she knew he was right and closed it without speaking.

"Enough of this," Leontius snapped. "I applaud your cleverness, but it has done nothing but ensure your own destruction."

Azerick barely had time to register the awesome power he and his wife drew in and unleashed at the speed of thought. He had just enough time to feel foolish for having wasted precious moments talking. Somehow, despite knowing these two possessed near godlike power, he had still underestimated them.

The raw destructive magic lashed out at him, and he barely heard a muffled cry from Sylvianne before it struck. Instead of disintegrating him where he stood, the twin beams bounced up into the ceiling and probably tore through the air above the palace.

"What do you think you are doing, Daughter?" Noela shouted and sent Sylvianne sliding across the floor with an invisible blow.

Azerick did not hesitate again. He conjured his staff to his hand and buried the arcanum tip into the Source pool. The silvery surface began to roil as every rune on his staff flared with searing light. The wood haft began to smoke before it burst into flames and turned to ash.

"No!" Leontius screamed, and he and his wife struck out at Azerick once again.

Azerick raised as powerful a ward as he could summon, but he knew it was a pitiful thing compared to the awesome forces at their disposal. He prepared himself for death, content in knowing that even though would die, he had unraveled The Order's plans and their ability to dominate others. Besides, it would not be the first time he died, and he had a feeling it might not even be the last.

But death did not come, and Azerick was almost giddy with the thought. A colossal, silvery hand burst forth from the Source pool and caught both the destructive rays that may as well have been sun beams shining through a window for all the harm it did. The hand morphed and became roughly humanoid.

"We meet again," the arcanian said, it's voice nothing more than the vibration of magic suffusing Azerick's soul. "We thank you for returning what was stolen. Farewell."

The arcanian disappeared back into the pool, but the splash it created did not follow it down with rest of the liquid arcanum. It continued to rise and stretch until an exact replica of Azerick's staff floated in the air before him, only it was made entirely of the silver metal.

"Azerick, you have no idea what you have wrought this day," Sylvianne said in a trembling voice as she picked herself up off the floor.

Azerick met her mournful gaze with steely resolve. "On the contrary, I know precisely what I have done. I took away a power never meant for mortals. It was why I willingly surrendered my own Source pool, because the risk of…" Azerick waved his hands over head, "this was too great. I have restored the balance of power, and in doing so have given everyone you enslaved a real chance at freedom."

"You have destroyed us," Sylvianne whispered.

"No! It was the choices you made up until now that has caused your downfall. You sealed your fate the moment you threatened my family and dragged me into your war." Azerick turned his icy gaze onto the momentarily dumbstruck emperor and empress. "Knock, knock, assholes."

"You have also sealed your own fate, fool!" Leontius snarled.

He and Noela lashed out a third time. Their arcane strike was nothing compared to that of the first two now that they no longer possessed the Source pool upon which to draw power, but it was still significant. Leontius and Noela had been master sorcerers before creating the pool, and their magic had certainly not lessened over the decades.

Azerick raised his new staff before him and flattened it into a disc. The arcanum shield slapped aside the arcane strike with almost contemptable ease. Even so, he knew the pair were still a match for him at the very least, and if he attacked them, Sylvianne was almost sure to side with her parents against him. The three of them, once they gained control over their anger and momentary shock, would certainly outclass and overpower him.

"I would love to stick around, but I'm far from finished," Azerick said. "This is but the first phase of your downfall."

He opened a rift in the air and disappeared before Noela and Leontius' follow-up attacks had a chance to cut him down. Azerick ported twice more before sprinting toward the glider hangar. Word of some significant disruption spread quickly, and legionnaires were running about and forming ranks by the time he reached the hangar.

"Hold, sir, and state your business!" a legionnaire commanded at Azerick's approach.

Azerick slowed his steps but did not stop as he stalked toward one of the waiting gliders. "My business is to end your empire's incessant occupation and domination by destroying their secret source of power and unleashing their most-feared enemies upon them."

The soldier's eyes darted from side to side and his mouth fell open. "I beg your pardon?"

"Allow me to clarify."

Azerick brought the end of his staff up between the man's legs and felled him like a rotted tree in a wind storm. He leapt astride the aerial vehicle and lifted off the ground. His absconding and assault did not go unnoticed as a squad of legionnaires formed ranks in front of the hangar's large opening.

"Halt and dismount!" one of them ordered.

"Sorry, I've got things to do, empires to destroy, and hell to unleash," Azerick replied.

He swept his staff in a wide arc, flinging the men barring his way several yards and knocking down another dozen reinforcements rushing forward to stop him. Azerick supplied power to the craft and streaked out of the hangar too fast for anyone to make any further attempts to impede his departure.

Within moments, he was beyond the city walls and headed for Homegate. Something struck him from below, and his glider bucked hard before coming apart. Azerick continued to fly forward as gravity rapidly asserted itself upon him once more. He thought quickly and opened a portal in his direction of travel, angling the exit point in a way to reduce his substantial velocity.

Azerick struck the ground and rolled for several uncomfortable seconds, his ward flaring with every bounce. While the magical barrier greatly softened the numerous impacts, it came nowhere near eliminating the damage.

Sylvianne emerged from a portal and stalked toward him. "Do you have any idea what you have done?"

Azerick rolled onto his hands and knees and stood up with a groan. "As I told you, yes, I do."

"We cannot maintain the warlocks' prison without the Source pool!"

Azerick shrugged his shoulders and lifted his hands palms up. "Yeah, that was the plan."

Sylvianne hurled a lance of arcane force at Azerick that could have shattered a city wall. Azerick summoned his staff to hand and batted it away. The princess unleashed a torrent of elemental destruction, and Azerick had to pour power into his wards and port away before she shattered them and reduced him to a pulpy mess.

The furious sorceress turned in a slow circle until she found Azerick standing a handful of yards away looking more amused than concerned. Some of her fury leaked away as she realized how much she had relied upon the Source pool for her power. It was a sobering thought to be brought back down to the level of a standard mortal. Still a powerful sorceress, but a mortal one nonetheless.

"They have had decades to create all manner of horrors, which they will now unleash upon us in an act of revenge," Sylvianne said with a heavy breath.

"Then I suggest you recall all your legionnaires, or at least the ones still willing to follow your orders once they realize you no longer wield godly power, and prepare to defend yourselves. It seems a much better use of your time and energy than going after me."

Sylvianne shook her head in stunned disbelief as a look of genuine heartache flashed across her face. "All we wanted was to put an end to the horrors plaguing this world and make it a better place."

"Better in the eyes of you and yours," Azerick countered. "All you did was replace one horror for another. Such is often the way of the self-righteous."

"Horrors? You think us, me, a horror? After all you have seen, you still cast us as the villains."

Azerick shrugged. "If you won't accept my view, go ask the families torn apart, those whose loved ones you stole away and sacrificed to create your *better world*."

"It was cruel but necessary!"

Azerick's eyes were as cold as his voice. "As are my actions. Do you wish to continue wasting your time and effort in fighting me, which I assure you will not turn out like the last time, or will you return to your people and lead them through the dark time that is coming, as a good leader should?"

Sylvianne stared hard-eyed at Azerick for several heartbeats before lowering her gaze. "What will you do now?"

"I will depart and make sure your people never again take away another person's freedom. Then I will go home never to return—unless you force me to."

"What manner of demon are you?" Sylvianne asked, her voice quavering and thready.

"The worst kind. One that will never bend, never yield, and never surrender."

Sylvianne's words came out heavy and mournful. "You have done far more than break our empire, Azerick Giles, you have broken my trust, and by doing so, my heart. I hope your victory this day haunts you for an eternity."

Azerick slowly nodded and said, "I will add it to the list of those that already do."

Sylvianne turned and disappeared into a portal. Azerick watched her leave and let out a heavy sigh before turning and walking the other direction. He had hurt, possibly even crippled The Order, but he had to make sure they never rose again.

CHAPTER 28

Gliders streaked by overhead, and skimmers laden with legionnaires zipped past as fast as they could manage toward the capital city. Azerick hid in the surrounding foliage and laid illusion spells over himself to remain unseen as he approached Home Gate.

It appeared that his timing was almost perfect. The number of soldiers streaming through the massive portal had dwindled to a trickle, and he doubted they would leave it functional once the last of them passed through. Their ability to move tens of thousands of legionnaires over such vast distances so quickly was what made them a nearly unstoppable foe.

The royal family's power was daunting, but it was their amazing logistics that enabled them conquer everyone in their path. Azerick had crippled that ability now that the power needed to operate the craft was limited to whatever the operators could supply on their own.

A handful of arcanus stood near the massive archway, likely there to shut it down or even destroy it once given the order. That would not do for Azerick's plans.

With the shackles no longer connected to the Source pool, Azerick was unsure of how much they now suppressed the mages' abilities, and he did not want to test his meager illusion magic to get him past them unseen. Boldness was his best gambit.

Azerick strode toward the men with purpose and determination in his step. A squad of legionnaires moved to block his path, and a few of the arcanus looked prepared to aid them.

"You men step aside!" Azerick commanded with an imperious tone.

His decades of being the demon lord of the Fifth Circle of the abyss had not been idle times. It had taught him how to command and control even the most recalcitrant of beings without having to resort to violence. Sometimes. Demons were a special case and often required savage displays of strength to keep them in line, but over time, even they balked at the power of his voice and presence alone.

The young optio swallowed nervously, but to his credit, did not yield ground. "By what authority to you command us?"

"By the authority of the emperor and empress. I am to assist Prince Phaidros in ensuring our legions can pass through the gate without fear of the Olmul taking advantage of our dire situation."

"But where are your shackles?" one of the arcanus asked.

Azerick turned fiery eyes onto the mage. "Shackles? The warlocks' prison is failing, and you are worried about shackles? They march upon Arkala within the next few hours, and you bother me about shackles?"

"It's just we've never…there's never been an arcanus allowed to go without them," the optio stammered.

Azerick took a few steps forward and placed his face inches from the junior officer's own. "I am to relieve Prince Phaidros from guarding our rear so that he may add his might in defending the homeland. How effective would I be were I still shackled?" He took a step back and laid a hand on the legionnaire's shoulder. "These are desperate times and they call for desperate measures. The Castracene are a threat to all, and all must answer the call to arms."

The optio bobbed his head. "Yes, sir."

Azerick gave his shoulder a clap. "Good man. Make sure this gate stays open until I return. No one other than the royal family has authority to countermand these orders without facing charges of treason. The very survival of the empire depends upon it. It depends upon you good, brave men."

"Yes, sir!"

Azerick returned the optio's sharp salute and strode through the gate. The garrison on the other side was a contradiction of ordered chaos. Legionnaires formed ranks and marched through the gate one legion at a time. It appeared most of them, the ones that would make the trip anyway, had already passed through. Other soldiers held the civilians back who feared to be left stranded in a hostile nation once the last of the legions crossed over and the Olmul arrived in force to slaughter the few who remained.

"Hey, you can't take that!" someone shouted when Azerick climbed onto a glider.

Azerick turned to look at a legionnaire running toward him and waggled the fingers of his free hand. "Shoo. I don't have time for anymore grand speeches, and I don't feel like kicking your ass. Go...march around or polish your spear or do whatever it is you do when you aren't invading foreign lands and tearing families apart."

The casual dismissal left the legionnaire stunned, and he simply stood and watched Azerick fly away without further challenge. Azerick sped toward the frontlines at a somewhat sedate speed. Timing was crucial in achieving the best outcome to his plans. Arriving too early would fail to achieve the desired impact he wished to impart. Too late, and far more people would die as a result and might cause the entire thing to unravel. That would not do at all.

Twenty minutes into his flight, he spied two or possibly three legions quick marching toward the gate garrison. Azerick was impressed at their pace, particularly if they had maintained it the entire way and could do so for the remaining miles to come. Skimmers carried at least half the legionnaires, and Azerick thought they probably swapped out to allow the marching soldiers to rest. Even so, it was an impressive feat of endurance and discipline, and he suspected there was magic involved as well.

Azerick kept his eye on several gliders flying above and a short distance ahead of the infantry. He made a wide circuit around them even as he did his best to cloak himself in concealing magic. It took only a couple of minutes before he began leaving them behind.

The sorcerer focused on the ground between him and the horizon, and it nearly cost him his life. A shadow fell over him, and that split second was all the time he got before a shimmering blade cut through his meager ward, which was meant to do little more than keep the wind out of his eyes, and sheared through the front section of his glider.

Azerick threw himself backward out of the saddle, a move that saved his life. The glider spat arcane sparks and fell away from beneath him. Once again, Azerick found himself plummeting from the sky.

"You have got to be kidding me," Azerick grumbled as he fell, more perturbed than frightened of the ground rushing up to meet him.

He rolled in midair and saw a man astride a glider making a sharp turn to chase Azerick to the ground, obviously not trusting gravity and terra firma to complete his execution. There was no mistaking Phaidros or his near-maniacal sneer as he nosed down his glider and chased after his prey.

Azerick opened a portal beneath him without looking and was suddenly flying back up at the prince. He enjoyed the look of surprise before lancing Phaidros' glider like an airborne jouster. The glider practically exploded beneath Phaidros, and his dive became an uncontrolled crash that ended with a curse, the clanging of destroyed metal, and a massive cloud of dust.

Runes flared on Azerick's staff, and he floated gently to the ground. He recognized all the runes from his old staff, but there were now many more that would require a good deal of research when he found the time. A form appeared in the cloud of dust and snapped Azerick's attention back to the battle.

Phaidros strode out of the haze none the worse for wear and wore a look of absolute hatred on his face. "You have brought us to ruin, and I will take great delight in destroying you for your audacity!"

"You and your Order forced me into this war. I simply mean to put a stop to it," Azerick replied.

Phaidros snorted. "You and your high and mighty words. The warlocks' prison has already failed, and even now they and their minions march on Arkala, slaying everything and everyone in their path. Thousands will die even before the battle is joined, and all because of your self-righteousness."

"Thousands are a drop in the bucket compared to the deaths just in your last vainglorious battle," Azerick countered. "How many will my self-righteousness save for putting an end to you?"

"That is war! They are soldiers. It is their duty and honor to fight and die for the empire."

"They are fathers and sons torn away from their homes and families to fight and die for your own selfish desires! You cloak your egotistic greed in the guise of creating a better, safer world, but in the end all of it is for nothing but your ascension to greater power. If you truly care about your people, you would do well to return to them, to help protect them instead of squandering your time and strength on seeking revenge against me. Your sister saw that, but she has always been the wiser of you two."

"It will not take but a moment to deal with you," Phaidros chuckled. "I have plenty of time to kill you, destroy the portal, and lead my legions to Arkala."

Azerick flashed him a cold grin. "Not if you die here."

Phaidros returned his impudent expression. "I am not my sister. I never relied upon the Source pool for my power, although I enjoyed its benefits. Even without it, I am more than a match for you."

"Many have made that claim. I'd tell you to ask them what came of it, but they're all dead."

Phaidros became a blur of motion, wasting no more time with words. His shimmering, ethereal blade arced toward Azerick's neck in the blink of an eye. His staff leapt up, seemingly of its own accord, and intercepted the strike that would have sheered through any other weapon, along with his head.

A glowing nimbus of light surrounded Azerick's fist, and he drove it into Phaidros' arcanum breastplate. The blow drove him back several feet with the sound of a single bell toll. His sandals dug twin furrows into the dry ground, but he remained standing. Phaidros raised a hand skyward and brought it snapping down.

Once again, Azerick's staff moved before his mind had formed the command. A weight like the stomp of a giant's foot struck his invigorated ward and created a room-sized divot in the ground. Azerick leapt from the shallow crater as more invisible stomps fell from the heavens, each one casting dust and detritus into the air.

Azerick opened a portal, but Phaidros met him the moment he emerged from its distant end. The ghostly blade swept in a dizzying array of flashes only to be repelled by Azerick's furious parries and sparking ward.

Phaidros lashed out with an arcane strike from his free hand and sent Azerick flying backward. Azerick leapt to his feet the instant his body ceased its tumble and rained down a hail of meteors upon the prince's head. Earth and fire exploded in a rain of destruction.

His foe sprinted out of the dust, battered but far from defeated. Azerick sent a swarm of arcane spheres at him, but Phaidros raised a massive wall of earth and stone before him. The orbs struck and created huge divots in the barrier, but the wall continued to rush at him like a tidal wave. Stoney spikes grew out from the wave's face as its mass increased with every inch of ground it consumed.

Azerick began forming a spell that would crush the oncoming wall as well as Phaidros, who he assumed was keeping pace behind it, but the spikes shot at him like a volley of crossbow bolts. His ward flared and failed. Shattered stone bludgeoned and tore his flesh. He opened a portal and fled from the unyielding bombardment. His staff once again shaped itself into an arcanum disc without conscious thought. Although less than a quarter inch thick, it sufficed to block the flurry of magical strikes that met him upon exiting his portal.

Azerick replied by sweeping his reformed staff out before him and sent a spinning crescent of energy streaking out at Phaidros. Phaidros raised the shimmering shield he formed on his left forearm and flashed Azerick a contemptuous sneer as he blocked the attack. His mocking grin fell when the arcane strike did not dissipate but instead began to lengthen and open like a crack in the ground formed by an earthquake.

Phaidros let out a strangled cry when a massive set of demonic hands reached out of the planar rift, enveloped his entire upper body, and dragged him inside.

"Say hello to my ugly friends, you arrogant prick. I am the demon lord of the Fifth Circle!" Azerick shouted at the dusty air before spitting out a gob of blood.

Azerick took a moment to get his bearing and began limping toward the former Olmul battlefield. He had only taken a dozen or so shuffling steps when the air crackled behind him. He spun around to find Phaidros covered in black, demonic ichor and looking even more furious than he had before.

Phaidros' eldritch blade flew from his hand toward Azerick—and then another and another until they looked like a swarm of giant, ghostly wasps. They hammered at Azerick's wards and cut through them almost as fast as he could conjure them. Even the now semi-sentient staff was unable to parry the onslaught.

Pain flared and blood splashed onto the ground as the blades began finding vulnerable flesh. A force struck him like a runaway carriage and sent him flying to lay in a crumpled heap. It was a devastating blow, but one that might have unintentionally saved his life. Azerick opened blood-crusted eyes and found Phaidros looming over him.

"Look at you," Phaidros sneered. "You called yourself a hero and claimed such grand titles, and yet here you lay, broken and pathetic. I am Phaidros Attar. I have the blood of an emperor flowing in my veins. I have legions of loyal soldiers at my command. I have unparalleled martial and sorcerous power. What do you have other than a shiny artifact and unworthy praise?"

Azerick coughed up blood and wheezed, "I have friends."

A shadow fell over them both, and Phaidros looked up just in time to see the fang-filled maw before it snapped down and engulfed him to his hips. The scaly beast whipped its head back and forth, savaging him before opening its mouth and sending his shredded carcass flying more than a hundred yards where it crashed to ground as so much carrion for the jackals and buzzards.

Azerick gazed up at the huge head and smiled. "Hello, Sandy. You've gotten even bigger."

The great sand dragon lowered her head and focused a shield-sized eye on Azerick. "That had better not be a fat joke."

Azerick managed to cough out a laugh. "Most certainly not. You are even more majestic than ever."

Sandy raised her head in a haughty manner. "Of course I am. You are very hard to find when you keep hopping about the world, you know. You may recall that sand dragons, despite their numerous admirable qualities, are not swift fliers, and I was quite far away."

"Well, your timing was impeccable nonetheless."

"Of course it was. We dragons are deeply tied to the strings of fate."

Azerick sat up with a pained groan. "Praise the fates then."

"And me," Sandy said.

"And praise be to you even more," he replied with a grin. "You truly did save my life, probably, and a kingdom and possibly a world as well."

Sandy rolled her huge eyes as if the declaration were too obvious to require a response.

"You look terrible," Sandy said.

"I feel even worse."

With a sigh, the dragon dug a talon the size of a two-handed sword and thrice as sharp beneath a brassy scale on her foreleg. Blood welled up from the superficial wound, and she directed it to drip onto Azerick's injuries. His bleeding wounds closed, deep, ugly bruises returned to a natural flesh color, and energy suffused his body.

Azerick stood with only a slight bit of pain. "Wow, that is incredible! I was unaware of the healing power of dragon blood."

"And it had better remain a secret," Sandy said with a slight snarl in her voice. "It's hard enough keeping stupid humans from hunting us into extinction for the godly gifts we possess that they already know about."

"I will take it to my grave," Azerick said, giving his solemn promise

Sandy glared down at him. "That is not a secure promise given the fact you cannot seem to stay there—for which I am glad."

"I have already forgotten it."

"Not surprising given the human brain is a sorry, grey lump of mud, especially when compared to that of a dragon's. But then nearly those of all creatures are," she replied with a sniff.

Azerick laughed, enjoying the fact that the best things in life never really changed.

"How would you like to help me a while longer?" Azerick asked.

"Hm, I don't know. Do you have any idea the cost of a dragon's time? Just providing this tidbit of assistance was worth a king's ransom, even with considering it being for family. What do you have to offer me in return?"

Azerick thought a moment on what might tempt her even though he was sure she would do as he asked, but he played her game. "Have you ever heard of an elephant?"

Sand pursed her scaly lips in thought. "Of course I have, but describe it so I know you know what you are talking about."

"An elephant is like…a cow the size of a small house but with a long nose that sweeps the ground and has hairless, grey flesh. I haven't tried it, but it looks delicious."

Sandy cocked her enormous head. "The size of a house and hairless? Very well, I accept your offer. What do you require of me?"

"Firstly, I need a ride."

Sandy's serpentine neck snapped her head up. "You do realize how grave an insult it is to a dragon to be used as a beast of burden?"

"I do, and I most humbly beg of you to tolerate such an imposition, but time is of the essence, and I do not think the timeliness of your arrival was happenstance. You know, dragons being so closely tied to the fates and all."

Sandy lowered her head with a grumble and allowed him to climb on. Azerick slid down her long neck and found a comfortable position just above her shoulders. She leapt into the air with power and grace that belied her enormous size. A single beat of her wings lifted them even higher, and they were soon flying over the vast savannah.

In little more than an hour, Azerick spied the formless shape of The Order's remaining legions, Sandy having spotted them long before he had. Another few minutes of flying brought into view the Olmul's horde of defenders. Azerick looked down at the legionnaires below and saw that most, if not all, were not of Syrna.

From the cheers that erupted from the soldiers, he guessed a large number were Valerians. The rest were likely from other kingdoms not trusted enough to defend The Order's homeland. They had been left to slow the Olmul should they attempt to capitalize on Syrna's sudden vulnerability.

It appeared that the Olmul were content to wait, at least for now, and stood prepared to meet any further advancement from the legionnaires still on the battlefield. Azerick found it curious since they now greatly outnumbered the invaders and could wash over them in a handful of hours. He doubted his own people were showing such forbearance at this moment and sought to hasten The Order's departure from Valeria and dealt harshly with any left behind.

Azerick had Sandy set him down near the prisoner pens and slid off her neck. Most of the legionnaires shied away from them and leveled weapons, unsure of their allegiance or purpose. Some took tentative steps toward the unusual pair, and one found the courage to speak.

"Lord Azerick, you've returned!" Amos cried. "Are you what made them turn back?"

Azerick smiled at the Valerian and nodded. "I told you I'd be back and that I would see you all returned home once more."

"Aye, you did, and I had faith in you. I just didn't think our deliverance would come so soon. I shouldn't have underestimated you."

Azerick clapped the man on the shoulder. "It's fine, Amos. Truth be told, I got lucky."

Amos snorted. "Man like you makes his own luck, and even the fates bend to his will."

Azerick pressed a finger to his lips and flicked his eyes from side to said. "Not so loud. Not even I dare tempt the fates lest they revoke my favored status."

"Aye, milord. Are ya to lead us home then?"

Azerick shook his head. "Not just yet. There is one final battle to come, and I must speak with the Olmul."

Amos bobbed his head and stalked toward the prisoner pens. "Move out the way, ya louts! Lord Azerick is here to take us all home."

Amos plowed a path through the crowd of legionnaires with his words and pantomimed threats with his spear. Azerick followed behind him until they reached the pens and Amos threw the gate open.

K'tar stepped toward him, an enormous smile spread across his face. "You are indeed a stranger man than I imagined. Is it you who has created such a stir and sent most of the invaders away?"

Azerick returned his smile and clasped his wrist. "I am."

"Have you come to free us then?" K'tar asked, turning his gaze toward the Olmul army in the distance.

"I have, but I want to collect on that favor now."

The Olmul warrior matched the white man's serious expression and tone. "If it is in my power, I will do whatever you ask."

Azerick took a deep breath. Everything depended on this moment. "I need your people to follow me, to fight one final battle so that The Order never returns to your lands with weapons drawn."

K'tar's expression became grave. "The favor you ask is no small thing, but neither is our freedom and sovereignty. I will speak to my people on your behalf. That is all I can promise. Whatever they decide, I will fight by your side as will my kin."

Azerick nodded. "That's all I can ask."

CHAPTER 29

Gloom cast a pall over the whole of Arkala and the surrounding land like a funeral veil despite the sun having crested the horizon. The capital lay under siege from a horde of spawn, Castracene warlocks, and their vile creations. The spawn's presence removed any doubt that their hated foe was in league with the old gods.

A handful of legions were all that stood between the populace and their imminent, horrific destruction. Although they fought valiantly, it was clear from where the royal family stood upon the walls unleashing their potent magic that they were losing. Already the enemy had breached their outer walls in a few places, and spawn and the warlocks' creations ravaged the inner defenders and any civilians into which they could sink a claw or fang.

The warlocks had also brought their dreaded plague with them, sending it ahead of their advancing horde as a black harbinger of doom just as they had decades before. By the time the invaders arrived, at least half of Arkala's population suffered from the horrific, fast-spreading disease. Thousands already lay dead, and the rest of the infected were miserable wretches covered in pustules and could do little other than bemoan their impending deaths.

But Syrna was a nation with an unmatched fighting spirit, and even the sickly picked up spear and stone and fought back until the last breath left their ravaged bodies. Syrna had conquered nearly the entire known world, had possessed power that rivaled that of the gods, but one man had brought their empire crumbling down around them. The thought was almost surreal in its absurdity.

A legionnaire officer hastened to the royal family's side and saluted. "Emperor, Empress, we have gliders awaiting you. You must take the princess and flee. Our legions will likely fall within the hour, and we must see you all to safety."

Noela snorted and shook her head. "Safety? There is no safety for the likes of us. Your emperor and I will fight with our people and die with them if that is what the fates desire. Sylvianne, it is time for you to go."

"No, Mother!" Sylvianne declared. "I brought this ruin to our doorstep, and I will pay the price as well."

Leontius hugged his daughter. "You acted with the best interests of your people in mind. You must now find those who were able to flee into the sea and lead them to a new home where you can rebuild Syrna into a better nation than ever. If you die, the last hope for our people dies with you."

A loud roar and blaring trumpets interrupted Sylvianne's continued protests. All eyes turned outward and took in the sight of another army approaching.

Leontius shook his head as tears streamed down his face. "They overrun us with their numbers and wasting pox, and yet more come to join the carnage. We are truly lost now. You must go, Daughter."

Sylvianne drew her hands apart before her face and gazed intently through the magical window she created. "They aren't Castracene. I see legionnaires—"

Noela clutched her husband's arm. "Perhaps it is Phaidros leading the rest of our legions come to deliver us from this evil?"

"And...Olmul," Sylvianne finished, the momentary excitement draining from her voice.

"The foreigners we left behind as fodder to slow them has instead joined our enemy. They now come to pick the meat from our bones," Leontius said, his voice heavy and weary.

War elephants crashed deep into the monstrous ranks laying siege to the grand city, and skin walkers in their animal forms leapt upon the monstrous minions and tore at them with tooth and claw. A huge, winged form appeared in the sky and unleashed a massive gout of fire in a hundred-yard stretch through the middle of the battlefield.

Sylvianne turned her attention to the figure astride the dragon's neck. "It is Azerick!"

Noela gave her a gallows laugh and shook her head. "He is indeed a clever one. He has no desire to unleash the Castracene and their monsters upon the world, so while he sends them to destroy us, he brings his own army to crush them once they have weakened us sufficiently so he can then finish us off."

Sickly green and black bolts of magic streaked skyward from the hands of the warlocks below, but runes etched into the dragon's scales flared, and the conjured ward turned them aside with ease. The dragon banked and scorched another line of fiery death through the enemy's center while Azerick unleashed arcane destruction with impunity.

With the Castracene's middle thoroughly ravaged, the outward ranks began to collapse, crushed between the opposing forces on both sides. There was little joy as the tide of battle turned. Once the Olmul and foreigners destroyed the warlocks and their minions, they would enact their revenge against an already defeated empire. The only glimmer of light was that they might be able to plead for some measure of quarter from the Olmul, which the Castracene would never allow.

A bestial roar reverberated from below, and a massive crash shook the wall beneath their feet. The colossal void drake took several ponderous steps back, lowered its head, and bashed its bulk against the crumbling stone barrier. Perhaps some of their people might survive the slaughter and plague, but it appeared the royal family would not be amongst them as the void drake deprived them of their magic.

Azerick turned his head toward the roar and tapped Sandy on the neck with the butt of his staff. "Sandy, down there! That thing negates magic. At least any from the outside."

Sandy's lips curled up. "Leave it to me. Nothing born or made can withstand a sand dragon's claws."

She turned and landed on the drake's back like a cat upon a rat, a rat nearly the same size as the cat. Her claws punctured the unnatural creature's steel-hard scales and sank deep into its flesh. She clamped her fangs into the back of its thick, stocky neck. Her bite was not nearly as effective a weapon as her diamond-hard talons, but they found purchase.

The drake roared and bucked, but there was no dislodging the grown sand dragon once she got hold of her prey. Azerick leapt from Sandy's back and onto the top of the wall as she dove at the void drake's back. He landed atop the wall with more grace than he might otherwise have achieved without help from his staff.

"Have you come to gloat over our defeat?" Noela asked, her tone as sharp as her piercing eyes.

"No…well, maybe a little, but later and mostly internally," Azerick replied.

"I should kill you where you stand!" Leontius bellowed.

Azerick shrugged, unconcerned. "You can try, but I recommend waiting until my friend dispatches the void drake. Even then your odds aren't great. None of us are the people we were just a day ago. As I told Phaidros, you can fight me, or you can defend your people as a good ruler should. His selfish nature urged him to choose the former, and people are dead who might otherwise be alive had he made a wiser decision."

Noela's voice caught in her throat. "My son is dead? You killed him?"

"I gave him a choice. He chose unwisely and paid the price for his arrogance," Azerick replied without a hint of remorse. "Will you do the same, or will you save your people?"

"Save them from the Castracene only to become chattel for the Olmul?" Noela snapped.

"A bitterly ironic choice given the fact it is almost the exact same two options you gave all the people you have conquered."

"Mother, Father," Sylvianne said, "we share a common enemy for the nonce. A vile and wicked one that must be destroyed for the betterment of all. Once that is done," she turned her pleading eyes to Azerick, "we can make terms with the Olmul, Valerians, and all those who now oppose us. As painful as it may be to admit, he is not wrong. I believe we lost sight of what began as a need for security and the betterment of the world. Instead of being the saviors we sought out to be, we became the oppressors, and there is a price to pay for our mistake."

Azerick felt the ambient magic in the earth and air return with the void drake's death. "It is time for you to choose."

Sylvianne had moved closer to Azerick's side and met her parent's gaze. The emperor and empress looked between Azerick and their daughter before dropping their eyes.

"Let us eradicate this scourge and come to terms," Leontius said.

The battle continued to ebb until the last warlock and monstrosity lay dead. A few may have escaped, but their days were numbered. Imprisonment was no longer an option, and they presented too great a threat for any to be allowed to live. The remaining legionnaires squared off against the Olmul and foreign soldiers, prepared to defend the city despite the hopelessness of their situation.

Tens of thousands of Olmul took up a chant, stomped their feet, and bashed their shield in unison for a full thirty seconds before turning about as one and marching away.

"Where are they going?" Noela asked as they all watched them depart the field.

"Home," came Azerick's simple reply.

"But we have not made terms," Leontius said, not understanding their actions.

Azerick smiled and shook his head. "They ask for none. They do not seek revenge or recompense of any kind. All they wish is to live in peace and make their own way in this world. You called them primitives, and most of us are compared to what you have created, but that does not mean they lack for honor or noble purpose."

He turned his gaze to the retreating Olmul and the conscripted legionnaires. "If you came to them with open arms tomorrow, they would welcome you. If you proved to be their friend, they would stand and fight beside you if your purpose was true and noble, as would my people, although they will require a little more time and proof of your good will. That is the power of friendship. That is what makes friends better than subjects."

Azerick held his audience captive with his words and steely gaze. "A friend will stand and fight with you no matter what. A subject might fight for you as long as you hold power over them, but the moment you don't, they will abandon if not turn on you." He waved his arms in the air. "That is the point I wanted to make with all of this. I wish so many people had not had to die to do so, but I saw no other way."

Leontius nodded. "I too wish my people, all the people, had not had to pay such a heavy price for me to learn such humility." He looked out at the sickness still ravaging his city and sighed. "Sadly, that debt has not yet been paid in full. Many more will die because of our actions, and there is nothing we can do about it. It would take a miracle to stop the plague."

"Then ask for one," Azerick said.

Noela's eyebrows shot up. "You can cure the sick?"

Azerick shook his head. "Not me, but there are beings who have been known to answer such prayers when the need is great enough."

Leontius' jaw fell open. "We couldn't! They wouldn't... We denounced them and even sought to usurp them."

Azerick shrugged. "You also sought to conquer the Olmul, and look what they chose to do when your need was great."

Sylvianne dropped to her knees and clasped her hands before her. The emperor and empress looked out at their dying people before joining her. Almost immediately, a fog began to form. It smelled sweet, like wild flowers. When it cleared, so did the pustules and boils that had stricken so many people so terribly.

"Now let us do something about this wretched pall so we might get a better look at this beautiful land," a deep, sonorous voice said.

All eyes turned to look upon the tall, muscular man standing resplendent in golden armor. Solarian raised a hand, and the sun destroyed the darkness and shined its brilliant radiance down upon them.

Ellanee appeared as if she had always been there and knelt next to Noela where she and her family lay prostrate and weeping. She wore a white wrap similar to the garb common among the people of Syrna.

She laid a gentle hand upon the empresses' shoulder. "Child, we did not forsake you. Although you call us gods—"

"Because we damn well are," Sharrellan said, emerging from a shadow that ought not have existed.

The goddess of nature rolled her eyes at her dark counterpart. "We are not all-powerful and omnipresent. We had to make a choice. While the Castracene's treachery was vile and brutal, it was a mortal threat.

One that came at a time when we had to face the old gods before they cast the entire world back into a place of pain and darkness."

Sharrellan jerked a thumb toward Azerick. "That's why we sent this one when you became too much of a pain in the ass." She smiled coyly at him. "Hello, lover."

Azerick shuddered beneath her gaze and the memories, not all of them terrible but certainly intense.

The goddess of death and darkness put her hands on her knees and bent down. "Had you made the attempt to cast us down, know that we would have kicked your asses across the face of the planet before I made you into my playthings, even with your little Source pool. I suppose I will have to content myself with your son. I need a new lord of the Fifth Circle, and I think he will do nicely. He might even be a worthy replacement for you," she said, giving Azerick a wink.

"My son..." Noela choked out. "He went to you?"

"Of course he did. He was a rotten little shit, and all rotten little shits go to me," Sharrellan replied.

"Sharrellan!" Ellanee snapped. "He is her son. Have a heart."

"I do, and it is as black as coal." She pressed herself against Azerick's side and ran a finger up and down his chest. "And like coal, it provides me with an inner fire, doesn't it, my sweet?"

Azerick cleared his throat and tried to move away, but the arm the goddess wrapped around his middle was as unyielding as steel.

Solarian fixed Sharrellan with a firm look. "I am sure Sharrellan will not take any punitive actions against Phaidros' soul, or we will take it upon ourselves to find him other accommodations."

"You can try, sun boy!" Solarian did not balk, and Sharrellan crossed her arms and huffed. "Fine. Like I said, I have a special position for him to fill. Many, many positions. You remember some of those, don't you, Azerick?"

Azerick blushed like a schoolboy, and he tried once more to break free of her grasp. Sharrellan let him go at the last moment, and he nearly toppled off the wall.

"I...should probably be going," Azerick stammered. "People back home need me."

Sharrellan laughed and disappeared like a shadow in the face of the approaching sun.

"Thank you for your mercy and divine intervention," Leontius said. "We are your most faithful servants and will never break faith again."

"And I hope we never again give you cause to," Solarian said before he ascended on a beam of sunlight.

Ellanee touched a hand to the rulers' brows and stood. "Continue to care for and lead your people with love and wisdom. Do not be afraid to trust and befriend others again. Friendship is the greatest source of strength one can have. Farewell."

The goddess of nature blew away as a whirlwind of leaves and flower petals.

"I should really be going as well," Azerick said. "The sooner I return home, the sooner I can help quell any issues that might arise with whatever legionnaires are still in Valeria. Our people need to know there is peace between us."

Sylvianne lightly grasped his arm. "Azerick, I hope you will return some day. I…there is much I would like to discuss with you."

Azerick smiled at her. "I'm sure I will. It would be cruel for me not to since I so thoroughly ensnared you with my irresistible charm."

Sylvianne grinned back at him. "It was another warning you gave me that I failed to heed to my great detriment."

Azerick scratched at his neck. "It is my curse to bear. The gods only know how many thousands of women across this world, and others, I have left in a similar state."

Sylvianne chuckled, and while her mirth was genuine, it still felt hollow. The death and pain around her were simply too great to feel real joy, and it would be some time to come before any of them could.

"Farewell, Azerick Giles," she said. "And, as crazy as it may sound, thank you."

Azerick nodded and whistled to get Sandy's attention. He stepped off the wall and floated down upon her back. The sand dragon took to the air, and they disappeared over the horizon.

EPILOGUE

Azerick sat at the table with his friends at an inn Rusty recommended. The last few days had been an intense time filled with sending messages and traveling to cities, towns, and campsites to deliver the news that the war was over and the legionnaires were allowed to depart without harassment.

The orders had mostly been obeyed, and there had been only a little more loss of life before the last of the invaders crossed through the archway. The portals remained to act as a bridge between them and Syrna and all the lands they now connected. Each side had their own lock, and it took both of them to open it.

"I hear you created a big problem for the invaders," Azerick said to Vera.

Vera smiled shyly into her wine cup. "Yeah, I guess so. Their defenses were not designed for alchemical warfare. It still wouldn't have been enough to drive them out, especially having heard how many soldiers you say they had. I cannot even imagine that many, and yet you defeated them by yourself."

"You saved the world yet again, Father," Daebian groaned and drained his mug of ale in a single gulp. "Gods, can you imagine the size of the fucking statues they'll make of him this time? I'll have to sail halfway around the world just so I won't be looking up into his stupid face every direction I turn."

Ellyssa punched Daebian hard in the shoulder. "What will you do now?"

Azerick sighed and shook his head. "I don't know. I haven't really thought about it." He gave Daebian a pointed look. "Maybe I'll try my hand at being a pirate and sailing around the world."

Daebian's eyes flashed between his father and his smiling wife. "Oh, hell no!"

Ellyssa scowled at him. "Admit it, you enjoyed fighting at his side. You two work well together."

Daebian pursed his lips. "Well, it would be convenient to have him nearby for when I decide to kill him."

Ellyssa snorted. "It's decided then. Wolf will miss you though."

"Miss who?" Wolf asked. "Him? Meh. I have my hands full with my six kids without having to go and save him from himself every other day. Time to pass that burden onto you."

"You have eight children," Azerick corrected.

Wolf set his mug down with a hard clunk. "Eight? Seriously? Poor Lynx. Man, I need to get a hobby."

The friends all laughed and boisterously ordered another round of drinks.

"So, you're really leaving again?" Rusty asked.

Azerick took a deep breath and nodded. "Yeah. I'm young, and I've seen a small part of what this big world has to offer. It would be nice to experience it in a more relaxed state. One where I am not having to fight for my or anyone else's life. I'll come back from time to time, don't worry."

"A little more often than every twenty years I hope," Rusty said.

Azerick clapped him on the arm. "You can count on it."

FROM THE AUTHOR

I hope you enjoyed this tale and will try my other works. Feel free to look me up on Facebook! You can also check me out on my website http://brockdeskins.com/ where I write serial fiction, free for your enjoyment, and answer questions!

Author page:
https://www.amazon.com/Brock-Deskins/e/B005M6VQ1O

Facebook:
https://www.facebook.com/brocksbooks/

Twitter:
@brockdeskins

PLEASE <u>**REVIEW**</u> **MY BOOKS** (Especially if you liked it). Customer reviews are the primary means of enticing others to purchase them. I am dependent upon the sales of my books to earn a living that will allow me to continue writing stories that I hope bring you some measure of entertainment. Thank you for your support.

OTHER BOOKS BY BROCK E. DESKINS

The Sorcerer's Path is an epic fantasy series.

The Sorcerer's Ascension: Torn from a life of comfort and luxury, his family destroyed by political intrigues and aspirations, a young boy must quickly grow into a man before the deadly streets of Southport devour him. Follow Azerick through a page-turning adventure that pits him against thieves, thugs, murderers, and men of power that will stop at nothing to achieve their goals.

Azerick must fight just to survive, but for him survival is not enough. A hunger to avenge the wrongs committed against him burns deep within. But that is not all that lies within the young man. There is a power waiting to be unleashed that may be the key to achieving the justice and security he seeks--if it does not destroy him first.

The Sorcerer's Torment: Azerick flees The Academy but quickly falls prey to powerful beings that use his skills and power for their own amusement. What these creatures do not understand is the power of the young sorcerer's will and the lengths he will go to for vengeance. Despite becoming a prisoner, Azerick finds his first true love, but can he keep it?

The Sorcerer's Legacy: Azerick has found himself a home and tries to settle down. He takes on an apprentice and tries to put all the death and desire for vengeance behind him. But when the Rook finds him, Azerick is once again pulled back into Ulric's schemes. Knowing that all he has worked toward and everyone close to him is in danger as long as these schemes are ongoing; Azerick decides to put an end to it, once and for all.

The Sorcerer's Vengeance: After narrowly avoiding being killed in his own bed by the land's most feared assassin, Azerick leaves his school behind to find out who sent him and to put an end to the threat once and for all. Azerick's search will take him to the very pits of the abyss and back to unleash hellish fury upon those that threaten him.

The Sorcerer's Scourge: With the siege broken and Ulric dead, Azerick can finally relax, study his magic, and run his school in peace. Unfortunately, Jarvin's reign is far from uncontested and the true usurper decides to make his move. Jarvin escapes with help from an unlikely source—a vampire named Landrin who still clings tenaciously to his own humanity. While Azerick and a large force from North Haven race to save the king in exile, evil forces are preparing to unleash a nightmare upon the kingdom that may well destroy them all.

The Sorcerer's Abyss: Now the master of the Fifth Circle of the abyss, Azerick is challenged by another demon lord for supremacy. Azerick must face this threat as well as his innermost demons, all the while searching for a way to escape his hellish prison.

Ellyssa fears she is going insane as she plagued by nightmares of her capture and enslavement. Deciding the key to saving herself lies in the total destruction of the object of her fears, she embarks on a crusade to find and kill the slaver, Captain Jake, and eradicate the slave trade.

Ellyssa's nightmares and battles spill out onto the streets of North Haven and gains the attention of The Academy. Fearing Azerick's school is turning out rogue wizards, The Academy decides to hunt down and destroy the rogue and place the school within their control.

The Sorcerer's Return: Azerick has come back from the abyss in order to try to unite all the races against the return of the old gods who seek to destroy them and subjugate the few they allow to survive a brutal purging. However, fighting ancient gods may be the least of his troubles as he battles to save a fractured kingdom, a brilliant son traveling a dark path, and the splintered soul of his own humanity.

The Sorcerer's Destiny: Brutally purged of his demonic influence, Azerick continues the struggle of uniting the kingdom to face the coming of the Scions, ancient gods banished by the mortal races during the Great Revolution two thousand years ago. The fallen gods' prison is crumbling, and Azerick is powerless to stop them from breaking free and enacting their cataclysmic vengeance upon the world.

The humans must ally with the other races in a final battle against impossible odds while their entire world crumbles to the ground and is trod beneath the feet of an unstoppable foe. How can they set aside their distrust of each other when they fear the very person trying to save them?

Rise of the Order: Banished to the abyss after helping defeat the Scions and saving the world from eternal darkness, Azerick languishes in perpetual misery as Lord of the Fifth Circle. The denizens of his hellish realm view him as a usurper and outsider. The chaotic creatures form an alliance with one goal in mind: destroy Azerick Giles, but Sharrellan stands in their way.

A powerful spell tears through the demonic planes, and when the dust settles, the dark goddess is nowhere to be found. It is up to Azerick to return her to her seat of power, but he has a price: return him to his mortal form and send him home.

Back home, a vast empire is on a crusade to conquer the world, and it has set its sights on Valeria. Their goal is to unite the world under a single banner, eradicate the spawn infestation unleashed by the Scions, and replace the gods who they feel have forsaken them with their mystical rulers.

Can Azerick save the dark goddess from the clutches of her demonic subjects and become mortal once again? Will he have the powcr to protect his people from The Order if he does?

Descent Into Chaos: The Order has arrived in force, and the fate of Valeria, and perhaps all the world, is poised to come under their iron-fisted control. Azerick and Daebian are forced to flee Southport and make a contentious alliance when King Miles capitulates to the invaders. Reduced to insurgent warfare, Azerick and his allies attempt to battle The Order's vastly superior forces in a series of hit and run strikes, but the enemy legions may not be his biggest threat.

Princess Sylvian Attar, daughter to The Order's godlike emperor and empress, has taken a personal interest in Azerick. Herself a powerful sorceress, Sylvian hunts Azerick in hopes of removing Valeria's legendary hero from the battlefield thus sapping her enemies' will to fight. Azerick decides there is but one course of action he can take against this unstoppable foe. It was time to inject a little chaos into The Order.

Brooklyn Shadows is a modern-day vampire tale. Full of action and snarky dialogue, Brooklyn Shadows is an enjoyable read for anyone who enjoys the supernatural underworld and butt-kicking vampires.

<u>**Shrouds of Darkness**</u> (Brooklyn Shadows Book 1) Leo Malone has been a vampire for the better part of the twentieth century. Once a prominent Sherriff (vampire cop), he now earns his living as a private eye and occasional bodyguard for anyone that requires some serious protection. Leo is hired by the daughter of a mob accountant who has gone missing.

The fact that her father is also a werewolf has Leo following a trail of grisly murders that will lead him through a web of intrigue and conspiracy involving his fellow vampires and the local werewolves that make New York their home, all the while trying to keep one particularly determined cop off his back and himself out of jail. Leo is not some pretty-boy vampire that all the girls ogle over, but a hard-eyed, remorseless killing machine who does not take crap from anyone.

<u>**Blood Conspiracy**</u> (Brooklyn Shadows Book 2): While dealing with the aftermath of the failed vampire council coup, Leo discovers that the modified Cure has fallen into the hands of a black ops government project designed to create vampiric super soldiers. When the inevitable happens, the off-book Homeland Security operation forcefully enlists Leo to help them resolve the situation. Worse yet, he has to work not only with an antagonistic werewolf named Meat, he is reunited with his hated creator, Lesile.

<u>**Primacy of Darkness**</u> (Brooklyn Shadows Book 3): Jack the Ripper, sadistic madman of old London, once thought long dead, has returned

to New York in an effort to quench his thirst for blood and mayhem. When the city's vampire enclave finds itself insufficient to deal with a madman of Jack's caliber, Vincent, the enclave head, enlists Leo Malone to put the maniac down before he reveals the existence of vampires as he throws the city into the throes of chaos and terror. Leo soon finds that Jack is not the only monster with which he must contend. A ghost from his past has also seemingly crawled from its grave and seeks to put an end to him and the rest of his kind.

The Transcended Chronicles is the story of an outlandish young man as he goes from being a troublesome youth to one of the kingdom's greatest secret agents. Blessed (or cursed) with an amazing ability to both fight and abuse his body with every conceivable vice known to man, Garran Holt is either the kingdom's greatest hero or its biggest embarrassment.

The Miscreant (The Transcended Chronicles Book 1): Garran Holt is a troubled young man. Unable to tolerate his self-destructive ways, his mother sells him into indentured servitude as part of a work crew building King Remiel's new trade road. When mercenaries sent to disrupt the road's construction attack his work camp, Garran discovers an inner power capable of turning him into a warrior of unparalleled ability. When the leader of his work crew recognizes Garran as being one of the transcended (a fighter able to slip into the swifter currents of time), he is trained as an agent, one of the kingdom's elite spies. Crude, abrasive, and deeply committed to destroying himself with drugs, alcohol, and debauchery, Garran might be the kingdom's only hope against falling to The Guild, the powerful trade cartel bent on becoming the true and undisputed power in the land.

The Agent (The Transcended Chronicles Book 2): The Guild rules the kingdom through their puppet monarch, and Garran must race to save the last living heir to the throne before the powerful syndicate's assassins complete their extermination of anyone who could oppose them. Garran and Prince Adam Altena struggle to find allies in hopes of rescuing Adam's sister, who was forced to marry the usurper in order to prevent even the thought of rebellion, and raise an army capable of defeating The Guild. With The Guild now in control of Anatolia's powerful army as well as their legion of mercenaries, their future is grim. How can a disreputable agent and a deposed prince convince their neighboring rulers to oppose The Guild, an organization that has had them cowed for decades?

Empire of Masks is an exciting and explosive new series that takes place in the world of Hedon and takes you across the land of Eidolan where ships sail through the skies and men and women wage war with magic, swords, muskets, and cannons.

<u>**Highlords of Phaer**</u> **(Book one of Empire of Masks):** Born a slave, descended of kings, Jareen Velarius just wants to provide the best life he can for his family, but Eidolan is a realm that challenges even the most stalwart of souls. Caught between his masters and those brave or foolish enough to strike against them, Jareen struggles to reconcile his role as a dutiful slave with that of a man who desires to be free. His goal: to return his people to a life stolen by the highlords more than a millennium ago.

Auberon Victore, sorcerer, alchemist, son of a powerful overlord, and Jareen's master, creates an alchemic compound he is certain will change the world; he just does not know how. Jareen sees it for the weapon that could break the sorcerers' iron grasp wrapped around the necks of every lowborn in the empire. It will change the world, but not in the way his master desires.

Across the Tempest Sea, a mighty storm has raged for a thousand years, keeping a terrible, long-forgotten enemy at bay, an enemy whose cruelty knows no bounds. Only the perpetual storm and their fear of the sorcerer highlords keep the Necrophages from returning to Eidolan and cloaking the empire in death and darkness. But the tempest is waning, and the dissidents' freedom may well come at the cost of their total destruction.

<u>**Nightbird**</u>**:** The Great Revolution ended the highlords' tyranny two hundred years ago, but the legacy of that epic war, and that of the principal architects' descendants, lives on. With the highlords' death and their taking magic, as it was once known, to their graves, Eidolan

fell into a time of darkness and its cities lived in isolation. However, some people, dubbed arcanists, discovered a new form of magic and the airships returned to the skies, rejoining the cities in trade as well as conspiracy, but a new darkness, more dreadful and deadly than any they faced before, is coming.

Kiera is a fifteen-year-old nightbird, one of many who flit about after dark, stealing whatever they can find in order to survive. She lives on a derelict airship in the poorest part of the city with Wesley, a young man who plies his trade as an escort to wealthy older women, and his little brother Russel, an autistic savant who communicates only through sign but who could secretly be the most powerful techno-arcanist the empire has ever known. Deep in debt to the underlord Nimat, Kiera dives into evermore dangerous schemes that put her at the heart of a secret war that could spell the destruction of not just the city, but the very empire.

Kiera is caught in the center of several factions on the brink of war. When she can no longer tell friend from enemy, there is only one side she can trust—her own.

Mourningbird: A creature of darkness lurks in the shadows of Velaroth, wearing the skin of its victims, and grips the city in terror. Dorian, a Necrophage bent on sowing chaos and paving the way for his people's invasion, has declared war on the humans of Eidolan, and there appears to be no one capable of stopping him.

Kiera's world is shattered by those who hold power, and she is forced to seek an ally. The nightbird is coming into power of her own, but can she stay alive long enough to seize it? Russel's behavior has taken a turn for the worse, and his actions have drawn the attention of those who would use his amazing talents for their own gain…and everyone else's loss.

The battle for Velaroth, and perhaps the world, has begun. Who will win? Who will live to mourn the dead? Will there be anything left for the victor to claim as their prize?

Standalone books

<u>**The Portal**</u> is a fun and exciting story of some less than popular teenagers that accidentally open a portal to a mystical land during one of their role-playing games. Drew, a dour and anti-establishment teenager, is pulled through and captured by evil creatures lying in wait on the other side. Now it is up to his friends and older brother to rescue him, but who will rescue Drew's captors from him?

<u>**Amelia (Battle for Ardentia)**</u>: Amelia is a precocious, ten-year-old girl with a powerful imagination. In her alter-ego guise of a demi-goddess warrior princess, Amelia fights against a powerful demonic sorcerer named Romut and his horde of monsters in a never ending series of battles to protect the people of her imaginary world. However, the true battle strikes home when Amelia is diagnosed with a brain tumor. Now Amelia must fight not just the evil living in her imagination, but for her very life.

ABOUT THE AUTHOR

Brock Deskins was born in a small town located in rural Oregon. At age twenty, he joined the army and served as an M1A1 tank crewman, dental specialist, and computer analyst. While in the military, he became an accomplished traveler, husband, and father of three wonderful children. His military career completed, attended college to brush up on his skills as a computer analyst and gain new skills as a writer. Brock received his degree in computer networking and is now devoting his full time and limited attention span to writing.

BIBLIOGRAPHY

THE SORCERER'S PATH
The Sorcerer's Ascension
The Sorcerer's Torment
The Sorcerer's Legacy
The Sorcerer's Vengeance
The Sorcerer's Scourge
The Sorcerer's Abyss
The Sorcerer's Return

The Sorcerer's Destiny
Rise of the Order
Descent Into Chaos

BROOKLYN SHADOWS
Shrouds of Darkness
Blood Conspiracy

THE TRANSCENDED CHRONICLES
The Miscreant
The Agent

EMPIRE OF MASKS
Highlords of Phaer
Nightbird
Mourningbird

OTHER BOOKS BY BROCK E. DESKINS
The Portal
Amelia: Battle for Ardentia

Curious about other Crossroad Press books? Stop by our website:
http://crossroadpress.com
We offer quality writing
in digital, audio, and print formats.

Subscribe to our newsletter on the website homepage and receive a
free eBook.

www.ingramcontent.com/pod-product-compliance
Lightning Source LLC
Chambersburg PA
CBHW020259200626
46816CB00001BA/373